Praise for the novels of Laura Caldwell

"Laura Caldwell writes remarkable, sexy, razor-edged thrillers that race to the finish and yet always make you stop to think. Chicago is brilliantly illuminated in *Red Hot Lies,* a book bursting with scandals and secrets. Caldwell's stylish, fast-paced writing grips you and won't let you go, making the Izzy McNeil trilogy a riveting must-read."
—David Ellis, Edgar Award–winning author of *Line of Vision* and *Eye of the Beholder*

"Caldwell's writing is always smart, sassy and sexy, with more suspense than a celebrity murder trial. In *Red Hot Lies,* her prose burns up the page, and you'll be still reading waaaaay past your bedtime. Highly recommended!"
—J. A. Konrath, author of the Lieutenant Jacqueline Daniels thrillers

"*Red Hot Lies* is a wonderfully plotted story, smoothly crafted, filled with striking characters and great narrative. Caldwell slips seamlessly between voices to deliver an emotional roller coaster of a thriller. A legal lioness—Caldwell has written a gripping edge-of-the-seat thriller that will not disappoint."
—Steve Martini, *New York Times* bestselling author of *Shadow of Power* and *Compelling Evidence*

RED HOT LIES

Laura Caldwell

MIRA®

MIRA®

Recycling programs
for this product may
not exist in your area.

ISBN-13: 978-0-7783-2650-2

RED HOT LIES

Copyright © 2009 by Story Avenue, LLC.

www.MIRABooks.com

Printed in U.S.A.

Dear Reader,

The Izzy McNeil series is fiction. But it's personal, too. Much of Izzy's world is my world. She's proud to be a lawyer (although she can't always find her exact footing in the legal world), and she's even more proud to be a Chicagoan. The Windy City has never been more alive for me than it was during the writing of these books—*Red Hot Lies, Red Blooded Murder* and *Red, White & Dead.* Nearly all the places I've written about are as true-blue Chicago as Lake Michigan on a crisp October day. Occasionally I've taken license with a few locales, but I hope you'll enjoy visiting them. If you're not a Chicagoan, I hope you'll visit the city, too, particularly if you haven't recently. Chicago is humming right now—a city whose surging vibrancy is at once surprising and yet, to those of us who've lived here a while, inevitable.

The Izzy McNeil books can be read in any order, although Izzy does age throughout, just like the rest of us. Please e-mail me at info@lauracaldwell.com to let me know what you think about the books, especially what you think Izzy and her crew should be doing next. And thank you, *thank you,* for reading.

Laura Caldwell

ACKNOWLEDGMENTS

My deepest appreciation to Margaret O'Neill Marbury, Amy Moore-Benson and Maureen Walters. Thanks also to everyone at MIRA Books, including Valerie Gray, Donna Hayes, Dianne Moggy, Loriana Sacilotto, Craig Swinwood, Pete McMahon, Stacy Widdrington, Andrew Wright, Pamela Laycock, Katherine Orr, Marleah Stout, Alex Osuszek, Margie Miller, Adam Wilson, Don Lucey, Gordy Goihl, Dave Carley, Ken Foy, Erica Mohr, Darren Lizotte, Andi Richman, Reka Rubin, Margie Mullin, Sam Smith, Kathy Lodge, Carolyn Flear, Maureen Stead, Emily Ohanjanians, Michelle Renaud, Linda McFall, Stephen Miles, Jennifer Watters, Amy Jones, Malle Vallik, Tracey Langmuir and Anne Fontanesi.

Much gratitude to my panel of experts— Chicago Police Detective Peter Koconis; Chicago Police Officer Jeremy Shultz; private investigators Paul Ciolino, Sam Andreano and John Powers; criminal defense lawyer Catharine O'Daniel; Gabriele Carles and Jason Billups for their help with Panamanian real estate; Dr. Richard Feely for explaining Chinese herbs; Dr. Doug Lyle for his autopsy and cardiology expertise; Matt Garvin for his computer hacking intel, and Chicago Lions rugby coach Chris McClellan.

Thanks also to everyone who read the book or offered advice or suggestions, especially Dustin O'Regan, Margaret Caldwell, Christi Smith, Katie Caldwell, Rob Kovell, William Caldwell, Pam Carroll, Liza Jaine, Morgan Hogerty, Beth Kaveny, Katie Syracopholous, Brooke Shawer, Clare Toohey, Mary Jennings Dean, Steve Gallagher, Les Klinger and Joan Posch.

*O*ne day can shift the plates of your earth.

One day can age you.

Usually, I pride myself on my intuition. I listen to that voice that says, "Something bad is happening…" or maybe, "Get out now, you idiot."

But on that Tuesday at the end of October, my psyche must have been protecting the one remaining day while I still believed that the universe was kind, that life was hectic but orderly. Because I didn't hear that voice. I never saw it coming.

1

Day One

"McNeil, she's not signing this crap."

"She told me she was signing it last week."

"She told you she was *considering* it."

"*No.*" I moved the phone to my other ear and pinned it there with my shoulder. With my hands free, I shifted about ten stacks of papers on my desk, looking for Jane Augustine's contract. I punched the button on my phone that would send a bleating plea to my assistant. "She told me she was signing it. Period."

"That's insane. With that lame buyout clause? No way. No. Way. You have no idea what you're doing, kid."

I felt a hard, familiar kernel of fear in my belly.

"It's the same buyout clause she had in her last contract." I ignored the personal comment he'd lobbed at me. I had gotten my fair share of them while representing Pickett Enterprises over the past three years and, although I acted like such comments didn't sting, I often thought, *You're right. I have no idea what I'm doing.*

I finally found the current contract under a pile of production- facility agreements. I flipped through it as fast as I could, searching for the clause in question.

My assistant, Q—short for Quentin—stuck his head in my

office with a nervous *what now?* look. I dropped the
document and put my hand over the mouthpiece. "Can you
get me Jane's *last* contract?"

He nodded quickly, his bald, black head shining under the
fluorescent lights. He made a halfhearted attempt to find it
amongst the chaos that was my law office—redwell folders
that spanned the length of my visitors' couch, file folders,
motions and deposition transcripts stacked precariously on
my desk. Throwing his hands up, Q spun around and headed
for his own tidy and calm workstation.

"I'm not messing around, kid," Steve Severny continued.
Severny was the biggest agent/lawyer in town, representing
more than half of Chicago's broadcasters and nearly all its top
actors. "Change the buyout or we're walking. NBC has been
calling, and next time I'm not telling them no."

I swallowed down the tension that felt thick in my throat.
Jane Augustine was the most popular news anchor at the
station owned by Pickett Enterprises, my client. The CEO,
Forester Pickett, was a huge fan of hers. I couldn't lose Jane
to another station.

Meanwhile, Severny kept rolling. "And I want a pay-or-
play added to paragraph twenty-two."

I flipped through the contract and found the paragraph. It
was tough, yes, and it was favorable to Pickett Enterprises, but
as much as I couldn't lose Jane, I couldn't simply give in to
anything her agent wanted. My job was to land the terms most
favorable to Pickett Enterprises, and although the stress of that
job was always heavy, sometimes so heavy I could barely see
through it, I would do my job. There was no alternative.

"No pay-or-play," I said. "It's nonnegotiable. I told you
that last time, and I'm telling you again. That comes from
Forester himself." It always helped to throw Forester's name
in the mix, to remind people that I was here, making their lives
tough, because he wanted me to.

"Then let's talk about the non compete."

"Let's do that," I thumbed through the contract, grateful to have seemingly won a point. Q darted into the room with Jane's previous contract, cleared a space on my desk and put it down.

I nodded thanks.

Q then placed a sheet of white paper on top of it, giving me a sympathetic smile. In red ink, he'd written, *Izzy, your meeting with the wedding Nazi is in forty-five minutes.*

"Crap," I said.

"That's right," Severny said, his voice rising. "That's what I told you before. It *is* crap. And we're not signing it!" And with that, he hung up.

"Mother hen in a basket!" I yelled, slamming down the phone.

I was trying not to swear anymore. I thought it sounded crass when people swore. The problem was it sounded great to me when I did it. And it felt so damn good. But swearing wasn't appropriate at a law firm, as Q had reminded me on more than one occasion, and so I was replacing things like *goddammit* with *God bless you* and *Jesus Christ* with *Jiminy Christmas* and *motherfucker* with *mother hen in a basket*.

Q sank into a chair across from my desk. "I know you're crazed, and I know you have to leave soon, but first I need some of your fiery, redheaded decisiveness."

I sat down, crossed my hands on my desk and gave Q my army-general stare. "I could use a quick break. Hit me."

Q was wearing his usual crisp khakis and a blazer. He tugged at the blazer to try to hide the slightly protruding belly he hated—his personal nemesis to the perfect gay physique. Not that this deterred him from sizing up the rest of the male species. Q had emerged from the closet six years prior, and though he had a live-in boyfriend, Max, he still enjoyed the "new gay" privilege of ogling every man he came across.

He paused dramatically now. "Max's mother is coming to town tomorrow."

"I see your problem." Max's mother was a former Las Vegas

showgirl, an eccentric woman with whom you'd love to grab a martini, but who wears you out after two hours. The last time she'd come to Chicago, Q nearly broke up with Max just for an excuse to get out of the house.

"How long is she in for?" I asked.

"Two weeks."

"That's not going to work."

"I know it's not going to work."

"You can make her help with your Halloween party this weekend."

He nodded, reluctantly conceding the point. "What am I going to do the rest of the time?"

"Watch a lot of football?" Q had retained many of his straight-man tendencies. A love of football was one of them.

Q had gray eyes that I'd always found calming, but they flashed with irritation now. "That's another not decisive, Izzy. There's a question mark at the end of that sentence. And you know she'll hover and talk, hover and talk. I won't see a single play."

"Okay, okay. Tell Max she has to stay in a hotel, and you guys will pay for part of it."

Q ran his hands over his head again. "I guess maybe that would work." He sighed. "God, I hate being in a relationship."

"No, you don't."

"Yes, I do."

Just then Tanner Hornsby, a high-ranking partner in his mid-forties, walked by my office. He was tall, with deep-black hair (dyed, I suspected) that arched into a widow's peak. He was rumored to run five miles a day, every day, before work, and so he was lean and wiry, but he had the tired, slightly puffy eyes of a career drinker.

He stopped now and frowned at us.

Q turned in his seat. "Oh, hello, Mr. Hornsby," he said in a breathy, effeminate voice, which he doled out only to annoy certain people like Tanner and his father.

"Hi, Tan," I said.

His frown deepened. No one called him Tan. He was Mr. Hornsby to most, and Tanner to the elite few, myself definitely *not* included, but I needed him to consider me his legal equal. I ignored his disdain and called him Tan because I wanted him to know he didn't scare me, even if he did. Behind closed doors, Q and I had other names for him—Toad Horny, Tanned Hide, the Horned One…

"I couldn't help but hear your phone conversation from down the hall," Tanner said. "Was that Steve Severny you were speaking with? Problems?"

Tanner Hornsby had negotiated hundreds of contracts with Steve Severny. Severny would never tell Tanner he didn't know what he was doing.

"No problems." I gave Tanner my dutiful-nice-girl look that served me well at the law firm of Baltimore & Brown. Though truthfully, I didn't need the look anymore. The ludicrous amount of dough I pulled in through the Pickett Enterprises work allowed me to get away with just about anything. I was my own little island amid a sea of associates who hadn't been as lucky as me and, as a result, were forced to be ass kissers and line-toers.

"How are your hours this month, Isabel?"

"Just fine, Tan, thanks for asking."

Ever since Forester Pickett had made me the lead attorney for Pickett Enterprises, taking the cases away from Tanner, Tanner had hated me. Tanner was lifelong friends with Forester's son, Shane. He'd originally gotten the Pickett Enterprises work because of that connection and thought he'd never lose it. Every so often, Tanner tried to throw his lean, wiry weight around and remind me that he was still my superior by asking questions about billable hours or continuing legal education. I felt bad for him. I felt guilty. I hadn't *tried* to take Forester's work from him. Forester had simply taken a shine to me, and I rode that windfall as far as I could. I knew many attorneys at the firm thought I'd gotten the work because I was a woman—a young woman with long curls of red hair who wasn't afraid to wear high, high heels and drink with Forester until the wee hours.

Even if that was true, I didn't care. I adored Forester. He was a smart, sweet man—not one of those older guys who oh so accidentally kept touching your hand…and your elbow… and your lower back. No, Forester was a prince, and like a prince he'd swooped in and saved me from the torment and agony of being just another associate slave. The job was hard, but I knew I was now doing good things for Pickett Enterprises. Still, that knowledge couldn't hedge my occasional yet powerful bouts of self-doubt or the feeling that I was an impostor, one who could be exposed at any time.

Tanner grunted. "Keep the hours up. We've got the end of the year soon."

I put a concerned look on my face, as if I didn't have the top billable hours of any associate at the firm, and nodded. "Sure. Will do."

He left. Thank God.

My cell phone dinged from where it sat atop a monstrous deposition transcript on my desk. I picked it up. A text message from Sam. Hey, Red Hot. Leaving for Cassandra's. See you there.

"Dammit." Cassandra was the wedding planner.

Q raised his eyebrows.

"Darn it," I corrected.

I swiveled around and started scrambling through the chaos on my credenza until I found my bag. I couldn't be late again. Plus, I needed to talk to Sam about this wedding stuff, which was starting to weigh me down as heavily as my job.

"Are you taking home the Casey research?" Q asked. "We have to file the motion by tomorrow."

"I know, I know." I stuffed a pile of case law and my Dictaphone into my bag.

"And don't forget Sam's work dinner tonight at the Union League Club," Q said.

I tried to ignore the mountain of panic taking over my insides. "Yeah, it's going to be torture. Those financial dinners always are. But I'll leave early and work on the motion."

"You can do it," Q said. "You always do."

"Thanks." I stopped and smiled, and he flashed one back.

As I kept stuffing things into my bag, I thought about how a big blowout wedding had not been my idea. In fact, when Sam and I got engaged, I was fine to book a trip to the Caribbean with a few friends, throw on a little slip dress and get married to the sound of steel drums. But my mother, who hadn't planned much of anything, or didn't usually care about much of anything, seemed stuck on a huge, traditional wedding. And my soon-to-be husband, who had legions of friends from grade school, high school, college, business school and work, said he was on board for that as well. *I want everyone to see how much I love you,* he'd said. How does a girl say no to that?

My phone rang. Q took a step toward my desk and we both looked at the caller ID. *Victoria McNeil.* My mother.

Q picked it up, handed it to me and left the office.

"Hi, Mom." I zipped up my bag. "What's up?"

"Izzy, I know you two picked out the plates with the silver border for the reception, but I think we should consider the gold again." My mother's voice was calm and smooth, as always. "I've been thinking about it, and the linens are a soft white, rather than a crisp white, and that really lends itself toward gold rather than silver."

"That's fine. Whatever you think." Reflexively, I extended the fingers of my left hand and glanced at my engagement ring, an antique, art-deco piece with an emerald-cut diamond. Looking at my ring used to make me grin. Now, it made me wince a little.

"Okay, and another thing. If you talk to your brother,

Charlie, give him a little encouragement, will you? We need him to try on suits."

"The wedding is still six weeks away."

"That's right. *Only* six weeks away."

My stomach hollowed. *Only six weeks.*

"Charlie has to stop dragging his feet," my mom said.

I murmured in vague agreement, but for once I felt simpatico with my brother. Mentally, I, too, needed to stop dragging my feet about this wedding thing.

"Don't forget, you have another dress fitting tomorrow night."

I tried not to sigh. "I know," I said. "Battle number five."

During the first visits with my bridal seamstress, Maria, it seemed she was trying to flatten my breasts and hide my hips, parts of my body I rather liked. I kept telling her, "I think the dress needs to be sexier," and so she'd been dutifully making the bustline lower and the waistline tighter, until the last time, when she'd taken the pins out of her mouth and said in her accented English, "You want to look like hooker on wedding day?"

I told her I'd think about it.

I realized that most women wanted an ethereal look for their wedding, but I liked wearing sexy clothes on a daily basis, so why not for my wedding day? Plus, Sam said he wanted me in something hot. So I was going to give him hot.

"Izzy, really," my mom said. "I don't want you showing nipple on your wedding day."

I laughed, and it felt good, like it was loosening up my insides. "See you tomorrow."

I logged off the computer, grabbed my bag and left to meet Sam.

It was just an average day.

2

The funny thing—although maybe *funny* isn't the right word—is that I already knew a single day could slap you around and send you reeling. I'd had such a day twenty-one years ago when my father died. It was Tuesday, and it was gloriously sunny and clear—I always remember the weather first—and Charlie and I were playing in the leaves in the backyard, making painstakingly neat piles, which we would dive into with a yelp and destroy in an instant.

My mother came out of the house. She was wearing jeans with a brown braided belt that tied at the waist, the ends of which slapped her thighs as she walked. Her red-blond hair was loosely curled around her face, as usual, but that face was splotched and somehow off-kilter, as if it had two different sides, like one of those Picasso paintings my teacher showed us in art class.

She sat us down on the scattered leaves and told us he was gone. He had been on a solo flight, training for his helicopter license when the helicopter experienced mechanical trouble and went down over Lake Erie. My father was a psychologist and a police profiler, but my mother would later tell us that he was always learning new skills. And now he was dead. It was as simple, and awful, as that.

Charlie seemed to take the news well. He furrowed his tiny brow, the way he did in school in order to avoid accusations of not paying attention. He nodded at her. He was six then, two years younger than me, and I could tell he didn't understand, or at least he didn't grasp the gravity of the situation. It was a trait Charlie would carry all his life.

After my mom and Charlie went inside, I raked the scattered leaves into neat piles and left them that way.

We moved from the small log house in Michigan to an apartment on the north side of Chicago, where my mother knew a few distant family members. We changed our wide swath of lawn for a concrete sidewalk. The air we breathed no longer smelled of pine or lake water, but of bus fumes and sometimes, when the wind was right, dark cocoa from the chocolate factory a few blocks away.

My mother, who had been a local radio DJ in Michigan, got some help from her boss, who found her a job as a traffic reporter. Every day, she ironically boarded a helicopter and floated above a city she hadn't known since childhood, telling people about the congestion on the Dan Ryan Expressway, the gridlock on the Northwest Tollway.

Sometimes at my new school, I would stare out the classroom window and into the sky, imagining her flying around up there, like an angel. My mother had taken on angelic properties, too. She was thin—so thin I sometimes imagined I could see her veins and muscles right through the translucent shell of her skin. She rarely played with us anymore. She never laughed. I thought she was probably thinking of my father, of his messy brown hair and mischievous eyes that made him look as if he was about to crack up, despite his serious round glasses.

I thought I'd grown up that day, sitting on those leaves. My mother would tell people afterward that I was an "old soul," a comment I took as the highest of compliments and a quality I worked hard to cultivate. It wasn't difficult given the fact that I had taken on many of my mother's duties. Every morning, I toasted two slices of bread, just like she used to. Every morning, I smeared them with peanut butter, and then, very carefully, striped the middle of the bread with a column of strawberry jam, just like my mother had when we were in Michigan. I would coax Charlie from bed and make him sit in the kitchen, where we would eat our toast, just like we used to.

And then one day, my mother came back, at least for a while. She smiled again, she had gained a little weight, she laughed when Charlie spilled chocolate milk on the couch.

As I got older, I felt stronger for having lost my dad at a young age. There was a certain relief in having experienced that loss, because I knew what pain was like; I knew I could survive. I laugh now when I think of that. The fact was I was only eight—old enough to be nearly destroyed, yet resilient enough to see no alternative but to march forward.

I'm not eight anymore, and the truth is, I grew lighter over the years. Maybe the old soul was still there, a piece of me that watched over my life, but my life had become fun again; I found friends with whom I could be silly and revel in it. Eventually, I found Sam, who had brought me so much joy. And then came that Tuesday—another autumn Tuesday— when the plates of my world screeched and shifted.

3

Forester Carlton Pickett loved being alone. Absolutely loved it. He was the youngest of eight from a poor Southern family. He had begun working steady jobs when he was eleven, and since his twenties, he had run Pickett Enterprises, which had some four hundred employees. All of this meant he was rarely alone.

At age sixty-eight, he now felt entitled to an occasional bit of solitude. So at a time like this—home early on a surprisingly balmy autumn day with no dinner parties, no date, no work occupying his mind—he planned to take advantage of that solitude.

His Audi hugged the long gravel driveway. At first, only the towering pines lining the drive were evident, but then they cleared, and his house, still far in the distance, came into view. Its style was Greek Revival, the kind Forester used to stare at in awe while growing up. It was made of white stone, the front protected by massive columns. Inside, the house boasted ten bedrooms, eleven baths, two kitchens, a gym and a movie theater. The place would have been ostentatious if it wasn't in the big-money area of Lake Forest and if it wasn't surrounded by acres and acres of lawn and trees. Forester had known the house was over the top, but he entertained frequently, and he felt he deserved it. He had never been shy about living a big life.

Forester entered through the garage door and came into the kitchen. His housekeeper stood at the counter, back turned, fixing his meal.

"Hello, Annette," he said. He remembered when it was Olivia he used to call hello to. He remembered that every day, even though she'd been gone thirteen years now, stolen by ovarian cancer.

Annette turned at the waist and bid him a subdued good-evening, then returned to her work.

Forester walked from the kitchen and through his large marble foyer. In the front living room, he opened the four sets of French doors looking out onto the patio, the vast yard and a small pond. For some reason, Annette liked to keep the house sealed up tight, a habit he couldn't seem to break. He glanced around the living room. The effect, he hoped, was one of eclectic elegance. The designer had packed it full of expensive rugs, couches and wall coverings that showcased Forester's unique and odd collection of objects collected on his travels—an oxidized brass bowl he paid two dollars for in Malaysia; the plaster statue of a radio microphone his mother gave him after he bought his first station.

Annette stepped into the room. "Cornish hen tonight," she said simply.

"Wonderful."

"They're in the warming oven when you're ready."

"Thank you, Annette."

In the study, he opened a bottle of DuMol Pinot Noir and poured it into a glass decanter. He turned on Ramsey Lewis. God, he loved jazz. He could still remember arriving in Chicago when he was twenty-one. He would hang out at the Green Mill, seeing every kind of jazz he could. His favorites were the southern, bluesy stuff that made him think of home, and the true Chicago style, guys like Franz Jackson that reflected the big, new, shiny city he lived in. In a way, it was jazz that had brought him everything he owned.

Looking back at his life, Forester was amazed at the apparent organization of it. He believed now that everything had happened for a reason—leading him to the next stage—but while he was busy living that life it had felt, at the time, like a convoluted, random mess. It was random that he had lost his factory job only seven months after moving to Chicago. It was random that a radio-station owner, a guy named Gus Connifer whom he'd met at the Green Mill, offered him a job as a "production assistant" at the jazz station, where he was essentially a glorified gofer. And it was decidedly random that after a year at the station, a year in which Forester had soaked up the world of radio the way the summer ground soaks up rain, he had a chance to buy the station.

Gus Connifer was a smoking, drinking, hard-living man who'd finally been diagnosed with emphysema and a host of other respiratory illnesses. He thought he would die soon, and he was fine with that, except for one little thing—he couldn't stand his wife, whom he suspected of cheating, and wanted her to inherit nothing. Gus was a Catholic, so divorce wasn't an option. He wanted to unload the radio station, and he didn't care for how much. He liked Forester, who over the last year had been a bigger help to him than his ten other employees combined. He told Forester he'd sell the station for exactly a thousand dollars. Forester got a loan and with it his first property. Later, he bought other radio stations, not to mention television stations, cable networks, production companies, newspapers, recording studios and publishing companies, making Pickett Enterprises the largest media conglomerate in the Midwest.

Forester poured wine into a long-stemmed glass. Thank God red wine was considered healthy these days. It gave him an excuse to indulge in one of his few vices. And hopefully it would give him a mellow buzz, maybe take away that vague sense that something was wrong inside his body. He was a fit, strong sixty-eight—that's what all his doctors said, and he had a few of them. Forester now believed in preventive medicine rather than a reactionary approach. Yet there was still this tiredness, this sense that his body wasn't exactly right. But he was nearing seventy. What did he expect?

He glanced at the framed pictures above the wet bar. He kissed the tips of his fingers and touched the photo of his late wife, Liv. He would give up everything to have her back. Were Livvie here, he would gladly give up his current preference for solitude.

The photo next to Liv's was of their only son, Shane. He often wished they shared the bond he saw and envied between many fathers and sons. That envy had worsened with the recent doubts he suffered about Shane—ever since the anonymous letters and peculiar occurrences that had happened over the past few months.

He picked up the photo of Shane. Looked closely at it. Was there any chance he was the source of the threats? Logically, it made sense, because Shane would take over the reins of his empire whenever Forester decided to hand them over. But they both knew and understood Shane simply wasn't ready yet. He *thought* they both knew and understood that.

He put the photo back. His doubts sometimes ashamed him. But who else could be behind the threats? He thought of Chaz and Walter, his two right-hand men at Pickett Enterprises. They knew Shane's limitations, and they knew they could pull his strings if he was CEO. If Forester was out, they could manage the company the way they wanted, which was often different from his way. But that's why Forester had hired people like them, people who didn't think exactly as he did. And until he figured out the source of the threats, he wasn't going to start axing people.

He heard a ding telling him a door had been opened— Annette leaving for the day. With Ramsey Lewis pounding the black and whites on "Limelight," Forester walked to the kitchen and made himself a plate with the Cornish hen and potatoes she had prepared. He took his dinner and wine through the French doors of his study and seated himself at the iron patio table.

In the deep-blue twilight his lawn took on a silvery hue, the edges of his estate blurring in the distance. He took a few bites of the hen, then a sip of the Pinot Noir. He sighed, anticipating the pleasure he got from such nights. But satisfaction eluded him. Why? He was alone, he had a perfect glass of wine and a delicious dinner, he had his jazz. He had everything he needed for a quiet night of contentment.

Yet that vague discomfort kept command of his body. In fact, it grew, and spread to his mind. Forester felt an overwhelming tiredness, even sadness, while something else—what was it?—caused his heart to race. His eyes swept across the acres of lawn, the old, drooping oaks and the stately pines. For the first time, he wished he had gated his estate. He'd never liked that concept, didn't like the thought of closing himself off from the rest of the world, but now it would have been a comfort against this strange dread.

He saw no one. He noticed nothing out of the ordinary.

Still, he took his cell phone out of his pants pocket. He hit a speed-dial number, not identifying himself to the person on the other end, and began to speak. "I know it's a lot to ask, but I'm just confirming that you understand what has to be done if…well, if something should happen to me." He paused, listening. "No, of course not. I don't anticipate anything. I just wanted to ensure your help and tell you how much I appreciate it. And I wanted to remind you that discretion, absolute discretion, is required."

He listened, then gave a short shake of his head. "No, really. It's nothing. I didn't intend to startle you. Everything is fine."

And indeed it was. The sky was turning a sultry blue-black now. "I'm sorry to have disturbed you," he said into the phone. "Thank you, and have a pleasant night."

He picked up his wine again. He speared a bit of scalloped

potato. He tried to force himself into the relaxed, almost euphoric state he would usually enjoy on such an evening.

The Ramsey Lewis CD came to an end, throwing his estate into cavernous silence.

Suddenly, he didn't like being alone. *What an odd thought.*

For the first time in a very long time, Forester Pickett was afraid.

4

Sam was distracted. I could see it when I walked into the office of Cassandra Milton, Wedding Creator. Sam and I both thought the title wedding creator was pompous, but Cassandra was one of my mother's best friends, and we'd heard her weddings always went off flawlessly.

"Hi, gorgeous." Sam got up from his seat on one of the white couches in the waiting room. He was wearing a navy suit over his short but trim, strong body. He was thirty, a year older than me, and he had cropped blond hair and the sweetest olive-colored eyes I'd ever seen. But those eyes were strained today, the faint creases at the corners somewhat deeper.

He hugged me just a fraction tighter than normal.

I pulled back, studied him. "What's up with you?"

"Just some complications at work."

"Forester Pickett kind of work?" Sam also worked for Forester Pickett. Specifically, he worked for a private wealth-management firm that handled most of Forester's investments, and Sam was one of the financial advisors assigned to him.

He nodded.

"Want to talk about it?"

"Not right now."

"Does Forester know about it?"

"Yeah. But I need to talk to him some more."

"Sometimes Forester likes determinations rather than discussions."

"I know. And it makes me nuts." Sam let me go and sank back into the couch. He dropped his head in his hands for a second, and his gold hair glinted under the muted overhead lights.

I sat next to him. "Are you all right?" Maybe it wasn't work. Maybe he was suffering the same issue I was—feeling as if the wedding was a speeding train that wouldn't stop. Hell, I was starting to feel like my life was that train. In a few short years, I'd gone from single girl associate with no responsibilities (except to bill some hours and have a good time on a Saturday night) to a nearly married, almost-partner, lots-of-responsibility woman with a fiancé who, just this past weekend, had started talking about houses in the suburbs.

Sam raised his head and put on the composed smile he used when he wanted to pacify his mother. "I'm fine."

"C'mon, tell me." *And then I'll tell you.*

I had a happy vision of us blowing off Cassandra and the dinner at the Union League Club. We'd flee to a dark bar on Roscoe near Sam's apartment. We'd drink beer and talk about how it had all gotten away from us, how we wanted to put the breaks on. We would decide that we wanted to be together, sure, but without all this formality and fuss. I would continue to get my sea legs at work. I would finally feel like I owned that job. And, in a few years, when we were both established and tiring of it all, maybe then we'd get married and think about a house in Winnetka.

Just then Cassandra Milton floated into the room. She was a tall, immaculately dressed woman in her fifties. "Well preserved," Sam once called her. He was right. All I knew was that when the time came, I needed to have the name of the surgeon who preserved her.

"Ready for a few details?" Cassandra said. She said this every meeting. "A few details" almost always consisted of an hour of excruciating decisions about shrimp forks and frosting.

"Absolutely." Sam stood and loosely clapped his hands in front of him, as if he'd just been in a huddle and someone had called *Break!*

I stood, too, telling myself it would all be worth it—eventually. I was just being immature about wanting to slow things down. I was a hundred percent certain I wanted to be with Sam. I'm not going to lie and say it had always been that way. When Sam and I first discussed getting married, I was struck with the enormity of the situation—no sex with anyone else ever again; having to see the same person every morning for as long as my life lasted; having to consult with someone about every major life decision from what blender to buy to what vacation to take. Being in the holy state of matrimony was nothing I'd ever romanticized. I didn't need it as a notch on my belt. But I was wild for Sam. I adored him in a way I'd never realized was possible. Monogamy required giving a lot up, but I was going to gain a hell of a lot more. I loved Sam in such a way, that my whole body said, *God, yes,* each time I saw him.

And now here we were at the office of a Wedding Creator. It was all going to be okay.

I glanced at him for the *hang in there* look he always gave me at Cassandra's, but he didn't meet my gaze.

"Sure, Cassandra." I stood and reached for Sam's hand, but he just sat there, staring straight ahead.

"Sam?"

He looked up. "Sorry." He stood quickly. "I forgot something. I mean, I've got to check on something. Can you handle this on your own?"

"You want to leave?"

"Yeah."

"I'll go with you. We can put this off."

"We *cannot* put this off," Cassandra said. "The contract with the restaurant requires we choose our appetizer selections by tomorrow."

"Can you do it?" Sam said. "Please?" With any other groom, I would assume he was wisely trying to shirk his duties. But Sam actually enjoyed all the planning that went into our wedding.

"Of course, but seriously, are you all right?"

He put on that practiced smile again. "Sure, yeah."

"Okay. I'll meet you at the dinner." We'd talk then. I would get the whole thing out—all my doubts—and the talking would dispel my panic.

He blinked. He seemed to have forgotten about the work dinner. He looked at his watch. "Right, okay. I might be a little late, but I'll meet you there."

"Shall we?" Cassandra said, in the voice I knew as her impatient tone, even if it was cultured and low.

I squeezed Sam's hand and kissed him on the cheek. "I'll see you at the club."

Later, I realized Sam hadn't answered me. He just watched me walk into Cassandra's office, and when I turned back to give him a reassuring smile, he seemed to be studying me, memorizing my face.

5

I sat in the ballroom of the Union League Club, an empty chair at my side.

"Where's Sam?" asked Faith McLaney, a woman from Carrington Associates, the wealth-management firm where Sam worked. Faith was ten years older than Sam and, in some ways, a mentor to him. Their boss, Mark Carrington, handled only a few exclusive clients, while Sam and Faith backed him up, dividing the clients between the two of them.

"I'm not sure."

I texted him again—Where are you? Still no reply.

I watched while a line of speakers from a newly formed venture-capital firm took the dais and eternally praised themselves for raising so much funding. I tried to make small talk with the others at our table—two people from a local accounting firm and their spouses—but because of my increasingly agitated worries about Sam, they were tough to tell apart save one woman's lazy eye and her husband's psoriasis.

"Sam's on his way," I kept saying to no one in particular, starting to doubt my own words with each second. Had he gotten held up with some emergency with Forester's work? It was strange for him not to text me and let me know what was happening.

I went to the bathroom, stood at the counter and called Sam's cell. It went to voice mail.

Q was someone I turned to for help with everything, not just work, so I called him to see if he had any ideas.

I'd been lucky enough to find Q while he was night staff at Baltimore & Brown doing word processing for attorneys, like me, who worked too much and too late. He had simply wanted to make some money until he could figure out what he should do with his life, having realized that his acting career wasn't exactly taking off. He was conscientious and meticulous, and as soon as he'd handled a few projects for me, I begged him to become my assistant. Yes, he'd be working for someone slightly younger, I told him, and yes, maybe "legal assistant" wasn't the day job he'd always dreamed of, but I'd get him as much money as I could, I'd let him go on auditions anytime he wanted and we'd have a blast. I told him that I needed him. Desperately. At the time, I was twenty-six. Only a year and half out of law school, and suddenly I'd found myself handling a large chunk of the legal work for Pickett Enterprises—and I knew I was in way over my head.

Q finally caved, and now, three years later, he was, as Sam always joked, my "work husband," a husband who could and would always make things better.

But oddly, Q's phone didn't ring either and went straight to voice mail.

I went back into the dining room and sat staring at my engagement ring, while the speakers droned on. I tried to figure out when it had happened—when the feeling had started that the wedding was getting away from us, didn't seem like *us* anymore. I had to talk to Sam about it. So where was he?

Whenever a dinner course was cleared, my eyes darted to my lap, where my cell phone sat, and I stared at the empty display. I texted him a few more times. Again, nothing. Something was wrong.

The desserts—glazed pears that were better suited for a Gerber jar—were served, but I pushed them away.

When the dinner ended I said goodbye to Faith and the rest

of the table, then I left and tramped down the stairway that was lined with an eclectic, expensive array of oil paintings. Once in the lobby of the club, I called Q again, but again it went right to voice mail. I tried Sam's cell phone…and his office… and his apartment number. Nothing.

I jammed the phone in my purse and wondered whether to keep being worried about Sam or move to pissed-off mode. This no-show was completely unlike him. In fact, he'd never done something this inconsiderate, this out of character, so my usual repertoire of fiancé-management techniques seemed inappropriate.

I walked back to my office, through the mostly empty Loop, now lacking its daytime vitality. I found my silver Vespa parked behind the building. My mom had gotten me started on scooters when I was sixteen. We didn't need a car in the city, and yet she constantly worried about me waiting at public bus stops and El stations. I'd used the scooter through college and bought a new one during law school. I thought that when I started practicing law I'd get rid of it. But then gas prices skyrocketed, and there was something about driving the Vespa I found not only convenient and energy saving, but cathartic. After a day spent in the stale stratosphere of the law firm, I liked the fresh air on my face, the feel of movement, of getting somewhere, sooner than later.

I got on the Vespa and pointed it in the direction of Sam's office. There was little traffic, so I was able to floor it up LaSalle Street. The dazzling lights of office buildings and restaurants bled past me into streams of colors. The wind tore through my hair, causing strands of orange curls to flick against my eyes and cheeks. I tried not to think of Sam. Instead, I let myself think how grateful I was that Illinois had no helmet law and, as a result, I could let my ears and my head fill up with the rumble and roar of city life.

In the lobby of Sam's building the security guard called upstairs, at my request, and said no one was answering. Everyone had gone for the night.

"Can I look at the log to see when he signed out?" Sam had told me about how the security in his building was woefully out of date. To make up for it, the building required every person, even employees, to sign in and out each time they left or entered.

The guard, an overweight, middle-aged man with a drooping mustache, shook his head. "Sorry. No one can see the log."

"Sure, sure." I flipped my hair over my shoulder. "How do you like the Bears this year?"

The guard waved a hand. "Ah, shit, that kid they got as quarterback doesn't even have gonads yet. We need somebody good."

"Somebody like McMahon?" Most Chicagoans had never emotionally recovered from the beauty of the Bears' mid-eighties victory in the Super Bowl. A reminder of such beauty was a guaranteed way to become best friends with anyone over forty who lived within a sixty-mile radius of Soldier Field. Name-drop a player from the '85 team to these guys and they were putty in your hands.

"Exactly!" the guard said.

"And they need a moral leader. Somebody like Singletary." At this point I was just spouting names I remembered from seeing the *Super Bowl Shuffle* video after we moved to Chicago.

"Right! Shit, that's exactly what they need."

"My fiancé and I are big Bears fans. He was at Soldier Field the day Payton broke the rushing record."

The guard's eyes narrowed. "You kidding me?"

"No." At the time, Sam had only been a kid, visiting a distant relative in Chicago, but he remembered it vividly.

"Wow," the guard said in a hushed, reverent tone. "Wow."

"Yeah, I gotta find him." I straightened up. "Can you check that log and just tell me when he left?"

The guard eyed me. Then he put the logbook on the counter, swung it around and pointed to an entry at the top of the page. There, Sam had signed out of the office ten minutes before I'd seen him at Cassandra's.

I looked up at the guard. "And he didn't come back?"

He shook his head then retracted the book.

"Thanks."

"Sure thing. Go Bears."

"Go Bears," I answered and left.

I called Sam's apartment, then mine. No answer at either. I started my Vespa, but I wasn't sure where I should go. What was I supposed to do now? *Sam, where are you?*

I called my best friend, Maggie, but only got her voice mail. Where in the hell was everyone?

As I clicked the Off button, my phone rang. I felt a tiny bit of relief rupture my worry. But it was a Chicago number I didn't recognize.

"Hello?"

"Izzy, it's Shane."

"Oh. Hi, Shane." Forester's son rarely called me, but then maybe Sam was out with him for some reason. God, let it be as easy as that.

"Izzy," Shane said. He seemed to choke, then I heard a snuffle. "My dad is dead."

6

The first time I spoke to Forester I'd been out of law school for eleven months. After living the student life, with natural built-in breaks of a week here, two months there, I had struggled to get my body and mind on what Grady, my friend at work, and I called the *coal-miner's schedule*. To us, it seemed that we labored as hard as coal miners with only a tiny light to illuminate the work ahead of us. As first-years, we were clueless about the law. We were given projects in piecemeal fashion, we worked until the wee hours to finish them, and then we turned them over to demanding partners, crossing our fingers that we hadn't just prepared a thirty-page memo on the completely wrong topic—something that happened more frequently than one would think. Often, the partners weren't clear about what they wanted, because they weren't even sure themselves. Other times, they were pompous jerks who believed that associates should be able to divine precisely what they needed without a lick of direction.

Tanner Hornsby fell into that second category, and so working for him, as I did, required lots of late nights in the office. But that first time I spoke to Forester, it wasn't even late. It was about five o'clock, and I'd just run downstairs to the lobby and bought myself a massive green tea with a shot of vanilla syrup to keep me sharp for the next few hours. Tanner had already left for the day. With the weather warming up, I'd heard him on the phone earlier making plans to sit outside at Tavern on Rush, where he and his buddies would no doubt ogle women and drink themselves silly.

I was jealous of Tanner that night. Jealous that he already understood the law, that he had the money and time to hit the town on a Tuesday night.

In my office, I sipped my tea and tried to focus on an option agreement Tanner had asked me to finish.

But it became hard to concentrate because of the ringing phone in Tanner's office, which was a few doors down from mine (and on the side of the building that actually had windows). Closer to me was the desk of Tanner's assistant, Clarice, and I could hear her phone chiming, too.

Finally, I got up, walked to Clarice's desk and picked it up. "Baltimore & Brown," I said in a quick, what-the-hell-do-you-want kind of tone.

"Tanner Hornsby, please." The man's voice was melodic, with a slight Southern accent.

"Mr. Hornsby is gone for the day. May I take a message?"

"Gone for the day? It's only five o'clock."

I thought of Tanner, probably already well into his second Bombay Sapphire. "Mr. Hornsby is in a meeting."

"Is this Clarice?"

"No, it's Izzy McNeil, one of the associates."

"Forester Pickett here."

I coughed involuntarily. Everyone at Baltimore & Brown knew Forester, at least by name, but the associates were typically kept away from the clients. "Hello, Mr. Pickett. May I help you with something?"

"Well, I'm calling about Steven Baumgartner, and I need some assistance ASAP."

Steven Baumgartner, commonly known around Chicago as "the Bomber," was the morning shock jock on a radio station Forester owned. We'd been working on his new contract, which he had been expected to sign for millions more dollars than before, but after a recent stunt that resulted in over a hundred listeners jumping into the Chicago River to win concert tickets (many of them ending up with a waterborne virus), the station had considered letting him go.

"I'm familiar with Mr. Baumgartner," I said. "What can I do for you?"

"I'm at Baumgartner's house. I've told the guy he's got to tone it down on air, and he's willing to do it. He's also willing to take a lot less money than we thought. But he wants to sign tonight. He thinks the bad press is going to lose him listeners, and he wants to turn it around as quickly as possible. His agent is on board. So I need you folks to get me that contract in the next two hours."

I felt a charge of energy. I'd always thrived under deadlines. "No problem, Mr. Pickett. I'll find Tanner, and we'll get this to you right away."

"I've tried his cell phone a number of times already."

"I know how to reach him."

I hung up the phone and called Tavern on Rush. I spent ten long minutes describing Tanner to the maître d', insisting they find him, asking him to look again, all to no avail. I tried his cell phone, but he didn't answer. Maybe they'd gone to Lux Bar? Or Gibson's? Or Hugo's? I tried each one. No one at any of these establishments matched Tanner's description.

Finally, I called Forester back, taking pains not to reveal my panic. "I'm having a hard time reaching Tanner, but I'm sure we can get this done first thing tomorrow."

Forester lowered his voice. "His agent is here now. They're in talks with stations in L.A. But if we get this done tonight, they'll sign with us. And I'll have just saved my company a truckload of money."

I thought about the contract. It was essentially ready to go. All I'd have to do was insert the new salary. "No problem, Mr. Pickett. What are the new contract terms?"

Forester named an amount, hundreds of thousands less

than the original. I pulled up the contract on the computer, typed in the new salary term and printed it out. Now I'd have to proof the thing. If I made one mistake, I'd be collecting unemployment in a week.

Thirty minutes later I called Forester. "Does Baumgartner still get a signing bonus?"

"Ah!" he said, sounding pleased. "Excellent point. No. No signing bonus anymore."

"I'll take that out. And what about the bonuses if he reaches certain ratings?"

"Keep in the ratings bonuses."

"May I have your fax number? I'll send the contract to you in five minutes." I took down the fax, gave Forester my direct line and told him I'd stay in my office for the next few hours in case any additional changes were needed.

I went back to my office with a pleased smile on my face. Making the changes to the Bomber's contract, although simple, had been the first time I'd felt any proficiency with the law.

Forester called back in an hour and a half. "So you said your name was Isabel McNeil, is that right?"

"Yes, sir."

"How do you spell McNeil?"

I spelled it for him. I could hear Forester murmuring, as if he was writing this down, and the notion that Forester Pickett—media mogul, founder and CEO of Pickett Enterprises—was writing down my name was thrilling.

"Well, Ms. McNeil, you saved Pickett Enterprises today."

I blushed. I couldn't help it. As a redhead, the blush is impossible to control. "I think that's overstating it, sir."

"It's the truth. That's all there is to it. Now, tell me, how long have you been a lawyer?"

"Only about a year. I've been working here with Tanner Hornsby most of the time."

Forester grunted at the mention of Tanner's name. I

interpreted this as a derisive grunt, which made me love him even more.

He asked me where I'd gone to law school, and I described Loyola University in Chicago. He asked about college, and I told him about the University of Iowa. And soon, I was talking about high school in the city and grade school before that and how we'd lived in Michigan before that. Forester was one of those great listeners. He chuckled at all the right times, and asked for clarification about this and that. He told me a few stories, too, like how he'd started in the business by buying a radio station, but how he'd gone to the University of Chicago at age fifty to get his college degree.

By the end of our conversation I felt, oddly, as if I was becoming friends with the man. The fact that he was a *bizillionaire* and I was a relative pauper didn't matter, nor did the fact that he was one of the firm's biggest clients and I was merely a peon associate.

When we were about to hang up the phone, Forester said, "You did well today, Izzy." It was the first time he'd called me that, and I blushed again, but this time with pride.

The next day, Forester sent a new case to the firm. The lawsuit wasn't anything big, just a simple torts case, a slip-and-fall accident at a theater Forester owned, and it arrived at our offices the same way all Pickett cases did.

The only remarkable thing was that the letter of retention wasn't directed to Tanner. Instead, it was made out to *Isabel McNeil.*

7

An emergency-room nurse in pink scrubs stepped in front of me and held out an authoritative arm. "Who're you here to see?"

"Forester Pickett."

She pursed her mouth. "Mr. Pickett is…" She glanced over my shoulder, as if looking for reinforcements.

"He's passed away. Yes, I know." I put on my courtroom face and refused to let the statement register. "I'm actually here to see his son."

"No one can go in except the family."

A green curtain that covered the entrance to one of the rooms was flicked back at its corner and Shane Pickett's face peeked out. "She's okay." He let the curtain fall closed.

"All right, go ahead," the nurse said. "Sorry about your loss."

The emotion hit me for the first time, and I felt as if I might gag on something large, something wrong, in my throat. "Thank you."

I pulled back the curtain and stepped inside. Shane sat next to a metal bed, staring at the form that lay there, covered. Shane was a small man, a sharp dresser, his brown hair always parted severely and combed precisely. He had recently started wearing glasses that were stylish, but I got the feeling he wore them so that he would somehow look older, smarter. When Forester had had a heart attack a few years ago and succession planning was done at the company, Shane was made president of Pickett Enterprises, so that if something happened to Forester or when he stepped down as CEO, Shane would run the place. Forester was determined to keep it a family company. (I think he hoped Shane would have kids and that those kids would work there, too.) But Shane hadn't been a "natural" in the business like his father was. There had been a lot of talk that he wasn't ready or worthy for the position of CEO.

Shane looked up at me now, then back at what was apparently the form of Forester Carlton Pickett, the kindest and most vibrant man I'd ever known, now covered with a white, hospital-issue sheet. Forester had been a simple man in many ways, but he'd loved luxury in all its forms, and in particular he'd often spoken about his 1500 thread-count sheets and how he always bought the best bedding money could buy. Something about the hospital sheet that now covered him struck me as deeply wrong.

"Shane, I'm sorry," I said.

Shane stood and launched himself into my arms, crying.

"It's okay," I murmured, rubbing his back. "It's okay."

But it wasn't.

As Shane's sobs continued, all I could think about was the discussion I'd had with Forester two weeks ago.

We were in my office for our "monthly roundup" as Forester called it. Forester met with his key professionals to find out precisely what everyone was up to. In the early days, I hosted him in the big Baltimore & Brown conference room with its view of the Sears Tower. I always ordered in a vast assortment of coffees, pastries and exotic fruit, but he'd soon had enough of that.

"You don't need to feed me, Izzy," he'd said. "And your office is just fine. Wherever you work, I work."

So each month, I sat at my desk with its stacks of documents and contracts, and Forester sat unperturbed on the other side, sometimes moving a large folder in order to see me better.

That day, a few weeks ago, Q had come into the office with Forester's usual cup of black coffee and a green tea for me.

"How are you, Quentin?" Forester said, standing to greet him. He was a little distracted that day, but as always, Forester took the time to speak with everyone.

"Great, sir, thanks." Q handed him his cup of coffee with a smile. If anyone else had called him Quentin, he would have grimaced, but Q loved Forester as much as I did.

"And how's Max?" Forester asked, even though being gay didn't quite register with Forester. "I *don't* understand it," he'd once said to me, almost under his breath, but not in an unkind way. Just in a bewildered way. Yet he dutifully and honestly asked about Max every month.

"Great," Q said. "He's fantastic."

"Good. Say hello for me." Forester patted him on the shoulder affectionately. "And thanks for the coffee."

We took our seats and spent the next hour discussing a lawsuit we'd filed against a delinquent contractor from a build-out of one of Forester's studios.

As we wrapped up, Forester shifted in his seat. "Look, Izzy, you've got to promise me something."

"I'll be nice to the contractor at his deposition. I promise." Forester hated needless nastiness, which was, I suppose, why he wasn't a lawyer.

"Thank you but, no, it's not that."

I closed my notebook and waited.

Forester shifted again. "Look, if something should happen to me, which of course it's not going to, but if someone tries to…I don't know…harm me, I want you to look into it."

"What exactly are you talking about?" I said.

"I'm healthy as a horse."

"Right, I know that."

"It's been three years since the heart attack, and you know everything I've done—how I've changed my eating, my exercising?"

"Right."

"And this morning, I had a physical with my cardiologist. Stress test, EKG, the whole rigmarole. I passed with flying colors."

"Good. I'm glad. So what do you mean about someone trying to harm you?"

Forester paused, which was unlike him. "I've had some problems at Pickett Enterprises. Over the last few weeks, I've been getting letters telling me I need to step down. That I'm too old for the job."

"Sent by whom?" I said, indignant.

"I don't know."

"Maybe it's a prank."

"Possibly." Another pause. "It's just the damnedest thing." Forester shook his head. "There's also the matter of this homeless man. Twice outside Pickett I've been approached by a homeless gentleman."

"And of course you gave him twenty bucks." Forester could never pass up an opportunity to help someone on the street.

"Something like that. But he spoke to me. He said something disturbing." Forester's face, perennially sun-kissed from hours at golf courses and gardening, seemed to pale slightly. I noticed the lines crinkling his face. "He said to be careful. Otherwise I would join Olivia."

I inhaled sharply. "Are you sure?"

Forester met my eyes. "Positive. The next time I saw him, I gave him money again, and he said the exact same thing."

I crossed my hands on my desk and squeezed them together. Suddenly, I felt my youth. As Forester's attorney, I was meant to advise him, but I had no idea what should or could be done. "Did you call the police?"

"No. There's no crime. No extortion or anything."

"We'll get you a security detail then."

Forester made a face. "Izzy, you know me better than that." He cleared his throat and sat taller, as if throwing off the conversation.

"Then let's call John Mayburn," I said, referring to the private investigator the firm hired for big cases.

"Don't worry about it. I'm handling this for now, and nothing is going to happen to me. I'm sure it's all a coincidence." He gave me the kind smile he was known for, and he changed the topic.

Since that conversation, I'd worried about Forester, but I did what he wanted, and I let him manage the situation. And now he was dead. I stared at his body covered by the hospital sheet.

"God, I can't believe it," Shane said, wiping his face. He took a step back. "Sorry about that, Izzy."

"Don't be." I sat in a chair at the foot of the bed, then pushed the chair back a few feet. "What happened?"

"Annette made him dinner and left. But she forgot something and came back about forty-five minutes later and she found him. He was dead. Out on the patio."

I put my hand to my mouth. Poor Forester. What had he gone through in those last moments? "What do the doctors say?"

"Heart attack. You know he had that heart attack a few years ago?"

"Yeah, but he had the angiogram after that and he's been so diligent about everything—his diet, the medications, the Chinese herbs, the exercise."

"You know about all that?"

"Your dad and I were close."

Shane nodded. "He thought of you like a daughter."

"I also know that he had a stress test a few weeks ago."

Shane looked surprised. "He did?"

"And an EKG. And he was told everything was fine."

"Well, I know if you've had a heart attack once, it can happen again."

"I guess."

We both looked at the covered form on the bed. I felt an intense urge to cry. I took a huge breath. "Shane, why is he still here? I mean, the body. Shouldn't they take him out or something?"

"They will. Any minute. We're just waiting." He laughed, a raw sound. "I guess *I'm* just waiting. He's not really here anymore is he?"

"Will they do an autopsy?" I asked.

"They say they have to."

"Good." My mind raced. Had someone hurt Forester or was it as tragically simple as Shane had suggested and just another heart attack?

Shane slumped forward, shaking his head back and forth.

"Shane, are you okay?"

He righted himself and nodded.

"Has anyone been here with you?"

"Walt just left to start calling people."

"Good." "Walt" was Walter Tenning, the chief financial officer of Pickett Enterprises and the most efficient of men.

"I called my aunts and uncles," he said, "but they all live down south. They're coming in tomorrow."

It seemed incongruous that Forester, a man who was loved by everyone he touched, would have so few people at his deathbed. I couldn't believe that Forester—wonderful Forester who had done so much for so many—was gone. He'd given both Sam and me our careers, and Sam had always said Forester had been the best teacher, not just about business, but about life.

"Where's Sam?" Shane asked, as if reading my thoughts.

I opened my mouth, then closed it. I thought about making up an excuse for my fiancé. But nothing came.

"I don't know," I said to Shane. "I have no idea where Sam is."

8

After Forester's body had been taken away, Shane and I hugged one last time in front of the hospital, and I went to my place in Old Town. I lived on Eugenie Street, in a brick three-flat converted to condos. I had bought the top unit, mostly because it gave me the rooftop deck with the city view, while the other owners had to make do with a balcony or patio. The downside was the three-flight walk up. Those stairs had never seemed so long as they did the day Forester died.

When I finally reached the landing and began to push open my door, I felt a twinge of optimism peek its head through my grief. Maybe Sam was here. He had spent less and less time at his place in Roscoe Village lately, and in a few short months, after our holiday wedding, he'd be living here officially.

But the place was dark, and over the kitchen bar top, I saw Sam's orange coffee mug, sitting at the side of the sink where he'd left it that morning. Now the kitchen was bathed in a cold pool of moonlight that filtered through the window. *Where was he?*

The only upside to not finding Sam was that I didn't have to tell him about Forester's death. Forester meant the world to him and he would take this news hard.

I turned on the overhead lights and stared around the condo. The polished pine floors and the marble turn-of-the-century fireplace with its bronze grate had seemed cozy when we left this morning. Now the place felt cold. I called Sam's two closest friends. Neither had heard from him that night. I called Sam again. It went right to voice mail without even ringing. Had his battery died or had he turned off his phone? If he had turned it off, then why? My head reeled with possibilities—an accident, a robbery, a sudden all-encompassing desire to scare the living shit out of me?

I tried his home phone once more, then the office again. I repeated the process five more times. Insanity is sometimes defined as repeating the same action over and over again, expecting a different result. I pondered this as I dialed Sam one more time.

Then a new thought hit me—it was Tuesday night, which meant the Chicago Lions rugby team practiced tonight, which meant the team would be out boozing at this moment. Sam had taken this season off, in preparation for the wedding, something that had drawn merciless taunting from his teammates. But maybe sweet, responsible Sam had flipped under the pressure. The team didn't usually go out after practice, but maybe they'd headed to McGinny's Tap, their favorite postgame hangout. Maybe Sam had gotten loaded, and maybe he was even cheating on me with one of the women who chased around the team.

Strangely, I was fine with this thought. Drunken debauchery I could handle right now. I could even forgive it. Yesterday, the thought of Sam cheating would have sent me careening around the city on my Vespa, a kitchen knife tucked in my fauxcrocodile clutch. Now, I actually found myself praying that my fiancé was throwing up too much beer into a gutter, his arm still around a big-boobed blonde. Because then he wouldn't be hurt. Because then, somewhere, he would be okay.

I scrolled through my phone to see if I had any numbers of the rugby guys, but there were none. There'd never been a reason to call them before.

I flicked the lights back off, went into my bedroom and stripped off my clothes. I pulled on a Jeff Beck–concert T-shirt of Sam's and crawled under the thick duvet. It seemed wrong to lie down, to be doing nothing, but the urge to escape the day was overpowering. Behind the grief of losing Forester and the worry about Sam, I felt inconsolably guilty. Today, I'd felt overwhelmed with my job—with everything Forester had given me. And I'd felt overwhelmed, too, with the wedding, with Sam, I guess. And now, they were both gone.

9

Day Two

I never slept. The phone never rang. I finally got up at 6:00 a.m. I got on my computer and checked my e-mail. The usual batch of messages appeared in my in-box—notes from other lawyers, one from Maggie about tickets to a concert at the Vic, announcements from local clothing stores where I spent too much money—but nothing from Sam.

I showered but couldn't deal with my hair and so I pulled it back in a low ponytail, and decided to go to the office where Q would help me, where I could figure out what to do next.

I had always liked the crisp quiet of Baltimore & Brown when the gray-white early-morning light filtered in the windows and hung there before all the troops descended. But at 7:05 it was too quiet. I texted Q and asked him to get in as soon as possible. I tried Sam's numbers again. And again. And again. This insanity was seriously fucking with my calm. I mean, *flubbing* with my calm. *Flubbing.*

I looked at my watch. It was too early to phone Sam's mom or sisters in California. I called the police and was told Sam hadn't been arrested and I could fill out a missing persons report if I came to the station.

"What would you do then?" I asked.

"We just take the report," the officer said.

"And then what?"

"We just take the report," he repeated.

I tried Northwestern hospital, along with Michael Reese, Illinois Masonic and every other hospital I could think of. Nothing. I tried his best friend, R.T., again, who answered sleepily and said he still hadn't heard from him.

From down the hall, I heard the swishing sound of a key card and then the click of the door opening.

"Q?" I yelled.

No answer.

"Q?"

Not a sound. It was too early for assistants to be here, and most of the attorneys didn't start arriving until at least eight. Goose bumps rose suddenly on my arms.

I stood from the desk and hurried to the door.

"Oh!" I said, colliding with someone turning in to my office.

Tanner's slicked-back hair had its usual sheen, but his blue eyes looked as tired as mine.

"You scared me," I said, a hand on my chest.

"Sorry." It was the first word of apology I'd ever heard Tanner utter. To anyone. "I saw your light on. Guess you couldn't sleep either?"

"No. You heard about Forester?"

He nodded. "Can I come in?"

"Of course." I sat at my desk, watching Tanner sink into a chair.

"I thought the old guy would live forever," he said.

"Me, too." I choked a little as I uttered the words.

Tanner shook his head, and we sat in a silence that felt both mutual and poignant. I wouldn't have thought Tanner capable of such a moment, and I never thought I'd share one with him, but grief, I suppose, makes for unusual buddies.

"Have you talked to Shane this morning?" I asked.

"I just got off the phone with him. He's a mess. Thank you for being at the hospital last night."

"Of course."

"I was at the opera. I didn't get the message until late."

I heard the outside door click again, then I heard Q's voice yell hello from down the hall.

A few seconds later, Q stepped into my office then stopped suddenly when he saw Tanner.

"Hiya, Mr. Hornsby," he said in his fake-effeminate voice.

When neither of us responded right away, Q's eyes swung from me to Tanner and back.

"Q," I said, "Forester died last night."

A beat went by. "What?"

"Yeah. Heart attack."

Q slumped against the back wall and put his head in his hands.

My phone rang, and I snatched it up.

"Izzy?" I heard a man's voice say.

Damn it. Not Sam. "Yes?"

"It's Mark Carrington." Sam's boss. I sat up straighter. "We've got a problem over here."

"Mark, is it Sam?"

"Yes."

Something sour and rotten twisted in my stomach. "Is he there?"

Mark paused. "No, he's not. Do you know where he is?"

I looked at Q and Tanner. Both were watching me curiously. "No."

"Well, there's something else that's not here. A series of bearer shares from Panama, owned by Forester."

"I'm not sure I understand."

"I was supposed to fly to New York this morning for another client, and I came in early to get something from the firm's safe. I saw that Sam had logged in to it last night."

"Sam logged in to the safe *last* night? You're sure?"

"Positive. We each have our own codes, so we can tell exactly who's been in there. I couldn't think of anything he would have needed, so I looked around the safe, and Forester's bearer shares are missing. They represent ownership of a corporation that holds about thirty million dollars of real estate in Panama. Whoever's in possession of those shares essentially owns them, and they're as good as cash."

My mind skittered back and forth. *Panama. Missing. Thirty million.*

"Something is screwed up here," Mark said. "*Really* screwed up. Because those shares aren't the kind of thing we usually keep in our safe. Just a month ago, Sam came to me and told me Forester wanted to move them from the safe-deposit box where he kept them. Something about switching banks and it being a temporary thing."

"Really?" Sam and I tried to be good about not discussing Forester's legal work or his financial holdings. I had an attorney-client privilege to protect, and Sam had a duty as his wealth manager not to discuss his portfolio. But there was something called the spousal privilege, and although we weren't married quite yet, Sam and I exercised it on a regular basis discussing Forester. It was impossible not to when Forester was the center of both of our professional worlds. But Sam hadn't mentioned anything about Forester changing banks or moving thirty million dollars of shares into the safe.

"Yeah, really," Mark said, his voice angry. "This is serious. You sure you don't know where Sam is?"

"I don't have any idea."

Mark exhaled loudly. "I called Forester, but he hasn't gotten back to me yet."

"Mark...Forester died last night."

"Are you kidding?"

"He had a heart attack."

"Oh, God."

"What time did Sam log in to the safe?" I asked.

I saw Tanner's eyebrows rise. I wanted to ask him to leave, but I couldn't wait even a minute to get some answers about Sam.

"Around eight-thirty."

A half an hour after I'd talked to the lobby security guard.

"What time did Forester die?" Mark said.

"I'm not sure. I guess around six or seven."

"When is the last time you saw Sam?"

"Five-fifteen or so."

We were both silent.

"Izzy," Mark said. "I think I'd better call the cops."

10

The day I met Sam I made him bleed.

We were at Forester's house in Lake Forest, at the annual end-of-June barbecue he threw for all his employees and business associates. Everyone was invited—from the execs to the valets.

The weather was crisp and sunny, a brand-new summer day with everyone conscious of how the Chicago climate would soon give way to sticky humidity and biting mosquitoes. Families were invited to the party, and many people rowed their children across Forester's pond or whacked the croquet balls across his rich, green lawn.

I had already spent the better part of a painful hour sipping a mimosa and listening to Tanner Hornsby talk at his pack of sycophants. Technically, I was one of those sycophants. I was a year out of law school, and although Forester had thrown me a couple of cases, he wasn't yet giving me the bulk of his files. I understood that my job as an associate was to perform grunt work, to smile about it and to murmur comments of thanks to Tanner for the great opportunity.

Tanner was repeating a story I'd heard ten times before about a caddy who'd given him bad advice on a putt. This story was always told with scathing scorn toward the caddy and a hero's verbal welcome for Tanner himself, since he'd seen through that awful recommendation and, using his stellar athletic intuition, read the green perfectly and sunk the putt.

That was how Tanner operated—he pumped himself up and up and up, so that his bloating, floating presence seemed akin to a Macy's parade balloon on Thanksgiving morning. Tanner only talked about three things—sports, the law and, most importantly, himself. The rest of us were supposed to scuttle along after him, guffawing and clapping him on the back. Some people liked getting their butts kissed, others despised it. Tanner *thrived* on it.

My buddy Grady was there, too, but Grady loved sports stories so he asked Tanner lots of questions and yucked it up. Meanwhile, my only contribution was a few saccharine chuckles, until I couldn't take it anymore.

"You know, Tanner," I interjected, "the word *caddy* comes from the term *cadets* after the men who attended Mary, Queen of Scots, when she played the game. Caddies are there to merely aid the golfer, not ensure victory."

This comment was the intellectual sports equivalent of flashing my tits, and Tanner stared at me, verbally stumped for a moment. A few of the other guys raised their eyebrows.

Tanner recovered by ignoring me and launching into a story about how he then went on to birdie the eighteenth hole. I was plotting my escape when Forester stepped up to our group. He was dressed in a cream linen jacket and a yellow tie, with a matching handkerchief tucked in his jacket pocket. His thick silver hair was perfectly groomed. He looked every inch the gentleman he was. Everyone immediately hushed, except for Tanner, who boomed to Forester about the *just fantastic* party and asked about "the Mouse."

"The Mouse" was Tanner's nickname for Forester's son, Shane, who was one of his best friends from childhood. I hated that moniker, especially since "the Mouse" was the precise reason that Tanner had all of Forester's legal work.

Forester smiled kindly and pointed to his son Shane—a short man in a seersucker jacket—who was speaking with a few other people on the limestone patio.

Forester turned to me. "Can I steal you away, Miss McNeil? I'd love you to meet someone."

I saw Tanner's face flash with surprise, then annoyance. Just as fast, the look disappeared. "Sure, sure," Tanner said, as if giving permission. "But don't keep my girl too long. Izzy's got a big Saturday night ahead of her, working on interrogatories for me."

Forester blinked a few times at Tanner's proprietary statement, which made me sound like a little lawyer geisha he only brought out at parties.

"That's right," I piped in, unable to stop myself. "I'll be working tonight, since Tanner will be too busy house hunting."

Tanner had just gotten a divorce from his third wife, a very public divorce in which she'd forcibly removed him from their home, a home the judge had awarded to her. The story of Tanner being ousted from his own castle had spread rapidly. We all knew that Tanner was living in a temporary apartment on Ohio Street.

I bit my lip as soon as I'd said it. Grady laughed loudly, then when no one joined him, shut his mouth. Tanner glowered.

"All right then," Forester said, like a dad on a playground. "Izzy will be back shortly."

Don't count on it, I thought as I followed him across the lawn.

Forester wore a bemused grin. "You know, you shouldn't have said that."

"I know. I'm sorry."

"No, you're not, and I don't blame you. The man can be insufferable. Has been since he was a kid. But then, I don't work for him." He looked pointedly at me.

I felt a flash of panic. I'd probably just set my career back by that jab at Tanner. It was one thing to toss in a random remark about golf history. It was another to attack him personally.

We passed the bar, and I swiped a beer from a tub full of ice. Enough mimosas. I needed something heartier, and I noticed Forester had a beer himself.

I'd just twisted the cap off when Forester stopped and tapped the shoulder of a man who swung around in mid-chuckle. He had blond hair that shone in the sunlight and eyes that were both soft and sparkling, like an olive in a martini glass. He was so yummy I wanted to mop him up with a biscuit.

"Forester, how are you?" the man said. I noticed he was about my age, but he spoke to Forester as if they were old and dear friends. Later, I would learn that Sam viewed Forester as a father figure. Sam's own dad was a jackass of epic proportions—a hard-partying, fist-flinging man who Sam's mom had finally divorced when Sam was in high school.

And, apparently, Forester felt the same way. "Son," he said to Sam, "I want to introduce you to a member of my legal team, Izzy McNeil. Izzy, this is Sam Hollings. Sam is one of my financial advisors."

Sam turned his gaze my way and held out his hand. He was on the shorter side, but he gave the impression of solidity and strength. He dipped his head slightly as if shy, yet a grin pulled at the corners of his wide mouth. And then the strangest thought occurred to me. *I could kiss that mouth. Forever.*

I'd really never had such a thought before. I could be hot for a guy, and I could think he might make a decent date to a wedding (i.e., drink enough to be funny, but not enough to embarrass me), but I usually didn't want to kiss—just kiss—someone so immediately. And I never used the word *forever.* I knew forever didn't exist.

I realized suddenly I was staring. I noticed Forester watching us, and it dawned on me that I hadn't shaken the guy's hand. I thrust my hand forward and gave him a fierce, tight handshake to cover up my lapse.

"Nice to meet you." I pumped his hand, squeezing it. "Really…nice."

Sam winced a little and looked down when I finally let go. There, on the tender pad of skin below his thumb was a small bead of blood.

"Oh my gosh." I opened my own hand and saw the bottle cap I'd forgotten I was holding, one of its sharp edges tinged red. "I'm so sorry…"

"No problem." Sam brushed away the dot of red with his other hand. "I'll live."

"He'll live," echoed Forester. "He's a tough one. He plays rugby, did you know that?"

Sam smiled. "She just met me, Forester, how is she supposed to know that?"

"I would have thought everyone knew about the great Sam Hollings." Forester patted Sam's shoulder. "Now if you two will excuse me…"

When he was gone, I gestured at Sam's hand. "I'm really sorry."

His eyes were fixed on mine. "I'm not."

Sam and I began our "forever" that moment, in the sun, on Forester's green lawn. Later, it became a ritual of ours—I would ask him if he loved me, and he would say, "Of course. I love you so much it makes me bleed."

11

After the phone call from Sam's boss, I had to get out of my office, away from the sad, sympathetic way Tanner was looking at me. I realized I liked his snarling criticism much better than his pity. And I also realized that the one place I hadn't looked for Sam was one of the most obvious—his apartment. I bolted out of the office, jumped on my scooter and headed to Roscoe Village.

Sam's apartment was next to a bar called the Village Tap. It was a cozy bachelor pad where we'd spent our early dating days.

I parked the Vespa and stood outside Sam's apartment building, shivering. The sky was a moody mix of white clouds broken up by occasional shots of sunlight that disappeared just as fast.

"Izzy!" I heard.

Maggie came trotting down the street, her tiny feet pounding on the sidewalk, her little arms swinging determinedly back and forth. Her light-brown hair with its natural streaks of gold hung in waves to her chin. She pushed it out of her face with an annoyed hand.

"What is going on?" she said when she reached me.

I'd left her a message, telling her that Sam was gone and that Forester had died, and that I needed to look around Sam's apartment but that I couldn't go alone. His place, which had once held me like a hug, scared me.

Maggie and I embraced. She was shorter than me by five inches, so I had to lean down. She was so delicate that she made me feel downright ungainly by comparison.

I pulled away and looked at her. "You cut your bangs again. You know you're not supposed to cut your own bangs."

Maggie had a habit of getting so irritated with her curly hair that she often took matters into her own hands and chopped away. It usually left erratic results causing Mario, her stylist, to throw a snit and swear he would stop cutting her hair if she didn't halt the self-mutilation.

"Yes, Mario will disown me. Now, what is going on?" She gave me that intent Maggie look—head bent down while her eyes looked up intently, her bottom lip dropping slightly away from the top.

I filled her in about Forester's death, about Sam not showing up last night, about the letters and threats Forester had received over the last couple months, about Mark Carrington's phone call and the missing Panamanian bearer shares.

"Holy cow." Maggie's eyes narrowed. "What's the deal with these Panamanian shares?"

"Mark Carrington told me Panama is big with retirees and people who want cheaper vacation homes. Apparently, Forester thought the country would be as popular as Costa Rica, so he was buying a lot of property there. Mark said that a common way to buy real estate in Panama is to have a corporation own the real estate. They issue shares of stock for the corporation, but the ownership of the corporation isn't recorded in any registry or database."

Maggie nodded. "The owners are anonymous."

"Right. And they don't have to report the transfer of ownership either. Panama is supposedly the last place you can get a truly anonymous corporation with no loopholes and no financial statements to file. Within the last few months, Forester put a lot of money into real estate there. With Sam's help."

"Did you know about this?"

"No. Mark said Sam came to him recently and asked to put those shares in the company safe. He said Forester wanted them moved from his safe-deposit box."

"And you're telling me that Sam now has those shares."

"Apparently."

We exchanged a look. I knew we were both thinking, *Why, Sam? Why, why, why?*

"Yesterday, Sam seemed worried about something," I told her. "He said it had to do with Pickett Enterprises, but I assumed it was the usual work stuff."

Was it possible he had felt the pressure of the wedding, too? He had said he was ready. He seemed a hundred percent about it. But maybe he was just trying to convince himself. Maybe the pressure had driven him to do something crazy. Maybe. But it simply didn't seem like Sam.

"Any chance Sam was the one sending those anonymous letters to Forester?" Maggie asked.

"No."

"You're sure?"

"I'm sure. Sam worshipped the man. Forester was the father he never had. Plus, what would Sam possibly gain from Forester stepping down from the company? He was one of Sam's biggest clients."

"What happened when Mark Carrington called the police?"

"They came to the office. He's talking to them right now."

"So, look," Maggie said, waving an arm in the direction of Sam's apartment, "maybe it's simple. He could be dead up there."

"That's helpful. Thank you. I'm glad I asked you to be here."

"You know what I mean. Maybe he came home and he fell or something."

"If he stole from Forester, I'll kill him myself."

"Maybe he was abducted."

"What?"

Maggie shrugged. "Who knows? I've heard of it happening."

"Yeah, to one of your drug clients. In *Colombia*." Maggie represented a host of drug runners. *Alleged* drug runners, as Maggie would say.

"I'm just throwing some possibilities out there."

"Let's not guess, okay?"

"Did he update his Facebook page or his MySpace?"

"You know neither of us have those." It was one of the things Sam and I had bonded over, our aversion to putting the tiniest details of our life on the Web.

"That's right. You guys are freaks."

"Really, you're so helpful."

"Okay." Maggie grabbed my arm and propelled me to the front door. "Open it."

Inside the front door, three metal mailboxes were attached to the wall. I stared at the second box—*Sam Hollings*.

We walked up the stairs and let ourselves into the second-floor apartment. It looked the way it always did. His leather couch was slouchy and slightly dusty. The blue afghan with the Cubs logo, which Sam's grandmother had knitted for him, was tossed over the side.

Maggie scoffed at the sight of the afghan. She was a Sox fan, a true-blue South Sider.

Sam's kitchen was typically unused looking, the refrigerator empty save for half a six pack of Blue Moon beer and a withered orange with a few slices cut out of it.

"Iz!" I heard Maggie yell from the bedroom. "Will you come here?"

Sam always made his bed in the morning and hung up his clothes at night, a trait he'd gotten from his mother. But Maggie was standing at the side of the bed, pointing at a blue suit that had been tossed there. "New or old?"

I walked to the bed and lifted it. I held it to my face and breathed in a faint smell—a little of the tea-tree aftershave he used and a little of something deeper, something pure Sam. "He wore this yesterday. He had it on at the wedding planner's."

"So…" Maggie said, trailing off.

"So he came home sometime after he saw me, and changed clothes and left."

"Not abducted, then."

"Probably not."

Maggie and I stood still.

I balled up the suit and hugged it to me.

I sat down hard on the wood floor. And then I started to cry.

"Oh, Iz," Maggie said, huddling her little form around me. "It's okay."

"It's not," I said between my tears.

"I know."

I wept for a few minutes and Maggie said nothing, just holding me.

Finally, I sat up straight. "I am okay," I said to convince myself.

Maggie sat back and watched me, saying nothing. Maggie always knew when to say nothing.

She hugged her arms around her chest, her black wool coat pooling around her, making her look like a little girl playing dress up. The difference was that Maggie was smarter than most adults I knew.

"The thing is," I said, "I really can't believe Sam stole those shares on purpose. He's the most honest man I know."

"We don't always know the people we love. I've seen that often enough," Maggie said. As an attorney specializing in criminal law, very little shocked her anymore.

"I know Sam." I shook my head. "Or at least I thought I did."

I closed my eyes and thought of Sam and me sitting on my rooftop deck, drinking Blue Moon, while Sam played guitar for me. He played songs he'd known for years—Buddy Guy and John Hiatt and Eric Clapton and Willie Nelson. He played songs he'd heard on the radio, since he could pick up almost anything by ear. And then he'd play songs he wrote for me. One was called "Wanting You Everywhere." At the bridge of the song, Sam would look at me with his martini-olive eyes, and he would say all the places he wanted us to go together—*Barcelona, Bangkok, Africa, Indonesia, Peru, Iceland, Tibet.* Panama had never been on that list.

Maggie pushed herself to her feet. "We'd better look around and see what he took."

"Is this a crime scene or something like that?"

"Not yet, and you need to figure out if he grabbed anything after he tossed off that suit."

I went into the bathroom and looked under the sink. "His shaving kit is gone." I opened a drawer. "And his toothpaste. And his deodorant."

"What about his clothes?"

Back in the bedroom, I opened the closet. "I can't really tell. It looks like a few things are gone, but I'm not here that much. Some stuff could be at my house or at the dry cleaner's."

"Is there anything he would take if he was going to be gone for a while?"

I stood in Sam's bedroom and glanced around. I tried to think like Sam. Like Sam standing in his bedroom with thirty million dollars in bearer shares.

I seized on a thought. I opened his nightstand drawer and reached under the small stack of rugby magazines. My fingers searched for the textured top of Sam's journal, a thin, green leather notebook one of his sisters had given him a few years ago. He wrote song lyrics in there, I knew, and occasionally thoughts about work or whatever else people wrote in journals. I didn't know for sure because I had never read it. Don't get me wrong, I'd thought about it a few times—once when Sam was pissed at me and stormed out of his house, another time when he'd been getting a few phone calls from his ex, Alyssa. But I wasn't a snooping kind of girl.

I knew exactly where he kept the journal, though, because

I'd seen him pack it when he went on vacation or long business trips. My hands searched through the drawer. I took out the magazines and a few books until the drawer was empty. The journal was gone.

12

Maggie offered to stay with me for the day, but I didn't want to just sit around, staring at the walls of Sam's apartment or mine, so I went back to work. Forester might be gone, but he wouldn't want the business of Pickett Enterprises to stop, or so I told myself, not sure if this thinking was for his benefit or mine.

Back at the building, I got off the elevator, ran my key card through the slot and hustled to my office. Was it a little quieter as I strode through the hallways? Were some of the assistants giving me looks?

Q sat at his desk, his bald head gleaming like a black globe under the lights. "Everyone's talking about it."

My eyes moved up and down the hall. "Talking about which part of it?"

"All of it. Forester. Sam taking those bonds."

"They're called shares." Why I was making the point, I have no idea. "How did everyone hear?"

"How do you think?"

"Tanner?"

"As far as I can tell. You shouldn't have had that conversation with him there."

"But I didn't really say anything out loud."

"He knew you were talking to Mark Carrington. Tanner used to be Forester's number-one guy, remember? He knows the inside circle. And you said something about 'the safe.' From what I can tell, he called Mark, who told him the whole story."

I groaned. Q was right. Talking in front of Tanner was a mistake. One I wouldn't have made twenty-four hours ago. I looked around. Down the hallway, a twenty-year-old assistant named Sheridan eyed me openly. The mail guy, pushing his cart, looked at me then quickly averted his gaze.

I turned back to Q's desk. "Where were you last night? I called you a bunch of times, but I couldn't get you."

"Out."

"With Max?"

"We didn't quite make it. His mother decided to come in early."

I groaned. "Oh, boy."

"Yeah. Oh, boy. I had to get the hell out of there."

"So what did you do?"

"Drank too much." Q looked down at his desk. "Look, Iz, I've got to tell you something. Elliot came down and got the Casey file this morning. Said he would finish the Motion to Dismiss."

"Great. I've been asking him to help me for weeks."

Elliot Nuster was an associate assigned to me. He had a stick-up-his-butt personality, but who could blame him when he also had to work with Tanner. Since Elliot was a year ahead of me, I often felt awkward giving him work, always having to ask nicely, and usually over and over again. But I simply couldn't handle all the Pickett work myself. Luckily, many of the projects or cases that came in the door from Pickett could be farmed out to the specialty groups—our intellectual-property people or the tax department—but the rest was mine and it was a struggle to keep on top of it, especially when I had to beg my associate to help.

"Yeah, it sounds good," Q said. "But it's weird, isn't it?"

"What do you mean?"

"He never offers to help."

"No lawyer ever *offers* to help, but if Elliot heard what happened, he's probably just chipping in, right?"

"Probably."

Q and I locked eyes.

"What are you going to do now?" he asked.

I looked at my watch, a Baume & Mercier given to me by Forester. The image of his covered form on the hospital bed made tears tug at the insides of my eyes. Then I thought of something equally unpleasant. "I have to call Sam's mom."

As I spoke the words to Lynette, Sam's mother—*gone since yesterday, no sign of him, looks like he took Forester's shares from the safe*—the sky outside my office window grew dark. Rain swooped into the area, bruising the sky with patches of deep gray.

"I don't understand." Lynnette said. "What?" Her voice caught. I could tell she was trying not to cry, struggling for an answer. Just like me.

I pressed the phone to my ear, giving her any details I knew, which weren't many.

"This isn't right," Lynette said. "I'm his mother. I brought that boy into the world, and I raised him. He is not a thief. There has to be a reason."

Silently, I looked out at the rain. I nodded. But what that reason was, I couldn't imagine.

When I was off the phone with Sam's mom, I called every other friend of Sam's I had a phone number for. Trying not to alarm anyone, I asked simply if they'd seen him yesterday. The answer was always no.

I looked at my watch. I called Mark Carrington to see if he'd learned anything new, but his assistant told me, in a frosty voice, that he was in meetings.

Panic started to rise in me, as much from futility as fear. Sam—*disappeared*. Forester—*dead*.

But Forester's company was still here. Which meant Forester needed me.

I picked up a contract I needed to work on—Jane Augustine's new one, but the words swam in front of me, like a bunch of tiny black fish in a white sea.

A memory crept into my mind of another day when I couldn't concentrate on work. A year ago, the day Sam and I got engaged.

It was the week after Thanksgiving, and we were each in our respective offices, ostensibly working but at the same time sending a bevy of flirty instant messages back and forth. Outside, the temperature had hit a bizarre sixty degrees, making everyone in the office gaze wistfully out the window.

I had just finished a letter that would be sent to the hundreds of employees of Pickett Enterprises, explaining the new paternity-leave policy, an easy task because it gave new dads a paid week off work. I called out to Q that I was e-mailing it to him, and I hit Send. But when I tried to move on to something new, I had a hard time focusing.

A message from Sam popped up on my computer with a pleasing *ding*. Hey Red Hot, it said, Want to play hooky and pretend we're rock stars?

I wrote back, It's 1:00 on a Wednesday.

Exactly. Let's pretend we're rock stars and we're just waking up from a gig last night. We'll get a hotel room and order food and champagne and drink it in bed.

I flipped open my calendar. No meetings scheduled that afternoon. Nothing to do, except attack the work that had been piling up, that was always piling up. I got back on the computer. You serious?

There was no message for three or four minutes. I opened a proposed contract for the renewal of a talk show Forester's company produced.

The computer dinged. James Hotel. Meet me in the lobby in thirty minutes.

That was something I loved about Sam—his ability to cut loose. He worked hard, and he didn't fear responsibility even a little. But he could also toss it aside and have a hedonistic amount of fun.

An hour and a half later, we were rock stars.

In the center of the suite, a huge room-service cart was piled with a strange mix of every single thing that had struck our fancy—popcorn, filet mignon, lobster salad, cheeses, champagne, beer and a huge ice-cream sundae that was chilling on a bed of ice under a silver cover.

Sam had brought CDs from his office, and we blared the tunes.

"C'mere," Sam growled at me at one point. He was standing at the side of the bed where I was sprawled in a haze of food and sex and music. He tugged me into a standing position and led me to the room-service cart. "We still have the ice-cream sundae, and I want to lick it off your collarbone."

"I won't say no to that."

Sam held my hand in his warm grasp and with the other, lifted the silver cover off the sundae.

"Yum." I pointed at the mounds of whip cream. "I can think of something better we can do with that."

I began to kiss his neck. I loved the way he tasted right then—a little salty, a little sweet, a little something darker.

"Can you think of something we can do with this?"

I looked. Sam was pointing at the top of the sundae. I blinked. Looked closer. Something was imbedded in the cream, and it was sparkling. I leaned forward, peered harder. It looked, oddly, like the art deco ring we'd seen in a window of a jewelry store.

I glanced at Sam, whose cute face was simply beaming. He nodded.

"Is that…?"

He nodded again. He took the sparkle from the top of the sundae and wiped it off with the edge of his robe. "Baby," he said, "you are a star. You're my star. I want you shining in my life forever."

Tears, like a cool, soothing rain, ran down my hot face. At the same time, I threw back my head and laughed. I had debated before about whether I wanted to get married. Sam and I had discussed the issue from every angle and we'd decided, in reasonable fashion, that we did want to get married eventually. But now, with Sam sinking to his knees, logic and reason were nowhere in the room. I was filled with a love so ferocious it seemed as though it could swirl around us and carry us out onto the street. I looked down at him, and my tears splashed his cheeks.

Now that Sam was gone, I started to doubt my memories of that day, the beauty of it, the beauty of us. Were Sam and I who I thought we were? Was Sam the man I knew? And without Sam, was *I* the same person I thought I was? I looked out the window into the rainy day and got no answers.

Grady Fisher pulled me out of my reverie when he stuck his head in my office. "Where have you been?"

I shot a look into the hallway. "Close the door, will you?"

Grady pushed the door closed and leaned back against it. His tie was loose, his shirtsleeves rolled high on his arms. "You all right?"

"I assume you've heard."

"Yeah. Everyone has heard, or at least heard the gossip." He paused. "I just want to know if you're all right. Give me a yes or no. You don't have to talk about it. You know that."

"I do know that. Thank you."

Grady and I had been buddies since graduation from law school. Professionally, we had been raised as brother and sister by our parents, the law firm of Baltimore & Brown. Grady was the sweetest guy—the kind who cleaned the firm kitchen when people left their microwave-popcorn bags out, the kind who bought a *Streetwise* newspaper from every homeless guy he saw, even though he already had a copy. When Grady and I were together, we didn't get deep with each other on a regular basis. We talked about the law firm and general stuff about our dating lives. We bailed out one another by covering court calls and depositions, but emotionally we never pushed too hard.

"So, are you all right?" Grady asked. He looked worried.

I blinked. "I don't know."

He moved into the office and sat down. "I can't believe Forester is…"

"Dead."

He winced.

"Yeah."

Everyone at the firm knew I was Forester's girl. People had been malicious at first. After that initial case he had sent me I'd gotten more and more of his work. Then the rumors started that I was sleeping with him. Such talk rattled me. I tried to point out to everyone that Forester hadn't even met me in person when he sent me the first case. No one cared. The talk continued.

It was only Grady who stuck up for me. I'd heard him once in a conference room, muttering, "Fuck you, dude, she's a great lawyer," to a clerk who had made a snide, sexual comment. It wasn't exactly true—I wasn't a great lawyer yet. The more I handled my own cases, the more I realized it took years, maybe even decades, to be a truly great attorney—but I appreciated Grady for saying it.

And it was also Grady who eventually told me, in his brief I-don't-want-to-discuss-this-much way, to get over it.

Lots of Forester's work was coming to me then. I'd gotten a huge bonus and a big office with a window and I got a portion of every new case I brought in. But I still was troubled about the way people were viewing me, and the pressure of the job was mounting.

"Izzy, enough bitching," Grady said one day over a beer. "You've got it better than any other associate at this firm. Better than any other associate in the city probably. You need to work hard and make a ton of cash and just let all those dickheads root around in their jealousy. Shut up and enjoy it, okay?"

It was a radical instruction. *Enjoy it.* There isn't a lot of talk about *enjoy*ment in the law. Some attorneys love the law and some put up with it for the salary and the prestige, but rarely did you hear someone speak about deriving actual pleasure from the whole experience.

I made a conscious decision to ignore the gossip and sink myself deeper into the work. I got to know Forester better, and I both adored and respected him. I wore suits that were sexy, not caring if such attire led to discussions about how I'd used my looks to get ahead. Soon after, I found Q, who made the work all the more fun. I sometimes missed the fraternitylike camaraderie that other associates experienced. But I had Forester, and I had Q, and I had Grady, and when I needed a little less testosterone in my legal world, I had Maggie, and then eventually, to flesh out my personal life, I had Sam.

But now, two of those pieces were missing.

"So, what have you heard?" I asked.

"Sam is gone and so is fifty million worth of some kind of corporate shares."

"Thirty million."

Grady blinked.

"*Allegedly,* it's thirty million," I said, channeling Maggie. I rubbed my forehead, wanting desperately, even for a moment, to be away from all this. "Look, for just a second, can we pretend it's yesterday. Before all this happened?"

"Sure." Grady sat back in his chair.

"So…" What would Grady and I usually talk about?

"Got any trials coming up?" Grady asked. "I have to make sure I'm there to mop up the flop sweat."

"Fuck you," I said, feeling the relief of using curse words knowing we were about to talk about something that normally embarrassed the hell out of me.

Like siblings, we knew the other's weaknesses. Grady's was billing. And like the brother figure he was, Grady saw it as his job to ridicule me about mine—acute nervousness I occasionally experienced at the start of a trial that resulted in extreme perspiration.

The first time it happened was during my very first trial for Pickett Enterprises under the most mortifying of conditions—as if the devil had taken a coal straight from the furnace of hell and plopped it onto my body. The results were worse than Whitney Houston at the Super Bowl. Panicked, I asked the judge for a recess, locked myself in a bathroom stall and, using a nail file and my teeth, I cut the shoulder pads free from my suit. I put the suit back on and kept the shoulder pads tucked under my arms for the rest of the morning. My hand gestures were probably a bit mechanical, but it did the trick.

The upside of my little dilemma was that it had happened only a few times, only under severe stress, and it seemed to last just a few hours.

"Okay, new topic," I said. "Dating anybody?"

Grady was a catch—dark-brown hair (most of it still there), a charming, wide grin and a great intellect that never made anyone else feel small.

"Ellen," he answered.

"Ellen is back?"

"Ellen is definitely back."

"Great." I liked Ellen. "Does she want a ring?"

"Yes."

"Are you going to give it to her this time?"

"I might."

Grady had told me over and over, *I don't want to be with the same person all the time. Plus, Ellen and I aren't like you and Sam. We're not in love like that.*

"So this thing with Sam…" Grady trailed off.

"I don't know anything." The image of his blue suit seared my mind. "New topic."

There was an uncomfortable silence.

"I don't know what else to talk about right now," Grady said.

I made an exasperated sound.

"Well, it's true. I feel like an ass talking about my dating life when you just lost the client you loved and your fiancé."

"I did not *lose* my fiancé."

"So where is he?"

"I've simply misplaced him. New topic, please."

Just then, the door flew open and Q sprinted into my office. "Iz," Q whispered. "The police are here."

13

Two men stepped into my office. Somberly, they introduced themselves as Detectives Damon Vaughn and Frank Schneider. They both wore pants and fall jackets that looked slightly bulky. When Detective Schneider unzipped his jacket, I realized they were both wearing bulletproof vests and guns in holsters at their waists.

The sight of those guns crystallized the intensity of the situation. This was serious. Deadly serious.

Grady left. I knew I should call Maggie—she was a criminal defense lawyer after all—but the problem was that Maggie would tell me not to talk to them. I had heard her tell people many times, *Don't speak to the cops. Never talk to them unless they arrest you.* Maggie had seen many interrogations go awry; she'd seen suspects confess to crimes they didn't commit. As a result, she viewed Chicago cops with the same wariness usually reserved for perfume-counter salesladies. *Just say no thanks,* Maggie would say, *and walk away fast.*

But I wasn't a suspect here. I couldn't see any way that I'd be considered a part in anything that had happened. More importantly, the detectives might know something about Forester. And Sam. If I just said "no, thanks," I wouldn't be able to find out what they knew.

"Have a seat, please," I said.

The detectives sank into their chairs. Schneider was a big guy, whose bulk draped over the chair. Detective Vaughn was lean, a runner, I guessed.

With hands the size of Frisbees, Detective Schneider held a form with white lettering while Vaughn sat motionless and watched me move behind my desk to take a seat. I was used to men looking at me, and yet his gaze wasn't as simple as being sized up by a guy hungry for a post-bar make-out. He was scrutinizing me.

Detective Schneider raised his eyes to me. He glanced at my hair and smiled. "My girlfriend in college was a redhead. Mindy Draper."

"Mmm," I said in a noncommittal way. For some reason, many people think all redheads are connected, maybe by a secret society that provided photos and contact information.

Detective Schneider dropped the chat. "We just have a couple of questions." His voice was low and soft, but there was a rumble to it that was almost menacing. "We're looking into the death of Forester Pickett."

"Good. Great." I felt a window of relief open in the room. Forester had asked me to look into the matter if something happened to him, and now I could be assured that someone was doing that.

"You were Forester Pickett's attorney," Schneider said.

"That's right."

"What kind of business was Mr. Pickett in?" I had the feeling he knew the answer already, but I explained that Forester was the Midwest's largest media mogul. He owned radio stations, newspapers, magazines, publishing companies and television studios. As his attorney, I did his contractual work, and I defended the company if it was sued.

"Was he involved in any takeovers?" Schneider asked. "Any corporate messiness?"

"No," I answered.

He asked a few more similar questions, all vague. I knew

he was fishing, which was what he was supposed to do, but I grew impatient.

"Look," I said, "I've got to tell you that Forester had been receiving threats."

"What kind of threats?" Detective Vaughn said, speaking up for the first time.

"He received anonymous letters saying he was too old for his job and that he should step down."

The detectives exchanged a glance, then looked back at me, and it was as if the air shifted into something brittle, crackling.

"Do you have copies?" Vaughn asked.

"No. I never saw them."

As I had that day Forester was in my office, I felt my youth then. As his attorney, I should have insisted that I get copies of the letters. I should have had them analyzed. But Forester said he didn't want to take action at that time, and no one told Forester Pickett what to do.

"How many letters were there?" Schneider asked in his rumbling voice.

I tried to think of the one conversation we'd had about it. "I don't know."

"What did they say other than he was too old?"

Why hadn't I asked to see the letters? "I don't know. There was also a homeless man who threatened him on two occasions."

"Tell us about that."

"Forester told me both times happened outside the Pickett offices. A homeless man came up to him and said if he wasn't careful he would join Olivia. Olivia was Forester's wife. She passed away from ovarian cancer."

"When was that?"

"He told me about the homeless guy two weeks ago. I got the impression the incidents had taken place recently."

Schneider blinked at me. Wrote nothing down. "What I meant was when did his wife pass away?"

I could easily remember Forester talking about Olivia, or

Liv, as he called her. They had met when he was twenty-three and about to close on his first radio station. Forester had gone to a men's clothing store to buy his very first suit. Liv's father owned the store, and she was working that day. Forester said he was immediately "smitten." For their first date, he took her to the closing. "She helped me with that suit," Forester had said, "and she helped me with that closing, and then she helped me with life." His face would always sag when he spoke about her.

"I believe Olivia passed away twelve or thirteen years ago," I told Detective Schneider.

"Did Mr. Pickett file a police report about this homeless guy?" Vaughn asked.

"No. He said no crime had been committed."

He grunted. "He was right. Doesn't sound like much of anything to me."

I crossed my fingers and leaned forward—the pose I always took during contract negotiations or depositions when I sensed things were about to get tough. "It doesn't sound like anything? He gets these letters and then a homeless guy tells him to be careful or he'll join his dead wife, and then he dies, suddenly, and that doesn't sound like anything to you?"

Vaughn raised an eyebrow. "What about you?"

"What about me?"

"Did *you* want him to step down?"

"No!"

Vaughn glanced around my cluttered office, then stared warily at my law-school diploma hanging on the wall. "You're pretty young to be handling all this legal work for Pickett, aren't you?"

"Technically, yes."

"How did you get it?"

"Forester. He chose me to be his lead attorney."

He glanced at my chest, then back to my face. "Why?"

A good question. He must have seen the hesitation in my face. He leaned forward, his eyes lasering onto mine. "You sure you didn't want him to step down?"

I was overwhelmed with the work. It was too much. But I didn't want it to go away. I didn't want Forester to go away.

"No, of course not. Forester is the reason I have this job," I said.

The detectives looked at each other again, then back at me.

Schneider shrugged. "Look, at this point, our investigation into Mr. Pickett's death is really just a formality, given the autopsy."

"The autopsy results are already available?" I knew from some medical cases I'd worked on during law school that autopsies usually took a couple of days, sometimes a week.

"Yeah." Schneider flipped through his notebook. "Mr. Pickett's son got somebody to push that through."

Why, I wondered, would Shane want to rush the autopsy? "What were the results?"

Schneider glanced back down at his notebook. "Acute myocardial infarction."

"Heart attack."

"Yeah. Likely caused by the usual—high blood pressure, age, history of smoking."

"But Forester's blood pressure was under control. He hasn't smoked in years."

"He had all the classic signs—he was slumped over when the EMTs found him, and he was clutching his chest."

I squeezed my eyes shut at the image.

"We did get a tip that something might not be right with this guy's death," Schneider said.

"Wait, you got a tip about Forester's death?"

Vaughn shot his partner a *shut-up* kind of glance, but Schneider just lifted his massive shoulders up, then let them drop. He nodded at me. Why did I get the feeling their little exchange was just for show?

"Who left the tip?" I said.

Another shrug. "Anonymous. We tested his food from that night. Clean. And Mr. Pickett's cardiologist saw him in the emergency room after he coded. He signed the death certificate saying it was a heart attack."

"But Forester had recently had a stress test. He said he passed with flying colors."

"The guy had a heart attack before. You're always at risk for another one. Could happen to anyone."

But Forester wasn't just anyone.

"Now, having thirty million dollars in corporate shares stolen," Vaughn said, speaking up, "that's a little unusual."

I met his eyes. I felt a blush creep over my neck, but I didn't move an inch. An uncomfortable silence filled the room as Detective Vaughn and I stared at each other. If he thought I would flinch first, talk first, he was absolutely wrong. I might doubt my legal abilities on occasion, but in a staring contest, I would always win.

Ten seconds passed, then twenty, thirty.

Schneider cleared his throat again. "You were engaged to Sam Hollings?"

"I *am* engaged to Sam Hollings," I said without moving my eyes from Vaughn's.

"When is the last time you saw him?"

"Yesterday. After work. We had a meeting with our wedding coordinator."

Vaughn chuckled, scornfully it seemed. Still, we stared at one another.

"He was supposed to take you to some shindig last night, huh?" Vaughn said with an upward flick of the corner of his mouth.

"That's right."

"Didn't show up?"

I felt my intensity melt away. "No, he did not."

Vaughn nodded, very slowly. Finally, he dropped his gaze

downward. But I felt no sense of victory. It was like winning a game deliberately thrown by the opponent.

"Any idea where he might be?" Schneider asked.

"No." My voice came out soft.

"Any idea why he'd take the thirty million in those shares?"

"I'm not even sure that he did."

Vaughn smirked.

Schneider looked at me for a long minute, then looked down at the form in his lap. He asked me a bunch of questions in a monotone voice. What was Sam's height, weight, build? Did he have sideburns? A beard? A mustache? What were his hobbies and pastimes? Did he have any skin disorders? What kind of car did he drive?

I answered all his questions quickly.

When he was done, Schneider placed his hand on top of the form. "We're going to turn over the Panamanian-share thing to the feds."

"What will happen?"

Schneider shrugged. "The feds will do whatever the feds do."

I took a breath and sat back in my chair. "And what about Forester's death. Will you look into those letters?"

"Nah," Schneider said. "Doesn't sound like much. We've got a man who died of natural causes. We're closing the matter."

"What about the homeless guy?" I couldn't believe they wouldn't be looking into Forester's death. If they didn't, who would?

"You find that homeless guy, you let us know, okay?" Vaughn said. He stood. The meeting, apparently, was finished.

Schneider shifted his heft to one side and fished a business card out of his pocket, handing it to me. It had the Chicago skyline on it. "Be careful if you see him."

"The homeless guy?"

"No, your fiancé."

"What do you mean, 'be careful'?"

"You didn't expect him to do something like this, right? Take off with those shares?"

"I'm not even sure he did."

"Well, you didn't expect him to disappear, right?"

"No."

"And he has. Apparently." Schneider opened his big hands wide. "So who knows what else he'll do. Maybe it's of his own volition, maybe not. Until it's all settled, keep your eyes open, be careful, and call us if anything changes."

I am rarely a speechless girl, but his warning had hijacked my words. Be careful of Sam?

Schneider stood with his partner. "Thanks, Ms. McNeil." His expression softened. If I read it right, it was one of pity. "And good luck."

14

John Mayburn followed the navy-blue Mercedes down Hubbard Street and watched as it turned in to the parking lot of the East Bank Club. He drove past the lot, found a spot on the street, threw quarters in the meter and hustled to the club.

When he was a few hundred feet away, he saw Michael and Lucy DeSanto entering the place. For once, he wouldn't have to sneak around or talk his way into an establishment in order to follow a subject. He was a member of the East Bank Club, although he rarely showed his face there anymore. He'd joined the club, the ritziest gym in the city, eight years ago when he was in his early thirties. The fact was, the East Bank Club, or simply "East Bank," as its members called it, was also a social club. It boasted a grill, lounge and spa and, in the summer, a rooftop pool that could have been outside a Miami hotel with all the beautiful bodies splayed around it.

Mayburn had joined East Bank when he'd first started out in the world of private investigations. Out of college he had initially started work as a claims analyst for an insurance company. He spent a few years there, then a few more following that as an independent adjuster, digging up evidence about malingering in personal-injury cases. It all bored him. So one day, when a lawyer he'd worked with asked if he did investigations for other types of cases, he lied and said yes. He quickly got his P.I. license and hung up his own investigative shingle. Once he was a P.I., he needed to meet potential clients in a discreet way and, when someone hired him, he needed to buy them drinks and meals in a not-so-discreet way. Which brought him to East Bank.

And now, years later, he'd been hired by Bank Midwest to investigate Michael DeSanto, one of its executives suspected of laundering funds, and Mayburn was pleased to discover DeSanto was an East Bank member. Before the DeSanto case, Mayburn had considered canceling his membership because it seemed he was too busy to use it, yet he carried around a tiny pipe dream that he would find time to start working out again, he would find time to sit in the grill and chat up a gorgeous female exec in high heels. In short, he dreamed of an ordinary existence, but he just couldn't seem to find the time to live it.

Mayburn ran his membership ID through the kiosk card reader and entered the gym, his eyes firmly on the black, curly-haired head of Michael DeSanto. When Michael and his wife, Lucy, a petite, elegant blonde with short hair, reached the locker rooms, they parted. Lucy called out to her husband as he walked away. She grabbed his arm and pulled him back for a kiss. Michael seemed to suffer through the gesture. Lucy stood for a second, watching his retreating back before she turned and pushed open the door of the women's locker room.

Mayburn had been watching the DeSantos for over a month now. They were ultrawealthy—definitely wealthier than they should be on DeSanto's executive salary. Mayburn had been trying to determine where the couple got the money that supported their high-flying lifestyle—a stunning home in Chicago, two others in Aspen and Grand Cayman, memberships on all the glitziest charitable boards and a small yacht they docked at Monroe Harbor in the summer. So far, he hadn't had a lot of luck finding the source. And Bank Midwest was getting anxious.

Just that morning, he'd gotten a call from Ken Cook, his contact at the bank.

"Look, I'll get to the point," Cook had said. "The board had a meeting yesterday. We're concerned as hell about DeSanto. We want him out, but we can't let him go without proof. If we fire him and accuse him of laundering funds for organized crime, he'll sue the hell out of us. We need something on this guy and soon."

Mayburn had been getting this message from them indirectly for the past few weeks, but now the real call. What Ken Cook was nicely saying was *Give us something fast or you're the one who's fired.*

"I need a little more time," Mayburn said. "This guy is smooth as hell, and his house might as well have a moat around it."

"We don't have the time. With the banking industry the way it is, we can't take on any kind of scandal, and we all think DeSanto is bad news and we want to cut him out. Quietly. We just need proof."

Mayburn wondered for a second if he should call it quits on this one. He'd had absolutely no luck getting inside their fortress of a mansion in Lincoln Park, nor had he had any success in getting close to Lucy, who he thought might inadvertently lead him to some piece of information about her husband. She was always at her husband's side, or else surrounded by women—usually other moms at the playground. Private investigations of this sort—with an intelligent subject who had protected himself like a medieval king—required sitting on one's hands, waiting and waiting and waiting, until the right moment of opportunistic light shot into your day. Unfortunately, there was little light breaking through the gloom in this case.

But if he quit, he'd have to give back the sizable deposit they gave him and then, most likely, he'd have to give up doing business with the bank ever again. Corporate clients were like that. If you couldn't produce the goods one time, they forgot your name.

"Ken," he said. "Just give me a few weeks. I'll find out what you need to know."

"You've got one week," Ken said. "That's it."

With this on his mind, Mayburn trailed DeSanto into the locker room and went to his own locker fifteen feet away. Using the mirror inside the door, he watched DeSanto change from a charcoal-gray suit into black shorts and a T-shirt. DeSanto had a toned body but for a pair of faint love handles. Mayburn had no real reason to believe this, but he imagined Lucy DeSanto was the type of person who actually liked that extra flesh on her husband's waist; thought it was sweet somehow, despite how DeSanto treated her—at least in public. In fact, it might be precisely because of how he treated her—like a possession he had little use for anymore—that Lucy probably found those love handles a sign of the humanity her husband no longer evidenced.

"Excuse me," Mayburn heard someone say.

He shot a quick look to his right, surprised. It was just another member, gesturing to get past him.

"Pardon," Mayburn said softly. He moved closer to the locker to let the man through. As he did so, he looked in the mirror again, and saw DeSanto glance his way.

Was he recalling that he'd seen Mayburn before? Was he remembering the guy behind him at the Starbucks on Armitage Avenue, near his home? Was he thinking of the man who'd sat two rows behind him while he was courtside at the Bulls game last week?

Mayburn turned his back to DeSanto. He doubted DeSanto could place him at either the coffee shop or the basketball game (or the bar at the Four Seasons or the men's bathroom at Bank Midwest), even though he'd been in all those places within mere feet of DeSanto. Mayburn had a knack for blending into his surroundings. His medium-size build, non-descript brown eyes and typical forty-year-old face worked perfectly to keep him inconspicuous. There was also his ability to change looks—jeans and a Jordan jersey for the Bulls game, a pin-striped suit and ivory handkerchief for the Four Seasons—that led subjects to occasionally think they'd met Mayburn. But rarely did anyone recognize him outright.

When he allowed himself to think about it, he wondered if this vagueness about him was the reason his personal relationships tended to suffer. His family in Wilmette thought of him as slightly odd, slightly standoffish, if only because he hadn't truly participated in their world. He hadn't gotten married despite a girlfriend here and there (he'd been dumped last year by Madeline, a half-Swiss, half-Japanese stunner), he didn't have children and he didn't work in the family's commercial-leasing business.

He left the locker room and followed Michael DeSanto to the cardiovascular room—a massive football field of a space lined with shiny silver treadmills, bikes and elliptical machines. The clientele here wanted a workout for sure—you could see the sweat and the rippling of toned leg muscles—but they were also here to be seen, hence the snazzy workout gear, the makeup on all the women's faces, the carefully constructed ponytails.

Mayburn trailed DeSanto from a wide distance for the next hour—first on the treadmills, later into the weight room. DeSanto spoke to no one, said nothing that could help Mayburn get into the guy's head or, even better, into the guy's house, where it was believed he ran the bulk of his laundering operations.

Mayburn left the weight room and went in search of Lucy, who he saw inside a glass-walled studio, her body held in an awkward V-shape, next to ten other women struggling themselves into the same position. Mayburn checked the class schedule. Advanced Pilates, it read.

Mayburn suppressed a sigh and turned away. Advanced Pilates was not something he was going to be able to fake, and besides, Lucy was once again surrounded by other women. He could usually blend in just fine, but not in Lucy DeSanto's world.

Something on this case *had* to give.

Mayburn left the club. As he walked toward his car, his cell phone vibrated. He reached inside his jacket pocket for the phone.

Baltimore & Brown, the display read.

He hit the Answer button, hoping to God it wasn't that dickhead Tanner Hornsby, who treated everyone who wasn't a lawyer as if they were distinctly second-rate. "Hello?"

"John, it's Izzy McNeil."

"Hey, Izzy." Now, Izzy McNeil was the rare kind of lawyer—the kind who didn't think her J.D. made her better than anyone else. And it didn't hurt that she was hot as hell. He'd worked with her a few times when she was still Tanner's associate and once when Forester Pickett was courting a well-known editor and Izzy wanted to know if the editor was in talks with other newspapers.

"You got a second?" she said.

"Sure." He found his silver 1969 Aston Martin DB6 coupe. It was a pain-in-the-ass car, always needing work, and when it got icy in Chicago, it was useless, but he loved the thing.

He slid inside and started the engine. He listened to Izzy's tales of woe—a fiancé who'd skipped town, apparently with a bunch of corporate shares of stock; the death of Forester Pickett; some business about letters Forester had gotten before he died and a freaky homeless guy.

"I'm really sorry about Forester," he said. He didn't meet the man when he'd handled the editor investigation, but he'd heard good things.

"Yeah." Izzy sounded on the verge of tears, which made Mayburn uncomfortable. He stared through the windshield at two girls, probably high-school students, eating bagels while they walked up the street.

He said nothing to Izzy. He'd found it more helpful to let people say what they wanted on their own terms.

Izzy got herself together and asked if she could hire him to find the fiancé—Sam, the guy's name was—and if he'd look into the matter of whether Forester Pickett had been killed.

"I thought you said he died of a heart attack." Mayburn put the car into drive and pulled out of the lot.

"That's what *they* say. But he'd been getting those letters. And what the homeless guy said to him—about how he'd join Olivia if he wasn't careful—I mean, it's clear someone was threatening him."

"I don't know about that." Izzy was sounding like a conspiracy theorist, and it depressed him that this woman he'd always thought of as sexy with her head screwed on straight was losing it a little.

She made a short growl, like she was irritated with him. "I promised Forester I would look into this if something happened, and now it has. I just don't think there's any way Sam would steal outright from Forester."

"But he logged in to the safe and now those shares are gone, and they're worth, what, thirty million?" He turned onto Franklin and headed north. "He made off with them in the middle of the night and disappeared. On the same day Forester died."

"Yeah, but—"

"Yes, but what?" he said.

They both fell into silence.

Lately, Mayburn had found himself simply wanting to do his work and go home. He knew this meant he was growing bored.

He only wanted cases that paid top dollar, or that gave him the street cred to continue building his résumé. Because if he wasn't personally drawn to the work anymore—and he wasn't, he was sick of the brain-stultifying effort that mostly involved sitting in a car with an audio surveillance system, listening to people taking a shit and having sex and just generally living their lives the way he wasn't—then he might as well get paid a heck of a lot of money to do it, and it better not depress the hell out of him. There was no way that Izzy's case—if he could even call it that—was not going to depress him. He would watch her go from a girl with exuberance and optimism to a bitter, pissed-off woman who'd been dumped and bamboozled.

"Hey, Izzy, I'm sorry this is happening to you, but I don't handle domestic stuff."

"This isn't domestic! It's not like Sam is screwing around on me, and I'm asking you to take pictures for evidence."

"Don't take this the wrong way, but that's probably what would happen. If I could locate him, I'd probably find him in bed with some sweet young thing, and I'd have to give you photos of it, in order for you to believe it."

"Screw you."

He chuckled, grudgingly. She had a mouth, he had noticed and despite his North Shore upbringing, he liked that in women. "Really, I'm sorry. I've got my hands full right now and, even if I didn't, you couldn't afford me." He reached Division, turned left and then right onto Clybourn, headed toward his house just south of Lincoln Square.

"Sorry," she said. "Look, I'll pay whatever it takes."

"I charge a retainer up front, and it's big."

"I remember. I approved your bills when you investigated the editor."

"That was small-time, and my rates have gone up since then. I've got more work than I can handle."

He mentioned a sum, the same he'd charged the bank where DeSanto worked. He explained how he then charged hourly, eating away at the retainer, but how he usually went well over it. He detailed the incidental fees that the client also had to pay—food, gas, copying, phone calls. He told her how his hourly rate soared if he worked nights or weekends, which was often, especially in a missing person's case. And then just to scare her, he told her how much he'd charged on his last case.

Izzy went silent. "We're getting married," she said, "and

so we've got a lot of money going out the door. I couldn't afford those fees."

"Right." Sad that the girl thought she was *still* getting married. "I really wish you the best, and if you hire someone else and you want to run things by me, give me a call, okay?"

"Yeah. Sure." Her voice sounded flat, which was hard to hear, since he'd always thought of her as full of life.

He'd watched her during the editor case. He was good at that—the watching. What he'd observed about Izzy was a quick ability to adapt. You could see her changing her vocabulary, her thinking, to fit whatever she was talking about or dealing with. She didn't seem like a natural at her job as Forester's lawyer, but he could also see that she believed she could be good at it if she just tried her ass off.

It would be an uphill battle for her now that Forester was dead. He'd gotten the feeling from everyone at the firm that they thought of her as the pretty girl who'd lucked into the gig.

He pulled into the alley behind his house and then into the garage. "Again, I'm sorry you're going through this, Izzy. Good luck."

"Thanks. Okay, thanks." Her voice sounded far away, fragile.

He hated to do it, but he hung up.

15

Between the meeting with the detectives and Mayburn's rejection I was feeling scared, my anxiety soaring. I paced my office. I picked up my phone over and over. I couldn't think of who else to call, and so I kept banging the phone onto the base.

Q opened the door and came inside. "Need anything?"

Behind him, I could see Holly, the assistant of the attorney next door, watching us. "I need you to get Holly to stop staring at me."

"Oh, ignore her." He looked over his shoulder and waved a hand. "She's two bad decisions away from being a crack whore."

I sat down. "I don't know what to do with myself."

"Sounds like what you need is a Halloween party with a lot of gay men."

I groaned. "I forgot." Q's annual party was that weekend.

"Max and his mother have been decorating for days."

"I don't think I can do it."

"I don't want to do it either. I'm so not in the mood. But you *have* to come. It wouldn't be the same without you."

"Sam was supposed to come with me." I swallowed. I was supposed to do everything with Sam. For the rest of my life.

"You can still wear the pumpkin costume," Q said.

I managed half a laugh. "I did *not* get a pumpkin costume, you pervert."

Q's big idea had been for me to dress as a pumpkin and for Sam to stick pumpkin seeds all over his face and wear a name tag that said, *Peter the Pumpkin Eater.*

"It's not for a few days," Q said. "Give it some thought."

"A few days. That seems so far away." For a long time, I'd been able to see my entire future before me—my work with Forester, my marriage to Sam. When it was all overwhelming me it seemed that the future was just a postcard—appealing and detailed on the front but flat when you really looked at it. And yet now that I had no idea what the next day would be like, I craved that pretty picture.

I glanced at Holly, then back at Q. "What are they saying? Does anyone know anything new?"

Q sighed. "It's just Tanner flapping his gums. But nothing new."

I felt a presence outside my door, I saw two first-year attorneys walking by, pausing for a second when they got to my office. One threw a nervous smile my way. The other glanced around.

"Hi, guys," I said.

I was usually a favorite among the law clerks, all of whom were stellar students from the local law schools. I was closer to their age than a lot of the other lawyers. I would sometimes drink with them after work, and I would give the straight skinny about whose butt to kiss and who to avoid.

But now they looked at me with curiosity and something approaching pity. "Hi," they said then kept walking.

I wanted to yell out, *Nothing to see here!* Instead, I stood, closed the door and grabbed my suit coat off the back of it. I put it on and looked in the mirror. My lightly freckled skin appeared pale with a faint gray hue, and my hair, normally bright and orange-red, looked faded. It was as if, in a twenty-four-hour span, I'd lost some of my luster. The thought only powered me into action.

I looked at Q. "I'll be back."

He squinted his eyes, probably sensing I could get myself into trouble. "Why don't you…"

"I'll be back." I turned, opened the door and stormed down the hallway.

I marched to the elevators and pushed the button repeatedly. I rode for two floors then made my way to the last door down the long hallway. Tanner's office.

Inside, Tanner was on the phone, his chair turned toward his windows so that he didn't notice me at first. I stood in the doorway, trying for patience, and looked around the place.

Every partner at Baltimore & Brown was encouraged to decorate their office in their own way and each got a small budget, but Tanner had clearly gone over his. His desk was a massive Oriental-teak affair, carved in detail and polished with a rosy, high gloss. His rug was plush, swirled in shades of crimson. Unlike most of the other lawyers who dealt with the overhead fluorescents, Tanner's office was lit by a trio of antique lamps.

He must have sensed me there, for he turned in his chair. The exhaustion in his eyes seemed to mirror mine.

"I've got to go," he said into the phone. "Hi to Peg. We'll talk tomorrow."

He waved me toward the brocade couch across from his desk. I closed the door and took a seat.

Tanner's eyes moved to the closed door, then to me. No one called the stage directions in his office except Tanner. I was past caring.

"How are you?" Tanner said. He looked as if he cared about the answer, which threw me.

"I've been better."

He nodded. He stared out his window for a moment, then back at me. "What do you need?" He glanced down at his watch.

There it was—the typical brusque tone, the usual attitude that assumed everyone would run around him like obsequious puppies. I was glad for the condescension. It put me right back in the mood.

"You know what I need?" I said, heavy on the sarcasm. "I need you to stop spreading rumors about my fiancé. The whole firm is talking about Sam and the bearer shares and the safe and Forester. And the only way they could be finding this out is from you or Q. And I know it's not Q. I'd have thought that you'd respect the privacy of another lawyer."

Tanner didn't say anything immediately, but his face softened into empathy. This left me feeling off-kilter. Tanner rarely listened or heard or thought about anyone apart from himself. Finally, he said, "I would think that you would appreciate my position."

"What position is that? This is none of your business."

His eyes narrowed, and he shook his head as if disappointed. "Izzy." He paused. It was the first time he hadn't called me Isabel. "What was I supposed to do here? I found out that the fiancé of one of my associates, one of the firm's *best* associates, appears to have stolen a lot of money from one of our biggest clients. I have to tell my partners about that. It is my fiduciary duty to do so. And if those partners tell their associates and the associates tell the secretaries, I cannot control that."

I blinked. He was right. "I'm sorry."

He shook his head, brushing off my apology.

"No, really, I'm sorry," I said. "It's just personal, what with Sam being gone, and then Forester. I'm having trouble seeing things correctly."

"Yeah. We're all having a tough time with Forester's death."

"I know. I realize you knew him much longer than I did. How…how are you?" I almost stumbled over the last few words. I'd never imagined being so personal with Tanner.

His mouth sagged a little. "Such a great man."

"He was."

He nodded. I nodded back. He stood, and I followed suit. It seemed we'd reached an impasse on our little come-to-Jesus moment.

"Izzy!" a woman's voice screamed. "Where you?"

Back in my office, I moved the phone away from my ear and sighed. On even the best of days, Maria, my wedding-dress seamstress, was hard to handle. First there was her energy level, which rivaled that of a Chihuahua on cocaine. Then there was her dual approach to life—one was Hispanic blue-collar, the other patrician elite. Maria only sewed and made patterns for the wealthiest and most fashionable of Chicago's crowd. I would normally not have been able to afford her, or meet her extremely high taste levels, but our wedding coordinator had railroaded her into making my dress, and my mother had graciously offered to pay. And every other Wednesday for the last few months, Maria and I been making each other crazy.

I looked at my watch. "Shazzer," I said, one of my replacement curse words for *shit*. It made no sense, but I liked it. My appointment had been at six o'clock, ten minutes ago, and I'd completely forgotten. Or maybe I'd forgotten on purpose. Yesterday, when the wedding had swamped my mind, I had wanted to forget. I was hit by guilt again now. Was I unconsciously borrowing trouble for myself?

"What you say?" Maria said, indignant.

"Maria, I'm sorry. I forgot our appointment." I breathed out hard. "This has been a terrible day."

A stumped silence. "Terrible day? We all have terrible day! I work hard. You work hard. But you go for appointment, you do what you say and you say you be *here*."

"Yes, Maria, I know." I paused. "A friend of mine died yesterday." There. I'd thrown the highest card. You can't trump death. *Everyone* gives you a pass for death.

Except, apparently, Maria.

"I no care that your friend die! You should call me if you want cancel. I have you book for one hour, and do you know what one hour of my time cost?"

"Yes, I do," I said forcefully.

But the truth was, I didn't know. Lately, I'd gotten so weighted down with the wedding and my job that I'd been somewhat avoiding my mother, who only wanted to talk about all things bridal. She was so wrapped up in the affair—what I would wear, what she would wear, what the tables would look like, what the place cards would say. She was not normally this frenetic or enthused about anything. She was normally the calmest of women, usually wearing a shawl of melancholy. But the wedding had jump-started her. Even her husband, Spencer Calloway, a well-known, now mostly retired real-estate developer, was surprised by how intense she'd gotten about it. But that's what mothers were supposed to do, he'd said to me.

Suddenly, with Maria prattling on, I was embarrassed by how strained I thought I'd been by the wedding and my work. I would have given anything to go back to that kind of stress. The kind of stress that had me worrying about what bikini to take on the honeymoon in Costa del Sol, Spain. The kind of stress that left me pondering truly momentous decisions like whether to have a jazz trio for the cocktail hour or a full band. The stress of being the highest-paid associate at the firm.

And how could I have been so dismissive to my mother? My kind, wonderful mother who had raised two kids by herself? I had never really known what she had gone through when Dad died, but now I had an inkling.

Maria railed on about appointments and the importance of keeping them.

"Maria," I said. She continued. Finally, I yelled, "Maria!" She stopped.

"I'll be there in fifteen minutes." And I called my mom.

* * *

Maria's studio was on a lonely strip of Clybourn Avenue, north of Fullerton. The sole indication that business was conducted there was a small, neon sign that spelled Maria's in magenta, cursive letters.

Inside, a team of seamstresses, mostly Hispanic, bent over the sewing machines. They looked up when I walked in. I often wondered what they thought of girls like me, spending so much time and money on one dress. The women quickly turned their gazes down when Maria strolled into the room. Maria was a steely sixty-year-old. She always dressed in timeless dresses—black, brown or navy shifts that could have been made today or forty years ago—and clunky, low-heeled pumps. Her black hair, which was giving way to silver, was pulled back in a chignon.

"You here. Okay," Maria said, waving me toward the fitting room in the back. "Come, come."

Just then the front door opened and my mother, Victoria McNeil, entered. The seamstresses glanced up again, but this time they weren't as quick to return their eyes to their work. They couldn't help but gawk at my mother. She had that effect on people.

Victoria McNeil was beautiful—in a willowy, elegant, strawberry-blond kind of way—but there were also some other qualities she possessed that drew people to her—that manner of melancholy combined with a hint of mystery. It was bizarre that we were mother and daughter. I was more brassy and flashy and quick to talk to everyone, while my mother was reserved and graceful and spoke quietly and only when needed. Then there were our looks—I'd gotten the bright red hair and freckles, while my mother clearly bore her ancestors' more Nordic aesthetic.

Even Maria's prickly face brightened at the sight of my mother. "Ah, Mrs. McNeil!" she exclaimed.

My mother greeted her, then turned to me and beamed. She

always beamed when she looked at me or Charlie, but I don't think I'd ever appreciated that open-eyed, unconditional appreciation as much as I did now.

"Hi, Boo," she said, calling me by the nickname given to me by my father.

"Come, come." Maria helped my mother out of her cashmere coat and dumped it in my arms. She took the purse from my mother's grasp and shoved that in my direction, as well. Then she took my mother gently by the elbow and led her through the workroom, while I trailed behind like a Sherpa.

The fitting room was swathed in white wallpaper and curtains, and contained two slightly worn couches and a carpeted pedestal in the middle of the room.

Next to the pedestal, my dress was hanging. And it was gorgeous. Even now, unsure of whether I would ever wear it, having not wanted to wear it for a while now, I let out a little gasp.

The dress, made of a creamy, ivory Duchess satin, had a strapless top with a bustline that curved gently inward. The gown was A-line with graduated bands of ribbon. The effect, I hoped, was sweet but fashionable. I also wanted it to be sexy, hence the eight hundred fittings so that Maria and I could argue about how low the neckline should be, how tight the waist.

My mother sighed with pleasure when she saw it.

"Oh, Izzy," she said. "Put it on."

Maria left the room so I could change.

I stripped off my clothes, lifted the dress off the hanger and slipped it over me. I saw myself in the mirror—a palette of ivory topped with the red of my hair. I saw myself standing like this, in this dress, with Sam in front of an altar. Now, it didn't seem so overwhelming. Now that he was gone.

The thought nearly flattened me.

I flopped back onto the couch.

"What's wrong?" My mother sat next to me.

"A lot of things." I gulped and looked at my mother's

face—smooth but for the faint lines around her eyes and throat. She had gone through so much when my dad died. I didn't normally confide much in her, not because she couldn't handle it, but simply because we had different styles of handling stress. Yet now more than ever, I needed advice from someone who had lost a spouse.

"It's Sam," I said. "He's…well, he's disappeared. And Forester died."

My mother's delicate lips formed an *O*. Her eyes, muted blue with flecks of gray, opened bigger. "What? My God."

"I know." I fell into her body and she wrapped her arms around me tight. For the second time in two days, I gave in to the tears lingering like unwelcome party guests. Apparently, the tears heard it was a big bash, because I cried huge gulping sobs. My mother squeezed me hard. I managed to tell her the story.

When I pulled back, she wore the same startled expression, but she was quiet. This was how my mother reacted to bad news—she went inside herself, she gathered evidence, she turned it over like a gem in her hand until she could determine its quality, its clarity.

"I can't believe this," she said quietly. "Why didn't you call me sooner?"

I shrugged. "I guess I thought it would end. But it isn't ending."

I told her about the safe and the bearer shares and the cops who'd visited my office.

"Sam wouldn't steal from Forester," she said in a strangled voice. My mother loved Sam.

"I know. That's what I think, too, but with him gone, with no other explanation…" I threw my hands up. "I don't know what to believe."

"Oh, Izzy, baby."

The words were said with such feeling, and my mother's eyes fixed on me like never before. We sat like that—two women who'd always thought themselves so different from one another, suddenly had so much in common.

My mother opened her mouth to speak again, when Maria stuck her head in the fitting room. "You ready now?" Her irritation was undisguised. She'd had enough of this.

"I don't know," my mother said. She grabbed my hand. "Do you want to do this?"

I sucked in a breath and thought about it. The doubts about Sam were starting to flood me, but I hated that. At my core, I believed he was a good man, but the evidence seemed so far the other way. I reminded myself the case wasn't over. All the evidence wasn't in yet. And so I would go forward, for now, with the wedding that just yesterday I didn't think I wanted.

"Yeah, I do."

I disentangled myself from my mom, gathered the cool, heavy satin skirt in my hands and climbed onto the pedestal.

Maria was already surveying me, pins at the ready on her wrist cushion.

Just then, my cell phone bleated from my purse. I jumped off the pedestal and scrambled for it.

Maria mumbled something in Spanish that I guessed were curse words.

Instead of *Sam, cell,* the display on my phone read, *Unknown.*
I answered it.

"Isabel McNeil?" It was a woman's voice, calm and confident. "This is Andi Lippman with the FBI."

I sat down hard on the pedestal. I felt bad news looming, large and black.

Maria cursed again and took the pins out of her mouth. My mother mouthed, "What is it?"

"Ms. McNeil? I'm calling about Sam Hollings."

"Is there any news?"

"The FBI is investigating the matter of the shares owned by Forester Pickett, which are missing from Carrington & Associates."

I blinked fast. *The FBI,* I thought. Once again, I was hit with how real this was, how severely momentous. "Have you heard anything new?"

She paused. "Well, I'm not exactly sure what you know and what you don't. I'd like to meet with you in person." She mentioned an address on Roosevelt Avenue. "Tomorrow at eleven."

I rooted in my purse for my date book. Most people I knew kept their calendars on their BlackBerries or computers, but I liked the old-fashioned hard copy. I liked seeing my months, my weeks, my daily appointments laid out and organized in front of me.

I found the date book—thin with a maroon cover embossed in gold. A gift from Forester, I suddenly remembered. "One second, please." I cupped the phone between my ear and shoulder and rifled through the pages for the end of October. I tried to think whether I had any meetings tomorrow, maybe a court call.

But as I reached the right page, everything blurred in front of me, because I realized it didn't matter. Whatever I had to do tomorrow wasn't important, not even a little bit, compared to Sam. And Forester.

I closed the book. "I'll be there."

16

Sam Hollings walked down Duval Street, sidestepping a woman sitting on the curb, talking on her cell phone, then one block later a pack of college kids pouring out of a bar, all drunk and happy and loud.

Sam gave the kids a wide berth. He hated how far away from them he felt, how much older. He easily remembered when getting loaded on a Wednesday night was not uncommon. God, the simplicity of those days, so unappreciated at the time. He was grateful for it now, feeling ancient and well past them.

He would have to remember to write in his journal about this sudden feeling of being old. He'd packed the journal, knowing he might be alone for a while, knowing the things he used to talk about to Izzy would have to remain silent, without a listener.

He kept walking up Duval, looking for a restaurant that wasn't bellowing Jimmy Buffett, one that didn't scream its name in neon lights. He was exhausted from the two days of driving, and he wanted something quiet and comfortable. But finding this was more difficult than he'd thought.

He and Izzy used to talk about coming to Key West. They'd expected it to be charming and eccentric. Being here, it felt more like a Disneyland version of the Key West they'd envisioned. The commercialization of the place was rampant—

each place boasted specialized frozen drinks and key-lime pie. The T-shirt stores bled one into another.

Finally, Sam found a restaurant in an old house set back from the street and flanked by a wraparound porch. He accepted a menu from the maître d' and allowed himself to be seated outside, his back to the door. He started to order a Blue Moon beer, then changed his mind. He drank Blue Moons with his buddies, with Izzy. He drank Blue Moon when he was happy. His Blue Moon days were over for now.

He ordered a glass of cabernet. Cabernet was what his asshole father used to drink. It felt, vaguely, as if he was punishing himself by ordering such a glass. When the glass was delivered, he stared at the blood-red of the wine, thinking about his dad, wondering if there was a reason he had used his fists on his family. It struck Sam now, in the middle of what he was doing, that maybe there were complicated reasons for just about any bad act. Maybe, for example, his father, by being a fighting man, was taking out frustrations that none of his family could understand, that no one could understand.

That might be true, Sam realized. His father might have had his own reasons for acting the way he did. There was a reason, for example, why he was here. He had to hang on to that idea, because it was too late to turn back now.

17

That night, with the bedside lamp the only light on in the house, I lay awake for a long, long time, Sam's side of the bed vast and cold. I tried to think of real possibilities about where he could be, of what had happened to him. I thought of Maggie earlier, saying he could be dead. Wasn't it only realistic to acknowledge this could be true? I wanted, desperately, to be logical. If I applied logic, maybe this wouldn't hurt so much, maybe it wouldn't be happening, maybe I could simply figure it out.

And right then, I was able to think logically about Sam being dead. I batted the concept around in my head. I imagined him, eyes closed, arms crossed over his chest. He'd be wearing the awful suit with the naval buttons his mother had bought him. His hair would be parted wrong.

Imagining this was easy because, the truth was, I didn't believe it. I didn't have any innate sense that the man I'd spent the last few years with was no longer in this world.

It was more likely that Sam was not dead, but rather sunning his annoyingly cute ass in Panama somewhere. I tried to imagine what Panama looked like. Jungly, perhaps? I saw Sam in a safari tent, attended by local women in Tarzan-like getups. Or was it beachy? I pictured Sam on a plush lounge chair, facing out toward crashing, blue waves, the bright sun turning his hair white. While he sat, he was counting the money he'd made—stolen, I should say.

I turned over in bed and pushed my face into the pillow. Was that true? Was Sam out there, wherever that was, already moving on to a new life? A new identity? A new girl? It didn't sound like the Sam I knew. And I could have sworn I knew that guy inside and out. But then maybe you can't know everything about a person. He hadn't known, for example, that I was scratching at the walls of my own wedding, wanting out. I hadn't said anything; I hadn't even written an e-mail—This thing is getting to me. What about you?

Then it occurred to me—Sam's e-mail. Why didn't I think of it sooner? I knew his passwords.

I launched myself out of bed and scurried through the dark apartment to the second bedroom, the room I used as an office.

I clicked on the desk lamp and turned on the computer, impatient with how long it took to power up. Finally, I got on the Internet and typed in GoToMyPC, which Sam used to get onto his work e-mail.

At the site, I typed in Sam's password—*grubber1228.* "Grubber" was a type of kick used in rugby; 1228 was the address of the house his family lived in when he was a kid.

I drummed my fingers on the desk while it took an interminably long time to connect to Sam's work computer. I'd seen Sam do this hundreds of times, and it had never seemed so long.

Finally, the site appeared to be connecting to Sam's e-mail, but then a message popped up—*Invalid e-mail address or password.*

Had he changed the password? I tried again. Same message.

Then it dawned on me. Sam's e-mail access had been shut down by Carrington & Associates. He probably no longer had a job there. Or maybe it had been done by the cops, the feds. I sat back hard, breathless by how swiftly everything had changed.

I remembered Sam had a Yahoo! account he used occasionally, usually for personal messages or things he didn't want to send through his work e-mail.

I got onto Yahoo! and typed his *grubber* password again.
And, voila, there was Sam's in-box.

Nothing looked out of the ordinary. It seemed it hadn't
been checked since Monday, the day before he disappeared.
I clicked on the *Sent* folder. Sam had sent a few e-mails from
Yahoo! last week. I let my eyes roam the names there. I
bristled when I came to one in particular—Alyssa Thornton.

Alyssa was Sam's ex-girlfriend, a woman whom I'd met
once at his ten-year high-school reunion. Before that, Sam
hadn't described her except to say that she'd wanted more out
of their relationship than he did. They stayed together for a year
or two in college then broke up. Until the reunion, I'd never
given Alyssa much thought. I wasn't the jealous type, and I
knew how much Sam loved me. But then I met her. She was
standing at the bar when we walked into the reunion, and she
was looking directly at Sam, as if she'd been expecting him, as
if she'd been standing there for *years* waiting for him to arrive.

She was ethereal, stunning and bony as a bag of door-
knobs. With her white-blond hair, she almost looked like a
miniature, female version of Sam. I could immediately picture
them together as the golden couple. Alyssa was dressed in a
silvery minidress. On me, the dress would have made me look
like a cheap, life-size Christmas ornament, but on her it only
made her look like a tiny silver light, shimmering amidst the
commoners. And she was nice, too, which only made it
tougher to stand there and talk to her and accept the fact that
Alyssa still loved Sam. She glowed when she gazed at him.
Just like I did.

I spent the rest of the reunion overcompensating. I worked
that room as if I were running for homecoming queen. I
wanted each and every person to tell Sam how fantastic his
fiancée was. They did, and he barely seemed to notice
Alyssa's adoration. But I had.

Her name came up once or twice after that. Sam would tell
me they e-mailed sometimes, usually as a group with the rest

of their buddies from high school. Her name always sent an eruption of jealously through me, which I hated. I never wanted to be the envious girl who couldn't handle past loves. I still thought fondly of Timmy, my college boyfriend, and Blake, a guy I dated during law school. But they were boys. Sam was a man.

Being the man he was, Sam chuckled when I made a jealous request that he not communicate with Alyssa, and he'd agreed. As far as I knew, he hadn't had contact with Alyssa for over a year.

But now here was her name, sitting in his *Sent* folder.

I clicked on the e-mail, realizing I was holding my breath. Had he been corresponding with Alyssa all along? Had they made some plan to take off together? Was that why he'd stolen Forester's shares? To fund some plan to run away together? My mind went crazy at the possibilities. I thought of every time I'd watched *Inside Edition,* fascinated by the stories of people who led double lives, never telling their family or friends.

Finally, Sam's e-mail appeared.

Hey Alyssa, it read, Sorry I haven't gotten back to you until now. Congrats on getting new funding for the research program. You might have heard that I'm engaged. I've been busy with the wedding coming up and with work. I won't be able to join the crew over the holidays. Izzy and I will be on our honeymoon. Say hi to everyone for me, will you? And hello to your family, too. Tell your brother he still owes me fifty bucks from that poker game. Sam.

I sat back and relaxed my clenched shoulders. Sam was just responding to a few e-mails he had gotten from Alyssa. That was all. But why couldn't I shake the feeling that there was more to it? I scrolled through his Sent box for the last year. There were no other e-mails to Alyssa; he'd honored my request to cut off contact with her. So why had he decided to e-mail her one week before he disappeared? Just a coincidence?

Suddenly, I felt the need for fresh air. I turned off the computer and put on running shoes and an old leather jacket of Sam's. I grabbed my keys and headed outside. Taking walks around my neighborhood always cleared my head, even at night. I knew the area well and usually felt as at home outside on the streets of Old Town as I did inside my condo.

I walked east on Eugenie Street, passing a grade school and a row of houses with wide front stairs. I thought about the days after Sam and I started dating when he began to take these walks with me. We spied into living rooms as darkness fell. We talked about how the red living room in that one apartment was too much to deal with every day. We studied the front porch on a house a few doors over and decided that, although it was a touch suburban, it gave a homey feel, and it would be a nice place to sit on summer nights. We planned to install a wall of bookshelves, like the ones we saw in the place on Sedgwick, as soon as we got the chance.

I reached Menomenee Street and walked south, drawn to a spot that held a shiny memory, the place where Sam and I had sat at picnic tables during the Old Town art fair last summer. Right there was where we had talked about getting married for the first time. I remember how his face was a little pink, and I wasn't sure if it was because of the sun or the topic.

I smiled, lost in the sun of that day, the thrilling nervousness of our conversation, the image of Sam blinking fast in the sunlight, saying how much he loved me, how he was shocked sometimes at how much he loved me. I could feel myself smiling at the thought, not pining to get married, but loving the fact that he wanted to marry me.

I heard a shuffle of feet behind me and the sunlit recollection of Sam disappeared. I jumped, startled. I spun around and saw a shadow stepping into a dim gangway between two tiny little houses.

I gulped. It was probably someone arriving home for the

night. But I heard no door opening and closing, no other sounds at all

I shook my head. I would *not* get paranoid. I might have lost Forester, yes. And I might have to give up a massive wedding deposit at the Chicago History Museum, true. But I would *not* become paranoid. At least not on a consistent basis.

I stared at the gangway for another second. Still no sounds; no one appeared. Time to go home.

Snap!

I didn't move, but I let my eyes run wildly. It was just another nice night in Old Town, yet abruptly I felt how truly alone I was, standing on a dead-end street amid homes lit from within but all locked and closed for the night.

I heard something that sounded again like the shuffle of feet. I glanced around, paranoia growing, my heart starting to thump, thump, thump.

Run, a voice in my head said. *Get out of here.*

I tried to tell myself again not to get paranoid. I tried to simply walk down Menomenee Street like it was any other day. But the shuffle came again, and again I heard my own voice say, *Run, Iz.*

I took a few fast steps. I could have sworn I heard a soft *tap-tap* of shoes behind me. I spun around. Nothing. No one.

I turned and walked faster. Again that shuffle sound.

I could feel the pulse in my temples. I could feel a little tremble of anticipation, and I cringed, as if I might be struck from behind.

Once more, I spun around. Still nothing, except that voice, insistent, in my head—*Run, you idiot.*

This time I listened, not caring what I looked like, not caring if I was being paranoid. I ran home and found myself all alone.

18

Day Three

Thursday morning, I went down the back stairs of my condo like I always did, desperate for normalcy. I would go to work. I would do my job. I would be grateful for it, and maybe that would help return things to everyday status. Maybe that would somehow return Sam. But at the bottom of the back stairwell, I dreaded having to step outside. My sleep had been spotty, jumpy, haunted by the memory of the *tap-tap* of shoes behind me.

With trepidation, I stepped outside my building and winced. Chicago had undergone a cold snap.

"Damn." I gathered the collar of my coat around my neck. The coat—chocolate-brown and thigh-length, with a large belt—was more about fashion than warmth, and I hadn't yet dug out my scarves or gloves. I looked around but only saw what I saw every morning—some houses still dark, others beaming with light and life as people got ready, a few commuters on the streets, walking to the El train.

I stuffed my hands in my pockets, jingling my Vespa keys as I walked from my graystone building to the detached three-car garage behind it. Maybe it wasn't as cold as I thought. Maybe I could floor the scooter and ignore the weather.

The garage backed on to the alley, and each unit owned one spot. In the garage sat my neighbor's cars and my little silver Vespa. I always rode the thing until it was ludicrously cold. During the winter I grudgingly took public transportation or cabs.

I touched the scooter and winced. It felt like a block of ice. Public transit it was.

I was about to close and lock the garage door when my eyes registered something unfamiliar. I glanced to my right, at the wall that faced our building, and noticed that the roller shade that hung over the middle window was open two-thirds of the way. When my neighbors and I had moved in, we decided it would be better to have a dark garage than to leave the windows uncovered and let thieves peruse the merchandise. We installed the blinds and always kept them closed. Always.

One of the neighbors could have just left the blind open, I thought. But then again, I'd been the last one in the garage yesterday night and that blind was closed. Neither of my neighbors appeared to have been in there yet today.

I walked to the window and went to pull the blind when I noticed that although a thin layer of dust coated the windowsill, a square imprint was clearly visible, as if someone had set something there. I swiped my finger over the square shape. It was smooth and clear of dust. Whoever had set something on the sill, marring the dust, had done so recently.

I peered through the window. The back of my building was visible, including the windows that looked out from each unit's kitchen and bedrooms. I stared up at my condo. When I'd finally reached home last night after my walk—or should I say *my run?*—I'd paced from kitchen to bedroom and back again, in front of those windows.

I looked at the windowsill again and heard Detective Schneider's words—*Be careful… Who knows what he'll do?* But was this anything to be concerned about? What exactly would I say—I've noticed a disturbing shift of dust in my grubby garage? I didn't see anyone, but I might have heard someone walking behind me in a city that has more than 2.8 million people?

Just then, I had the feeling of being, somehow, not alone. I spun around. The garage was the same as before—two cars, my silver scooter.

I yanked the shade down tight, pulled my collar tighter and left the garage, triple-checking the lock. I walked to the Sedgwick El platform. I got on the next train, stuffing myself inside with the rest of the crowd headed to the Loop. Everyone wore distant gazes or fiddled with their iPods, trying for the last few moments of personal time before beginning a bustling day.

I got out at Washington, walked to Madison and then west a few blocks until I reached the office. The whole time, I kept glancing over my shoulder.

Q was already at his desk. "Sleep?"

"Not much. You?"

He shook his head. "I've been here since six-thirty. I thought I might as well get some things done. Your brother called. Also, there was a message left last night from Shane's secretary. The funeral is tomorrow at noon. Up in Lake Forest."

He handed me a slip with the address of the church where the funeral would be held.

I felt like putting my head on the little wall surrounding Q's desk and having a good cry. Instead, I managed to keep a bland look on my face and nodded. "How are you?"

"Fine, fine."

"Why doesn't that sound genuine?"

He shrugged. "It's just—" he looked around "—everything. You know?"

I glanced around, smiling a tight grin at the assistants who were making no attempt to hide the fact that they were staring at us. "Right. Well, I'm going to…" I pointed at my office.

Q nodded and looked back at his screen. I stood a moment longer, looking at him. Something was different, but I couldn't put my finger on it.

"What?" he said, looking up at me, feeling my gaze.

"Nothing. Nothing." I finally turned and headed to my office.

I made some calls to a distribution company that wanted to buy the rights to a TV movie made by one of Forester's companies. I halfheartedly argued with the distributor's attorney about whether the company's rights should end on the expiration of term or whether they should have the ability to purchase the rights again at that time.

Contract negotiations were all about give-and-take. They were all about making the other side feel appreciated and heard, and then making them realize that while they'd given a little, they'd gotten a heck of a lot more.

But I couldn't give anything. I kept thinking about Sam's e-mail account. I kept thinking that I knew more than a few of his passwords.

"I've got to call you back," I said, interrupting the attorney on the phone.

I hung up and found the Web site for United Airlines. I put in Sam's frequent-flier number and then his password.

Hello, Sam, the screen read.

"Hello, Sam," I murmured. "Tell me where you went."

I clicked on My Itineraries. I held my breath while the screen shifted.

I blew out in a long, steady stream when I saw what was there—one itinerary.

Our honeymoon.

In a month and a half, the day after our wedding, we were supposed to be boarding a flight to Madrid and then changing planes to fly to Málaga, Spain.

I sat back, again resisting the urge to cry. Why had I taken the wedding, the honeymoon, for granted?

I swung my chair around and stared out my window, then swung it back just as fast. It dawned on me that if I knew Sam's passwords for his e-mail and the airline, wasn't it possible he used similar ones for other sites? Like his credit card?

But an hour later, all I'd learned was that Sam hadn't used

his credit card since buying lunch at Custom House restaurant on the day he disappeared. And there was nothing interesting in the purchases he'd made in the previous month or two—no airline tickets on other airlines, no hotel bookings, nothing other than the usual stuff I knew he bought, like protein bars from the health-food store on North Avenue and socks from Bloomingdale's.

My nerves about my upcoming meeting with the FBI started to grow. And grow and grow.

Then I had an idea.

"I'm out," I said to Q, leaving my office.

"Where to?"

"I have a meeting."

19

I left the Baltimore & Brown offices and walked to LaSalle Street. Again, I felt the weight of someone's eyes on me, but every time I spun around, no one seemed to be watching me.

I went north toward the Board of Trade until I came to an old high rise that housed a bevy of criminal-defense firms. The lobby inside used to be grand, but now the marble was yellowed and the lighting patchy. On the tenth floor, the firm of Martin Bristol & Associates wasn't much better. God knew they made enough dough to have a sleek office overlooking the Chicago River, but like many criminal-defense firms they didn't care about image. They only cared about the work and the clients. And, of course, the cash.

"Hey, Izzy," the receptionist called when I walked in. I waved. She hit a buzzer under the desk that unlatched the door to the internal offices and went back to her phone call.

The hallway was lined with courtroom sketches, mostly of Martin Bristol, Maggie's grandfather, prowling the courtrooms in his many cases. He'd been an assistant state's attorney for years and had prosecuted the infamous serial killer Keith Lee Baker. It was a case that continued to define him, even now, and he'd told me he was just fine with that. Keith Lee Baker, he always said, had brought him a hell of a lot of business.

Maggie's office had *typical overworked lawyer* written

all over it. The windows that faced LaSalle Street were mostly blocked with stacks of redwell folders bearing the names of various cases. Her desk was littered with motions and complaints and witness statements.

Maggie was seated in the black leather chair she'd inherited from her grandfather's old associate, who'd left years ago. The chair was faded and torn in spots, and I knew she'd been meaning to get a new one since she'd started practicing here after law school but, like many criminal lawyers, Maggie was superstitious. She'd somehow convinced herself that the chair was good luck, and now she couldn't get rid of it.

"Mags," I said.

She looked up, shocked. She always looked like that when someone came into her office, as if she didn't know that other people, like clients and friends, might visit her. She was always completely consumed in what she was doing.

She blinked once, and I could see her brain clearing off a clean space. She batted away a lock of honey-colored hair that had fallen in her eye.

"Iz!" She jumped and picked her way over the piles of documents on her floor. "What's up? Any news?"

"No."

She shut her door while I excavated one of the chairs. "Did you come from work?" she asked.

"Yeah. It's bleak. I can't get anything done."

"I can't believe you're still going to work."

"What else am I going to do?"

She sank back into her chair and stared at me. "I don't know."

"Actually, I've got an idea." I lifted my bag from the floor and took out my checkbook. I wrote a check to Martin Bristol & Associates for a thousand dollars. It was money we had earmarked for the honeymoon, but who knew whether I'd need it now.

I stood and put the check in front of her. "I'm hiring you on behalf of myself and Sam Hollings. This is a retainer."

Here's the thing about lawyers—everyone assumes that if you've graduated law school and passed the bar, you're a mini-expert on every area of the law that exists. The truth is that while law school indoctrinates and introduces, it doesn't truly educate. It can't. The legal world is simply too vast. Real education happens on the job. And so, if we lawyers haven't worked in criminal law (or patent law or real-estate law), we know as much about it as a CTA bus driver. I knew nothing about criminal law, and I'd realized that I'd better have someone on my side—on *Sam's* side—who did.

Maggie looked at the check, then at me. "You're my best friend. You and your fiancé get free legal advice. If you need it."

"Nope. I don't want you being half friend, half lawyer here. I want you, Maggie Bristol, tough-girl attorney, woman who pulls no punches. I want you to tell it to me straight. Just like Sam or I were any other client."

"Why do you think Sam needs a lawyer? I mean, right now?"

"I got a call from the FBI. I'm going to see them at eleven-thirty." I told her about my conversation with Andi Lippman. "Do you know her?" I asked Maggie.

"No. But I do know you're not going to that meeting."

I sighed. "Mags—"

She shook her head. "Never let yourself be questioned without a subpoena or an arrest."

"I know, I know, but that's the advice you give someone who has something to hide. Someone who might be arrested for something. That is not me."

She shrugged. "You never know what kind of story these people can cook up. The feds are no better than the cops."

"Right. Well…the cops seemed nice."

Maggie's eyebrows rose to the ceiling. "You didn't."

"They came to my office yesterday."

She briefly dipped her face into her hands. "Have you learned nothing from me?"

"I needed to know what they knew. And that's the same

reason I'm going to see the FBI. This time I'm taking a lawyer." I gave her a pointed look.

She nodded slowly, then her nodding picked up pace. "All right then." She looked at her watch. "It's time for a client-prep meeting."

With the facts as we knew them, Maggie told me, Sam could be charged with embezzlement, which was essentially stealing property owned by someone else but which had been entrusted to his care.

"Like the Enron guys," Maggie said. "They rightly possessed all that money due to their positions in the company, but when they started using it for their own personal benefit, then it became embezzlement."

"Didn't one of them get a twenty-four-year prison sentence?"

"Oh, yeah," she said, her voice getting a little louder, a little excited. "The judges smack those guys hard. I mean *hard*. There's no mercy anymore for white-collar criminals."

I flinched.

"What?" She raised her eyebrows. "I thought you wanted a tough-girl attorney? The woman who pulls no punches?"

"I do."

"Okay, well, look, there are a lot of positives. I mean, number one, they haven't found him."

"Precisely how is the fact that Sam is missing a 'positive'?"

"I'm just looking at it from the perspective of a defense attorney, okay? And the truth is, if I get a retainer and I work the case as hard as I can and then one of my clients disappears, I'm not too upset. I get paid, and I don't have to deal with sentencing. Also, I get a soft spot for my clients, even if they sold thirty kilos of coke to an undercover cop. When they're gone, I can imagine a better life for them."

This always fascinated me about Maggie—she was part tough cookie, part legal scholar and part plain old softy. *Scholar* wasn't even the right word, but there was no appropriate term for someone who simply *loved* the law like Maggie did. I was surprised to find out after graduation that most attorneys didn't adore the law. Sadly, *I* didn't adore the law.

"With Sam," Maggie continued, "it's possible the feds will lose interest if he stays gone. They're human, too, and everyone wants to close cases."

She caught my look. "Okay, obviously not finding Sam wouldn't be the best result for *you*."

"Moving on. Other positives?"

"Well, Forester may have given Sam the right to take those bearer shares. If he did, then it's not embezzlement."

"How would we know if that's true? Forester is gone." I felt a vacancy in my heart, right in the warm spot where I used to hold Forester.

"I know. That makes it tricky. But if we can find some evidence that Sam had the right to take the shares, he's in the clear."

"Sam handled Forester's investments under Mark Carrington's supervision. According to Mark, there was no reason for Sam to take those shares."

We sat in silence, thinking.

"Forester died the night Sam took those shares," I said finally. "That doesn't look good, right?"

"At this point, there's no reason to think the two are related." Maggie dipped her head to one side. "But it's not great."

"They *can't* be related. I mean, to say they're related would be to say that Sam had something to do with his death. Plus, the autopsy said Forester died of a heart attack."

Maggie stared at me. I could see the friend, not the attorney. I could see she felt sorry for me. "You told me about the threats Forester was getting," she said. "Do we know anything more about those?"

"No. But Sam just isn't that guy. He had no reason to want Forester to give up the reins of his company. Forester was Sam's biggest client, same as me."

Maggie was quiet. She blew a strand of hair away from her face.

"What?" I said. "I'm listening."

"Well, it doesn't seem like Sam had anything to do with Forester dying." She paused. "But if I'm a federal prosecutor looking to pin him for embezzlement, I'm sure as hell going to make it sound like he did."

20

Instead of being located in the midst of the jostling and crowded Loop, Chicago's FBI office was housed on bland Roosevelt Road, in a characterless steel-girded building, as if to give the distinct impression that the agency was separate from the city and would tell you nothing about its secrets.

Maggie and I went through a revolving door marked One Way and stepped into a glassed-in booth with three armed guards.

"Bulletproof," Maggie said, pointing to the glass. "The whole place is made of it."

The cold looks of the guards put fear in my belly. *Sam*, I thought, *what have you gotten us into?*

"Appointment?" one guard said.

"Andi Lippman," Maggie answered. She gave both our names.

The guard studied a printout, then stared at Maggie. "You're not on the list."

"I'm her lawyer."

"You're not on the list," he repeated. He was a thick man, all muscle, with an expression that was absolutely flat. He reminded me of a dog that was none too smart, although something told me I was wrong about that.

"Well, let's get me on the list," Maggie said, "because if I'm not on the list, neither is she."

Silence from the guards. Irrationally, I felt trapped, nervous. The guard nodded slowly.

"Great." Maggie gave the guard her attorney ID and driver's license. She pointed at me to do the same.

We both signed our names on a login sheet, then we were asked to remove every item from our bags and pockets and place them on the conveyor belt. There lay our lipsticks and wallets and mints and cell phones and errant tampons. The guards studied each of them like aliens discovering objects in a new world. We were patted down and wanded. We were walked through a metal detector, then through a machine that puffed out massive breaths of air and sucked it back in, apparently in an effort to detect gunpowder. As the machine roared and my blouse billowed around me, I felt illogically guilty again, as if I might have accidentally hidden a bomb in the underwire of my bra.

Once we were cleared, we were led through a hallway covered in slate-blue carpet that resembled Astroturf.

In the reception area, a woman hidden behind a massive pane of bulletproof glass asked for our names again. She consulted a printout, similar to the one the guards had, then typed something into her computer.

A minute later, she passed us badges through a steel drawer. On them, our names were printed and below that, in orange letters, Visitor, Not To Be Unescorted.

We took a seat on steel chairs, the cushions made with the kind of tough, ugly fabric that covers seats in a cheap car. And there we sat, and sat, and sat. We leafed through periodicals that were outdated by a good eight months. We looked at each other. With each passing minute, my anxiety grew like a steel ball in my chest that was taking up more and more room.

"Relax," Maggie said in a low voice. "They're just icing us."

"Seriously?"

She nodded and fired a murderous glance at the impervious receptionist.

"But why would they want to make *me* nervous? I'm just here as a witness." I stopped, realizing that being a "witness" made it sound as if a crime had been committed.

I tried to think about work, but it was impossible. I thought, instead, about Sam.

Ten minutes later, I turned to Maggie. "I have to tell you something."

Her eyes narrowed a little. "Is it something about Sam's case?"

"No. It's something about Sam. And me. And the wedding." I exhaled loudly. "This has been torturing me, but before this all happened, I was thinking of telling Sam that the wedding was too much."

"You were thinking about calling it off?" Her eyes went big.

"I don't know. I'm not sure what I wanted to do about it, but it was just getting so out of hand, so overwhelming, and…yeah. Yeah, I guess I was thinking, in the back of my head, of calling it off. I was going to talk to him that night. But then he disappeared. And I can't help feeling like I caused this somehow."

Maggie moved a strand of hair away from my face and turned so that she was looking directly in my eyes. "You did *not* cause any of this, Iz. Not a bit. I mean, maybe the pressure was getting to Sam, too. Maybe he took off and got a little goofy because of it. But *you?*" She shook her head. "You didn't cause anything. You didn't do anything wrong."

"The thing is, I don't think the pressure was getting to Sam. The opposite, actually. He was excited about the wedding. He was so good-natured about planning it. He liked doing all that stuff. That's what was making me feel bad—that I wasn't as enthused about it as him. I wasn't very enthused at all."

The door of the reception area opened and a brusque brunette entered the room. "I'm Andi Lippman. Sorry I'm late."

Maggie stood. I followed suit and shook hands with Andi. "I'm Izzy McNeil. This is my…"

I had started to say the word *friend,* but I saw the sharp glance Maggie gave me.

"…lawyer," I said. "Maggie Bristol."

Andi Lippman frowned, as if she hadn't been advised of Maggie's presence. "Lawyer? You don't need a lawyer, do you?"

More irrational guilt.

Maggie held out her hand. She had to hold it up a bit, since Andi Lippman was taller than me, which meant she towered over Maggie. Still, if Maggie had any feelings of insecurity about the height difference she certainly didn't show it. "I'm just here to listen and learn," she said congenially.

"Sure." Another frown.

She led us down three different hallways, all covered in the blue Astroturf carpet. She turned this way and that so that we'd never be able to find our way out on our own, which, I realized, might be the point. As we followed Andi, I noted her fitted, dove-gray suit coat, her black skirt, her stylish pumps, her long brown hair that fell past her shoulders.

Andi's office was all government, all the time. The desk was steel with a wood-grain Formica top. Utilitarian as you could get. The windows were set high up, higher than even Andi Lippman's head.

She caught me looking at the windows. "They place them up there," she said, "so that if someone shoots from outside, even if they could crack the window, they wouldn't hit anyone."

I nodded, wondering what it was like to work every day in a job where getting shot at was a possibility.

Andi took a seat behind her desk and gestured at the chairs. We took our seats, and I noticed that there was nothing personal on Andi's desk, not a framed photo or even a mug. The desk itself was clean, but for a stack of plain manila folders and some white legal pads. Andi sat back and picked up the top folder.

She opened it, glanced at what appeared to be a few sheets of paper, then replaced the folder on her desk and picked up a pen and a pad of paper.

"As you know," she said, "we're investigating the disappearance of Panamanian bearer shares from the office of Mark Carrington, along with the apparent disappearance of Sam Hollings. What is your relation to Mr. Hollings?"

"He's my fiancé."

"Had you set a wedding date?"

"Yes. A couple weeks before Christmas."

Andi asked me a series of questions about when I'd last seen Sam and the day that he disappeared. I told her everything I remembered. There had been nothing remarkable, I told her, except that Sam seemed distracted when I'd seen him at the wedding coordinator's office and he'd said there were complications at work. I told her how I'd searched for Sam—looking at his office and his apartment the next day. I told her how I'd called his friends and family.

"May I have the phone numbers of those friends and family members?" Andi asked, pen poised.

I pulled out my address book and read off the numbers.

"Did Sam have any enemies?"

"Enemies?" The word almost made me laugh. It seemed like something out of a *Star Wars* movie. "No, everyone loved Sam."

Andi squinted.

"It's true. His friends adore him. So does his family. As far as I know, everyone at work loves him..." I faltered for a moment, thinking that Sam's boss probably didn't love him so much right now. "And everyone in his rugby club, they think he's the best."

"Rugby club?"

"The Chicago Lions."

Andi squinted some more, as if she found this business about rugby utterly suspicious. I found myself racing forward with my words, explaining about the practices every Tuesday and Thursday, how Sam had taken some time off from the club because it was too much to handle with the wedding and work.

"And what does Sam do for work, exactly?" Andi asked.

I explained that he worked for Mark Carrington, who owned a private wealth-management firm. Forester was one of those clients, and Sam was the adviser who backed up Mark to manage Forester's money, assets and investments.

Andi didn't write anything down. She clearly understood already what Sam did for a living. "Did you and Sam discuss the investments he was making on Forester's behalf?"

"Sometimes."

She gave me a stern look.

"He hadn't told me anything about the Panamanian shares."

"And what about Sam's finances? Was he a big spender?"

"No. The only thing Sam really splurges on is guitars. He plays music." I thought of all the time I'd spent in the acoustic lounge of the Guitar Center on Halsted, while Sam tried out every Martin or Gibson they carried.

"Was the wedding costing you a lot of money?"

"Yes, although my mother was helping us out with a few things."

"Did you and Sam have joint bank accounts?"

Maggie leaned forward a little. "Ms. McNeil's finances aren't in question here."

"They're not in question *per se*," Andi said. "But if they've got joint accounts and there's been a big deposit lately…"

I looked at Maggie, who gave me a look that said, *It's up to you.*

"Sam and I do not have a joint account. Not yet."

"Why not?"

"We planned to do that after we get married." I glanced at my engagement ring, thinking of the platinum band sprinkled with tiny diamonds that was supposed to go under that ring.

"Where does Sam bank?"

I had to think about that. "Um…I think Chase?"

"You think?"

"Sam received his bank statements at his apartment. We'd

talked generally about how much money we had, but I never asked to see his statements."

"Did he have any debt?"

"A student loan from his MBA."

"How much?"

"I'm not sure."

"Cars?"

"He has a Volvo that's five years old. I think it's paid off."

"But you're not certain?"

"I'm pretty sure it is."

"Credit-card debt?"

"No."

"Where do you do your banking?"

"That's not pertinent," Maggie said.

"Do *you* have any debt?" Andi asked.

Maggie held up a hand. "Her financial status is not in question here. Not in any way. I'm going to advise her not to answer that."

"It's okay—" I said.

Maggie looked at me pointedly and shook her head, then turned back to Andi. "I'm going to advise her not to answer any questions about her financial status. If you have other questions, fine, but let's move on."

Andi regarded me.

"I have a small student loan," I said quickly, before Maggie could stop me. I knew that she was thinking it was an invasion of my privacy, a completely unnecessary one, to answer questions about my finances, but I didn't care. I had nothing to hide. "And I've got three grand to pay off on my credit cards," I continued. "I got in a little trouble with a store on Damen that won't stop selling me clothes."

"Did Sam ever talk to you about Panama?"

"No. We talked about a few places in South America when we were planning the honeymoon, but we never discussed Panama. I don't know anything about it."

"An interesting country," Andi said. I got the feeling she knew more about Panama than from just working on Sam's case. "They've made it very attractive for expatriates to buy there. Affordable luxury housing, low taxes on all levels."

"Explain something to me," I said. "How is it possible that someone can just take possession of your luxury property and sell it? I mean, that's what you're accusing Sam of, right?"

"We're not accusing anyone of anything right now."

"Fine, but how does this Panamanian-property thing work? Are people just snatching people's shares and running around selling them?"

Andi shook her head. "It's not as simplistic as it seems. Many people there buy property like we do here, with a title that's transferred to the buyer's name."

"But it's different if a corporation owns the property?"

"Right." She paused. "You're a lawyer, you know how it goes."

"I'm an *entertainment* lawyer. If you're a cabaret singer on the side and you want me to negotiate your recording contract, let me know. But this stuff?" I shook my head.

"Well, look, I don't necessarily have to share this with you, but here's how it works. If the title is in the name of a corporation, there is no transfer of title, only a transfer of shares of the corporation."

"So whoever has the shares can sell the corporation and essentially the property."

Andi nodded. "The buyer can then keep the same officers of the corporation or appoint new ones."

"Aren't there safeguards against the wrong people selling the shares?"

"If you can provide legal documentation that you own the corporation, and not someone else, you can put a lien on the property, eventually have your shares reissued and the others voided, but that takes time. So if the person who has the shares acts quickly, they can essentially do what they want with them."

"But there's no evidence at this point that Sam has sold the shares, right?"

"I can't really say." Andi eyed Maggie, then me. "We're just trying to figure out why your fiancé would steal the shares. Do you have any answers for us?"

"I don't."

Andi pulled her pad of paper closer to her. "We'd like to compile a list of the people Sam was closest to. People he would turn to if he needed help."

"He would turn to me," I said without thinking.

There was silence in the room. Obviously, I was wrong about that.

"R.T.," I said. "R. T. Rubinoff. They're friends from MBA school at U of C. But he says he hasn't heard from Sam."

"Who else?"

I mentioned Tom and Don, Sam's rugby friends.

"Tom's last name?" Andi asked.

"Uh…" I could see Tom's ruddy face. Over beers one night, I'd talked to him about his mom who'd recently passed away. But what was his last name? Sam had been handling the gathering of names and addresses for the wedding invitations, and so I had never really asked.

"Don's last name?" Andi said.

"I can't say. Cavanaugh or something like that?"

She gave me a face, one that was expressionless, at least to the observer, but I knew there was something different behind it. Her face turned back to her notes.

"If there's nothing else…" Maggie checked her watch.

"Look," I said. "Can you tell me what you know? About Sam being gone or about Forester's death?"

"I've already told you what I know about the Panamanian shares." She paused.

I inched forward in the seat of my chair so that I was now a foot closer to her. "Do you know something else?"

"I'm sorry…"

My eyes bored into hers. "If you know anything else. *Anything.*"

She shook her head. "Ms. McNeil, seriously, I don't know anything more than you do at this point. We're at the very early stages of our investigation. And we're doing everything we normally do at the beginning of an investigation." She put the top back on her pen.

Silence in the room.

Finally, Andi exhaled loudly. "Look, I will say something. Sam sounds like an okay guy. At least what you know of him sounds great, right? But from what we can tell, he's stolen a heck of a lot of money. And when we see that, it tells us that Sam is probably involved in some bad stuff. Or mixed up with some bad people."

"Like who?" I said incredulously.

"We don't know at this point. But I've seen this kind of thing before. Too many times. And the wives and the mothers are the worst. They can never believe something bad about the guy. And they're always the ones who pay the most. Then there's the fact that an investigation like this, and any resulting litigation, will take years and years to complete. So seriously…" She nodded fast like she was very certain about what she was saying. "If I were you, Ms. McNeil—" more nodding "—I'd move on with my life."

We stepped outside the FBI building. Across the street, a gray Honda sat at a light. The light turned green, but the car didn't move. Maggie stood, staring at it. "That car," she said.

As if it had heard her, the Honda finally hit the gas and sped through the light.

The minute we got into a cab, Maggie turned to me. "Have you noticed anything…well, *off* the last few days?"

"Aside from the fact that my fiancé is MIA with a small fortune and people think he might have killed Forester?"

She looked at me intently. "Right. Aside from that."

"What do you mean?"

"Something Lippman said in there about 'we're doing everything we normally do at the beginning of an investigation.' What they normally do is tail a person when they believe a suspect might contact them."

I told her about the garage and my paranoia last night.

"Yep." Maggie nodded. "That's probably the feds."

"Are you serious? I'm being followed?" Oddly, I felt momentary relief. My mind *wasn't* slipping into some suspiciously obsessive realm.

"Sure," Maggie said. "Best way to find a fugitive is to watch the wife or girlfriend."

I flinched at the thought of Sam as a "fugitive." "Don't they have to tell me?"

"God, no. They can tail you to their heart's content. The only thing they have to let you know is if they tap your phone. And, even then, they don't have to tell you until they're done. Later, you might be entitled to see the logs under the Freedom of Information Act. But now? During a new investigation? Nah. They get to look wherever they want for Sam."

"So what should I do?"

"Don't dance in front of your window in your underwear."

"There's nothing I can do?"

"Not really."

I stared out the window as the cab entered the Loop and drove down Franklin Avenue. I dropped Maggie off and kept going toward my office. *This is baloney,* I said to myself. Bullshit, actually. I wasn't just going to "move on" the way Andi Lippman had said; I had to do *something,* but what?

I didn't know the answer to that, but I knew someone who might be able to help me.

When the cabdriver pulled over to the curb in front of my building, I leaned forward. "Keep driving, please."

21

Whenever I need a sharp slap in the face or swift boot in the teeth, I go in search of Bunny Loveland.

Bunny was the housekeeper my mother hired when we first moved to Chicago following my dad's death. When we'd lived in Michigan, no one we knew employed a cleaning lady or any household staff. You scrubbed your own toilets. And if you needed someone to watch your kids while you ran an errand, you called the neighbors, who said, *Sure, we'll stop over and check on them every so often.* But in Chicago, it was different. My mother was a single mom, a *working* single mom. She needed someone to keep the apartment reasonably germ-free and to be at the house if she worked late.

When she heard the name Bunny Loveland my mom must have thought she'd hit it big. Surely this woman was an affectionate grandmother type. She certainly looked the part—gray polyester pants with the built-in seam and once-a-week beauty-shop hair that lay in rounded, steel-gray rows. Alas, Bunny wasn't what my mother was hoping for. I'm not sure my mother even truly interviewed Bunny, because a quick conversation with the woman would have made it obvious that she was a cranky, mean-spirited person who cracked a smile only when she saw a Polish sausage from Vienna Beef.

Bunny came to our house twice a week from the time I was eight until I was a sophomore in high school. She brought groceries, mopped our floors and eyed my brother and me with a wariness that said, *I know you little motherfuckers are up to something. Knock it off.*

For the most part, Charlie and I stayed out of her way. Yet, as the years went on, Bunny started to toss out her opinions. They never came when you wanted to hear them, and they were always harsh, but you were glad for them when you recovered from the punchlike trauma.

I remember being eleven years old and tortured with the early advent of puberty. Something *bizarre* was going on with my body. It wasn't the boobs—I wouldn't get those until late, a surprise arrival senior year—it was simply that something seemed to be cooking inside me, boiling over, making me hot, making my red hair curl in sweaty ringlets around my face.

Bunny glanced over at me one spring afternoon and seemed to really see me for the first time in months. She frowned deeply, the motion making the thin skin around her mouth hang in folds. She crossed the room in a flash and grabbed my shoulder with a tight grip.

"Bunny! What…" I said, trying to squirm away from her.

"Come here." She tightened her grip until it cut into my skin, pulling me closer. She leaned down and sniffed. "You smell ripe, girl."

I froze, hoping this was all a mortifying, horrifying, terrifying dream.

"Has your mother bought you anything for that?"

"For what?"

She sighed—the same sigh that Moses must have made when he pondered the pickle of the Red Sea. "Watch your brother."

She grabbed her keys and left the apartment. She returned twenty minutes later with a brown paper bag. She took out a blue tube that read Secret on the side. "Put this under your arms before you get dressed," she said, plunking it down on the counter. "Every morning. Got it?"

We stared at each other. I knew she wasn't steering me wrong. "Sure, got it."

I quickly learned that when Bunny said something, she was rarely incorrect. And at the very least she was always atrociously honest, which was exactly what I needed now with Sam gone and no clue what, in my life, was worthy of belief.

Bunny was in her late seventies now and had only stopped cleaning houses a few years prior when a number of deaths in her distant family resulted in one cousin's money being left solely to her. She still lived on Schubert Avenue in the place she'd bought in the sixties with her first (and only) husband, and which she had kept in the divorce a few years later.

I stood in front of the house now. It was a squat, old, brown cottage, overgrown with trees and surrounded by soaring brick brownstones, all built within the last ten years. Bunny had been offered loads of money to sell her place to developers who would raze her outdated shack. She could move to a bigger and better house with that kind of money, they told her. And she told them to shove it. I was sure her neighbors gritted their teeth every time they looked at the straggly bushes at the perimeter of the property and the little windmill outside Bunny's front door.

I knocked. I hadn't called, but I knew she'd be home. Bunny rarely left the place these days.

She opened the door, the smell of vinegar (her favorite cleaning solvent) wafting from behind her. She looked much the same as she had years ago—same hair, although it was white now; same grim set to her mouth.

"What are you doing here?" she asked by way of a greeting.

"Great to see you, too." I kissed her on the cheek, and she quickly wiped at it with the back of her hand.

The front room of Bunny's house was a sitting room decorated with sixties furniture—curved leather couches and mod coffee tables, stuff she and the husband had purchased way back when. For years, it was painfully dated, but now that retro was hot again, the room made Bunny seem like an elderly woman with extremely hip tastes. The *Chicago Trib* lay in sections on the table next to a cup of coffee.

Bunny nodded at the table. "Want some coffee or tea?"

"Sure."

"It's in the kitchen." She sat down on the couch.

When I was back with a cup of tea, Bunny put down the paper and stared at me with a frown, waiting.

"It's Sam," I said.

The corners of her mouth lifted for the briefest second before dropping again. "I like that boy."

This was true—I'd brought Sam around a few times and Bunny had taken to him like she didn't to most people. He didn't try to butter her up, and he shared her love of hot dogs and Polish sausage, and the two of them could go head-to-head for hours, debating Sugerdawg vs. Vienna Beef vs. Nathan's vs. Portillo's vs. Red Hot.

"Sam seems to have taken off," I told Bunny. I told her what I knew.

Bunny's gaze moved away from mine toward the light coming through her front window. She stared out, looking almost wistful in a way I'd never seen before. "I miss having a man around."

I held my breath. Never, ever, ever had I heard such a sentiment from Bunny's mouth, and I would have bet my favorite True Religion jeans that I never would.

"Bart was a shithead," Bunny continued, still staring out the window. "I'm glad I divorced him. But it sure is nice to have someone to spend your life with." She turned and met my eyes. "Sam was pretty special."

"He *is*." I shrugged. "Who knows, maybe he's a pretty special con man."

"You believe that?"

"No."

"I don't believe it either," Bunny said. "So what are you doing about it?"

"I tried asking the cops and the feds, but they don't know anything more than I do. I called this detective I know, but it doesn't seem like he's able to help me."

She scoffed. "So try harder, Izzy. You're no stranger to getting your hands dirty. Do it."

"How?"

Her eyes narrowed with annoyance. "*I* don't know."

"But what if Sam *is* a thief? What if he stole Forester's money?"

"Then when you find him, you can cut his little pecker off."

"It's not little, actually," I said before I could stop myself. I slapped my hand over my mouth. "Sorry."

Bunny tossed her head back and laughed, one of only a handful of laughs I'd ever heard from her. "Well then, all the more reason to track that boy down."

I nodded. Nodded again. Thought of what I had to do. "Thanks, Bunny." And I left.

22

From a distance, John Mayburn followed Lucy DeSanto as she pulled out of the garage behind her Lincoln Park mansion. Compared with the other brick or wood-sided houses on the street, the place was a monstrosity. It was made of white-gray stone, took up three full lots on Bissell Street and was shaped like a huge *L*. From what Mayburn could tell from studying its aerial view, the inside of the *L* opened to a large courtyard, a luxury in Chicago.

The problem, at least for Mayburn, was that a massive wall made of the same white-gray stone surrounded the place, which made it impossible to see inside from the street. To add to the overkill, the wall was spiked on top.

He needed to be inside this house. Working with the auditors at the bank he'd been able to detect a pattern, his only lead on this case. Whenever DeSanto worked from home he predominantly handled transactions for a business called Advent Corporation, whereas when he was at the bank his transactions were easily spread among the thirty clients in his portfolio. Something funky was going on with DeSanto and Advent Corporation.

Advent claimed to do corporate business consulting. They actually had the nerve to call themselves "process reengineers," which Mayburn found freaking priceless. Really, what did such people actually do?

There was one interesting thing he and the bank had pieced together about Advent—the year before, they'd had twenty-five million in sales and netted eighteen, and yet they did about thirty-five million in transactions with Bank Midwest. Always through Michael DeSanto.

Mayburn was starting to suspect Advent was a mob-owned corporation, and DeSanto was laundering funds for them. Why he always ran such transactions from home, Mayburn wasn't exactly sure, since he could access the same network from work. What was probably happening was that DeSanto got instructions from Advent while at home, either through a secure phone line or through a different secure network. That was why Mayburn needed to get into the guy's house and, in particular, onto his computer.

He wanted to crack this case, not just because the bank was jumping on him to do so, but also because it annoyed him that some smug jerkoff like DeSanto got the fat crib *and* the girl *and* the family *and* probably a pile of money in an offshore account. DeSanto seemed to have a full-fledged life, something Mayburn realized he was missing.

Since he hadn't figured out a way to get inside, he was tailing Lucy again.

Her car was a ninety-thousand-dollar Mercedes; glittering navy-blue with ivory leather interior. She looked pretty in the car. Whenever she parked it by her florist, whom she visited every week, it seemed that sunlight flooded out of the door when she opened it, as if the sun had been trapped inside by those ivory seats and Lucy's finespun, blond hair. Mayburn wondered if Lucy's husband ever noticed these things. He doubted it.

Mayburn trailed Lucy's car down Armitage Avenue and onto Clybourn. He knew then where she was going, and he groaned. He trailed her for another two blocks, then drove past her as she pulled in to the parking lot of Gym Matters, a business that taught gymnastics and movement skills to toddlers. Lucy had a three-year-old, and she took her here two afternoons a week. So far Mayburn hadn't followed her inside. Too risky. But maybe the break he needed on this case was inside Gym Matters. Maybe he could get closer to Lucy this time. Maybe her friends would be there and she would discuss plans to redo her kitchen or her bathroom. If so, Mayburn could find out when that work would take place and he could show up early in the day, posing as a plumber. Or maybe Lucy would talk about a vacation they were planning, and while they were gone, Mayburn might be able to start a contained fire near the house and get inside with the firefighters. Mayburn had thought about doing that when the DeSanto family was in town, but he hated to scare Lucy and the kids, and from what he could tell, DeSanto was such a control freak, he'd get right inside with the firefighters, which would mean Mayburn wouldn't get a chance to look at his computer.

Mayburn turned his car around and doubled back toward Gym Matters. He pulled in, parking far away from Lucy's Mercedes. Inside the front doors was a long, narrow waiting area that overlooked a large room with a matted floor, where two instructors led around a pack of hyped-up kids. Lucy sat by herself at the far end of the waiting area. She had a pile of hot-pink thread in her lap, and it looked as if she was knitting a tiny cap. When Mayburn stepped up to the front desk, only six or so feet from her, she raised her head. For a moment, Mayburn was both anxious and thrilled that she was about to see him, and for the first time.

But Lucy DeSanto only looked through the glass wall until her eyes found her tiny daughter, Eve. She smiled—one of those contented private smiles that people make when they're lost in their thoughts. Then she returned her attention to the bronze knitting needles, which made a pleasant *click-clacking* sound.

Mayburn told the clerk he was looking for information about programs for his daughter.

The clerk put a promotional sheet in front of him and invited Mayburn to watch the class in progress. He took a seat about four feet from Lucy.

It was exciting to be so close to her without her husband or girlfriends around. But the problem with her current solitude was the fact that he couldn't learn anything from her that would help him get inside the DeSanto house.

He sat for a tedious hour, watching the group of toddlers race from one station to another, jumping on mini trampolines, climbing on large blocks, throwing themselves onto the padded floor in a fit of giggles. If anything, the kids seemed to pick up energy as the hour went by, as if someone had slipped speed into their juice boxes. He wondered how Lucy was ever going to get that kid to take a nap.

Lucy kept to herself and her knitting. Once, she answered her cell phone, giving Mayburn a burst of hope that some detail would filter through the room, but from what he could hear, the caller was her sister, and the discussion consisted only of what gift to order for their mother's birthday.

When the hour came to an end, Lucy and her daughter went to the car.

He followed, frustrated, and got in his own car.

His cell phone vibrated from inside his jacket pocket. He took it out and saw the display, *Isabel McNeil cell.*

"Hi, Izzy," he answered in a flat tone. "What's up?"

He watched Lucy get in the front seat and start the car. She was about to drive off. And again he had no leads on this case.

"Mayburn, you're *going* to help me."

"Excuse me?"

"I know you turned me down yesterday, but I need some serious assistance here. The cops aren't looking into Forester's death. The feds are investigating Sam, but they've pretty much told me to move on with my life. The thing is, I think Sam must be gone for a reason. I've got to figure out what that reason is. And I have to find out if someone hurt

Forester—whether it was Sam or someone else—because I told him I would. This is the last thing I can do for him."

"Look, take a breath. Can you log in to Sam's e-mail?"

"I did that already. He hasn't sent anything since he disappeared. Doesn't seem to have received any e-mails that are suspicious."

"Okay, try to find out if he took any flights."

"He usually flies United. I got onto their site with his password, but there was nothing except the flight for our honeymoon."

Mayburn grunted, impressed by Izzy's tenacity. "Credit cards?"

"Checked 'em. Nothing. C'mon, help me. Give me a discounted rate or something."

Mayburn watched Lucy's glittery blue car pull out of the parking lot. He thought about how to package his rejection to Izzy. But then, the spark of an idea came to him.

"I might be able to pool together some money for you," Izzy was saying. "It won't be much, but—"

Lucy's car disappeared into the two streams of traffic flowing down Clybourn. He smiled for the first time that day. "Izzy," he said, interrupting her, "I think I know a different way you can pay me."

23

An hour after I'd called him, I was sitting with John Mayburn at RL, the restaurant owned by Ralph Lauren, right around the corner from Ralph's store on Michigan Avenue. It was apparently a favorite of Mayburn's, which kind of surprised me. It was an elegant, refined place, and although Mayburn wasn't exactly coarse or unrefined, I wouldn't have expected him to suggest it. The place was cozy and cavelike, decorated in deep, rich mahogany. The walls were packed with oil paintings and photographs, to which there was little continuity of theme. A canvas showing a turn-of-the-century hunter hung next to a black and white of Mick Jagger.

Usually a table was hard to come by, but since it was between the lunch and dinner rush, we scored a banquette in the back. Still, the tucked-away positioning couldn't stop the paranoid feeling I had that someone was watching me. Except it wasn't paranoia. The feds probably *were* watching me.

I grabbed the chair with my back to the room, so that if someone was tailing me, they wouldn't be able to see what I was saying. The thing was, although I didn't have anything to hide, the thought of someone observing me, studying me, was unsettling. As Mayburn took a seat on the banquette, I couldn't help but swivel my head around. Was the man by the door an agent, the one looking into the crowd as if searching for another diner? Could it be the guy in the blue business suit getting seated by himself?

"What's wrong?" Mayburn asked.

I turned back to him. "Nothing." I wasn't sure if I was supposed to talk about the fact that I was probably being followed.

"I have a proposal for you. I'll work your case if you work mine."

"You need some legal work?"

"No, I need a female operative to assist on a few cases, one in particular."

"A female operative?" The waiter came and took our drink orders—sparkling water for me, an iced tea for Mayburn.

"Here's the deal." Mayburn pushed aside his leather menu and leaned forward on his elbows. He was wearing a nice camel sport coat over black pants. "I'll help you try and track down Sam, and we'll look into what happened to Forester Pickett. If he was killed, we'll try to find who did it. In return, I want you to work a case of mine."

"I'm not even sure what that means."

"Let me explain something. A lot of times I'll conduct surveillance, and I'll find myself in a place where it would be much, much easier to collect intel if I were a woman."

"Like a women's locker room?"

"Sure, or at a coffee shop during the day where there are a lot of young moms, or at a pilates class that's taken mostly by women."

"You take pilates?" I laughed.

"No, I *don't* take pilates. That's the point. There are a lot of activities or venues that are populated predominantly by women. The other point is that if anyone has even the slightest instinct they are being followed, they rarely look for a woman. Women slip by easier in this world."

I looked around. How surreal that I was likely under surveillance by the feds, while Mayburn seemed to be asking me to conduct surveillance on someone else.

"So, I've been hiring freelance female operatives," Mayburn continued. "Usually someone who's got a P.I. license."

"I don't have that."

"I know. But what you have is a look—a young, professional look. A look that says, 'I live in Old Town or Lincoln Park or Gold Coast and you wouldn't catch me dead on the South Side.'"

"Hey, that's not true! I go to the South Side with my friend Maggie to visit her family."

"Fine, but you're not there a lot. You have a gentrified Northside look, and that's what I need here. You're not going to testify in this case. You'd just help lead me to evidence I might use in the future."

"What about the freelancers you usually work with?"

"Those women aren't a help to me with this situation. They're a little tougher around the edges. They don't always blend so well."

"But they've got the training. I wouldn't know what I was doing."

"I'll teach you."

"I don't have any background." But it occurred to me that instruction from Mayburn might make it easier to tell when I was being watched.

"You actually have a lot of background," Mayburn said. "One of the key skills an operative needs is how to listen. Most lawyers, although they never shut up, know how to do that. Of course, there's a different kind of listening involved with this work, but I can teach you that."

The waiter came to take our food order. I looked at my menu, but I couldn't concentrate.

Mayburn ordered the lobster club. "I always get that," he said.

I kept studying the menu, trying to let the last few minutes sink in. I was being asked to act as a private investigator. How had that happened? Mayburn said he'd teach me, but did I have the time to pick up the skills I'd need? I didn't even know what those skills were.

But what other option did I have? Sam seemed to be slipping away from me fast. And I owed it to Forester to do anything I could to look into his death.

"Ma'am?" the waiter said.

I focused, ordered the first thing my eyes landed on, and then looked at Mayburn.

He stared back at me. "What do you think?"

"When would we start?"

He glanced around the restaurant and grinned. "Right now."

24

"**Y**ou've *got* to have impeccable listening skills," Mayburn said. To flex my listening muscle, he said he wanted me to tune in to a conversation in the restaurant and tell him what was said.

Just then, two women were led into the dining room. They were dressed expensively—one wearing a brown fur jacket, the other in a black coat with a hem of sparkling beads—and their hands were weighed down with shopping bags. The maître d' seated them at the table behind us.

"Those are your subjects," Mayburn said.

I started to twist around to get another look, but Mayburn said, "No, no, you don't get to look at them. Staring at them signals you might be listening. You have to be able to do it without using your eyes."

"No problem." I took a sip of my water and began listening.

"Oof," the one said, apparently sinking into her seat. "I'm exhausted."

"Me, too."

"Thank God I found something to wear to Beth's Thanksgiving dinner. That was hanging over my head. I mean, you can't just throw something on for that thing."

"Absolutely not. Last year I wore a dress that I'd worn only once before, but she knew."

"She gives you that look."

"Exactly!"

Mayburn crossed his arms over his chest. "I'll tell you another thing that's really important in investigative work."

"Great," I said.

"Assumptions."

"What do you mean?"

"Never make them. You're going to have to watch that. I can see the tendency in you."

"What are you talking about?"

"You assume that Sam must have had a reason for lifting those shares and taking off."

"So?" I couldn't keep the annoyed tone out of my voice. "I want to believe in the man I'm supposed to marry." I had to. Or at least I had to try. I had doubted the wedding, which meant I doubted Sam and me. I doubted *us*. And now look what had happened.

"I respect that," Mayburn said, "but you've got to wear two hats now. When you're working on this case with me, you have to separate yourself from it. You have to look at Sam objectively."

The waiter delivered our food. I cut a piece of the fish I'd ordered and put it in my mouth, but I couldn't really taste it.

For a while, Mayburn ate and I pushed food around, and we made small talk.

Mayburn picked up the last bite of his lobster club and popped it in his mouth. "I hope you're still listening to them," he said, chewing.

"Listening to them? Oh, *them*." I jerked my head back in the direction of the women. "No problem."

"Yeah? You were listening to them the whole time?"

I dropped my voice. "Sure, they're talking about whether they should have bought the jeans they both tried on."

"And before that?"

I shrugged. "Before that you were talking to me about assumptions."

"And you should have still been listening to them at the same time."

"I was."

Mayburn gave me a mild grin. "So what did they say? From the beginning."

I pushed my plate away. "First, they talked about Nordstroms, and they said the saleslady was a bitch."

"What else?"

"One of them wanted to return a pair of shoes. She told the saleslady she'd worn them twice, and they hurt her feet. She said the saleswoman wouldn't accept the shoes she'd worn twice, which is *priceless,* don't you think? I can't believe she was trying to return used shoes."

Mayburn crossed his hands on the table. "Izzy, focus for me. I need you to be able to remember *exactly* what she said. It's like when you have a witness on the stand—"

"Right, right," I interrupted him. "I get it. Every word is important. It's like taking a deposition or cross-examining someone. You have to listen to each word, and to precisely how they phrase things."

Mayburn gave me a pleased nod.

"Dude, seriously," I said, leaning toward him. "Maybe you think this is hard. Maybe *guys* think it's hard, but for me? For most women? I could listen to two more conversations. No-brainer."

He paused, looked at me, shrugged. "Glad to hear it. I've got a couple of assignments for you on your case."

I leaned farther in, more interested now.

"You need to talk to Shane Pickett," Mayburn said. "Always look at the family first when someone dies. Especially when the family inherits a lot of money or assets."

"Okay, I'll see him tomorrow at the funeral—"

Mayburn shook his head. "You won't be able to have a long discussion at the funeral. You've got to meet with him privately. Use those deposition skills. Ask him about his dad's death, where he was that night, what's been going on since, how he's handling everything."

"What am I looking for?"

"There are ways to cause a heart attack. We need to rule that out."

"But even if Shane did something to hurt his dad, he's not going to tell me, right?"

"Of course not. Look, the way investigations work is that you put lots and lots of little pieces together. So, this is your first piece—get Shane Pickett's explanation of the whole thing now that his dad's been gone a few days. Shane Pickett's demeanor. Anything that comes up when you talk to him."

"Should I tell him I'm working with you?"

"Never tell a subject you're investigating them, unless it's to your advantage. With Shane Pickett, you're in a key position. You're already on the inside. There's no reason to tell him anything."

"Okay. What's the other assignment?" I felt motivated by these tasks, by the thought that something was being done about Forester's death. At last.

"I need you to find the names and addresses of the doctors Forester was seeing—both his cardiologist and that Chinese whack job. We'll need to establish whether his health was as good as he was telling you."

"Got it."

Mayburn wiped his mouth with a napkin and cleared his throat. "Anything else you haven't told me about Forester? Or Sam?"

I glanced around, feeling that creeping paranoia again. "There is something." I told him about how the blinds in my garage were up that morning and how it looked as if something had been placed on the sill. I told him about my meeting with the FBI.

"Shit. Are you serious? You're probably being followed by the feds. When were you going to tell me this?"

"Now."

"Jesus, Izzy."

The restaurant was getting louder now that the happy hour crew was descending.

"Does that screw everything up?"

"Well, I really don't like the thought of the feds tailing one of my operatives..." He bit his lip, and his words trailed off. Then he shrugged. "What the heck. I guess it really doesn't matter. If the guy I'm investigating really did what we think he did, the feds are going to find out anyway." He waved for the check. "Let's get out of here."

"So," I said as we waited, returning to the small talk, "what are your plans for tonight?" I realized that I knew nothing about John Mayburn from a personal perspective, other than he was in his early forties.

"Not much." But I noticed he looked uncomfortable for the first time today.

"I guess I've never asked, are you married?" I glanced at this left hand. No ring.

"Nope."

"Girlfriend?"

"Not right now. So tonight, I'll probably go home and return the calls I've been getting from my family." He gave an embarrassed look. "Tomorrow is my birthday, and they want to make some grand plans."

"What?" I clapped. "Your birthday? Let's get some dessert!" The waiter arrived with the bill, and I asked him for a dessert menu.

Mayburn took it from my hands. "No dessert," he said with quiet force. He handed the menu back to the waiter. "Just the check, please."

I crossed my arms and looked at Mayburn. "No wonder you don't have a girlfriend."

He scoffed. "Fuck off. I do fine with the ladies. I didn't want you to order cake or a dessert because I'm trying to teach you something, and that's when you can keep a low profile."

"Oh, please. What's a little cake going to do to your low profile?"

"You told him it was my birthday. What do you think he was going to do with that information?"

"Stick a candle in your cake?"

"And he would light that candle, and people in this room would turn and watch where that cake goes, and then you clap again and maybe sing, and people at the next table say, 'Happy Birthday!' and I don't know what part of that sounds like a 'low profile' to you."

I sat back. "Understood."

"And, by the way, 'low profile' also means that you aren't going to be telling anyone that you're working for me."

"No one?"

"No one. If you're really going to be of any help to me, I can't have word getting around that you're a part-time P.I."

"But I could tell my friend Maggie, or my assistant, Q?"

He shook his head. "No one. You'll swear them to secrecy, but they might let it slip to one person and that person slips and then another. The whole reason I need you is because you're a typical, normal Northside Chicago woman. If there's any inkling that you're not, it won't work. That's how it's got to be if you're on this team."

"Are there any other team members?"

He laughed. "No."

"All right then, so we're the team?"

He nodded, and held out his hand.

I shook it, and I felt a flowering of something inside of me, something I hadn't felt for the last few days. Hope.

25

I gave my name to the front-desk clerk at WNDY, a television station owned by Pickett Enterprises.

"Jane Augustine is expecting me," I said.

The clerk looked at his computer screen, then glanced at his watch. "You'd better get up there fast." It was fifteen minutes before five, and Jane was the star of the five o'clock news.

I pushed through the double doors behind the desk and stepped onto the cavernous television set. On the far side, raised on a platform and bathed in bright klieg lights, was the anchor's desk. Jane's coanchor was already seated there, being dotted with powder by the makeup artist. All around the set, people moved quickly, wearing headphones and clutching clipboards, none of them seeming to notice what the others were doing.

I stopped a tall woman with short black hair and dark-rimmed eyeglasses. C. J. Lyons. Jane's producer.

"Izzy!" She patted me on the shoulder. "How are you? Doing okay?" She wasn't usually so friendly. But she'd obviously heard about Forester.

"I'm hanging in there."

"Yeah, God. Can't believe all this."

I wasn't sure exactly what she meant by "all this," but I didn't feel like talking with her about it. I was here to see Jane about her contract. She'd called today and left a message with Q, saying she was ready to sign and asking if she could talk to me about one thing. All I really wanted to do after my lunch with Mayburn was go home and decompress, but if I had any kind of an "in" with Jane, I was going to take it. I wouldn't let Forester down by letting Pickett Enterprises grind to a halt.

"Jane's waiting for you in the dressing room," C.J. said.

I walked in front of the anchor desk, waved at Jane's coanchor and made my way down a short hallway to the dressing room. Jane was sitting on a high swivel chair, her shiny black hair hanging in a sheet down her back, her eyes heavenward while a makeup artist added a little more mascara to her well-known mauve-blue eyes.

"Izzy!" She leaned forward from her stool and gave me an air kiss. The tissue they'd stuck around the collar of her suit brushed against my neck. "Sit down."

"You heard about Forester?" I took a seat on a matching chair.

Jane glanced at her makeup person. "Give me a minute?"

"You're done anyway," the woman said. "See you out there."

Jane turned back to me. "I'm sick about Forester. I cannot believe it."

"I can't either."

"I feel stupid now." She shook her black hair over her shoulder, a patented Jane move that was both sexy and elegant.

"What do you mean?"

"I've been drawing out this contract stuff."

"I noticed."

She smiled. "Sorry. I just wanted to make sure I'm getting the best deal possible. This is my career, you know? And my agent plays hardball. He gets off on that stuff. I should have stepped in and stopped him, but that's what he's paid for, and... Well, now with Forester gone, it seems pointless to have been fighting."

"We weren't fighting. We were negotiating."

"Well, I'm ready to sign it. Just finalize everything, will you?"

I nodded.

Jane went silent. It seemed she was studying me. "I heard about Sam."

The hair on my arms rose. "You heard what about Sam?"

Jane and Sam had met only once, at a benefit at Café Brauer, where Forester was being honored for his charity work.

"I heard about those shares of Forester's," she said, "and I heard Sam is gone."

"Who told you that?" A cold lick of premonition swept over me like something bad was looming.

She pressed her lips together for a moment. "I can't reveal a source."

"A *source?*" It sounded so official. They'd had Forester's death on the news, but so far there had been nothing about Sam or the shares.

"Yeah. C.J. is all over it."

Just then someone made a short rap on the door. It opened and C.J. poked her head in. "How's it going?"

It hit me. I looked at Jane. "You didn't have me here to talk about your contract, did you?"

A flash of sympathy from her mauve eyes.

C.J. stepped into the room. "We've already covered Forester's death. And now we've learned about the shares that were stolen. C'mon, it's good stuff. We can't ignore this story."

"So you had me here to interview me about it?"

"We're just getting started. But we'd like to put something together for the ten o'clock."

The lights over Jane's makeup counter seemed glaringly bright and hot suddenly. How strange that I was always here in an official capacity—as Forester's lawyer, someone distinctly behind the scenes—and now this.

"I don't know anything." I was getting sick of saying that. Sick of it being true.

"You must."

"I don't!" I couldn't help it, but my voice boomed loud into the small room. "And if *you* know anything—*anything*—you guys have to tell me."

C.J. and Jane exchanged looks.

C.J. shrugged. "On the same night Forester died, Sam took off with some kind of corporate shares that give him control of millions of dollars of real estate in Panama."

I bit the inside of my cheek to stop myself from talking. They had it right, but I didn't want to go on the record as having said anything. I wanted her to keep talking.

"That's the gist of it," C.J. said. "The assumption is that Sam will try to unload the property by selling the shares, and he'll end up with a lot of money."

"Whose assumption is that?"

"We did some research on these Panamanian shares," C.J. said. "From what we can tell, Panama is about the last place you can still get an anonymous corporation with no loopholes or tax returns to file when you sell. And apparently, the assets are generally nonsequesterable which means nonfreezable, so there isn't a whole lot anyone can do to stop it. At least not in the short term."

C.J.'s eyes gleamed from behind her dark-rimmed glasses. This was exciting for her, a challenging story. "So, right now, Sam is the owner of that corporation," she continued, "as well as the real estate that the corporation owns. He can sell it whenever he wants."

"Who told you that Sam took off?"

She said nothing.

"Who the hell told you guys any of this?"

"We got an anonymous tip," Jane said.

In my brain, I scribbled a list of everyone who knew about this—me, Q, Tanner, Mark Carrington, Shane. But then I realized that anyone who worked for Baltimore & Brown knew about it, and anyone who worked for Mark Carrington's office knew, and most likely a number of people at Pickett Enterprises knew. Then there were the cops and the FBI.

Probably, at this point, hundreds of people knew the story, or what little there was to know.

"You guys can't air this," I said. "You don't know anything, and you don't have any footage, right?"

Silence. I'd hit it. How ironic. I'd had such a conversation hundreds of times, but I'd never cared so much about the decision we made. Usually, C.J. called me and asked if they could run a story that was thin. If it was based on rumors and suppositions, if there was no one to interview to make it a solid story, I told them no. Pickett Enterprises was the cleanest of companies, and we didn't want the threat of a slander suit.

"You're not getting an interview or a confirmation from me," I said. "Mostly because I don't have anything to give. I really don't know a thing. This is an ambush, and I'm not taking it. But also, as your lawyer, you can't run this story."

Now, I was bringing personal stuff into my work, something lawyers were always warned against, but I also knew I couldn't let Sam be tried and found guilty by the press before we really knew what he'd done.

C.J. looked pissed. "Someone else is going to run with it."

"Have you heard that?"

"No, I'm just saying. Eventually. Eventually, some other station or paper is going to cover it."

I looked from C.J. to Jane and back again. It was funny that Jane was the beauty, the face, the person everyone in Chicago knew. It was C.J. with the brains *and* the brawn. Unlike most of the newscasters who wrote their own stories, writing had never been Jane's strong suit, and as she worked her way up to anchor, she chased the stories, and she conducted the interviews, but she left the writing and the fighting to C.J.

I stood up. "You have a broadcast to do. Good luck."

Jane scrambled to stand with me. "Thanks for coming, Izzy." She gave me another guilty smile. "I did want to talk to you about that contract. I wanted to tell you I'm signing it."

"Good. And please do me a favor. As friends. Tell me if

you learn anything. If you've got solid information, I won't stop you from covering the story, but I need you to give me a heads-up."

Jane looked at C.J., who bit her lip. "Yeah, we'll do it," C.J. said.

I left the dressing room and walked through the newsroom. I'd always been struck by how vivid the anchor desk looked on air, and yet when you pulled back, you saw so much shadowy emptiness around it, so much messiness in the form of wires and lights and people. Was the same true of Sam? Had I been using a zoom lens, focusing only on the image of him that I saw and wanted, without ever really looking at the dark chaos surrounding him?

I felt numb as I took a cab to Old Town. The people on the streets seemed full of levity, zest. I was flattened by the questions about Sam and me that kept reverberating in my head, ones I couldn't find the right answers for. Should Sam's absence call into question whether the love I thought we had was ever there to begin with?

As lawyers, we take very seriously something called precedence—that which came before and which, in large part, dictates the future. We study laws that were written before and cases that were decided before, and as long as there is a precedent, there's a good chance it's true in the future, as well.

I had to keep reminding myself that Sam and I had precedence. I had doubted the wedding, yes, but never the love. Which meant that love, or whatever you want to call it, had been real then. That was precedent. Therefore *we* were still real at this moment. We must be.

And yet. And yet. It had been days now since Sam disappeared, and when I thought about that fact, our precedence seemed flimsy. How could Sam and I have been as wonderful as I'd believed if he'd simply taken off with thirty million dollars of Forester's property apparently with no thought to me or my feelings?

I got out of the cab by Twin Anchors, an ancient corner barbecue joint. The place glowed with golden lights from within, and something about it drew me to the windows, made me gaze inside. People sat laughing at the bar, or stood behind it with mugs of beer, waiting for a table. Everyone looked happy. Everyone looked normal.

I glanced behind me and saw a guy ambling slowly toward me. Too slowly. Almost as if he didn't want to reach me. He was short, wearing a tan jacket, zipped up part of the way. His hands were in his pockets, but his elbows jutted out at his sides, as if he was trying hard to appear nonchalant but was really ready for a fight. His hair was black and wavy.

Run! That voice insisted. But this was *my* neighborhood and being followed was fast becoming an annoyance, so I stood my ground.

When he saw me watching him, he slowed even more, the elbows jutting out farther. And then, casually, he turned and disappeared down one of the tiny side alleys.

Get out of here, Izzy.

I hurried to my house, my shoes loud on the pavement. I dug in my bag for my keys. A car slowly passed my building. It was a Honda. Gray. The same car Maggie had seen outside the FBI office.

The car passed under a streetlight and although I couldn't see the face of the driver, I saw the license plate. Illinois. I memorized the number and repeated it in my head as the car disappeared down the street.

I hurried up the stairs. *Call Mayburn, call Mayburn,* I thought.

I reached the door, and as soon I put my key in the dead bolt, I knew something even more was wrong.

I knew someone had been inside my condo.

26

My pulse throbbed in my head. I couldn't get my thoughts straight. *Is he home? Is Sam home?*

Sam usually left the dead bolt unlocked and simply locked the doorknob on his way out of the condo. And now the dead bolt was unlocked. I pushed the dead bolt key to the left again. And then again to make sure. Definitely unlocked, and I was positive I had locked it when I left home this morning. I always did. The fact that Sam often didn't annoyed me.

You're on the third floor, he said, *and you need a key to get inside the main door. Don't worry about it.*

But I did. I was a relatively new home owner, and I wanted to protect my castle.

I'd finally gotten Sam trained—mostly—by guilting him about it. *How will you feel when someone breaks in and attacks me?* I said, joking.

He locked the dead bolt after that, unless he was in a hurry. But here it was, unlocked.

I found the key for the doorknob and shoved it in the slot, opening it.

It was dark inside.

I reached to the right and found the light switch, flipping it on and bathing the condo in soft, recessed lighting.

No one. No Sam.

But, but… An intangible feeling gripped me, a sense that

another person had been in my house. My eyes roamed, searching for confirmation, but everything seemed in order. The pulse in my head quickened, beating at my temples.

I went to the bedroom and stood in the doorway. I reached for the lamp on the dresser just inside the door. A dress and skirt lay on the bed, where I'd left them this morning. Nothing seemed out of place.

I walked back through the kitchen and to the office. The computer was off, as usual. I always shut down the computer after I used it, a habit I'd gotten from Q. He swore computers needed sleep like humans. But something in the office felt moved or disturbed. I let my gaze search the place. Files I'd brought home Monday night—only three days prior; how far away that seemed—still sat piled next to the desk. The photo of Sam and me in Puerto Vallarta sat to the right of the computer. In it, we looked sun-kissed and ecstatic. I studied the picture for a second, trying to discern signs of unhappiness in him, some signal of unease I'd previously missed. I saw nothing.

I sat down at the desk and immediately noticed it—a faint static around the monitor, the same slight crackling sound it made when it had been recently turned off. My hand shot to the hard drive on the floor. Sure enough, it was warm. I hadn't used it since last night. It should have been cool to the touch.

I turned on the computer. While it powered up, I raced around the condo, Sam's orange mug in my hand as a pathetic excuse for a weapon, trying to determine if anything else had been touched. Nothing appeared to have been moved or taken. I went to the closet in the master bedroom and found the clothes of Sam's that I'd shoved out of the way that morning. They looked the same.

Sam, I thought, *were you here?*

But if he had been here, why come in and leave again? Was there something here, in the place we spent much of our time that he'd needed? If all he wanted to do was use the computer, surely he could have done that anywhere. Unless there was something saved on this computer that he needed.

I hurried back to the office. The computer was on now, and I opened the browser Sam preferred. I clicked to see what sites had been recently viewed. ChicagoLions.com, ESPN.com, Netflix, Amazon, GoToMyPC and a few others. These were the sites that Sam regularly accessed. Nothing new.

Time to check his e-mail again.

I opened GoToMyPC, but the same message popped up— *Invalid e-mail address or password.*

I got onto his Yahoo! account. New messages that had accumulated over the course of the day—e-mails about rugby, junk e-mails from the flower shop on Wells where he often shopped for me, a few messages from a group of college friends trying to get together, one from a cousin in San Jose.

I read each of the e-mails closely, trying to discern hidden meaning beneath the mundane text. Until I suddenly remembered that someone had been in my apartment and on my computer, it appeared. I opened the browser I usually used. But that only showed the Web sites I viewed often— JPMorgan, AOL, OpenTable.com, PickettEnterprises.

I stopped and looked back at the first one—Morgan Stanley, my bank's Web site. I paid my bills online, but I hadn't done so for two weeks. The bank's site shouldn't have been the last one viewed. My pulse picked up once again.

I logged on to the bank's site, then clicked on Login History.

"Oh my God," I said aloud, sitting back.

According to the history, my account had been logged in to a half hour before.

27

I paced my apartment, clutching my cell phone.

I called Mayburn, who answered on the second ring. "Someone was in my house." I told him the whole story— how the dead bolt wasn't locked, how the place felt recently inhabited, how the computer had been warm. I told him Sam knew my passwords and that my bank's computer had been logged in to an hour before.

"Any funds missing?" Mayburn asked.

"No."

"Any transfers?"

"No, nothing. Why would Sam log in and then just leave?"

"Assuming you're right about someone breaking in."

"Are you saying I don't know when someone has been in my house and on my computer?" My voice raised in irritation. "Look, I know I'm supposed to be your protégé or something, but now you need to return the favor. Now you have to help me. Trust me on this one."

Silence.

"What?" I said.

"You're being a pain in the ass," he said calmly.

I stopped pacing. "No, I am not."

"Yes, you are, but you're entitled."

I groaned, ignored the slam and told Mayburn about the guy outside Twin Anchors and about the gray Honda I'd seen twice. I gave him the plate number.

I heard clicking from his end, the sounds of a keyboard. "I'll see what I can find about the plate number," he said. "Meanwhile, if someone was in your place, and someone was on your bank's site, why are you so sure it was Sam?"

"Because he knows my passwords."

"He knows your login name and your password?"

"Yes." I started pacing my apartment again. It had seemed so spacious when I'd bought it. Now it felt constricting.

"Do you change the passwords often?" Mayburn asked.

"No. I know you're supposed to, but I never get around to it."

"And do you use the same password for the bank that you do for other sites?"

"Yeah."

"Pretty easy to get them, especially if they're on your computer."

"Great," I muttered.

"Do you keep valuables in the house?"

"I have a small safe where I store some of my good jewelry and some savings bonds."

"That still there?"

I went to the hall closet and peered past the pile of sheets and towels to the small safe. "It's here."

"Open it and check."

I got the key and complied. "Everything is there."

"Then I doubt Sam was in your apartment."

"Why do you say that?" Disappointment flooded in. I hadn't realized how much I wanted Sam to have been there. Even if he'd taken off again, I would know he was okay.

"Well, if Sam was going to come back into the apartment and take off before you got there," Mayburn said, "one of the reasons might be that he was looking for something he left behind or something he needed, right?"

"I guess."

I heard him typing on his keyboard again. "And none of his stuff was taken, right?"

"As far as I can tell."

"Okay, let's think about another reason. If he was coming back to get some quick cash—maybe the jewelry to pawn or the savings bonds to cash—he knew where to get that stuff, right?"

"Yes."

"And if it was he who got onto your computer and got onto your bank's Web site, then he would have had some purpose in doing that. He would have made a wire transfer or done something to get himself some cash but, as far as you can tell, someone was just looking at your bank records. No action was taken."

"Right, but what about the dead bolt? He always leaves it undone."

"Someone probably bumped your lock."

"Bumped? Is that like picking?"

"Sort of."

"I had expensive locks installed when I moved in here."

"Expensive ones are easier to bump, actually. They're smoother."

I walked to the door and peered at the dead bolt. "Wouldn't there be damage to the lock?"

"Not if the guy was good."

"What about the lock downstairs?"

More clicking sounds from his keyboard. "Is the downstairs one a dead bolt, too?" he said, his voice a bit distracted.

"Yes."

"And does it lock again automatically when you close it?"

"Yes. And there's also a back stairway that you can't access from outside. It locks from behind as well. No dead bolt or anything."

"Well, they could bump the front door in two seconds."

"So you think it was the FBI?"

Mayburn exhaled a long audible sound. The sounds from his keyboard stopped. "Well, it was the feds following you today in the gray Honda."

"How do you know?"

"That's a government plate."

"Then maybe the feds were following me tonight and got in the house, too?"

"Maybe, but I doubt it."

I finally stopped pacing and sank into the chair in front of the fireplace.

"What do you mean?" I said.

"I think you've got somebody altogether different tailing you."

28

Mayburn explained that since September 11, the feds no longer needed a warrant to search a home, just probable cause, so it was entirely possible they'd been in my condo that night. But the reality was the bureau usually reserved their breakings-and-enterings for suspected terrorists.

"If it wasn't the FBI, then who else would be following me?" I asked.

"That's what we have to figure out."

"Should I call the cops?"

"Up to you, but then you're signing up for yet another group who will come into your house and go through your stuff."

"What do you mean?"

"Well, the Chicago PD no longer has a case open, not about Forester or Sam. You call them about a break-in, and *bam*, they've got a case open, which means you've essentially given them the go-ahead to search your place. Sounds like you already know exactly what happened—someone got on your computer. I can sweep the rest of the house for prints. And I can get a locksmith there tomorrow to install a keyless lock with a push-button pad. But I don't think the cops will help right now."

I stayed silent, mulling over the information.

"In the meantime," Mayburn continued, "you shouldn't be alone. The fact that they didn't lock your place back up means they probably had to leave fast, and that makes me nervous. Do you have anyone who can stay with you?"

"I suppose my friend Maggie could come over."

"Is Maggie a tough chick?"

I laughed. "She is when she's in the courtroom."

"Is she a big person?"

"She's five-foot-one and weighs about a hundred pounds. After she jumps in Lake Michigan."

"Yeah, I thought so," he said dryly. "Got anybody else?"

I started to say no. Then I thought of the perfect person.

Ten minutes later, my buzzer went off. "It's me," I heard my brother, Charlie, say through the speaker.

I buzzed him in and went to the kitchen to see if I had any red wine. If he could, Charlie would spend his whole life drinking red wine and reading. He was a lazy intellectual, but not a snobbish one. He found joy in anything creative and stimulating—from quirky commercials to quirky cabaret music—just as long as he didn't have to work too hard to enjoy these things.

I found a bottle of French red. A soft knock sounded from my front door. I went and opened it.

My brother stood on the threshold, giving me his sweet, empathetic smile. He had brown hair that was longish and grew into loose spiral curls. It was a chestnut-brown, and when he stepped into the sunlight, or when an overhead light hit him like now, you could see the red hue that we both shared.

"You okay, Iz?" He knew Sam had disappeared, but I hadn't told him anything else tonight when I called. Just that I needed him.

Charlie was my little brother, someone I was supposed to watch over, and technically I had done that. I was the more industrious of the two of us, the more responsible. But Charlie was the one who looked into people's eyes and understood everything about them in an instant.

I launched myself into his arms and had a good cry. He patted me on the back. He held me, not flinching, not saying anything. Finally, I wiped my eyes and we moved inside. Charlie shed his old leather jacket and dropped it onto my yellow chair as if this were any other day. Then again, it was hard to shock Charlie—he was that laid-back. In fact, all of his friends (and sometimes even my mom and I) called him "Sheets" because he spent much of his time in bed.

Charlie had graduated from the oddly named college Miami of Ohio with a degree in English and a desire to do absolutely nothing. He seemed mystified that he had to work for a living. My mother and I tried to put the fear of God into him, telling him he'd end up homeless if he didn't find work, and yet Charlie was unconcerned. He had this innate belief that life would work out, one way or another, and it wasn't worth worrying about.

Since he couldn't figure out what to do with himself, Charlie took a job on a construction crew with one of his high-school buddies who hadn't gone to college. Charlie didn't have much aptitude for tuck-pointing or electrical work, but everybody loved him. They finally gave him a job driving a dump truck to and from work sites. When there was nothing to haul, he napped in the trailer or read his well-thumbed copy of *Dorian Gray.* One day, while he was on the Dan Ryan Expressway, a semi cut him off, causing a rollover. He suffered internal bleeding, broke his femur and screwed up his back. I had to get him an attorney to make sure he collected workers' comp, and I found him a personal-injury lawyer to get a settlement from the other truck driver's insurance company.

An accident like that would have set most people back, but Sheets took it as a windfall. Sure, he was in a full leg cast for two months, and yes, the physical therapy was grueling, and true, he might still have to undergo surgery for his discs, but hey, at least he didn't have to work for a while. He was going to make that settlement money stretch as long and as far as possible. As a result, my brother had essentially spent the last two years sitting on his butt.

Charlie walked to the kitchen and saw the open bottle. He reached into my cabinet, pulled out two glasses and poured the wine. Then he walked to the fireplace and began making a fire. "Tell me," he said simply.

I gave him the whole story—Sam not showing at the Union League, finding out about Forester, what I'd learned from Mark Carrington, Sam's boss, and my meeting with the cops and the FBI, someone following me and breaking in. I told him how I'd asked for advice from Mayburn. I started to tell him more about Mayburn—how he was going to help me, how he was going to train me so that I could help him on some cases, but then I remembered his warning—*You aren't going to be telling anyone that you're working for me... No one.*

"So that's pretty much it," I said as Charlie raised himself from a newly burning fire and sank onto the yellow chair. His frame crushed his jacket, but he didn't move to right it.

"I wonder what in the hell Sam has gotten himself into," he said.

"That's what I can't figure out." I took another gulp of wine.

Charlie let his head fall back against the chair and stared at the ceiling. "He seemed fine at his bachelor party."

I sat forward on my seat, excited. "That's right, the bachelor party. I never got to ask you about that."

Sam's bachelor party last weekend had consisted of a mess of guys—his rugby buddies, friends from MBA school and friends from college—all descending on the Viagra Triangle for a night. The Viagra Triangle is a little pocket of bars and restaurants in the Gold Coast populated by drunken suburbanites, frat boys and middle-aged divorcées on the prowl (hence the "Viagra" title). It's a perennial favorite for bachelor parties, and since Sam didn't want a strip club, off they went to the Triangle. Afterward, he crashed at his Roscoe Village apartment, and I didn't see him until the next night when I found him still there, avoiding bright lights and loud noises.

"He was typical Sam," Charlie said. "He drank every shot somebody threw at him, but he wouldn't do any of the stupid bachelor-party games the rugby guys wanted. He just got hammered and talked to his buddies. He seemed happy. Same old Sam."

"And yet only three days later, same old Sam took off with thirty million dollars of Forester's property."

Right then, there was a soft shuffle from the end of the hallway, near the second bedroom.

Charlie cocked his head at the sound.

"Did you hear that?" I whispered.

He nodded, slowly putting his wineglass down.

Another scuffle sound, so quiet I wouldn't have heard it if we were talking.

"What *is* that?"

Charlie stood from the chair and tiptoed silently toward the noise. I followed. When he stopped, I cupped Charlie's ear to whisper into it. "I think it came from the back stairs." I pointed to the door at the end of the hall.

The back stairs led to the garage behind my building. You could walk down those stairs and get out the door, but as I'd told Mayburn you couldn't reenter. It was designed to be opened only from the inside, to protect against break-ins. This meant if there was someone behind that door and on that staircase, they didn't get there from the outside. They would have come from my apartment. Or from one of my neighbors'. And I'd never known my neighbors to linger on the back stairwell.

So who was it?

Charlie and I stood frozen for a moment, listening for more sounds. None came.

Charlie bent down, whispered, "Maybe it's mice?"

"They would have to be damn big mice, don't you think?" I whispered fiercely.

He shrugged.

Some bodyguard.

We heard another scuffling sound, then a creak of stairs.

"Someone is on the stairs!"

Another slow *creak*. Then another. And another.

"Someone is going *down* the stairs," I whispered.

Charlie blinked a few times, his expression hardened. His generous mouth formed a grim line, and he took a deep breath.

And then my brother, the one they called Sheets, charged toward the door, ripping it open and disappearing through it.

29

Everyone wonders how they'll react in a crisis. When we hear a news story—like the one about the man lost in the wilderness who finally stumbled home after eating tree bark and moss for two weeks—we wonder if we could do the same. We think that maybe tree bark would be a healthy weight-loss plan.

Now my crisis was here. I'd finally get the opportunity to see what I was made of. My house had been broken into, my computer searched and my brother was chasing the likely intruder down the stairs.

I'd always been concerned that my usual unflappable self would crumble in times of crisis. It turned out I was wrong. I didn't exactly spring into action, like a saucy rocket scientist in a Bond movie, but I did stand there and quickly sifted through the potential courses of action in my head.

First possibility—*Run after Charlie.* I rejected it as soon as I thought it. If he got into trouble, and I ran directly behind him, then whatever fate befell him would happen to me, too, and I wouldn't be able to help him.

Second possibility—*Call the cops.* Earlier, when my poor apartment seemed violated but unharmed, it was easier to agree with Mayburn about not phoning the police. Now the possibility of cops crawling around my condo seemed a welcome image. But that would take too long.

Third choice—*Call Mayburn.*

Fourth—*Get Sam's bat and run down the front stairs.*

I decided to go with number four. I raced to the front closet and grabbed Sam's baseball bat. I hurtled myself down the front stairs.

I stopped and sucked in air when I got to the front door. I opened it gingerly, peering outside.

Nothing. Just a normal fall night, most of the houses lit up and happy looking. I peered to the right, toward the side of the house. Again nothing.

I stepped through the door and closed it softly behind me. I was still wearing my suit from the meeting with the FBI. I raised the bat at the ready. It struck me that I looked ridiculous, creeping around with a raised bat. I wasn't entirely sure how to use the thing. I'd never even played softball. But then I thought about my brother, my kind, sweet brother, and I knew that if someone was hurting him, I'd turn into Sammy freaking Sosa.

I hurried around the side of the house, bat still raised. I heard heavy breathing when I was almost near the back.

I paused, listening more intently. Someone was panting, hard. And they were only a few feet from me, I could tell.

I raised the bat higher, tiptoeing now. I walked one, two feet, and finally I dashed around the side of the building, yelling like a banshee and racing with the bat.

"Whoa!" My sweet brother fell to his knees, hands raised over his head in a gesture of self-protection.

I dropped the bat and sank to my knees with him. "Oh my gosh, I'm sorry. Are you okay?"

He raised his face and looked at me with big eyes and a laugh starting to bubble up in his throat. "Remind me to take you next time I get into a street rumble."

"I wasn't sure if it was you or someone else."

"Whoever was on your stairs..." He paused to pant some more. "They took off. When I chased after them, I heard them all the way down the stairs..." More panting. I'd never known my brother to exert himself this much. "When I got outside, I saw him running."

"A guy?"

"Yeah, I think so. Jeans, jacket, baseball hat."

"Tan jacket?"

"Uh... Not sure. It was dark in the stairwell."

"Did he have black hair?"

"Couldn't tell."

"Was he short?"

"Not sure. He was below me, so I couldn't tell, and then he got away so fast."

"Did you see *anything* else about him?" I asked, although I knew the man on the stairs probably wasn't the same guy I'd seen on the street outside Twin Anchors. He wouldn't have been able to get in my apartment sooner than I did. How many people were following me?

"It was too dark on the stairs," Charlie said, "and you don't have many lights out here."

We both looked around the small backyard. One weak light hung above the rear door, another over the entrance to the garage.

"I never noticed that before." I felt how vulnerable we were out there in the dark.

I helped Charlie to his feet and dialed 9-1-1.

It went pretty much as Mayburn predicted. The cops were at my condo within five minutes of calling them. They poked around, radios squawking about DUIs and bar brawls.

"Is this a typical night for you?" Charlie asked one cop, a squat guy with a belly as wide as he was tall.

"Thursday night," he said, as if that explained everything.

"What exactly are you looking for?" Charlie asked the cop, who was opening and closing the backdoor, looking at the door joints.

The cop glared at him.

"I'm curious," Charlie said. "Seriously."

The cop turned his attention back to the door. "Looking for signs of breaking and entering."

"They must have broken in downstairs just to get in the building," I said. I'd explained this all earlier.

"Got it." He opened and closed the door a few more times, then turned to me with a bland expression. "You said you talked to Detective Vaughn this week?"

"And Detective Schneider."

The officer unhooked his radio from his belt and spoke into it, asking whether Detective Schneider or Vaughn was on duty.

"Off duty," came the response.

Twenty minutes later, an evidence tech and a different detective showed up. The detective was an older black man in a red fleece jacket. Sitting in the living room, Charlie and I once again went through the details of the night. The detective told us that the locks showed little damage, which meant they'd either been bumped, as Mayburn had said, or someone had left the front door open.

"We never leave the door open," I said, "and it's set to close and lock automatically."

"Yes, ma'am, but nothing was stolen." He looked at me with kindness. And obvious boredom.

"I explained to the other officers that it looks like someone had been on my computer and in my bank records."

"Any idea why someone would want to do that?"

I told him the FBI had questioned me and were probably following me.

As soon as he heard "FBI," he flipped his notebook closed. "You should have told me that earlier."

"Why?"

"Sounds like they've got jurisdiction." He asked a few questions about whom I'd spoken to. I gave him Andi Lippman's name from the FBI. "I'll contact the feds," he said.

"And they'll look into it?"

"Up to them." He stood up, his tall frame looming over me.

"What should I do in the meantime?"

"The door is secure."

"But if they got in once, can't they just come in again?" Charlie asked.

"Technically," he said. "You'll want to change those locks."

A uniformed policeman came up to us. "Ma'am." He handed me a clipboard with a police report. "Can you sign this, please?"

I took the clipboard and the pen he offered. "So this is it?" I asked the detective.

"Unless you want us to barricade the door."

"Then how would my neighbors and I enter the building?" The detective nodded gravely, as if to say, "good point."

"So there's nothing else you can do?"

He shrugged. "You're on your own."

30

Day Four

Usually, everything looks better in the morning. Usually, the crisp, cool light that grows over Lake Michigan and spreads over the city fills me with hope and possibility.

But after a night spent alternately watching the front door, and dozing fitfully in the yellow chair, trying to tune out my brother's snoring, life seemed nothing but bleak. When I remembered that Forester's funeral was today, I felt the loss of him like a hard kick to my gut.

Mayburn texted me. Called the locksmith. We're on our way over.

Charlie began moving around, shifting his body from its awkward position on the chair. "Mmm," he said, sounding distinctly satisfied, as if he'd just slept in a luxurious bed covered with the most expensive linens.

He yawned, stretched his long limbs. Finally he opened his eyes. "Hi, Iz," he said, sounding pleased to find me in front of him.

"Sleep well?" I asked in a wry voice.

"Yeah, great." Then he caught my expression. "Sorry, I fell asleep."

I waved a hand at him. I should never have expected my

brother to stand guard over me. He and I didn't work that way. "I've got a locksmith coming over. You're off duty."

We hugged at the door. "Call me if you need anything," he said. "Anything at all."

Mayburn arrived twenty minutes later with the locksmith.

I waited until they climbed the three flights of stairs. Mayburn wore dark jeans and a long-sleeved T-shirt that said something about Smashing Pumpkins at Soldier Field. He had on beat-up brown boots that managed to look cool. I liked this casual look of his better than the blazers or suits he wore for work.

I shook hands with the locksmith then looked at Mayburn. "Thanks for coming."

"No problem. I'll check the place out," he said. "See if I notice anything the cops missed."

While the locksmith went to work, Mayburn poked around the apartment. He searched for prints using a battery-powered light source strapped around his head.

"Very cute." I nodded at the thing, which made him look like a high-tech coal miner.

"I don't care what it looks like," he said. "It's a hell of a lot easier than dusting. And a hell of a lot cleaner."

When Mayburn was done, he told me that there were prints all over my house, which was typical, since Sam and I lived there, we entertained occasionally, and we had a cleaning person who came every few weeks. Mayburn also said that if the person who'd broken in was a professional, which was probable, they wouldn't have left any prints.

"So there's nothing to find?" I stared around my apartment, feeling nervous again.

"Not right now, but remember what I told you. Investigations are made up of lots of little pieces of information that you put together."

"And what piece of information did we get here?"

"Someone definitely broke into your house."

"I knew that."

"You *suspected* that. Now that we've seen the locks and the cops have seen the locks, we know they were bumped for sure."

"Great," I said.

"Sorry to be the one to tell you, but this stuff takes time."

I sighed. "Well, I appreciate you being here."

"That's what we're doing, right? I'm working for you and you're working for me?"

"Yeah."

He crossed his arms over his chest. "Good, because I've got another assignment for you. One that's for my case. Can you borrow a kid?"

"Excuse me?"

"A friend's kid. Is there somebody you could offer to baby-sit for, like, for an afternoon?"

I ran my mind around everyone I knew. "My friend Maggie has brothers and sisters who have kids. I've never babysat before, but they'd probably be thrilled if I offered."

"Excellent." Mayburn's eyes went a little brighter, and I could see him thinking. "Sunday afternoon, I need you on a playground."

"But the Bears are on." I knew the Bears game didn't matter in the scheme of things, not anymore, but I liked saying that, as if I still lived in a day when my world ran around social outings and court calls and sporting events, rather than FBI visits and funerals and private-investigation assignments.

Mayburn shook his head. "TiVo it. Because on Sunday, Izzy McNeil, you're going to be a mother."

31

After Mayburn left, I called Maggie. She had a virtual day-care center of nieces and nephews.

I heard the phone being picked up at her apartment. "What courthouse? What's the bond?" She barked the questions, but she couldn't mask the hoarse sleepiness of her voice.

"It's me, Mags." Maggie loved to sleep as late as possible, but was constantly awakened by her drug clients who landed in the clink.

"Iz?"

"Yeah."

"Are you in jail?"

"No."

"So why are you calling me right now?"

"It's Sam." I knew that would wake her up.

"What happened?" I could almost see her in her contemporary South Loop apartment. The drapes would be drawn across the floor-to-ceiling windows, and she would be only a mere bump in her big, sleek bed, but now her head would be popping out of the covers; now she would be sitting upright, springing out of bed.

"No news," I said quickly.

A pause. "Then why are you calling me?"

Now it was my turn to pause. How to do this without telling her that I was working with Mayburn, that in order for

Mayburn to look into Sam's case and Forester's death, he
wanted me to borrow a kid and hang around some woman
named Lucy DeSanto? Apparently, every Sunday afternoon
Lucy and her daughter met a friend and her kid at a Lincoln
Park playground. While he could technically hire a female operative to get close to them, to listen to them, it was hard for
such an operative to fake certain things, like the neighborhood
where you lived.

"Like I told you at lunch," Mayburn said, "you have a
Northside feel to you."

"I'm still not sure exactly what that means."

He shrugged. "It's intangible, but you know how it is—if you
meet someone you can tell immediately if they're South Side."

"Sure."

"Or you can tell if they're from the burbs."

"Right."

"So these women live on the North Side, and if you start
talking to them and don't seem like you're from their world,
you won't be able to get within ten feet of them. And most of
the women investigators I know definitely don't have that feel."

I was dying to tell Maggie all this—*I'm going undercover!*
But Mayburn's rule was I couldn't tell anyone. And truthfully, I didn't even know why he wanted me to loiter around
Lucy DeSanto. He was going to bring me up to date if I could
find a child.

"I wanted to see if anyone in your family needed babysitting," I said to Maggie.

"Huh?"

Charlie had left behind a pile of dishes. I tucked the phone
under my chin and started cleaning up. "Like your sisters. Do
they need someone to watch one of their kids this weekend?"

"What in the hell are you talking about?"

"I want to babysit. You know, as practice for having kids.
Maybe Sunday?"

"For starters, the Bears are playing on Sunday. And more

importantly, I'm just going to say it again—what in the hell are you talking about?"

This was going to be harder than I'd thought. Maggie knew me well. And she knew I didn't envision myself having kids anytime soon or possibly ever. Maybe something in my past gave me the instinct to delay the child-rearing process; like maybe it was some response to the fact that I'd helped raise my brother, and I'd felt rather grown-up when I was young. Sam, on the other hand, definitely wanted kids. He wanted to try in the next few years, he'd said. My response to that was always, "Okay, we'll *talk* about it in the next few years." Then Sam would ask, "Where do you see us in five years? What about in ten years?" Those kinds of questions confounded me. I simply didn't look that far ahead.

"Look, honey," Maggie said in a serious tone. "I know you miss Sam, and I know you're freaking out. But practicing taking care of kids, or even pretending you want to have them, won't bring him back."

"I know." I started loading the dishwasher. It felt like a relief to do something normal.

"It seems like you're reaching for something to hold on to. Something that Sam wanted."

How to convince her? "Here's the deal," I said. "I'm lonely without Sam."

It was the truth. I glanced to the right of the sink, where I kept a tiny framed photo of Sam and me at a boat party a few years ago. Just looking at our happy faces gave me an ache in my stomach. I lifted the photo and placed it facedown.

"And normally, Sam and I would watch the Bears game together," I continued, "but with him gone, I…I'm just lost. I think being with children would ground me. Remind me what's important." Now, I had no idea what I was saying, but it sounded good.

"Oh, honey," Maggie said. "All right, well, I'll get my

niece Kaitlyn tomorrow—she's four but she's cool—and we'll come visit you."

"I'd like to take her by myself. It'll be nice to spend time with her. And my inner child."

Silence. Had I pushed too far with the "inner child" bit?

"I miss Sam," I said again with a sigh.

And that seemed to do it. "Okay, I'll give Mary a call," she said. "She'll be excited to have Kaitlyn out of her hair for a few hours." She gave me her sister's phone number and told me to work out the details with her later.

"What are you doing today?" she asked.

"I guess I'm going to work. Then I have to go to Forester's funeral." Another kick to my gut. This one so swift and intense I had to go into my bedroom and sit down on the bed. "I can't believe he's gone. I can't believe they're both gone."

At the office, with the door closed, I managed to get through two hours of work on the final details of Jane Augustine's contract before my mind wavered. The loneliness I'd been telling Maggie about was slowly edged out and then finally given a sharp elbow by another feeling—anger. *What in the hell had Sam done?* I got out a legal pad and decided to take on an entirely different task.

A few minutes later, Q opened the door and stepped inside. "What are you doing?"

I held up the yellow pad. "Making a list."

"Of what?"

"This is a list of red flags. Things that, in retrospect, could have tipped me off that Sam was a schmuck."

"Sam wasn't a schmuck."

"Don't refer to him in the past tense."

"You're the one calling him names."

"He's a *potential* schmuck. That's what the list is for."

Q crossed his arms. "All right. What do you have so far?"

"Number one—he gets moody when his rugby team loses. Even when he's not playing."

"He's competitive, so what?"

"Number two—when we watch dumb movies, he always laughs, and I mean really hard, at the poop jokes."

Q rolled his eyes. "All men, gay or straight, think those are funny."

I tapped my pen on my notepad. "Three—he gets those hairs that grow out of his nose."

Q pointed at his nostrils. "Same answer. All men."

"Next—he makes this loud smacking sound when he eats something that he thinks is delicious."

"Okay, that's enough. These are all just things that bug you about Sam. And it's normal for things to bug you when you're in a relationship." He exhaled. "God knows, I could make a list two pages long about Max."

"Is that true?"

"It grows longer every day."

"Then why—"

Q held up a hand. "We're talking about you, not me. And none of those things on your list mean Sam is a schmuck. Or a criminal."

I pushed the notepad away. "I know."

"So what are you doing?"

"I guess I'm trying to remind myself of the things I don't like about him."

"In case you have to let him go."

"Yeah."

"Oh, Iz." Q took a step and perched on the edge of a visitor's chair. "How are you holding up?"

I was about to tell him about the break-in, when Tanner stuck his head in my office. "Do you need a ride to the funeral?" Tanner said without pleasantries, without addressing Q.

"I brought my car," Q said.

"Izzy?" Tanner said, still looking at me.

"I'll ride with Q. But thanks for thinking of me, Tan."

Tanner disappeared without another word.

"Will wonders never cease?" Q said.

"He's never been so nice to me," I whispered.

Q shrugged and looked at his watch. "We should get going."

In the hallway, we could see the office beginning to empty out as many left for the funeral. Q and I got his car from the garage and headed north.

When we got off Highway 41 and began to drive through Lake Forest, I noticed for the first time that it was a beautiful day—not as cold as the day before, many of the trees still vibrant, the color of marigold. Yet I kept turning around, trying to determine if any of the cars that had been near us on the highway were still there.

"Was that blue SUV behind us a mile ago?" I asked Q.

He glanced in the rearview mirror. "I don't know. Why?"

I wondered if I should tell him I was probably being followed. On one hand, I usually told Q everything. On the other hand, there was something off about him lately, and I had the strange feeling he was holding back from me. Plus, the truth was, I was still craving normality. I wanted it to be like it always was with Q and me.

"No reason," I said. I tried to enjoy the falling leaves. "Nice day for this, I guess."

"I guess." He was quiet, his eyebrows hanging low over his eyes, the way he got when something was weighing heavy on him.

"You okay?" I asked.

"Yeah, of course. It's just…you know, it's hard. Forester meant a lot to so many people. I guess I'm nervous for everyone. For how this is going to go."

"It's going to be tough."

"Yeah."

I kept swiveling around and memorizing license-plate numbers while we drove through the hills and woods of Lake

Forest. It was one of those towns where people moved when they made a lot of money and wanted out of the city.

The funeral was at Saint Mary's, a grand old church near the downtown area, and the front lawn was blanketed with media. News trucks topped with satellite dishes lined the streets. Reporters broadcasted from every corner. A few chased after funeral attendees, hoping for a sound bite to put them ahead of the rest.

"What will you miss about Forester Pickett?" a reporter shouted at everyone who passed.

"Care to comment on Mr. Pickett's death?" yelled another.

"What will happen to Pickett Enterprises now?" from another.

It was a bizarre thing to watch. It seemed so disrespectful of Forester, intruding on everyone's grief. Yet, Forester would have understood implicitly. I could hear him say, "Let them get their story."

Inside the church, it was quiet, hushed. Massive wooden beams curved skyward and impressive, stained-glass windows scattered ethereal shards of light. We spotted Max, who rushed forward when he saw us. Max was of Chilean descent, a small man, and he had a sad face matching the rest of the congregation's. He'd met Forester at his summer barbecues and he, like so many of us, had adored the man.

Max hugged me tight, and I thought of how lucky Q was to have someone wonderful like Max in his life, someone who wouldn't steal thirty million of your boss's money and hit the road.

Grady came in and patted me on the back.

"*Please* step into the church," we heard a voice say behind us.

I turned and saw it was Annette, Forester's housekeeper who'd been with him for nearly as long as I'd been alive. She was one of those women who appeared bland at first glance—she wore her silver hair in a plain bob; her ears adorned with small pearls; she was always in a simple dress—wool in the winter, linen in the summer. If you looked closer, though, you saw that her eyes were clear and shrewd and missed nothing. You noticed that beneath the unpretentious dresses, she had a thin, womanly body that must have taken time to care for.

"Oh, hello, Izzy," she said when I turned.

"Annette, how are you?"

I made the bold gesture of squeezing her wrist. I'd never touched the woman before, and she always gave the impression that personal contact was not encouraged. But I knew she adored Forester and it must have been awful for her to have found him dead.

"Things are moving well," she said in a brisk tone. "It seems we'll start on time."

"Great."

I wasn't surprised that she was brusque. It was her usual MO, and I wondered if she'd heard about Sam and the bearer shares. I knew she and Forester were close, but I had no idea whether that meant close in a housekeeper sort of way, or close in a more personal way.

"The Baltimore & Brown section seems to be forming." Annette gently pulled her wrist from my hand and gestured toward a few pews filled with our law-firm personnel. Tanner sat on the aisle next to his secretary.

Annette led us to a pew a few rows behind Tanner, then she quickly made her way back down the aisle toward other guests.

I watched her back for a moment, wondering what she would do now that Forester was gone. This was the last big hurrah she would handle for him.

As Grady, Max, Q and I moved into the pew, organ music boomed from the back of the church, and grief flooded in.

But then a familiar feeling—I was being watched. I turned and scanned the congregants. There were lots of people I didn't recognize. Forester's friends, family and business associates were a vast group.

I felt a poke on my side, and I jumped.

"Oh, hi, Erin," I said to the woman sliding into the pew next to me. Erin Mayer was an associate in B & B's estate-planning section.

"Did you hear how much she got?" Erin whispered as she sat.

"Who?"

"Annette. She got a *big* chunk of change in his will." Erin's brown eyes flashed.

I debated whether to continue the conversation. In theory, attorneys in the same firm shouldn't talk to each other about a client when one attorney wasn't working on the file or being consulted about it. But theory doesn't always worm its way into practice, and some lawyers were pretty loose-lipped. They not only talked to everyone at their firm about what their clients did and said, they talked to other attorneys at court about it, and when the five o'clock bell rang and the beer started flowing at Petterino's (the bar next to the courthouse) they talked to just about anybody about it.

When some piece of information, like the one Erin was about to impart, came my way, I usually tried to divert the conversation, even if I was interested in the topic. But now I found it impossible to take the higher ground. "How much is she getting?"

"Two mil." Erin smoothed down her short black hair and angled herself closer to me so she could talk low in my ear. "That's a nice take-home for someone who used to make fifty grand a year, huh?"

I glanced over my shoulder and saw Annette greeting Walt Tenning, the CFO of Pickett Enterprises. "Does she know?"

"Oh, she knows. Everyone in Forester's life knew what they were going to get, roughly at least. We told him not to say a word, but you know how Forester was. He spelled it out for everyone after he had the first heart attack. He didn't want anyone to worry about their future."

I crossed my hands and looked down. Forester was exactly that way—always taking care of everyone, never wanting anyone to worry about a thing. Even in death, he would tend to his loved ones.

Yet it made me wonder about Annette. Had that two million been tantalizing to her? A way to escape being someone's servant? And yet it couldn't have been her who sent Forester the letters about stepping down from the company. What good would that have done her? She would simply have had to deal with Forester being around the house all the time.

But what about the others who had benefited from Forester's death?

My curiosity grabbed me. "What about Shane?" I asked Erin.

"Well, he's supposed to get a large portion of the estate and control of Pickett Enterprises."

Forester told me that he intended for Shane to take over the company, but he'd envisioned that there would be years and years to teach him the business. And now Shane was on top. Had that been what Shane wanted all along? Had he wanted it enough to threaten his father? But Shane was such a mild-mannered person, such a shadow of his dad, it was hard to imagine.

"I say, 'large portion of the estate,'" Erin said, as if correcting herself. "Except…"

"Except what?"

The salacious tint to her eyes died away, and she looked almost sheepish. "Well, no one is getting that real estate in Panama."

I could feel my insides tightening and a blush creeping over me.

"Those shares were supposed to be an easily liquidated portion of the estate," she continued. "Until they're recovered, and especially if they're liquidated by someone else, the rest of the estate can't be administered, which means we can't disperse *anything* from the estate or make any official moves until those shares are accounted for. There are some very unhappy people, I guess."

"Like who?"

"I don't know for sure. That's just what Joel said." Joel Hersh was Erin's boss and the head of B & B's estate-planning section.

Erin watched me with interest. Sometimes I hated that about lawyers—how we were trained to study people like specimens under glass.

Meanwhile, I needed to come up with a party line about Sam and the bearer shares. Word was spreading like a virulent virus.

"I don't know anything about the shares," I said, because a good party line was not yet forming itself.

One side of Erin's mouth lifted in a smirk. "C'mon."

"I'm serious." Why did no one believe me? I had a feeling that Jane and her producer, C.J., hadn't bought it either, which was unbelievably frustrating.

The organ player finished, sending the church into momentary silence. I watched as Annette walked Walt Tenning toward the front of the church.

Walt was a tall, reed-thin man, probably fifty-six years old, with a high forehead and a monk's cap of gray hair. He was very patrician, both in his impeccable appearance and also in his reserved demeanor, yet I knew he and Forester had butted heads along the way, as any CEO and CFO might. Walt, along with Chaz Graydon, the chief operating officer, had thought Forester too kind when it came to bonuses, medical leave and things like that. They thought Forester was bleeding money away from the company. But Forester cared more about the contentedness of his employees, asserting that their happiness would make them more money in the long run. It was a debate they'd never finish.

But now with Shane at the helm of Pickett Enterprises, Walt and Chaz could probably twist him any which way they wanted. Shane was not known for his confidence or resolve.

And yet, fifteen minutes later, Shane was at the lectern of the church, looking emotional but confident.

He was wearing a dark charcoal suit and a navy blue tie. His normally pale skin looked even more so today, almost bordering on translucent, which only made his blue eyes sharper and brighter under his glasses.

"My father loved all of you," he said. He gripped the side of the lectern momentarily, as if holding himself up, then he took a breath and looked up, meeting the collective gaze of the congregation. "I know that sounds cliché. How could one person love hundreds of people?" He shook his head. "Not many can. But as you know, my father was not average. He *loved* all of you. He truly did. He saw you for who you were, not who he expected you to be. He didn't always understand everyone. He was old-fashioned in many ways. Yet he loved everyone with an open heart, sometimes to his detriment."

Shane's eyes had been roaming the mourners, but right then they stopped on my face. He paused. A long pause.

I felt Grady and Erin shift uncomfortably on either side of me. The pause went on. I tried to look down, but Shane still wasn't talking. When I looked up, his eyes were still on me. A few people started to glance between Shane and myself. I felt a blush creeping from my toes up to my face. I wanted to shout, *What? Are you talking about Sam? Are you implying that Forester's love for Sam was to his detriment? I don't know! I don't know anything!*

I almost let my mouth fall open to shout.

And then, as if giving me a reprieve, Shane moved on. He talked about his dad's upbringing in a town outside New Orleans. He pointed out some of his relatives present in the church, and he talked about Forester's charity work. He talked about how Forester had started Pickett Enterprises and thanked people—including Walt Tenning and Chaz Graydon—who had helped make the company a success.

I had been keeping my gaze squarely in my lap, not wanting to draw Shane's gaze again, but I glanced up when he mentioned Walt and Chaz. Walt acknowledged Shane's words with a barely perceptible bow of his domed head. Chaz, a flashy guy in his late forties, who wore cuff links the size of quarters and a huge silver watch, nodded appreciatively and glanced around the church as if accepting applause.

Shane thanked Annette for years of service to his father. He thanked his dad's close friends whom he'd known since his early days in Chicago.

Then Shane took a deep breath and stared upward toward the yellow bands of light streaming through the high, stained-glass windows. "My father lived his life in a grand way. He squeezed every bit of joy out of it. And he didn't shy away from pain because he knew that pain was only a path to more joy. I hope we can learn from him. I hope…"

Shane's words died away here, and he began to cry. Softly at first, almost soundlessly, but then a hand covered his eyes, his shoulders hunched and Shane Pickett began to sob like a lost little boy.

The sniffles began to pick up throughout the church. The sounds of soft weeping joined that of Shane's.

"Thank you," he said, finally getting himself together. "Thank you so very much."

He raised his head, and just then the sound of a lone bagpiper crept into the church, its soulful tone curling through the congregation. Everyone turned. At the back of the church, on the second landing, stood the bagpiper, his instrument gaining volume, gaining strength.

Another bagpiper stepped from the shadows and joined him. Then another…and another…and another…until twelve bagpipers stood, their instruments joining one somber note that twisted into a single song—"Amazing Grace." Forester's favorite.

It seemed everyone in the church began to cry then. I watched in awe as Grady wiped a tear from his eye, and Q cried openly without bothering to cover his face. I let myself cry too, feeling the sensation of finality settling into my bones. *Goodbye, Forester.*

We walked from the church into a gorgeously sunny fall afternoon, a steep contrast to the bleakness everyone felt. The reporters still reported and the cameras still rolled, but they weren't hounding people now. Mourners stood in groups on the church steps, unable to let go of the last traces of Forester.

I felt a tap on my shoulder and turned. "Mom!"

"Hi, Boo." She and her husband, Spence, both hugged me.

"I didn't realize you were coming," I said.

I had introduced Forester to my mom and Spence, and she'd gotten him to donate to a charity she'd started called the Victoria Project, an organization that helped widowed women with children.

"We wouldn't have missed it," Spence said. He was a pleasant-looking man with brown hair streaked with white. It fell longer on the sides to compensate for the slight balding up top. He wore a blue jacket and tie over slacks. He rarely wore a suit. His light-blue eyes, his most striking feature, looked into mine. "How are you holding up?"

"Hanging in there," I said.

Annette came up to us. "We're having a reception at the Deer Path Inn."

"Thank you," I said, but I wondered at her use of the word *we.* I'd never heard her use that word when referring to Forester or his family. She'd always said things like, *Mr. Pickett would like you to join him at his home.* But then, the only Mr. Pickett around now was Shane.

As if he'd heard my thoughts, Shane appeared, his lips pursed. Behind him were Walt Tenning, who looked typically unflappable, and Chaz Graydon, who stood with his meaty arms crossed over his chest, the sun glinting off his watch face.

"Izzy," Shane said. "We need to talk to you."

32

I followed Forester's son and his two closest advisers to the lawn at the side of the church, away from the media. My high heels sank into the grass, forcing me to walk unsteadily on tiptoe. I saw Tanner on the steps of the church. He was surrounded by Baltimore & Brown people, but his eyes were on me. Finally, when it seemed as if we were clear of the reporters, Shane and the others stopped. They turned to face me.

"You did a very nice job in there," I said to Shane.

He seemed to have lost the hostile attitude. Instead of staring me down, his eyes glistened with tears now. "Thanks. Thanks a lot. It was tough." He shook his head. "It's just hard to believe."

"I know. My father died when I was young, and sometimes I still can't believe it."

Chaz cleared his throat, as if he'd had enough of all this talk about dead fathers.

"Izzy, we need to talk to you about Sam," Walt said. "What he's done is an egregious act."

"We need to know what you know," Chaz said in his deep, gruff voice.

"*Everyone* needs to know what I know. And I know precisely nothing. I've discussed this with the Chicago PD. I've discussed this with the FBI, and I've told them all the truth—I have no idea where Sam is or why those shares are missing."

"We've talked to the authorities, as well," Walt said, "and we're not convinced they're efficient enough. This matter needs to be concluded quickly. Forester's estate can't be administered until all the property is accounted for and, ultimately, that could affect the running of Pickett Enterprises and, of course, Shane's inheritance."

Yeah, I thought. *And now Shane is your puppet with Forester gone. Is that what you wanted all along?* I studied the men. Shane looked to be in pain. Chaz looked like a pissed-off bulldog ready to snarl and bite. Walt bore his usual concerned look.

"I'll do whatever I can to help the investigation along," I said. "I want to get Forester's estate in order, too. I still consider him my main client, and as such I'll do everything I can to serve him well."

"Don't be so sure about that client thing," Chaz said.

"Excuse me?"

Walt threw Chaz a glance, and he went quiet.

"Keep us apprised if you learn anything," Walt said. "Anything at all."

"Of course. I have to tell you that, although it looks bad, I just keep returning to the thought that Sam wouldn't do anything that would have harmed Forester or his estate."

Chaz scoffed. "For all we know, sweetheart, he killed him."

We all froze at the word *killed.* My gut intuition screamed, *Wrong. Sam didn't kill him.* Yet what did I know anymore? Was my intuition something to be believed, or had Sam duped me and everyone else? Meanwhile, another internal voice insisted, *Sam didn't kill him, but someone else did.* It seems too coincidental that Forester got those threats and two weeks later dropped dead.

I threw Chaz a withering look.

The silence between us crackled. I looked at them, wondering if it was Walt and Chaz who had killed Forester. Was it them, in additon to the feds, who were having me followed?

They might have hired their own investigator to track down Sam and those bearer shares so that the estate could be administered, so Shane could step in closely behind him and run everything the way they wanted. Or was it someone else— Shane maybe? Should I tell one of them about the letters, in case they didn't know? Their positions inside the company could help determine who had sent the threats and maybe who had paid the homeless guy to say something to Forester. But then I was back to the possibility that the threats had been made by one of the men I was standing in front of.

"I'll let you know if I learn anything." I faced Shane and put my hand on his arm. "I'm so sorry for your loss."

I walked across the front of the church, picking my way past the reporters and cameramen who were packing up, until I found Q, Max and Grady.

"Your mom said she'd meet you at the reception," Q said.

"I'm not going. I remind everyone of Sam, and that will cause more stress for everyone."

"I'll drive you home," Grady said.

The two of us walked away from the church. A block away, Forester's hearse crossed in front of us, followed by a long string of cars. I watched the hearse, with its yellow flag that spelled *Funeral,* as it disappeared down the street.

33

Grady and I drove toward the city. The first fifteen minutes were spent in silence. I watched out the window as the large, tree-filled lawns of Lake Forest gave way to local Highway 41, crowded with strip malls, and then eventually to the Edens Expressway. Every so often, I twisted around, studying the road, and I swore I saw the same blue SUV. I squinted to get the license plate, but could only make out that it was from Illinois.

"What are you doing, Iz?" Grady asked when I had turned around for the fifth time.

I looked at him. His eyes were still on the road, one arm draped casually at the top of the steering wheel.

"It's starting to get to me," I said.

He glanced at me, then returned his eyes to the road. "Well, of course it is. Sam's gone. Forester's dead."

"And people are wondering whether Sam might have had something to do with Forester's death." In my mind, I saw Shane's eyes boring into me from the pulpit.

Grady's mouth pursed for a second. "I'm not going to lie to you, it doesn't look good."

"What are you saying? That *you* think Sam did something to him?"

"I'm just saying he took off with the guy's property."

"Allegedly. *Allegedly* he took off with his property. And even if he did, he didn't need Forester dead to do that."

"That's true."

"I know it's true." I sighed. "I just wish I knew what else was true."

Quiet. Then, "Let me buy you a drink?"

This was the Grady I loved. "Yes, please."

Twenty minutes later, Grady parked in front of a corner pub in Lincoln Park. Inside, the place was typical Chicago—pool table, long wooden bar, state-of-the-art TVs at either end showing college-football highlights on ESPN.

The place was mostly empty. We took a seat at the bar. Grady ordered an Amstel Light. I got a Stoli O and tonic. I drank two gulps. Then a third.

"Whoa, tiger." Grady took the glass and moved it away from me.

"I need it." I pulled the glass back and stared into it. Maybe the events of the week would push me into becoming a raging alcoholic. I'd never thought I had the potential, but anything seemed possible after this week, including the scary, the far-fetched and the wretched. Maybe Sam would never come back. Maybe I'd never get over him. Maybe I'd never have sex again.

The last thought made me start to sweat. I lifted the glass and gulped once more.

"Look at me," Grady said.

I turned on my stool to face him, drink at the ready in one hand.

Grady's brown eyes studied me more intently than usual. "Want to talk about it?"

"No." I took another gulp and gestured at the bartender for another. "Let's talk about something fun."

Grady was silent.

"Seriously, let's talk about what we usually would. Let's talk about football. How about those Bears, huh?"

Grady studied me again.

"What?" I said.

"You underestimate me."

"What are you talking about?" The bartender delivered my drink, and I pulled it toward me.

But Grady put his hand around my wrist. "Stop for a second and look at me."

Reluctantly, I turned away from my drink and swiveled so that my body faced his. "Okay, I'm looking."

"I can handle more than sports talk and law-firm chat."

"I know that."

"No, you don't. We haven't talked about much else in the past, but I'm telling you, I'm here for you, okay?"

Now it was my turn to study him. Had he grown up since I last really took stock of him? Were there little lines by his eyes that weren't there before? Did his jaw have a harder edge? It seemed so. Somewhere along the last few years, Grady had started to look like more of a man, not just a college boy.

"Thanks," I said.

"I'm serious. You don't have to talk about it now. You don't have to ask me for any favors now. But I want you to know that I am always, always here. Got it?"

"Got it." I smiled. "You're a good friend."

He nodded. "I am if you let me be. That's the kind of people you should have in your life right now—good friends. You've got no room for anyone who won't be honest with you and won't help you when you need it."

I nodded along with him. He was right. I needed to keep my good friends close. I mentally made a list of such people—Grady, Q, Maggie, my mom, Spence, my brother. The thought of these people in my life—solid, wonderful people—relaxed me. But with the relaxation, and the drink I'd been chugging, utter exhaustion slipped in. The adrenaline of the break-in last night had carried me through the funeral, and now it was gone.

I stood. "I'm sorry, Grady, but I have to go."

"Where?"

"Home. I didn't sleep much last night."

"Do you need me to drive you?"

I started to say that I'd grab a cab. I wanted desperately to stop talking, to just sleep. But then I remembered that someone could be in my apartment. Again.

"Yeah, that would be great," I said. I'd ask Grady to walk me up to my place, but I didn't want to tell him about the break-in. If I did, he would never leave me alone for the night, and more than anything, I felt I needed to be alone to think.

Grady accompanied me upstairs on the pretense of borrowing a book I wanted him to read. I grabbed the mail, untouched for days, and unlocked the front door. The locks seemed fine. I walked quickly around the apartment, sweeping it with my eyes. I touched the computer to check for warmth. Nothing. Everything appeared as I'd left it that morning.

I gave Grady a book my brother had recommended, something about a guy who falls into a ravine coming down a mountain and somehow claws his way out, alive. Guys always love those tragedy-on-a-mountain stories. I hugged him at the door. "You're the best. Thank you."

"Anytime. Hey, you going to Q's Halloween party tomorrow?"

"No. I can't go to a party with everything that's happened."

"What else are you going to do?"

Helplessness surged through me. "I don't know."

"Might be good for you."

"You're not going, are you? It'll be all gay guys."

He shrugged. "You told me last week I had to go."

"I was trying to guilt you into it. You never fall for that."

"We'll go together. I'll pick you up."

"You must be worried about me."

"Nah, I'm just being a good sport."

"Really, I don't think I'm up for a party."

"Too bad, I'm picking you up at eight."

"I—"

He held up his hand in protest, then turned his back on me. "See ya at eight," he called over his shoulder.

I went into the kitchen and began to sort through the mail— a tax bill from the city, an invite to a charity event, a thank-you note from my mom, a flyer from a clothing store I loved.

And then I got to a postcard. From Indianapolis of all places. On the front was a photo of a white capitol building with Corinthian columns and a green dome.

And on the back was Sam's handwriting.

34

The postcard wasn't signed, but there was no mistaking Sam's printing—short and square, all in caps. I'd been reading his handwriting for years on notes he left in my pockets—*Good luck today on your deposition. Kick some ass like you always do*—or those propped against my teapot when he left early for rugby pitches on Sunday mornings—*You're beautiful when you sleep. I wanted so badly to wake you up. If we lose, I won't be as patient when I get home.*

But now. Now, that printing on the postcard. His handwriting twinged something deep in my gut. Why in the hell would Sam be sending me a postcard from Indianapolis?

Red Hot, the postcard said. *Remember when we came here a few years ago? The hellish weekend that turned out to be heaven?*

I remembered. It had been only a few months after we'd met, a time during which we were mad for each other. We sent each other sexy text messages all day and rushed to one of our apartments at night, frenzied to get into each other's arms. When Sam remembered he had to spend a weekend at an investment seminar in Indianapolis, we were tortured at the thought of being apart. It was a cold and rainy week and, as Friday approached, Sam kept grumbling, "This is gonna be hell." But then he came up with the idea that I join him. He upgraded to a suite, rented me a stack of DVDs, made sure the minibar was stocked, and I was happy to stay in bed all weekend, watching movies and waiting for him.

What's happening now has nothing to do with us, the post-card continued. *Know that. Trust me. And please don't tell anyone you got this.*

And that was it. No signature, no "I love you." I studied the card, relieved that at the very least he was okay—*he was alive*—but I realized that there wasn't anything in the card, other than his handwriting, to give away the fact that Sam was the author. The words he printed there were vague and gave away nothing. He'd been careful about what he wrote, I could tell. But why?

What have you done, Sam?

I studied the postcard some more. The only real information it revealed was the fact that it came from Indy.

What was he doing in Indy? I struggled to recall whether he'd ever mentioned any investment opportunities there, maybe something he was working on for Forester. Nothing came to me.

I looked at the postmark. It had been sent two days ago on Wednesday, the day after Forester died, the day after Sam failed to show at the Union League Club. He must have driven there that night.

But again—*why?* Did he know anyone in Indianapolis? I searched my mind for any friends, business contacts, anyone he might know there. Something was bothering me, something tickling my brain.

Then it struck me—a recollection of Sam's high-school reunion, a bunch of Sam's friends standing at the bar and talking about the Indy 500.

The next thought struck harder. I remembered *why* they were talking about the Indy 500. Because Alyssa, Sam's ex-girlfriend, had just moved to Indianapolis for a project.

Calm down, I told myself. I reminded myself that Alyssa said she was living there only temporarily while she was conducting research in something called geriatric thermoregulation. I remembered this because I'd Googled her extensively when we returned from the reunion. All I'd really been able to understand was that Alyssa went around the nation conducting research that improved the quality of life for the geriatric population, particularly those who were bedridden. She was an angel of mercy, essentially, which was tough to compete with from a girlfriend perspective.

Was she still in Indianapolis? I thought of Sam's recent e-mail congratulating her on new funding. I raced to the computer and found her e-mail address—*AThornton@ICCR.com*. I searched the Web for "ICCR" and "geriatric research." It took only a second to find what I was looking for. The Indianapolis Center for Clinical Research, also known as the ICCR, was still conducting a trial on geriatric thermoregulation. Which meant, as far as I could tell, Sam might have gone to Indianapolis to see Alyssa.

35

I went on a crazy tear to find her.

First, I e-mailed.

Hi Alyssa, This is Izzy McNeil, Sam's fiancée. I'm wondering if you could call me as soon as you get this. Thanks much, Izzy

I typed in my cell-phone number, my home phone number and my work number and hit Send.

I sat by the computer, watching it, glancing at my cell phone, praying she was still at work, even though it was after five on Friday. I prayed she would call me back. I prayed that she wasn't in bed with Sam and his thirty million dollars' worth of bearer shares.

Nothing.

I tracked down the number for the Indiana Center for Clinical Research and went through an exhaustive round of number-punching to access their directory and get Alyssa's voice mail.

Her voice sounded sweet and smart. I hated her more by the second.

"Hey Alyssa, this is Izzy McNeil," I said. "I wanted to ask you a few questions…"

I paused. How much to say about Sam? About the fact

that he'd disappeared? If he was there in Indianapolis with her, would she be more likely to call me back if I mentioned him?

"It's about Sam," I said finally. "If you could give me a call, I'd really appreciate it." Again, I left my cell, home and work numbers.

I sat at my desk, waiting for the phone to ring or an e-mail to pop up in my in-box. Nothing happened. I called Information and found there was no listing for an Alyssa Thornton in Indy.

Despite the postcard, my exhaustion started choking me. As I stared at my in-box, the images and letters on the screen blurred. But I didn't want to go to bed too early and wake up in the middle of the night, my thoughts racing.

I tried to think of something productive to do. There had to be *something* I could do.

I thought of the first assignment Mayburn gave me. I picked up my cell phone and found Shane's number.

"Shane, it's Izzy."

Silence. "Hi, Izzy," he said finally, with weight in his voice.

"How was the reception?"

"Still going. I'm downstairs, hiding from everyone."

"I meant what I said earlier. You did a great job at the funeral. Your dad would have been proud."

A pause. "That's all I've ever wanted." His voice sounded hollow now, far away, almost as if he was musing to himself.

"Shane, do you think we could meet?"

He was silent.

"I just think we should talk…privately," I said. "I mean, after today."

"I'll be in the office tomorrow morning for a few hours. You could come by there if that works." He named a time.

"See you then."

I got back on the Internet and ran a few more searches, looking for video, images, anything that could get me some information on Alyssa Thornton and where I could find her. Nothing.

My cell phone rang. *C. J. Lyons,* the display said. Jane Augustine's producer at WNDY.

"You asked me to give you a heads-up," she said in typical C.J. form without any pleasantries. "Channel 5 is running something. I just heard. I don't know anything else. Newscast starts in a few minutes."

I jumped up and headed for the living room.

"Now I need a favor from you," C.J. continued. "Tell me straight—is Pickett Enterprises selling WNDY?"

"Not that I know of. Why?"

"Because I heard that the Pickett board approved the sale of ten radio stations and five TV stations. We weren't in that group. For now. But I want to know if we're next."

I was shocked. Forester's business model had been all about building the empire, rather than selling it. But then again, Forester wasn't there anymore. The people who were running the board were Walt and Chaz. And now Shane.

"I haven't heard anything," I said.

"All right. Gotta go."

I grabbed the three remotes, frantically pressing the ten different buttons that were required to turn on the TV ever since Sam, who considered himself an electronics genius, had set up our system.

The soaring sounds of Channel 5's opening music filled the room. The lead story was a news conference held by the mayor to address allegations of a hiring scandal at City Hall.

"C'mon, c'mon," I muttered. The city of Chicago ran so well it was hard to care if some DMV worker got his job because his cousin knew the mayor's dentist's dog walker.

The next story was more familiar.

"Today the city mourned one of its most well-known and respected businessmen," said the male newscaster. "Funeral services were held this afternoon in Lake Forest for Forester

Pickett, founder and CEO of Pickett Enterprises, the largest media conglomerate in the Midwest. Pickett died this week of cardiac arrest."

A smiling photo of Forester filled the screen, then the picture shifted to a shot of his casket being carried down the steps of the church, a stream of mourners trailing behind. I caught a glimpse of Forester's housekeeper and Chaz Graydon.

"Pickett's death has been overshadowed by allegations that one of his financial advisers stole millions of dollars in corporate shares owned by Pickett."

"Oh, no," I said.

"Samuel Hollings, age thirty," the anchor continued, "is an employee of Carrington & Associates."

"No!"

A photo of Sam took over the screen.

I stared at a photo I'd never seen before, but which was now being broadcast to millions of people. Sam was wearing a suit I recognized as one of his old ones. Other people had clearly been cropped out of the picture, because Sam looked disembodied. His arms, which must have been around people on either side, were cut off.

The story kept going—*Panama corporation...real estate... safe...missing.*

When he was finished, they returned to a wide-angle shot of the anchor desk.

"That's a significant amount of money," the anchor said, turning to his coiffed female companion.

"Son of a motherless goat!" I yelled, using one of my replacement curse phrases. It didn't cut it. "Son of a bitch!" I yelled, my voice boomeranging around my condo.

"It certainly is significant, Bill," the other anchor answered somberly. She swung her body to face a different camera and began a new story.

"Son of a bitch!" I yelled again. Now that Forester's missing shares were news, as well as Sam's apparent part in the disappearance, I wouldn't be able to stop the rest of the media from covering the story. Whether he deserved it or not, Sam was about to get crucified.

I hit the Off button. I trembled from the sense that everything was spiraling out of control with every passing moment.

I threw the remote at the TV. I missed and instead the remote hit yet another framed photo of Sam and me at one of his rugby games. The frame teetered, our smiling faces wavering. The frame fell, and the glass shattered.

36

Day Five

Sam Hollings stepped out of the elevators and walked through the lobby of the hotel. He'd gotten in so late last night he hadn't noticed much except that the hotel was a tall, reflective tower, like those in any big city. It was a welcome relief after the kitschy, cottagey place he'd stayed at in Key West, where the air-conditioning never worked and a host of cockroaches set up camp in the tub every night.

Now he took in the polished floors of the lobby and the restaurant at the far end, where low-slung red couches were dotted around sleek ebony tables.

He straightened his tie and made his way toward the front doors. It felt good to be in a suit. It felt good to be working again. But really, it was much more than work, and he knew it.

Outside the hotel, he tipped the bellman, who hailed him a cab. He gave the driver the address. He had memorized it, but just to be certain he pulled a small notebook from his briefcase and double-checked.

The drive was short—maybe fifteen minutes or so—but even a few seconds was enough time to let his mind swirl around what he'd done. What he still had to do.

The problem was, he wasn't the only part of this riddle, and he couldn't be sure how much of the situation had been organized or how much had yet to be initiated. He would have to watch and wait, assessing and adapting to each change. How long that would take, he had no idea.

Just focus on today, on this morning, he told himself. This piecemeal approach—always looking at the smallest goals right in front of him, rather than the big picture—was how he'd gotten through college and B-school and the early years at Carrington when he was learning the business. Focusing only on what was right in front of his face allowed him to believe he could handle such tasks. Accomplishing them one by one got him to the end of the big picture without ever having to contemplate the momentousness of what he was doing. He was grateful that somewhere along the way he had stumbled on this style of tackling his duties. He needed it now. Because the big picture was terrifying.

When he arrived at the address, he studied the nondescript three-story building with its frosted-glass windows.

He went inside and gave his name to a doorman, who gave him a slow but aggressive stare that traveled up and down his body. Finally, the doorman handed him a badge and directed him to an office down the hall.

He walked down a hallway—as nondescript as the building itself—the doors all closed, probably because it was a Saturday. He stopped when he came to the office where he'd been directed.

He knocked.

"One minute," the woman's voice said.

But it was only ten seconds before she let him in.

37

When I think of autumn, I think in reds and oranges. But that year in Chicago, after the hot, long summer we'd had, it was more about yellows and golds. When I stepped outside my condo that Saturday morning, I made myself stop and look around at how the city appeared gold-spun and glowing. It was only sixty degrees, and I was grateful I could ride my Vespa. The El train on a Saturday would take too long and after twelve hours of sleep the night before, I was raring to go. I would work for Mayburn, I would figure out if someone had harmed Forester and I would find Sam, for better or for goddamned worse. First stop—my meeting with Shane.

I opened the garage door and started the scooter. As I let it warm up, I looked at the blinds. All down the way they were supposed to be. I looked around some more, and I noticed something on top of the storage shelves—my silver helmet. I rarely wore the thing. Illinois was one of the few helmet-free states, and the helmet tended to flatten my hair. I'd rather have windblown curls than matted fuzz. And there was always the problem of where to put the thing, especially at a restaurant or bar. It was unwieldy to walk around with; it wouldn't fit in a handbag.

But now, those reasons seemed silly, especially when lined up with the reality that if I had an accident, I could be seriously injured. Or worse. How had I taken life so lightly before? With Forester dead and Sam gone, the fragility of the world as I knew it was readily apparent. Leaving the scooter running, I put the kickstand down and crossed the garage to the shelves. Standing on my tiptoes, I took down my helmet.

With a rag from one of the shelves, I wiped off the dust that had accumulated. The helmet fit snugly over my ears, the way it was supposed to. I fastened the strap under my chin, not caring that it made me look like a Teletubby or that my hair would be ruined for the day.

I got back on the Vespa and headed for the offices of Pickett Enterprises.

"Did you see the Channel 5 news last night?" Shane said, opening the frosted front doors of the office, which was in a building on Michigan Avenue that bordered the river. Forester hadn't tried to save money when he decorated the place and, as a result, the hardwood floors gleamed, the expensive artwork was well lit and the eclectic furnishings, collected from around the world, were top of the line.

"I saw the segment," I said. "C.J. called to give me the heads-up."

"The press has been outside the offices every day. I thought they'd be worse today after the news about Sam, but I guess because it's a Saturday they didn't expect anyone to come in."

Shane turned his back, while I trailed behind him. Even on a weekend, he was dressed impeccably in a houndstooth jacket and perfectly pressed pants. "Who's C.J., by the way?" he asked.

"The producer at WNDY. She works mostly with Jane Augustine."

He said nothing and I was reminded how little Shane knew about the details, the people that made up his father's company.

"I heard Pickett is selling a bunch of its radio and TV stations," I said. "Is that true?"

He stopped, turned sideways. "Who told you that?"

"C.J. She's scared you're going to sell WNDY."

He looked at a loss. "Actually, they're thinking about it. Chaz and Walt. They think the company needs more cash to operate, and selling off some stations is the easiest way to get it."

"It's not what your dad would have wanted."

He gave me an agonized expression then shook his head. He turned and began walking down the hallway again.

After a few feet Shane stopped, and I almost crashed into him. His office, the place I'd thought was our destination, was much farther down the hallway.

"C'mon in," he said.

That's when I realized it—Shane had moved into his father's office.

The lights were on, and a mess of paperwork was spread over the desk. Forester would never have been able to work with his desk like that.

I went to the window and looked down at the sidewalk bordering the river. I wasn't sure what I was searching for—the guy with the tan jacket I'd seen in Old Town? Maybe someone with a sandwich board reading, *I'm Following Izzy McNeil?* I hadn't noticed anyone following me on my scooter ride from my apartment.

I moved away from the window.

"Let's sit here." Shane pointed to a sitting area at the right of the room. Four bucket chairs in rich, brown leather were grouped around a glass coffee table. Three televisions were placed between books on every topic imaginable on the shelves.

When I hesitated, Shane looked at me, then his eyes swung around the room. "Sorry. I guess I should have told you I moved into my dad's office."

"When?" I took a seat.

"Last night. After the funeral."

Cold, I thought.

He sat in a chair opposite me and seemed to be looking at me for approval. I said nothing.

"I just want to do what he would want me to do," he continued. "That's *all* I've ever wanted. And he always told me he wanted me to take over the company. I'm not ready, but I want to carry out his wishes."

I nodded in a noncommittal way. Behind his head, the sun glinted off the river and the majestic *Tribune* tower.

"So I'm glad you called me," Shane said. "I wanted to talk to you because, as Walt said, the estate is tied up because of the problems with Sam."

I gave another slight nod. I heard Mayburn in my head telling me, *When you're interrogating someone, never let them know it. Stay on your schedule, not theirs.* "Why did you ask for the autopsy to be rushed?" I asked.

"Walt and Chaz wanted me to. They were afraid that if something was wrong with my dad's death it could tie up the estate even more, and I wouldn't be able to move into the position of CEO. There was concern that everything at Pickett would grind to a halt and the company could go downhill."

"You're CEO already?"

We both looked around the office, Forester's office.

"The bylaws of the company put me in this position," he continued. "Yes, I'm the CEO now." He said this simply, with no triumph or embarrassment, but I got the sense that saying it out loud was helping him believe it.

"Wow. Well, congratulations."

I settled back in my chair and remembered all the times I'd been in exactly the same seat, talking with Forester about a contract negotiation or a new deal. That would never happen again, I realized. Forester had been replaced already.

"The story about Sam is going to be on the other stations tonight." Shane's mouth turned down at the edges. His pale skin had a bit of a flushed look today, as if he'd been running around all morning. He swiveled back and forth in his chair like a kid.

"Probably," I said.

"You know how my dad hated publicity."

"I know. He thought a company's good reputation should be publicity enough."

"How did Channel 5 get the story?"

"I have no idea," I answered.

Shane gave me a strange look.

"What?"

"Did you leak it?"

"Are you crazy? Why in the hell would I want to leak a story about my fiancé disappearing with Forester's property?"

Shane's face softened. "I don't know. I don't know what to think anymore. This whole thing is so surreal."

We both looked around the office. *Is it surreal, Shane, because you've wanted this all along? Is it surreal because you threatened your own father and somehow caused his death?*

But then I reminded myself that the only indication I had that Forester's death wasn't natural, aside from my intuition, were those threatening letters, along with the information he'd given me that his cardiologist had given him a clean bill of health.

"Shane," I said, "who was your dad's cardiologist?"

"Dr. Donald Loman. Why do you ask?"

"Your dad told me that he'd recently had a stress test and EKG. He said he passed with flying colors."

"Yeah. He seemed so healthy."

"He did. Have you talked to Dr. Loman?"

"He came to the emergency room after my dad was brought there. He said it was a classic presentation of a heart attack."

"And what about that Chinese doctor Forester saw?"

Shane scoffed. "If you can call her a doctor. Her name is Song Li, I think."

"Have you had any discussions with her?"

"No. What's with all the questions?"

I gave a nonchalant shrug. *The investigator I'm working with wanted me to ask you.*

I thought of the other things Mayburn told me to learn from Shane. "So," I said, trying to make my voice pleasant, "I do have another question. When was the last time you saw your dad before he passed away?"

"That afternoon. He had meetings all over the city, but he came into my office to check in." Shane blinked and looked down. It seemed he might be on the verge of tears. Guilty ones, I wondered, or just grief?

"Did he say anything about what he was going to do that night?"

"Yeah, he said he didn't have anything going on. He was happy about that. Annette was going to leave him dinner, and he was going to go to bed early. He asked me a question about a project I was working on and told me I was doing a good job." Shane gave a mirthless laugh. "That's the last thing he said to me—that I was doing a good job."

I had no idea how to read Shane's laugh or the despondent look on his face, but I recorded it in my head, the way Mayburn had taught me. "What did you do that night?"

A pause. "Nothing."

"You just stayed home?"

"Actually, yes," Shane said, his voice almost clipped. "Yes, I did stay home."

"Were you with anyone?"

"What are you, a cop?" he said with an edge to his voice.

"Did the cops question you?"

"Of course. Didn't they talk to you, too?"

"Sure. Were you alone that night?"

"Yes."

I didn't believe him. There was no pause this time. Now he'd answered quickly, and his eyes had flicked to the bookshelf and back. So maybe he wasn't alone that night. But then again, why did that matter? It wasn't as if Forester had been tied up and physically injured, something that would have required a few people to achieve. I'd asked Mayburn why we needed to know where Shane was that night and with whom.

Mayburn had explained, once again, that it was just one piece of a big puzzle.

Shane crossed his arms. "Now why don't you tell me why you're asking these questions? The truth is, I should be asking *you*. Like where were *you* that night before the hospital, and where was Sam, and where the hell is he, and why did he take those bearer shares?"

Shane's voice had risen with each of his words, and when he stopped, the silence rang like a bell in the room. His eyes glittered underneath his glasses. It was the most emotion I'd ever seen from him.

"Sorry," he said, quieter now.

"For the record, that night I was at the office of my wedding coordinator and then a dinner at the Union League Club." I thought of Sam's empty seat next to mine. "Sam was supposed to be there, but he never showed."

"You know, Forester and Sam were getting really...I don't know...chummy before he died."

"Chummy? What do you mean? Sam worked for him. He looked up to Forester a great deal, but it wasn't like they hung out on weekends."

Shane dipped his head forward, as if agreeing. "But Sam knew everything about my dad's money."

"Sure, Sam was one of his financial advisers."

"I don't understand why my dad didn't trust me with that kind of information."

"What makes you think he didn't?"

Shane shook his head. "He didn't talk to me about that stuff." He stopped. He looked as if he was considering his words. "You know my dad was always generous with me."

I nodded.

"I've worked for Pickett since I got out of college," he continued, "and I've always drawn a good salary, but my father also gave me access to pretty big sums of cash whenever I needed them.

"The thing is," Shane continued, glancing down now, as if embarrassed, "my dad became a little less… How should I put this? Well, he became a little less liquid with the funds over the last few months. At least with me." A small shrug of one shoulder. "It was like my father didn't trust me."

"He trusted you enough to leave you his company."

"Yes. My taking over Pickett Enterprises has been part of the plan for a while. It's just that no one thought we'd need to execute that plan anytime soon…" Shane's voice trailed off and, as he had at the funeral, he looked like a lost little boy. "I'd just hate to think that my dad died not believing the best about me. He was old-fashioned, you know?"

"I guess." Shane had said something similar at the funeral about Forester being old-fashioned. I wondered what he was getting at.

There was a silence in the office. Down the hall, a lonely phone rang and rang.

Shane cleared his throat. "I wanted to talk to you about the future of Pickett Enterprises."

"Okay."

"As CEO, I'm going to be making some changes."

My breath involuntarily froze in my lungs.

"And one of those changes," Shane said, "is that you…" He closed his eyes briefly as if in pain. "You…" He met my eyes, then his glance dodged to the floor. "You will no longer be handling Pickett's legal work."

My breath completely left me then, as if someone had stomped on my chest.

I stared at Shane, my mouth open. I thought of Q telling me how Elliot Nuster, the associate who worked mostly for Tanner, had picked up the Shepard file. I suppose I could have seen this coming, but once again, everything was happening way, way too fast.

"You know, Izzy," Shane said, "I never really understood why my father gave you all that work."

I hadn't either, but I wasn't about to admit it. "You *know* I've done a good job for this company."

"Yeah. From what I could tell, it took you a while to get up and running, but now I think you're representing Pickett Enterprises very effectively."

"And I'll continue to do that. The last thing the company needs is more change."

Shane shook his head. "If I'm going to take over this company, I need to have experienced representation. I don't know as much about the company as my father did."

I nodded, barely. The truth was, I understood what Shane was saying. He was probably unqualified to run the company, so he wanted staff and advisers who were eminently qualified. I managed a short exhale. "You're giving the work back to Tanner."

Shane stared down at his lap. "I'm sorry, Izzy. I really am. But Tanner is my best friend from way back, and he's much more experienced than you."

I had no response to that. There was no doubt that Tanner was a great attorney. A horse's ass, sure, but an excellent lawyer nonetheless.

"I've made up my mind," Shane said.

I opened and closed my mouth, no words forming.

If the Pickett cases were taken away from me, if I wasn't getting any new files, my career, as I knew it, was over. In the past, every time I brought a new case in from Pickett, I got a percentage of whatever money we made on that case. This made me the highest-paid associate at the firm. Plus, I was on track to be the youngest partner ever. I could say goodbye to all that if I lost the Pickett work. Worse, I would no longer be my own ship amid the choppy waters of Baltimore & Brown. I'd have to go back to being an associate slave and work for one of the partners, many of whom already resented me.

I tried again, but found myself completely unable to speak. I felt a suction motion, a loosening and a pulling away of all things important—Sam, Forester, my work. Those things represented the biggest parts of my life, the best. And now, it seemed, I had lost them, all in the span of a few short days.

I stood and held out my hand to Shane. I didn't know what else to do. He shook it.

"We'll talk more about how to handle the transfer of cases," he said. "It will be gradual."

"Sure," I managed to say. I turned and left Forester's office—*Shane's office,* I corrected myself.

Out on the street, I scanned up and down for signs that someone was watching me. But really, I didn't care any longer. What was there to see?

38

I drove my scooter down Michigan Avenue. Too slowly, apparently. Cabbies honked and zoomed around me, cars cut in front of me and then sped away. I turned left on Chicago Avenue and drove down to State Street. I stopped at a light and readjusted the helmet, making it even tighter.

You will no longer be handling Pickett's legal work.

The car behind me bleated its horn. I wasn't even sure where I was going, but I turned right, since I was already in that lane. A few blocks later I realized I was close to my mom's place, an elegant graystone near State and Goethe.

My mother had moved into the house after she married Spence fifteen years ago. As a prominent real-estate developer, Spence had bought the place when it was falling down. He'd given it some much-needed TLC and restored the structure of the house, along with its walls and floors and stairs, but apparently it had still lacked character and decor, which my mother saw as the ultimate challenge. After they met, she and Spence traveled the world collecting furniture, art, vases and tapestries. The place was now stunning—soothing colors of ivory and gold permeated the place, and it was often where I went when I was feeling down.

I knocked on the front door. My brother answered it. Charlie hangs out at my mom's place a lot. "Iz!" He pulled me into the house and wrapped me in a hug. "I was just telling Mom about the other night. Sorry I was good for nothing."

I laughed. "You were fine. It was nice to have someone there."

We went into the front room—a big, beautiful living room with ivory couches and muted Oriental rugs over wood floors that were wide-planked, honey-colored and glossy. The only thing my mother didn't like about the room was that it faced east and got dark in the afternoons. My mother was prone to depression, and when the sun swung over the building and the living room fell into shadow, she had to head for the back of the house.

But now it was sunny and cozy. My mother walked into the room. She was wearing a fitted, white button-down shirt, pressed jeans and bare feet. Thin silver bracelets jingled faintly from her wrists as she looked at me with crossed arms.

"Why didn't you call me the other night?" she asked. "You didn't even mention the break-in at the funeral."

"I didn't want to worry you. And I had Charlie there."

My mother pursed her lips. She didn't want to disparage her son in front of him, but we both knew what Charlie was like.

"It was fine, Mom."

She walked over to me and pulled me onto a silk couch, and then she drew me into her arms. I clung to her, felt myself melting.

"Any word from Sam?" my mother asked.

I thought of the postcard. I thought of what Sam had written there. *Trust me. And please don't tell anyone you got this.*

I would do what he asked. For now. But the trust I had in Sam was starting to wane. I didn't want that to happen, but I didn't want to be a fool either.

"No word," I said.

"What do you want to do about the wedding?"

"Do you think I should call it off?"

"Not yet. You've got time for that if you need it."

Something inside me said, *Do it now. You have the perfect excuse.* Then I felt guilty for the thought.

"I know you've been so excited about the wedding, Mom."

She tutted. "Oh, I was, but that doesn't matter now." She stroked my forearm, something she'd done since we were kids when she wanted to calm us. "How are you?"

"I just found out that I'm losing the Pickett Enterprises work."

My mother straightened. "What?"

"I saw Shane. He's running the company now and wants someone more experienced. He's going to gradually pull the work from me and give it to Tanner."

My mother shook her head. "Forester wouldn't have wanted that."

"It doesn't matter what Forester wants anymore. Shane is CEO. He wants to work with Tanner, his friend, and he wants to make sure he's got an experienced panel of consultants on his team. I can't blame him, really. He's not very experienced himself."

"But Forester trusted you, and you did exceptional work for them, that's what he always said."

I shrugged. "It doesn't matter anymore."

"Of course it matters." My mother's face looked drawn. She hated to see her kids in pain.

"It should matter," Charlie said. He took a sip from a can of cranberry juice, his during-the-day substitute for red wine, and stared thoughtfully at the can. "Forester was one of the richest men in this town, but he was also the nicest. He cared about people. And he built that company from the ground up. It shouldn't be dismantled so quickly."

"It's not being dismantled," I said, wondering why I was arguing for Shane. "It's just that someone has to run it now that he's gone, and that someone is Shane."

"I wonder about that man," my mom said in a musing tone.

"What do you mean?"

"I've always thought there was something a little different about him, something that wasn't quite authentic. I've never been able to put my finger on it."

Just then my cell phone rang. I took it out of my bag. The display showed a local number I didn't recognize.

"Hello?"

"Isabel McNeil?"

"Yes."

"This is Ernesto Rosario. I'm a producer for Fox News. We'd like to interview you about the disappearance of your fiancé and the death of Forester Pickett."

"I'm sorry, but I won't be commenting."

"If we could just ask you a few questions. We'd be happy to meet you wherever—"

"No comment." I'd gotten good at saying that during the times Pickett Enterprises had landed in the press, like after the radio stunt when listeners jumped into the Chicago River, but I'd never had to say it on behalf of myself.

I hung up the phone. It rang again. A different local number this time. "Ms. McNeil? This is Tiffany Millstone with ABC."

"No comment." I hung up. "Fox and ABC," I said to my mom and Charlie.

Charlie took a final sip of cranberry juice and then crushed the can with his hand. "That's not good."

He was right. For the next half hour, my phone kept ringing with calls from reporters and producers all over the city. Finally, I changed the outgoing message to say that I would not be giving interviews or making any comments about Forester Pickett or Sam Hollings.

"I wonder if they're going to be outside your house," my mom said, looking worried.

"My address is unlisted, remember?" When I'd bought my condo, I had just finished a few dates with a guy who showed up at my apartment way too often and without notice. I unlisted the address to deter him.

I turned off the ringer because the calls wouldn't stop, but then I saw Mayburn's number flash across the phone.

"Hello?" I stood and took the phone into my mom's kitchen. It had high ceilings, beautiful woodwork and a cozy breakfast nook that overlooked the small, landscaped backyard. I sat at the nook and turned my back to the room.

"Hey," Mayburn said. "I have a buddy who's with the government, and I asked him to run a search on the passenger lists for all the major airline carriers this week."

"And?"

"No air travel by anyone named Sam Hollings."

"Which means he drove wherever he went." *To Indianapolis, probably.*

I struggled with whether to tell Mayburn about the postcard. Sam had asked me not to. But what did I care anymore what Sam wanted? I had been battling in my head with this since the moment I'd gotten that damn postcard. I wanted to trust Sam. Desperately. If I didn't, and this thing somehow got resolved, wouldn't I have then betrayed him? I decided to track down Alyssa before telling anyone about the postcard.

"Or he flew under a different name, or he might have chartered a private plane," Mayburn said. "I'll keep looking into it. How was your talk with Forester's son?"

"Aside from the fact that I'm going to lose their business, it went fine." I told him Shane was already in Forester's office and making some major decisions.

"I thought you told me he wasn't very decisive," Mayburn said.

"He never was before."

We were both silent for a moment.

"I found out Forester's cardiologist was Dr. Donald Loman," I said. "He signed the death certificate at the emergency room and told Shane that Forester had the classic presentation for a heart attack. The Chinese doctor he saw is named Song Li."

"We've got to get all the records and talk to those docs. I want to see if what Shane says about his conversation with Loman is true. We need to find out if Forester's heart attack was as simple as that. If it was, Sam is in the clear, at least on that front."

"And I can stop worrying that someone was out to hurt Forester."

"I've been thinking, what did Forester do with the letters he told you about?"

"I'm not sure. I'd guess they'd be at work or in his home office."

"And what about any medications he was taking, or those herbs from the Chinese doctor? Where do you think he kept those?"

"Same. But his desk at Pickett has already been cleaned out."

"Anybody living in the house?" Mayburn asked.

"Not that I know of."

"Then we're going to have to pay a visit. What are you doing tomorrow?"

"I'm babysitting, remember?"

"Yeah, that's right, and I've got to prep you before that. But tomorrow night?"

"Nothing."

"Are you familiar with Forester's place?"

"I've been there a bunch of times, but how would we get in?"

"Leave it to me."

"I don't like the sound of that. I'm an attorney, remember? An attorney who might have to start looking for another job soon. I can't be getting arrested for breaking and entering."

"I never get arrested."

"That doesn't make me feel better. Seriously, I don't have the stomach for criminal activity. I had to steal something once when I was pledging a sorority, and it nearly killed me."

I told Mayburn how I still felt nauseous just thinking about it.

"That was a senseless, dumb-ass theft," he said. "The only thing we're looking to take from Forester's place is those letters, if we can find them, and a sample of the medications and herbs he was taking so we can test them and see if someone slipped anything in there. We'll make a copy of the letters if we find them and we'll replace them, so really we won't be stealing anything."

"I can't believe *you* do stuff like that. I would never have hired you on actual cases if I'd known that."

"Yes, you would, because I get results, and those are always on the up-and-up. I only bust into someplace to start the flow of information. Think about it. We'll take some of those herbs from Forester's place and have them analyzed. If there's anything suspicious, we'll do it by the book then. We'll subpoena them and have them tested officially, so the results can be used in any litigation in the future, or we can turn the case over to the cops and let them do it."

"I wouldn't exactly describe that as on the 'up-and-up.'"

"Of course it is. Like I said, sometimes you just need to get the ball rolling."

I said nothing for a moment. Mayburn was not the boring, by-the-book investigator I thought he was. And obviously Sam wasn't the person I thought he was either. In truth, they were both much different than the way I saw them. It made me wonder who else in my life I'd underestimated.

"Look, Izzy, we need to get in Forester's house. You got a better idea?"

I thought for a second. "What about Annette? His house-keeper? I could tell her I just wanted to say goodbye to Forester in my own way. Say I wanted to look at his house one last time or something like that. Maybe she'd let me in."

"That would work. Even if she only lets you in for two minutes, as long as one door isn't locked for a bit, I can put something on it to make sure it won't lock properly on her way out, and that way we can get back in."

"But there's the alarm. She'll turn it on when she leaves."

"If I've got access to the panel, I can figure out the code. I'd need a few minutes in there before she leaves."

When we hung up, I called Annette.

She picked up after the second ring and said a soft hello.

I told her my story of wanting to say goodbye to Forester in my own way. I told her that I'd been thinking of all the parties he'd had on his back lawn, and I wondered if I could get one more look at the lawn and say my own private farewell there.

"I don't think that's appropriate. I don't have authorization to let anyone in here, and your fiancé apparently stole a lot of money from Forester."

"Annette, I know nothing about that. *Nothing.*" I paused to try and let that settle in. "Who would you have to get authorization from?"

She sniffed, then cleared her throat. "Well, I don't know. The estate can't be administered because of your fiancé's crime, so it's unclear who owns this house right now, although I'm sure it will go to Shane."

"Will you stay on to take care of the house?" I asked.

"At least initially," she said stiffly, "but I have no idea what will happen."

"I'm sure Shane will keep you on if you want." I wasn't exactly sure about that, but suddenly I felt terrible for her, and I wanted to make her feel better. She was a sixty-two-year-old woman who might lose her job, while in the meantime unable to rely on the money Forester had left her. It occurred to me that maybe what most upset her was the two million. Was it possible she'd done something to Forester, knowing she'd get money after he died?

"I'm sorry for everything you're going through," I said. It was vague, intentionally. I was trying to work up a way to ask her if, or how long, she'd known she had two million waiting for her, but there seemed no polite way to do so.

"Thank you." Again, her delivery was stiff, but then suddenly she softened. "I'd be happy to let you into the house to say goodbye. When were you thinking?"

"Tomorrow afternoon? Maybe about five?"

I'd be done with my babysitting job then, and dusk would be settling in. I could pretend to look at the lawn, while Mayburn would have some darkness to do his work.

"I'll see you then, Izzy," she said, and hung up.

39

At eight o'clock on Saturday night, my buzzer rang. When I pushed the intercom, I heard, "Hey, baby, it's the King."

"Grady?"

"No, baby, it's the King. My Caddy is all warmed up and waiting for you."

Downstairs, Grady held open a cab door for me. He was dressed as a seventies Elvis—fat suit with chest hair, white jumpsuit, a black sweeping pompadour and huge gold sunglasses.

When he saw me, he swiveled his hips and sang, "A hunk, a hunk of burning love." A couple walking arm-in-arm laughed at him from across the street. I looked around to see if there was a gray Honda, a blue SUV or any other suspicious car or person. But the city was full of suspicious people on Halloween.

Grady swung his hips around again and gave me a lascivious grin.

I laughed and it felt so good.

"C'mon, baby," Grady said. "Get into the King's car."

I got into the backseat.

Grady kept singing "Burning Love" then switched to "Hound Dog," then lifted the gold sunglasses. "What are you supposed to be?"

I pointed to the devil's ears on my head and opened my coat to show a slinky blue cocktail dress.

"Devil with a blue dress," Grady said.

"You got it."

"It's not that original."

"Oh, and Elvis is original?"

"At least I'm going all out. I've got a fricking fat suit on. You're just wearing a dress you know is hot and then you stuck those things on your head."

"May I remind you, my fiancé took off this week?" I ignored the lump of nausea that fact sent to my belly. Why was I going out tonight? The same reason I'd been doing so many things lately—I didn't know what else to do.

A pause from Grady. He reached into his fat suit, from somewhere in the direction of his armpit, and pulled out a flask. "You'd better take a nip of this."

"What is it?"

"Cinnamon schnapps. It's a seasonal drink."

I took a sip, winced at the spicy burn trailing my insides. But it felt good to feel anything. On second thought, I drank some more.

Five minutes later, we pulled up to Q's place. The house he shared with Max on Cleveland Avenue was all lit up—candles burned inside pumpkins, orange string lights were twisted around black railings and every light in the house was on.

Grady and I walked up the front steps, and I opened the door. But as I pushed, it hit someone on the inside.

"Hey, watch it!" It was Max's mother, Simone, dressed in her Vegas-showgirl costume, complete with a purple feathered headpiece that towered a foot above her and plumed out in all directions. "Sorry," she said, patting the feathers. "It gets in the way sometimes."

"Hi, Simone, it's Izzy." No matter how many times I'd met Simone, she never remembered me. I had long stopped taking it personally. She never remembered anyone.

"Oh, Izzy! How nice to meet you!" Simone hugged me. I could feel her tiny waist and her ribs. The woman was in amazing shape. Well over sixty and still able to rock a show-girl outfit.

Simone grabbed a passing waiter, who was dressed in tight black pants, no shirt and a Venetian catlike mask. "Two, please," she said, relieving him of a couple martinis, which she shoved at Grady and me before she disappeared into the crowd.

"Simone, this is Grady," I said to her retreating back.

"Don't worry," he said. "I'm not staying at this party long." He glanced around. "Man, I thought gay men were supposed to have tons of straight girlfriends."

"Hey," I said, taking a sip of the martini, which tasted of apple and cinnamon, "you're not looking anyway, right? You said it was going great with Ellen."

He eyed a guy dressed as Little Orphan Annie, wearing a sign that read, *You're Only a GAY Away.* He shook his head and returned his eyes to me. "Things are great with Ellen. But I'm always looking."

We made our way into the thick of the crowd. I began to wish I was a single, homosexual man. It seemed every hot, gay guy in the city was in Q's living room, most of them shirtless and greased up. One guy was dressed as a Chippendales dancer, another as an Indian (replete with feathered loincloth), yet another as a trapeze artist. And the flirting that was going on—*Jiminy Christmas.* Everyone seemed to be batting their eyes at one another and squeezing biceps. I started to feel ignored in my sexy blue dress.

We found Q in the kitchen, talking with a black guy cross-dressing as Marilyn Monroe. Q wore white footie pajamas and sheep ears.

"Iz!" he yelled when he saw me. Q got *loud* when he drank. And he had clearly been drinking. "Izzy, baby, how are you?"

He lurched over to me and hugged me big. "How are you?" he hollered again.

"Fine. What's with your costume?"

"Max is Little Bo Peep. I'm the sheep." He turned me to face Marilyn Monroe. "Iz, have you met Timothy?"

Timothy/Marilyn licked his lips and swished the skirt of his white dress back and forth. "Lovely to meet you," he purred. "So tell me something…" He pointed to my red hair then down toward my waist. "Does the carpet match the drapes?"

"Dude, shut up!" Grady said.

I laughed. "It's okay." I'd been hearing that question, in one form or another, since I was thirteen, usually from drunk assholes at a late-night bar. Coming from Timothy/Marilyn, it didn't bother me.

I turned and pulled Grady forward. "This is Grady Fisher."

"Yum." Timothy/Marilyn looked him up and down.

"Yeah, hi." Grady put his martini on the counter, grabbed a beer from a drinks tub and disappeared.

"So," Timothy/Marilyn said, dragging his eyes up and down my body now. "You're sexy."

"*Thank* you," I said. I was struck by how truly flattered I was. And then immediately struck by how truly low my self-esteem must have dipped for me to be eating up attention from a man dressed as Marilyn Monroe.

Q threw his arm around my shoulders and pulled me close. "So, Timothy, Izzy is my boss."

"Shut up," I said. "We work together." *Or we did. Before Shane took the Pickett work from me.*

"Yes, but you make the big money."

"Wait a minute, I direct a portion of my salary to you, so you make more than enough."

"But I'm still just a lowly assistant," Q said. "Hey, I'm okay with it. It's like being in AA." He pulled away and threw his arms out. "I am Quentin David Briscoe. And I…am an assistant."

"Oh, have another drink."

He grabbed a bottle of Corona off the counter. "You and

I need to have a talk about that fiancé of yours." Q tugged me though the living room, up the steps to the second floor and into his and Max's bedroom. The space was cool and calm, done in charcoal gray and decorated with contemporary artwork, many painted by Q.

"Sit," he said, half gesturing toward the bed, half shoving me in that direction.

"Watch the devil ears!" I tumbled back onto the bed.

"Spill it. I've called you four times since the funeral yesterday, and I got nothing. What's been happening?"

"Everything." I threw a hand over my eyes, *Gone With the Wind* style.

He didn't laugh. I didn't either.

I couldn't tell him about working with Mayburn, so I told him about getting followed, probably by two people. I told him about the break-in, and how I'd met with Shane Pickett today. I stopped short of telling him everything about the meeting.

Q listened intently. "How was Shane doing?"

"Seems to be great. He's moved into his dad's office already."

"Really?"

"Yeah, that was fast, huh?"

He shrugged. "I guess he's just doing what he has to do."

I knew I should tell him that Shane was giving my work back to Tanner, but I was hoping to come up with a plan, some way to meet with Shane and maybe the entire board and convince them that I should remain as one of the company's attorneys. It had slipped from me too fast. Last week the work was too much. In some ways, I had wanted out. And now I was out. If I told Q, it would make it reality.

"I don't know what to think about Shane," I said. "I've always really liked him, but it was weird to see him in his dad's office. Has he always wanted to take over Pickett? Is it possible that he did something to make that happen?"

"Forester had a heart attack."

"There are ways to cause a heart attack," I said, mimicking Mayburn's words.

"The guy was almost seventy, Iz. He'd had a heart attack before. Don't insult his family members by implying they might have done something to get him there."

"I'm not trying to insult anyone. I'm just trying to make sure there was no foul play. Forester had been receiving death threats before he died."

Q narrowed his eyes. "You didn't tell me that."

"Yeah. He was getting threatening letters, telling him to step down from the company." I told him what they'd said. I told him about the homeless guy outside Pickett Enterprises. "I want to make sure that his heart attack was natural and not caused by something else. Or anybody else. I have to look at everyone. I know Shane is a nice guy." *A nice guy who just gave me the ax.* "But I'm just trying to keep my eyes and ears open. I thought Sam was the nicest guy, too, right? I mean, I *still* think that. But sometimes it gets hard to ignore what I'm seeing."

Q was silent for a minute. "How can I help?"

"I might ask you to stay at my apartment with me, although I did get new locks put in."

"That wouldn't be a problem. Anything to get away from Simone. Max is tense as hell with her around."

"How are things with you guys?"

He looked away. He seemed to be staring at a painting of his that was deep-yellow and tinged with orange. I knew he had painted it when he first met Max, and he said that being in love made him feel at the center of the sun.

He looked back at me. "Not good."

"What's going on? Is it just Simone?"

"That doesn't help, but the main problem is Max thinks I'm cheating on him."

"Did you finally cave and fool around with someone else?" Q had a wandering eye, but I never thought he'd give in to the impulse.

He waved a hand. "I can't talk about this with two hundred people downstairs. Plus, you've got enough going on. Tell me what else I can do other than crash on your couch once or twice."

"How hard would it be to get our hands on Forester's autopsy?"

Q thought for a second. He gave me a long look. "I think you're being paranoid, but I can get you the report from the estate department if you really want it. I'll just say we're closing up something for Forester and we need it for our records. I'll copy it and have it Monday morning."

"What about Forester's records from his cardiologist?"

"Hmm. Well, I'd guess those would be part of the autopsy records. If not, I could subpoena them under the court number of the estate."

A knock came from the door and Fat Elvis stuck his head in. "There's my hunk of burning love."

Q stood and put his hands on his hips. "I'm glad you're coming around to the good side, Grady."

Grady guffawed. "Not you, man. I wanted to see if Izzy was okay."

"She's a conspiracy theorist." Q adjusted the foot of his pajamas. "Get her drunk and onto a different topic." He left the bedroom.

Downstairs, through the open doorway, I could hear the thumping strains of the song "It's Raining Men."

"What's the conspiracy?" Grady shifted the heft of his fake belly to the other side and sat on the bed next to me.

"I can't take you seriously in that outfit."

"Wait a second." He pushed the gold shades up on his pompadour and peeled off the top of the jumpsuit and the fake belly. "Better?"

"Much."

He put his beer on the floor. "Iz, remember I told you that

you could rely on me? That I could handle more than sports and law-firm talk?"

"Yes."

"Well, I want to tell you something else I can handle."

I held my breath. There was something weighty moving into the room—some kind of energy that felt serious.

"I could handle me and you," Grady said.

"Me and you? But we're friends."

"Exactly. We're great friends, and it's not like I've thought about this for years or anything, but since last week, since everything has happened, it's killed me, absolutely killed me, to see you sad. And I started to wish I could be more than just your friend."

"So you want…" I couldn't even finish my sentence. I'd never thought Grady was interested in me.

"I don't really want anything. You've got too much on your plate right now. The only thing I want is for you to know I'm thinking about you, and I'm into you, and if you are ever ready for that, you let me know. And if you just want to be friends, that's great, too, and I'll do anything I can to help you get through this. Anything. Ask me anything."

I remembered that tomorrow morning I had to pick up Kaitlyn, Maggie's niece. "Well, um, could I borrow your car tomorrow morning?"

"Sure. I'm going to the gym in the morning. I'll leave it outside your place and put the keys under the doormat." He stood. "I'm getting out of here before I say anything else. Are we okay?"

"Yeah, I guess. I mean, sure."

He zipped up his jumpsuit and put his wig back on. The huge gold sunglasses came next.

I started laughing.

"That's not exactly the response I wanted from a girl I hope to date."

I put on a serious face. "Sorry."

He swiveled his hips. "Don't feel sorry for the King, baby."

Grady left, leaving me to sit alone in a room, wearing devil ears, listening to the thump of too much bass and pondering how life never failed to surprise.

40

Day Six

Sleep had come easy the night before, thanks to the vast quantities of apple-cinnamon martinis that Simone kept handing me and I kept chugging, liking how reality receded with every sip.

I woke up on Sunday morning to the persistent sound of a thudding bass drum. I tried to tune it out, but the thumping only got louder, to the point where I could feel the reverberation through my body.

I sat up and yelped with pain. The drum was, I realized, in my head.

Lying back down, I concentrated on quieting it. Impossible.

I investigated and saw that there was a tiny hangover band in my brain that was playing really, really, *really* loud. On closer inspection of the band members, I saw that Simone was playing the bass drum with one hand, holding a martini in the other and grinning. Grady was also there, banging away on some kind of bongo. Q and Max played matching snare drums.

I groaned and rolled over, which only made the pain worse and the noise louder.

"Go away," I muttered.

No such luck.

I got out of bed and stumbled into the kitchen. Reaching

into the cupboard for a box of green tea, I stubbed my toe—hard—on the corner.

"Fudge!" I yelled, hopping around, trying out one of my swearword replacements. Definitely wasn't working. "Fuck!" For some reason, I stubbed my toe on that corner at least twice a week.

I started smiling a little through the pain when I thought of how Sam always laughed when I did this. He'd come into the kitchen to find me bouncing around, clutching my foot and cursing. And then I remembered, again, that I had no idea where Sam was, that I might never see his laughing face again.

I stopped hopping and sank abruptly to the floor. I sat there, staring around my kitchen, seeing Sam make his coffee in the morning, shirtless and with his blond hair rumpled. I could hear him whistling the fight song of USC, where he'd gone to college. Was he somewhere else making coffee right now? Was he laughing at someone else's hangover or stubbed toe? Was that person Alyssa?

With that thought, I left the kitchen and quickly checked my home phone, cell and e-mail. Nothing from Alyssa. *That brick,* I said, trying out another swearword alternative. It wasn't working either. "Bitch," I muttered.

I looked at the clock on my phone. I had to meet Mayburn in twenty minutes, which meant that a few hours after that I had to pick up a toddler. In my head, Simone grinned bigger, banged louder and raised her martini in a toast.

Walking to the Starbucks on Wells and North, I was jumpy and nervous. I kept looking over my shoulder for signs that I was being followed, but with all the commotion of the city, I didn't notice anything out of the ordinary.

The Starbucks was a huge one with two walls of glass overlooking the street. Mayburn was already seated in a maroon velvet chair with his back to a far wall, away from the windows. I waved, then beelined for the counter where I ordered a Venti green tea with three tea bags.

"Three?" said the barista with a dismissive lip curl. "We usually do two."

"Three," I barked. "Charge me whatever you want."

As I waited, I looked at my phone and saw a text from Grady. Just left the car outside your apartment. Key's under the mat.

You are the best, I wrote back.

A few minutes later, I was in the chair next to Mayburn, sipping the tea, my sunglasses firmly on my face.

"What's with you?" he said.

"Tough night."

"Ah. Want to talk about it?"

"Nothing to talk about."

"Okay, then," he said, "let's get this done so I can leave your charming company, and you can go make friends with Lucy DeSanto."

"You often make friends with your subjects?"

"Normally, no. I try not to let them even see me, or one of my operatives, unless I have to, but I'm almost out of time on this case. I have to make something happen by the middle of next week. I need a break so I can get into their house."

"Who's your client?"

"A bank. Lucy's husband might be involved in some fraudulent activity, and I'm trying to get evidence about it. I'm just collecting intel. But really, what I need to do is get into their house. It's when he works from home that the bank picks up some interesting activity. He's been able to explain it away, but they're not buying it anymore."

"So, what do you want me to do?"

"Be a nice, cool, friendly mom who has her kid on the playground. Don't talk to Lucy right away, though. Listen to her and her girlfriend for as long as you can. I'm looking for any information about work on their house, a vacation they might be taking, really anything at this point that can get me in."

"How will I know who she is?"

He reached down and pulled a manila envelope from a black bag at his feet. He looked around before he removed a five-by-seven photo of two women sitting on a park bench, strollers next to them, cardboard coffee cups in their hands.

Mayburn pointed to the woman on the right, a blonde with a pixie haircut and a big smile. She wore a T-shirt and white pants, her arms thin, toned. Her designer sunglasses were pushed back on her head.

"She's cute. What's her husband like?"

"A total asshole who doesn't know how to treat her."

"Geez. Have an opinion?"

He didn't respond.

"Do I sense a crush?"

Mayburn looked at me sharply. "What are you talking about?"

"Sounds like you have a crush on her."

"She's a subject."

"So?"

"Of course not." He took the photo from my hand and placed it back in the envelope. "Once you've listened to her for a while, angle yourself so you can talk to her. You don't have to intrude too much or be best friends. I just need you to have met her so when you see her again on Tuesday night, you can strike up a conversation."

"What's happening Tuesday night?"

"A presale party for the holiday benefit ball that Lucy is on the board for. It's at the Prada store. Very invite only, but don't worry, I'll get you on the list."

"And what am I supposed to do there?"

"Well, if you can talk to Lucy enough you might be able to wrangle an invite to her house. Actually, that's what I *need* you to do. Get a playdate or something so we can get inside that place."

"Why would anyone invite a stranger into their house?"

"You won't be a stranger by the time you see her at the

Prada party, and this is what these moms do all the time. They make friends and set up playdates."

"What do you need once you're in the house?"

"To get on his computer."

"Wouldn't that be unlawful search and seizure?"

"It's just like going to Forester's house. I need to get on that computer to see if he's guilty of what we think he is. If so, *then* we can build a case with evidence that can be used at litigation."

I shook my head. "I had no idea you operated this way."

"You didn't care how I operated as long as I got you what you wanted."

I shrugged. That was true. "Why don't I just try to get invited to Lucy's house when I see her today? Why wait until Tuesday?"

He shook his head. "The DeSantos have big money, and they run with a very select crowd. She's not a snob, but from watching her, I can tell she's private, and she'll never invite you over just because she met you at the playground. But if you're at this exclusive party on Tuesday, she'll know you're in the same crowd."

My green tea was cooler. I gulped it, hoping for a large infusion of caffeine.

"It would help," Mayburn continued, "if you could bring a guy to the party, like a husband type. You know, really show that you're the family type."

"I'll have a kid today."

"I know, but Lucy always hangs around married women with kids. Anything you can do to bolster your cover helps. So bringing a guy who looks like your husband would be good."

I looked across the shop. It was full of people, but I wasn't really seeing any of them. "Sam was going to be my husband."

Mayburn said nothing.

I looked back at him. "Why don't you just go to the party with me on Tuesday?"

"I've already been in Lucy's sightline once, and that's

because I was getting desperate. Can't do it again. Who could you take to the party?"

"Q?"

"Your black, bald, gay assistant? Not going to work. You want to seem like you're a perfect married couple. Don't you have a guy who can play the nice husband?"

I thought of Grady. I heard his words—*I'll do anything I can to help you get through this.*

"I think I know someone," I told Mayburn.

41

Mayburn made me pick a different name for my cover, something easy to remember, a name that wouldn't make me balk when I introduced myself to Lucy DeSanto. I chose my first name combined with the last name of Maggie's niece—Isabel Bristol.

"What if Kaitlyn says something that makes it obvious I'm not her mom?" I asked Mayburn.

"Just run with it. Make anything up. They'll believe whatever you're saying if you believe it. That's the number-one ticket to a successful cover—believing every word of it. No stumbling with your words, no embarrassment, just be confident about it. Now, let's practice."

Mayburn and I ran over the rest of my story ten times—I was new in town, having moved with my husband from L.A. I lived in a three-bedroom penthouse apartment on Lincoln Park West. I was an entertainment lawyer. I had practiced in L.A. before I met my husband, a widower, and adopted my daughter, Kaitlyn. My husband, Grady, was also a lawyer. (How I was going to explain to Grady that we had to pretend we were *married,* I wasn't sure).

I spent ten minutes with Maggie's sister when I picked up Kaitlyn, but Mary seemed excited to get me out of the house and have some time to herself. After some profuse speeches of gratitude, she put Kaitlyn's car seat in the back of Grady's car and off we went to a kids' park on the North Side called Adam's Playground.

Kaitlyn, it turned out, had gotten a little sassier since the last time I'd seen her. Back then she was a wide-eyed two-and-a-half-year-old. Now she was four, going on thirty-five, and she knew exactly what she wanted. With her curly hair and big eyes, she resembled her aunt Maggie but, with her bossy attitude, I had a feeling she could kick Maggie's ass in court.

"Change the channel!" she yelled every minute or so when she tired of a song on the radio. If I didn't do what she was asking, she would kick my seat so hard I feared she'd break a leg.

"Are you hungry?" I asked, for lack of anything better to say. The truth was, I was *starving*. I should have gotten something to eat at Starbucks, but at that time the thought of food had conjured up the real possibility of projectile vomiting.

"Thirsty!" Kaitlyn screamed with a voice loud enough to land her a job on a trading floor. "I'm thirsty!"

"Just a minute." I rooted with my right arm into her pink backpack. Kaitlyn's mom had loaded me up with enough gear and food to make a push for the summit on K2. There had to be some kind of drink in there. I wasn't finding anything. Then suddenly I remembered "the juice-y" that I'd left on the table.

I realized I had slowed down inadvertently, and I looked in the rearview mirror to make sure a trucker wasn't about to run me over. No truck, but there was, about a hundred yards away, a gray Honda. The same one I'd seen in front of my house. The same one that Mayburn said was a government car. The feds.

"Thirsty! Thirsty!" Kaitlyn yelled. Honestly, her vocal power rivaled Celine Dion's.

"We're almost there." I tried to make my voice cooing and calm, but the truth was the sight of that car behind me filled me with shots of anxiety. I sped up. The Honda stayed well behind me but kept pace.

I shifted into the left lane and passed three cars. Behind me, the Honda did the same.

I called Mayburn on my cell. "I think someone's following me. That Honda again. What should I do?"

"Nothing."

"What do you mean, nothing? I've got a child in the car that's not mine, and I'm about to take her to a playground."

"So what? You're not doing anything wrong. The feds don't care if you babysit for your friend's kid. Out of curiosity, see if it's the same license plate."

I slowed down. The gray car did the same. "Yeah, it's the same."

"Good. Seriously, the feds just want to know if you can lead them to Sam. If you can't, they don't care what you're up to."

"I want juice!" Kaitlyn screamed.

"Gotta go." I hung up with Mayburn and tried to say anything to calm Kaitlyn.

But nothing would shut her up. The kicking on the back of the seat was so insistent the band in my head decided to play a second set.

The playground was just north of Armitage, a few blocks from Lucy DeSanto's home. When I got off at the exit, the Honda did, too. And right behind it was a blue SUV.

My hands started to shake, whether from the caffeine or Kaitlyn's screams or the fact that it seemed I was being followed at that very moment by two different people, I couldn't tell. By the time I got to the playground, Kaitlyn had worked herself into an absolute tizzy, her face red from shouting, her voice bordering on hoarse. I found a parking spot right next to the large playground, jumped out of the car and tried to extract a wailing, kicking Kaitlyn. She was thrashing so much I couldn't disentangle the Houdini-like straps that held her into the seat.

I glanced around as I wrestled with the car seat. No sign of either the SUV or the Honda now.

Finally, Kaitlyn seemed to sense my ineptitude and managed to unlatch all the straps herself. She fell out of the car, still wailing.

Out of the corner of my eye, I saw people in the playground stopping their activities to stare at me. I blushed what must be a deep fuchsia. I glanced around at them, trying to give an I've-got-it-under-control kind of smile. One guy shook his head dismissively and turned away from me. Another woman glared.

I looked around again for the cars. Nothing. Were they on foot and watching me from somewhere? The thought was creepy as hell.

As I slammed the car door, I could see Lucy. She was sitting on a bench in jeans and a stylish, puffy down jacket, talking to another woman. They both held coffee. Three kids played angelically in front of them. How was I supposed to use the tyrant known as Kaitlyn to talk to Lucy? She probably didn't want Kaitlyn within ten feet of her kids.

Kaitlyn kept yelling that she was thirsty, which gave me an idea.

"C'mon, Kaitlyn," I said. "We're going to find you something to drink."

I tugged her through the metal gates of the playground and made a beeline for Lucy DeSanto. Mayburn had told me to listen first, then try to befriend her, but there was no way. We skirted a green jungle gym and a red, tubular slide.

Lucy and her friend both stopped talking and looked up as I approached. Kaitlyn continued to yell, but it was no longer making me crazy. She was going to help me.

"Hi," I said when I reached them. "I'm so sorry to bother you, but we spilled our juice on the way here, and as you can see she gets a little upset when things like that happen."

Lucy's friend, a woman with black wavy hair, eyed Kaitlyn,

who was now crouching next to their kids and trying to take a toy train from one of the boys.

Lucy laughed and gave me a smile. "I've got a few extra juice boxes." She went digging in a leather bag on the bench next to her and withdrew a box of organic apple juice.

"Thanks so much." I took it. "Kaitlyn, leave that little boy's train alone."

Lucy smiled again. "Don't worry about it. Noah likes to share, don't you, Noah?"

Noah, who looked about five, nodded and seemed fine to let Kaitlyn commandeer his toy.

"He loves having other kids around," Lucy explained. "Sometimes his little sister, Eve, just isn't enough stimulus."

"They've all got their personalities," Lucy's friend said.

I got the straw in the top of the juice box and tried to hand it to Kaitlyn, who had completely lost interest now that she'd taken over the train. I placed the juice box next to her.

As I stood, I felt a shock go through me. Across the playground was a man—short with black wavy hair. He wore a tan jacket. I knew immediately he was the guy who'd followed me through Old Town that night, right before I discovered my apartment had been broken into. If Mayburn was right, he probably wasn't one of the feds, but someone else altogether. My eyes scanned the playground around him. He was standing near two dads and some kids, but he wasn't talking to anyone. As if he felt me looking at him, he turned and walked away and passed through an exit on the far side of the playground.

"I'm Lucy DeSanto," I heard. "And this is Bethany Larsen."

I tried to watch where the guy was going, but he disappeared into a row of brick three-flats on the other side of the playground. Was he looping back around? Was he going to watch me from someplace else? Who in the hell was he?

"I'm Lucy," I heard again.

I turned, offering a hand. "Uh…sorry. I thought I saw

someone I knew. I'm Isabel Bristol. Izzy." I shook her friend's hand as well. "Do you guys come to this playground a lot?" It was sort of the parenting version of *Come here often?,* but I couldn't think of anything else. Meanwhile, I checked the edges of the playground, looking for signs of the guy.

When I turned back, I saw that Bethany appeared annoyed I was still hanging around, and I couldn't blame her. Whenever Maggie and I were able to get together I was protective of our time. But Lucy seemed happy to chat.

"I live a few blocks away," she said. "There are a couple of playgrounds closer, but this is the best one."

"This is my first time. It's amazing." The place was huge, probably half a city block, with groupings of slides and swings and bubble-like climbing stations. No sign of the guy.

"Are you new to the area?"

I took a breath for bravery and launched into the cover story Mayburn and I had concocted.

"I was in L.A., too," Bethany said when I had finished. "For eight years. Where did you live?"

Uh-oh. "Manhattan Beach." It was the first place I could think of. A college girlfriend had lived there.

"How funny. I was in Manhattan Beach for three years. Where was your place?"

I made an exaggerated shrug. "Oh, God, we lived all over. Truth is, I'm not a big L.A. fan. I'm so glad to be back in Chicago."

"Isn't Chicago the best?" Lucy said. "It's so easy to live here."

"Especially with kids," I said. "You have to be in the car so much in L.A."

"But at least in Manhattan Beach, you can walk a lot," Bethany said.

"Yeah, true. It's just not the same vibe, you know." I don't think I'd ever uttered the word *vibe* before, but it seemed like something an ex-Los Angeleno would say.

"We used to be on Pine Avenue," Bethany said. "Do you know where that is?"

Jiminy Christmas, would she give it a rest with the Manhattan Beach stuff? "Sure, sure. Pine is great."

I got a flash of panic. What if Pine Avenue wasn't great? I could get myself into trouble with this L.A. stuff. And really, what else did I need to do here? I'd met Lucy. I'd see her on Tuesday and introduce myself again. Mission accomplished.

"Okay, Kaitlyn," I said. "Let's leave these ladies alone and go to the swings."

She looked up at me with abject horror. "No! No! I don't want to go!"

"We're not leaving, we're just going to swing."

She bashed a fist on the train and began to sob impressively, all the while yelling, "No, no!"

I shot Lucy and Bethany an apologetic glance. "Sorry."

Bethany sighed.

Lucy just laughed. "Don't worry about it. We've all been there."

Lucy had such a breezy, sweet smile. If Mayburn did have a crush, I could see why.

When I looked down, Kaitlyn was starting to put wood chips in her mouth.

"Kaitlyn, no!" I grabbed her, and she fell crying into my arms.

"I want to go home!" she wailed.

Thank God. The thought of the dark guy watching me from behind a tree was freaking me out.

I crouched, swooped up the juice box and stuck it in her hands. The pink backpack still on my shoulder, I started backing away, calling, "Nice to meet you!"

Kaitlyn sobbed the rest of the way home. I kept searching in my rearview mirror for the Honda or blue SUV, or the black-haired guy in another car, but I saw nothing.

The minute we got in Kaitlyn's driveway, she shut up, and by the time I'd gotten her in the house, much to the chagrin of Mary, who was on her couch with a stack of celeb magazines and what looked like a Bloody Mary, Kaitlyn was a smiling little princess again.

I promised Mary I'd try to babysit again soon, and got in the car, praying that Mayburn wouldn't force me to make good on that promise.

42

I'd barely been able to shower and recover from my eighth circle of hell with Kaitlyn when Mayburn arrived to pick me up. Downstairs, I found him idling in a small, silver muscle car with shiny rims.

"What is this thing?" I slid into the low, low passenger seat, glad I was wearing the black pants and jacket that Mayburn had recommended and not a skirt.

"Nineteen sixty-nine Aston Martin DBS coupe." There was pride in his voice.

"I thought the plan was for you to hide when we got to Forester's and let me drive up to the house."

"It is."

"Where are you going to hide in this thing?" I looked in the backseat. There was none.

"We'll swap seats. I can get on the floor."

"Do you conduct surveillance in this thing?"

"Quit calling it a 'thing.' And no, I have an Acura for surveillance."

"So why didn't you drive that?"

He turned in his seat and gave me an annoyed look. "I like taking this baby on the open road, okay? And we've got a forty-five-minute drive to Lake Forest. I don't have many pleasures in my life, so forgive me."

He put the car into gear and floored it down my street.

I couldn't help myself. "I hope you don't take women for dates in this thing."

He gave me a concerned look. "Why?"

"Because the seats are low and hard to get out of and, inevitably, somebody's going to pull a Britney and flash their delicates."

"Their *delicates?* Where do you live? Victorian England?"

."Hey, I'm trying to be a lady."

He guffawed.

"What's that for? I *am* a lady."

"Yeah, a lady who talks like a fucking truck driver, excuse my French."

"I do *not* talk like a fucking truck diver." I held on to the door as he veered around a few corners and shot up North Avenue, heading west. "I say 'God bless you' instead of 'Goddammit.'"

"What nationality are you?" Mayburn said, throwing an inquisitive face at my hair.

"A bunch of stuff—Scottish and Italian on my dad's side, Welsh and English on my mother's."

"That explains it. The Scottish and the Italians both swear like truck drivers."

"So if you don't like the word *delicates,*" I said to Mayburn, "what do you want me to call it? Coochy? Crotch?"

"We don't know each other well enough for this discussion. Besides, don't worry about girls in my car. I don't date girls who don't wear underwear." He stopped laughing and grunted. "Actually, I *wish* I dated girls who didn't wear underwear."

"Who do you take out?"

"Anyone who will say yes."

"C'mon, seriously. Do you have a girlfriend?"

I was curious now that I'd gotten to know Mayburn a little better. Today, he had on dark-blue jeans that were almost black, a black sweater jacket that zipped up the front and a black baseball cap. He looked tough and, I had to say it, kind of hot. I also liked the no-bullshit way he had about him. I liked that he drove this oddball little car, and I kind of even liked that he broke into places in order to break a case. He was tenacious, ambitious, confident. None of this made me *like* him in a romantic sense, but he was simply not the dreary private investigator I once thought I knew.

"I'm getting over a girlfriend." He slipped on a pair of sunglasses and continued to power down North Avenue toward the expressway.

"How long ago did you break up?"

"Ten months. I know. Time to move on and all that, but if you knew this girl, you'd know how hard it is to move on from her."

"What's her name?"

We got onto the Edens Expressway, which was blessedly wide open on a Sunday afternoon. Mayburn kept frowning and looking in the rearview mirror.

"See anybody following us?" I asked.

"Nope. And if they are there, I'm about to lose them." Mayburn went through each gear quickly until he was going well over seventy. He zigged and zagged from lane to lane. I could tell he wanted to go faster by the way he drummed his fingers on the leather steering wheel.

"Her name was Madeline," he continued. "It *is* Madeline. Madeline Saga. And God, was it a *saga.*"

"Why does that name sound familiar?"

"She owns an art gallery."

"She got in trouble, right? Because she had nude guys handing out flyers?"

He laughed. "That's her."

"Wow." I had even more respect for Mayburn now. He was a book whose cover I shouldn't have prejudged. "How long did you date?"

"A year and a half. She was the most incredible person I'd ever met. She didn't believe in anything but art. Well, that and sex." He threw me a look, seeing if I was okay with the topic.

I nodded for him to continue. Having been unexpectedly

celibate for a week, after a few years of frequent sex, I was jonesing, even if it was just for the stories of other people.

"Seriously," he continued, "she didn't believe in food or wine or drugs. She ate so that she didn't fall down, and she had a glass of wine occasionally just to be social, but her whole world was art." Mayburn paused and punched the gas a little higher. "When I met her, she made me part of that world for a while."

"What happened?"

"Dumped me. In a nice way. I just wasn't passionate enough for her. And to me that seemed crazy, because I was more passionate with her than I'd ever been. I hardly knew myself, but in a good way." He changed lanes again. "Anyway, enough about The Saga. Tell me how it went with Lucy."

I laughed. "My kid was a train wreck, but it gave me the opportunity to walk up to Lucy and ask for her help."

"Right away? Like you didn't collect any intel at all?"

"No, and I don't feel bad about it." I told Mayburn about it.

He gave me a grudging nod. "It's not the way I wanted, but it's better than anything I've gotten in two months. And you're on the list for the party at Prada Tuesday night. Got a date?"

I thought of Grady. "I'll figure something out." I could take my brother, but he was too much like a curious puppy dog. He'd talk to everyone about everything. He'd never be able to pretend we were married.

Soon we were pulling down Forester's long gravel driveway lined with pine trees. It wound and curled until the house was revealed, like a wedding cake, looming in the distance.

"Quite the place." Mayburn pulled over. "Let's switch before we get close enough for anyone to see us. You drive stick, right?"

"Sort of."

He froze and glared. "You better drive stick *well*. This car is my baby."

"Let me at her." I got out of the car and swapped places

with Mayburn. He crouched on the floor of the passenger seat, looking foolish as he curled up in a ball and tucked his head down.

"Ease into the clutch really, really lightly," he said. He began spouting off a bunch of other instructions, which I let fly past me. Too much coaching tended to leave me confused rather than focused.

I didn't tell him I hadn't driven a stick-shift car since college. *Like riding a bike,* I told myself. I stepped on the clutch, put it into First and with the confident push on the gas that my college roommate had taught me, I was heading toward Forester's mansion.

"Nice," Mayburn said grudgingly.

As I reached the house, the front door opened. Annette came outside, her arms crossed over her black dress.

I parked on the right of the circle driveway, where Mayburn was shielded from her view. I jumped out and scampered to the front door before she could approach the car. "Annette, thanks for meeting me here. How are you?"

She frowned a disapproving glance at the car. "I'm fine, thank you."

I looked over my shoulder. "I don't have a car," I said. "I had to borrow this from a friend."

She gave a nod, then shook her head slightly as if to toss off the sight of the shiny little spitfire.

Annette held open the front door and gestured for me to come inside. I had a shot of nervousness. How was I supposed to ensure that she didn't lock the front door or that it wasn't one of those doors that locked automatically? Mayburn needed to be able to get at it so we could get back in later. I couldn't think of a way, so I simply followed her inside. She led me past the foyer, which was like a marble basketball court it was so huge, and into the living room decorated to the hilt, the French doors overlooking the back lawn and pool.

Annette sat on a wingback chair covered in soft taupe

leather and gestured for me to sit on the couch. How strange it was to see her there, as if she owned the house. In the past, I'd only encountered Annette as she moved through the place like a ghost, a phantom who brought food and wine and cleaned up clutter before you knew it was there.

"Would you like something to drink?" she said.

"No, thank you. I don't want to take up your time." I glanced at the front door. I needed to make sure it was open, and I needed to get Annette to the backyard so Mayburn could work his magic. "On second thought, I would like some water. And I forgot my cell phone from the car. I'll be right back."

As hoped, Annette nodded and left for the kitchen. I hurried to the front door and went outside, letting the door close behind me. I couldn't see Mayburn, which was good. I waited a moment, then tried the front door, which was blessedly open. I gave a thumbs-up in the general direction of the car, in case Mayburn was watching, and went back inside.

I stood in the living room instead of taking a seat, and when Annette returned, I asked her if she wouldn't mind going outside.

She gave a one-shouldered shrug, as if she cared little, and began leading me from the room.

"So, how are you?" I asked.

"About the same."

"The same?"

"The same as when we spoke yesterday."

"Ah. Right." I suppose Annette's statement was accurate—she still didn't have her two-million-dollar inheritance.

We went through one of the sets of doors and out onto the lawn.

"I'll leave you alone for a moment," Annette said, starting to turn.

"No, no, no!" I couldn't let her go back into the house without giving Mayburn a chance to do a number on the front door and the alarm. He'd told me to give him at least five minutes.

I grabbed Annette by the elbow. "Please, come with me," I said. "I don't think I can be alone."

She pulled her arm away and gave me a sharp glance but then, with a terse nod, she followed me.

We walked toward the pond, the grass spongy under our feet. In between the pine trees, the oaks stood tall, but there were few leaves on the ground, as if the groundskeeper had just been there that afternoon.

At the edge of the pond, we fell into silence. I tried to keep rough track of time in my head, wanting to give Mayburn what he needed, but I found it hard to care. Suddenly, I could see Sam on that day we met, the sky an ocean-blue color behind his head, his martini-green eyes staring at me with delight and a knowing—a knowing that seemed to suggest he understood me, or that he soon would. I could see Forester, too, his silver hair glinting in the sun, holding court at his summer party, always gracious, always truly glad to see everyone—whether they were one of his execs or one of his doormen. He loved his estate. It was fitting, in a way, that he had died out here.

"I can't believe he's gone." My words sounded small out on that big lawn.

"Yes," Annette answered simply, then after a few seconds, "I couldn't believe it when I found him."

I watched her face. It was completely composed—the way it always was. "I'm so sorry for you. I know that must have been awful."

"Yes. It was very shocking, but already I am growing accustomed to him being gone."

I narrowed my eyes. I couldn't help it. Was it so easy for her to move on because she'd done something to Forester, and now the stress of the situation was eased by the two million she hopefully could soon enjoy? But the cops had said they tested Forester's food. Of course, that didn't mean that she hadn't been in the house the whole time and simply swapped out his meal after he died.

She seemed to catch my look. "I'm old enough to know that this is the course of death, Isabel. And of life. No matter who it is that passes, the loved ones can never grasp it at first, even though we know that everyone dies. And then, sooner than we think, we work the reality of the situation into our daily lives. Later, what is surprising to us is not the death but the fact that we have continued to walk on."

I'd rarely heard her speak so many words in a row. "That's how it was when I lost my father," I said, "but then again, I was so young."

"It works the same. It's always the same."

"I'll never get used to Sam being gone."

She looked at me with some suspicion. "You really don't know where he is?"

"No."

A pause. She looked back at the pond, at the warbled reflection of our bodies and the trees behind us. "You will get used to his absence. Whether he returns tomorrow or never, you will grow accustomed to what has happened. You will work it into the fabric of your life, because that's what we do. Adaptation—it's an undeniable human reaction. You don't even need to control it for it to happen."

She turned, and we shared a long look.

"Thank you, Annette. I appreciate you letting me come here."

She gave a brisk bob of her head. "Forester would have appreciated it."

43

Lovell's, a restaurant located in a French provincial-style house, was a place where Forester used to like to eat steak and drink red wine. I took a seat at the bar there and, as arranged, waited for Mayburn's call. For two hours I munched on peanuts and sipped tonic and lemon, constantly looking at my cell phone. Finally, ready to float away on peanut salt and carbonated beverages, it rang.

"Jesus Christ," Mayburn said. "You'd think Annette had nowhere else to go."

"She probably doesn't."

"Well, she's gone now. No other staff around."

"I'm heading back."

"Go slow and quiet on the drive. And park halfway down under that bunch of oaks."

The night was heavy and still as I parked the car and walked through the long, inky blackness toward Forester's house. The gravel crunched under my feet, like someone chewing ice with their back molars. Tiny lights lined the driveway, but they were thirty yards apart, and in the spaces between I had the sense of being off kilter, as if the ground under my feet could turn to sand and suddenly give way.

Forester's house was dark when I reached it except for a few floodlights that highlighted the massive front columns and surrounding trees.

"Mayburn?" I whispered into the night.

I heard the snap of a breaking branch, and I swung around. No one there that I could see. "Mayburn?"

Silence answered me. A breeze swept through the estate, making the trees whisper and the hair on my arms stand up.

I walked to the front door and tried it. It swung open easily.

"Mayburn!" My whisper was more fierce now. But all I heard were a few creaks, the house settling for the night.

I stepped inside. *Thud!*

I swung around, my eyes veering, dodging at everything around me. What in the hell was that?

Then I realized it was the door, which had slammed shut. My heart pummeled my ribs. Had it closed by itself? I felt trapped in that big, dark house.

"Hey!" The word, whispered from somewhere deep in the house, made me jump again. "Izzy!"

I took a long breath. "Where in the hell are you?" I whispered back, afraid to move too far from the door, feeling the paranoid need to flee.

"In the library."

I made myself walk the marble hall, past the living room and through wooden pocket doors that led to the south wing.

I found Mayburn with a flashlight, going through the drawers in a desk.

"Forester called it a study, not a library." I didn't like the sight of Mayburn pawing through Forester's belongings.

"Whatever." He kept rummaging. "When did you say he got those letters?"

"I'm not sure. He told me about them a few weeks before he died."

"He's got a lot of stuff organized by date." Mayburn seemed to decide on one drawer. He propped up his flashlight, angled it at the drawer, kept rifling through it.

"What's that?" I pointed to a device the size of a jewelry box that was attached to the phone. A display on one end showed a lighted number.

"It's downloading all the calls made in and out of the house for the last month. Sometimes you find something interesting." He stood and took a small, red flashlight from his belt. He put it on the desk, along with something soft and white next to it. "Here's a flashlight for you. And gloves."

I crossed the room, put the gloves on and picked up the flashlight. I stood, my arms at my sides, feeling entirely inadequate and fighting the feeling that being here, in the midst of the remnants of Forester's life, was simply wrong. "What do you want me to do?"

"Give me one second to see if this is going to be easy."

I felt in the presence of a grave robber. To get my mind off it, I moved to the wet bar and looked at the shelf above it. There, Forester had placed a number of pictures—one of his wife, Liv, another of Shane, a few group photos with extended-family members.

I moved across the room to the bookshelves behind his desk.

I looked at Forester's wide selection of books, everything from Buddhist texts to Graham Greene to Dostoevsky to contemporary thrillers. I ran my finger, encased in the rubber gloves, over the spine of the books.

"Almost done here," Mayburn said. "But we've got no easy answer. Look on those shelves for the letters, will you? Maybe he kept them inside something."

The two upper bookshelves held all sorts of knickknacks, vases and bowls. I picked up each one, looking inside them, looking under them. At the end of the shelf, I found a white scalloped bowl made of coarse ceramic. Nothing was inside. I started to place the bowl on the shelf, but something tickled my brain.

I picked up the bowl again. I had the sensation that I'd seen it before, or something like it. Maybe even recently. I'd been in the study more than a few times, yet there was something about the bowl that seemed even more familiar than that.

"You got something?" Mayburn whispered.

"No, nothing. This reminds me of something, but I can't remember what."

Mayburn swung his flashlight and moved toward me. He took the bowl from my hands and turned it over. "Handmade." He shrugged. "But amateur. There's probably a bunch like it out there."

"Probably." I took the bowl from his hands, looked it over one last time and placed it on the shelf.

Mayburn went back to the desk, and I continued my search. When I came to the highest shelf, I reached up and found a large, flat, enamel box. I lifted the cover.

"Bingo," I said, excitement leaping through my body.

Inside, was a small stack of typed correspondence. I flipped through the letters, looking at the words. *For the good of Pickett Enterprises, you need to step down... We all know you're too old for the job... Please don't make this more difficult than it has to be...* And lastly, something in quotes. *"It is better to be violent, if there is violence in our hearts, than to put on the cloak of nonviolence to cover impotence."*

"What's with that quote?" I said.

"Never heard of it." Mayburn was reading over my shoulder.

"Who would write this to him?"

"Shane? Is he the kind of guy who feels impotent?"

I thought of Shane in his father's big, gorgeous office. "Not anymore he doesn't." I thought about it. "Maybe Walt Tenning, the CFO, or Chaz Graydon. Life is easier for them with Shane at the helm of Pickett Enterprises."

"We need to make copies of these letters and leave the copies where we found the originals," Mayburn said. "Then I'll check the originals for prints, as well as printer and paper type."

I pointed to a closet door, where I knew Forester kept a copier.

"I'll handle the copies," Mayburn said. "You go look for the medications he was taking."

"They're probably in the master bath." Which was in the north wing of the house, far away and bathed entirely in darkness.

"We need his heart medications. I want them analyzed, and I want a sample of those herbs you said he was taking."

"I'll wait for you."

"No way. The phone numbers are still downloading and the copies will take a few minutes. You never have a few minutes to spare in these situations. The sooner we get what we need and get out, the better."

I hesitated.

"Go, Izzy," Mayburn said.

Reluctantly, I left the study and tiptoed down the hallway, past the formal living room again.

I froze when I reached the pocket doors that signaled the entrance to the north wing where I'd only been once before when Forester had given me the tour.

Just then, I thought I saw a light swing by in an arc outside.

Turning off my flashlight, I scampered to the glass next to the front window. Careful to keep my body in the shadows, I peered through the windows. Nothing. It was as dark as when I'd walked down the driveway. Had it been lightning? The weather forecast had called for an evening storm. Or had it been the car light of someone following me? Or had Annette returned? I readied myself to run for Mayburn and tell him we had to bail.

But the light didn't return. Forester's estate looked calm and dark outside.

I went to the other side of the door and looked through the glass there. Again, nothing. I listened, trying to make my ears as keen as a dog's. I heard no sounds at all.

I must have imagined the light. But if it was my imagination, then my imagination was making my heart pound. Hard.

I took a deep breath and thought about Mayburn's words about having no time to spare. But maybe I should tell him about the light and let him decide if we should leave or not. I felt frozen with fear and indecision.

"Let's get this done with," I whispered to myself.

I broke into a trot and headed to the north wing. This time I didn't hesitate. I went from room to room, swinging the flashlight into each, hoping desperately we weren't being watched by someone outside.

The master bedroom was located at the end of the wing. The ceiling was vaulted and two stories high. The French doors overlooked the dark backyard. I went to a door on the other side. It led to a massive walk-in closet bigger than Sam's apartment and an equally large master bath. I rushed to the cabinets and opened them quickly. In one, I found a small army of pill bottles. I picked them up and examined them as fast as I could. A few I recognized were muscle relaxants, all very old, probably from a back injury I knew Forester had suffered. A few were for high cholesterol, also old. His cholesterol was a condition that Forester had beat, he said, and he attributed that success to the doctor in Chinatown, who Shane said was Dr. Song Li.

I didn't recognize a number of the other medications, and I started to get nervous about taking too much time. I decided simply to look at the dates of the medications. Finally, I found one that had been prescribed only three weeks before. The name of the medication sounded familiar, a heart drug.

Just then, I heard the soft shuffle of feet from the hallway. My arms, one still holding the medication, the other holding the flashlight, froze.

Mayburn stepped into the bathroom. "What do you have?"

"You scared the crap out of me," I said. "How about giving me some signal?"

He shrugged. "I never do this with other people."

"I thought I saw a light outside."

"Whoa, when?" His voice was alarmed.

"When I was walking past the front door."

"Why the hell didn't you tell me?" His head swiveled both ways, as if looking for someone.

"Because it went away. I thought I was imagining it, and I just wanted to get everything we need here before we leave."

He gestured at my hand. "Heart stuff?"

"I think so."

He took the bottle. "Let's do this and get the hell out of there." He shook out three tablets. "We'll take these for analysis, and hope they're the same as the rest in here." He dropped them in a small, plastic box he'd pulled from the pocket of his coat. "Now, what about the herbs?"

"I'm not even sure what they look like." I rooted around in the cabinet some more.

Mayburn shined his flashlight in the cabinet for extra light. "Let's go, Izzy." I heard impatience there, and if I wasn't mistaken, a little fear.

Finally, I found a small bottle that was a third full of dark-brown liquid. The white label listed the name of Dr. Song Li. "Got it."

"Great, I've got something for that." Mayburn took out a small white bottle capped with a medicine dropper. He used it to extract two droppersful of the liquid, which he squeezed into the bottle.

Just as I was putting the brown liquid back on the cabinet shelves, I heard a low rumble and the crunching of gravel.

"Shit," Mayburn said. "Turn your light off."

We both switched off our flashlights, shrouding the bathroom in shadow.

I felt something touch my hand, and I jumped.

"It's me," Mayburn hissed. "Stay behind me. We'll leave through the back."

"But we have to turn the alarm on or Annette will know someone was here."

"I've got it."

I followed Mayburn, so close to his back that a few times, I almost bumped into him when he slowed.

He went to the alarm panel near the kitchen door. "Quiet a minute."

We both stood in absolute stillness. I concentrated with every cell in my body to hear something.

Mayburn punched a series of numbers into the alarm. "Okay, it's armed. We just have to leave in forty-five seconds. There's a door in the garage that leads to the backyard. Let's go."

I followed him again, trying hard not to make any noise with my shoes, jumpier now. The garage had no windows and was entirely black.

Mayburn took hold of my hand. "This way," he whispered. He flashed his light on, for one second illuminating the door at the back, behind six of Forester's cars. Just as quickly, the light was off, and we were sneaking through the darkness. "We've got to hurry. We've got about fifteen seconds to get out or the alarm will go off."

When we stepped out into the backyard, I breathed a sigh of relief. We crept around the side of the house toward the front. Mayburn peeked around the corner at the front driveway.

He stepped back and spoke into my ear. "I don't see anyone, but let's stay in the trees."

We slunk into the trees and headed away from the house, keeping the driveway in our sight. Finally, we came to Mayburn's car.

"Stay here," he said.

I watched him move around the car, shining the flashlight. "C'mere," he said. On the ground, near his back bumper was a vague imprint in the gravel. "It's a footprint."

"It could be ours."

"Did you walk around the back of the car when you got out?"

"No. So whose is it?"

"Someone who wanted to get my license-plate number."

"The cops?"

He shook his head. "They wouldn't be so quiet about it. Get in the car."

With the lights off, he rolled down Forester's driveway, and I was left feeling like a thief, one who had come very close to getting caught.

44

Day Seven

Monday, I woke up yearning for Sam so intensely I felt physically sick by his absence. I had gotten used to seeing him every morning and at the end of every day. Each time I saw that cute, sweet face, it was like getting into a hot bath—that initial disappearance of breath, followed by a tingling of every inch of my skin, then the breath rushing back to fill up the lungs, and then the utter relaxation, the utter bliss. Without him, my body didn't seem to know how to loosen up. I couldn't remember what it was like to take a full, satisfied breath of air. My guilt over the wedding hit again, closely followed by the hard stabs of a million questions—*Was he overwhelmed, too? Was he a bad guy and I never saw it? What in the hell is going on?* And more. So many more.

I swung my legs over the edge of the bed and tried to breathe deep. No luck.

I called Q. He was already at the office.

"You have a meeting with Jane Augustine and her agent at eleven," he said. "Jane left a message to finalize everything. She's ready to sign the contract."

"Great." I would have to tell him I was losing the Pickett work. But I had time. *Gradual.* That's what Shane said. And as long as the work was still mine, I was going to give it my all. I'd go to the meeting. I'd keep doing my best for Forester until they wouldn't let me anymore. I liked pretending that this was any other Monday morning. "Fun party on Saturday," I said. "How was the aftermath?"

Q groaned. "Simone hooked up with some guy that Max's sister brought."

"What? How old was the guy?"

"Late thirties."

"And how old is Simone?"

"Sixties."

"Jiminy Christmas, that's impressive." And oddly hopeful, I thought. Life, apparently, does go on and on.

"Did you see the news last night?"

No, I was going through Forester's house right about the time the news was on. I thought of that white, scalloped bowl again. For some reason, it kept lingering in my mind. "I missed it. Anything new?"

"Same recap of the Forester and Sam stuff. New picture of Sam, though."

"Which one?"

"Looks like a professional thing. Just him. Wearing that brown suit he looks so hot in."

"We got that at Bloomie's." I thought of that night—we'd gone shopping for Sam and then to Pane Caldo for dinner. We sat in a cozy front-window booth and talked about wedding plans. That was when the planning was still fun.

I told Q I'd see him at the firm. I went into my home office and got on the Internet. I checked my bank accounts and other sites. No one seemed to have logged in, and there was no sign that anyone had been in my apartment since I'd changed the locks. I went to my e-mail. Nothing from Alyssa. No voice mails.

I looked up the number for the research institute where she worked and called. This time a receptionist answered. I remembered that Indianapolis was an hour ahead of Chicago. I asked for Alyssa and was connected.

As the phone rang, I planned on leaving another message but, on the third ring, it was picked up. "Alyssa Thornton."

My body tingled with a bizarre mix of excitement and utter jealousy. "Alyssa, it's Izzy McNeil."

Silence.

"Sam Hollings's fiancée," I added.

"Right, sure." More silence.

"So, I don't know if you got my e-mail and messages over the weekend…"

"Yeah, I did. Just about ten minutes ago."

"I'm looking for Sam, and—"

"I don't know where he is."

My excitement dissipated. "Oh. Well, it's just that he's disappeared, and—"

"Disappeared?" she said with alarm.

"Yes. No one has seen him since last Tuesday."

She was quiet.

"Look, Alyssa, I have reason to believe that Sam was in Indianapolis recently. Obviously, you're there, and so I thought you might have seen him."

"No, I haven't." It sounded like a practiced response.

"Have you spoken to Sam recently?"

More quiet.

"Alyssa, Sam is in some very serious trouble. It appears that when he left, he took off with thirty million dollars of property belonging to a client of his."

"What? Sam would never do that!" I heard the disbelief in her voice, and I recognized it as blind devotion, something I knew well myself. Was I being stupid to keep returning to the response that said—*There must be a reason. Sam is a good person. And Sam wouldn't have done anything to harm Forester?*

"Look, Alyssa, I believe he wouldn't do something like

that, either. At least not without very good reason. But it's pretty clear he took these shares. There's also the fact that the person who owned the shares ended up dead on the same night Sam took off. People are asking questions about whether Sam had anything to do with his death."

"This is insane. He would never hurt anyone. And if he stole that money then why would he be borrowing from me?" She stopped abruptly.

I felt my pulse quicken. I stood from the chair and began to pace the office. "When did he borrow from you?"

Nothing.

"Have you seen or talked to Sam this week?"

"I...I don't know what to say."

"What you should say is the truth! Look, I'm sorry to raise my voice, but this is serious. Sam has disappeared without a trace. The FBI is investigating him."

"Oh, God."

"Please, tell me what you know. Have you heard from Sam?"

More infuriating silence, and then finally, "Yes. I saw him last Wednesday morning."

45

"You saw Sam last Wednesday?" I said to Alyssa. The day after he disappeared.

"Yes."

I squeezed the phone so tight I thought I might break it. He had gone to Alyssa. He had disappeared, and he had headed for Indianapolis and Alyssa, the one person he knew made me jealous.

I felt a crushing weight. I sat on the floor, right in the place I was standing and slumped back against the wall.

"I told him I wasn't going to say anything, but I had no idea all this was going on," Alyssa said.

I had so many questions, but at the same time I wondered if any of them mattered. Sam had betrayed me, that much seemed true. "Are you…involved with Sam? Is that what this is?"

"Involved?" She sounded confused. "No. Not at all. You guys are engaged."

"I thought we were. Now he's gone. Why did he go to Indy?"

"He said he needed help. He called me on Tuesday and asked if he could borrow a credit card and a passport."

"From you?"

"From my brother. Sam actually looks a lot like my brother. He said he needed them, just for a week or two, and that he'd return them."

"Your brother handed over his credit card and passport? What are you guys thinking? He could be a terrorist!"

"Sam is not a terrorist," she said with scorn. I had to agree, but *still.*

"My brother loves Sam," Alyssa continued. "I mean, Sam was like a big brother to him. He grew up with Sam around. My brother is on the college football team now at Indiana. That's why I'm here, to keep an eye on him and give him some family nearby. But anyway, we've known Sam forever. We trust him. Or we did."

"When was the last time you talked to Sam before last week?"

"I guess it was after the reunion. We'd always kept in touch. Loosely, I mean. But then he just dropped out of the picture."

Because I asked him to. "And then you got a phone call out of the blue?"

"Yeah, Tuesday night—I guess it was early in the evening—and he asked if there was any way he could borrow some cash."

"How much?"

"Seven hundred dollars."

"And then he asked for the passport and credit card?"

"Right. My brother got a passport last year to do this exchange program, and it's not like he needed it right now. Anyway, Bloomington, where my brother goes to school, is only an hour away, so I drove there and picked up the passport and credit card."

"And then you met Sam?"

"He said he was driving to Indy and asked me to meet him first thing Wednesday morning."

If Sam had driven Tuesday night to Indy, where had he slept? In his car? In a hotel? It was surreal that a week ago I knew every detail of Sam's life, down to what he ate for breakfast, what time he intended to work out, what he discussed with his mother when he called for one of their biweekly discussions. At least he hadn't spent the night with Alyssa. If she could be believed.

"We met in a hotel for breakfast on Wednesday," Alyssa continued. "It's on the southwest side of town, by the airport."

"How did he look?"

"I don't know. Tired, I guess. And worried. But he was Sam."

He was Sam. I knew what that meant. We both did. Gorgeous Sam. Funny Sam. Sam, who lit up everyone's room and everyone's life. Or at least that's what we *thought* we knew of Sam.

"Did he tell you why he was asking for the money and stuff?"

"He said he had some things he had to take care of and it required that he not use his own ID. He said he might charge a few things on the credit card, but he promised he would send me a money order paying everything back within the next two weeks, along with the passport and credit card."

"Have you received anything?"

"Not yet."

"I need your brother's name."

She didn't respond.

"And his address and credit-card number," I added.

"I don't want to get him in trouble. Or myself."

"It's Sam who's in trouble."

"But if the FBI knows I gave my brother's passport to someone to use…"

"I've got an investigator working on the case. I'm just going to give him the information. I won't turn this information over to the FBI unless I have to."

A sigh. "Okay, here it is."

I grabbed a pen and scrap paper off the desk and sat back on the floor, scribbling the information Alyssa gave me. Her brother's name was Alec Thornton. Was Sam somewhere, introducing himself as Alec?

"Did Sam give you any kind of information about where he was going or what he was doing?" I asked.

"Nothing. He said he couldn't tell me anything, and he asked me not to tell anyone he'd seen me. Then we just talked for the rest of the time."

"About what?"

"You know. Small talk. What's going on with my family and his."

I felt the burn of jealousy sear its way into my belly. *Alyssa* had gotten to have small talk with Sam last week.

"When is the last time *you* saw him?" she asked.

I told her the basics of what had happened over the last week. When I was done, Alyssa said, "My God, Izzy. What do you think Sam is doing?" Her voice was empathetic and low, and I thought that maybe in a different life, Alyssa and I could have been friends.

"I have no idea. It doesn't make any sense to me."

"Or me. And I know Sam better than anyone."

That jealous burn returned, along with my usual disdain for her. I opened my voice to correct her to tell her that it was *I* who knew Sam best now. But as soon as I started to say it, I realized the inaccuracy of that statement. If I knew Sam best, I would be able to understand some little part of what he had done, and yet I was still very, very much in the dark.

Alyssa seemed to sense my turmoil. "I'm sorry. I shouldn't have said that, and I'm sure it's not true. I know you and Sam have something very special. 'Extraordinary.' That's the word he used, anyway."

I laid my head back against the wall behind me. "When did he say that?"

"At the reunion." A pause. "I'll be honest with you, I went back to that reunion hoping to rekindle things with Sam."

"I know. I could tell."

"Really?" She laughed softly. "I guess subtlety isn't my forte. I've always worn my heart on my sleeve. And I didn't even know he was engaged until I got there. But Sam wasn't having any of it. You could probably tell that, too. All he was doing was talking about you or gazing across the room at you. Even when I saw him last week and we were making small talk, it was mostly about you."

I closed my eyes. "What did he say?"

"That you guys have an amazing relationship."

"I thought so," I said, my voice barely audible.

"And he said you were smart and sexy and that you weren't afraid of anything."

I hung up the phone a few minutes later, thinking that Sam was wrong. I was very afraid.

46

In Grady's car heading to the office, I called Mayburn.

"Sam borrowed a credit card and passport from an ex-girlfriend's brother," I told him.

"Damn, that's good info. How did you find out?"

"I didn't tell you, but I got a postcard from him."

"When?"

"Friday."

"*Why* didn't you tell me?"

"Because in the postcard he asked me not to."

"Jesus, Izzy, you have to—"

"I know!" I said, cutting him off. "I have to tell you everything or you can't help me. I get it. I wanted to tell you, but he asked me not to in the postcard, and I just wanted to see what I could find out first. Now I've learned something, so shut up and listen, will you?"

"That's a hell of an outburst."

"*Please* shut up."

"Go ahead."

"The postcard was from Indy." I told him what the postcard said, and the fact that I'd remembered that Alyssa lived there. I told him about my conversation with her and how Sam had borrowed money, along with her brother's passport and credit card. I gave him the credit-card number and Alec's address in Bloomington.

"I'll start tracing it. And I'm leaving in five minutes to drop off Forester's herbs and heart medication at the lab."

"I'm hoping to get the autopsy and the records of Forester's cardiologist today."

"Will you be able to read them?"

"Not well, but I know someone who does."

"Can you get the records for the Chinese doc?"

"Not sure, but I'll try. Meanwhile, do you think I should call the FBI about Sam and Alyssa's brother?"

"Are you under subpoena?"

"No, I was questioned informally."

"Did they tell you to call if you learned anything?"

I thought back to the conversation at FBI headquarters. "No, I don't think so."

"Then it's up to you. Hey, I checked out that quote in that one letter to Forester. The one about how it's better to be violent than to cover up impotence?"

"Yeah?"

"It's a quote from Gandhi. So keep your eyes out for any Gandhi groupies."

We hung up, and I watched out the window as LaSalle Street rolled by. The tourists were already in line outside what was known as the Rock-N-Roll McDonald's. I usually rolled my eyes at such a sight. Why were these people coming to town and visiting a freaking McDonald's? But now I felt only envy. I wished I was in a foreign city, with nothing to do except buy an Egg McMuffin.

I decided I wasn't going to call the FBI. At least not yet. So far, Mayburn was making more of an effort than the feds. Mayburn and I were at least looking into Forester's death, which, to all appearances, the police and the feds weren't doing. And at least Mayburn kept me in the loop about what he found.

At the office, I got the usual stares and whispers from the assistants as I made my way to my office.

Q was there, a nervous expression on his face.

"What's up?" I asked.

"Can I talk to you?" He gestured toward my office.

Inside, we closed the door. I sat at my chair, and Q perched on the edge of the desk. His usual blazer was already off, and his blue button-down shirt was rolled up at the sleeves, as if it was six at night instead of eight-thirty in the morning.

"Do I want to hear this?" I asked.

"Probably not. Elliot came down with a memo from Edward Chase saying Tanner is taking over all the Pickett cases." Edward Chase was the head of the firm's executive committee. He called the shots. "Except the Jane Augustine contract because they know you're close to finishing that."

I placed my fingers on the bridge of my nose and rubbed, then harder, trying to rub away the time—speeding past me like a fast storm, picking up everything and tearing it all apart. "God, I didn't think this would happen so soon."

"You didn't think *what* would happen?"

I pulled my fingers away. Looked at Q. "I should have told you at the party, but I was hoping to come up with some way to stop it. We're losing the Pickett cases."

Q stood, his arms tense, giving him the look of a boxer about to get in the ring. "Why?"

"Shane wants to give the work to Tanner."

"You've got to be kidding me! How could he do that?"

I told Q about the rest of my meeting with Shane, how he felt he had to build the best team for himself, in order to run Pickett.

"He can't do this."

"Well, it seems he can. I'll try to get him to back off. I was thinking that maybe he'd let us keep a fraction of the cases, while I go looking for other entertainment-law work."

Q gave me a doubtful look. We both knew that the market for entertainment law in Chicago was small. Most artists and creative companies found local counsel in Chicago, but when they got big, they went to one of the L.A. or New York firms. The work that remained was sought after and picked over by the many people in Cook County who wanted to call themselves entertainment lawyers, if only because it sounded cool.

"I can't blame either Tanner or Shane too much," I said. "Tanner has always wanted this work back, and who wouldn't? And Shane, well, he doesn't know what he's doing with this job, and he needs people to help him."

"Why are you so calm?" Q moved aside some file folders from one of my chairs and fell into it.

"Am I? It's just that I can only do so much. I'm trying to get my head around the fact that Forester is gone, and I'm trying to figure out where in the hell Sam is, and I've got…" I paused. I wanted to say, *And I've got Mayburn, who I'm working with.*

"I know." Q looked away. "You've got a lot on your shoulders."

"It's hard to care about work when I don't know what's going on with Sam." Although my phone call with Alyssa had somewhat alleviated the feeling of loss. He had turned to her. Not me.

"Look, I know this is hard on you, too," I said to Q. "And I'm going to find something else for us."

"Sure." He didn't sound sure of my words at all. "Hey," he said, sitting up straight, "if it helps, I got the autopsy and records of Forester's cardiologist."

"You did? Great."

Q left and brought back a file folder about four inches thick.

I groaned. "It's bigger than I thought." I flipped through the file, trying to make sense of the EKG slips and the office notes and the operative reports. Reading medical records was an art form, one I'd never had reason to master.

I called Grady's office. "Can I come for a visit?"

"Please. I'm in the middle of a dep summary that's kicking my ass."

I took the elevator up to the floor we commonly called the "med mal" department. There, Grady and his group represented hospitals and doctors who had been sued or gotten themselves in disciplinary trouble.

Grady's office was near the end of the hall. It was a mess, like mine, but he had hung some interesting art on the walls—one a pop-art piece he'd bought at the Old Town art fair, another a colorful postmodern scribble his mother had done.

"Hey!" He walked around his desk and greeted me with an awkward hug. Grady had never stood for me before, much less come around his desk. His declaration of sorts from the party lingered in the air between us.

I pecked him awkwardly on the cheek and then quickly sat on the small couch in front of the window.

"How are you?" His brown eyes were earnest, and strangely it made me sad. As much as I appreciated how Grady apparently felt about me, I longed for normalcy again, for the days of yore when he would simply mock me about my flop-sweat and head off into the night to date some twenty-year-old.

"I'm okay." I paused. Did I need to deal, somehow, with what he'd said Saturday night? "Remember on Saturday when you said you'd do anything you could to help me get through this?"

"Yeah. You going to give me my car back?"

I reached into my pocket and put his key on his desk. "It's in the garage. Fourth floor."

He looked at the key, then me. "Need anything else?"

I put Forester's file on his desk. "Help me read these records?"

He picked up the records and leafed through them. "Don Loman," he said. "I know him. I've used him as an expert on a few cases. What do you want to know from these records?"

"The autopsy says Forester had a myocardial infarction, but Forester had told me he'd had a number of tests recently and that he had passed with flying colors. I guess I'm just trying to find out if these records say something different."

"Give me a second." Grady pushed his chair back, crossed a leg and started perusing the file.

I watched him. I liked how his concentration shifted so intently into work mode, liked how he flipped from one record to another and back again, his eyes flicking easily over the medical hieroglyphics that would have boggled me. I felt a rush of affection for him then, for someone who truly liked me. And was still in town.

Grady raised his eyes, and they fastened on mine. "You're staring."

"Sorry. Do what you have to do. I'll just be over here." I stood up and lifted a *Code of Civil Procedure* from his shelf.

"Exciting reading," he said.

"The provision on 619 motions is particularly interesting."

Grady went back to flipping through the records. Ten minutes later, he said, "Well, it looks like Forester's cardiovascular health had improved greatly since he had that previous heart attack. At that time, they did an angiogram and a cardiac cath and believed he didn't need surgery. He was a good patient. He took all the meds he was supposed to. He changed his diet and, just a few weeks ago, he had a battery of tests, all of which were normal."

"So then how did he die of a heart attack?"

"Once the heart is weakened, you're always at risk."

"I wonder what Loman thinks about his death."

"We can call him and find out."

"We can?" I slid back into a chair across from Grady. "I thought you couldn't talk to doctors without a subpoena."

"You're allowed if you're representing the patient or the estate, which the firm does."

Grady flipped through a Rolodex and dialed his phone. "Hi, Gwen," he said. "Is Dr. Loman around?" A pause. "I've got a new case I want him to look at."

He gave me a thumbs-up. "These guys charge six hundred an hour to review records. They always get on the phone for a new case. I'll put him on speaker."

A minute later, a deep voice came through the speaker. "Morning, Grady."

"Good morning, Dr. Loman. I want to talk to you about a new case, but I have a few questions first. About Forester Pickett. I've got another attorney here with me. Izzy McNeil. She was Mr. Pickett's lead attorney."

He had that right. I *was* the lead attorney. Previously. No longer.

"My condolences," Dr. Loman said. "I'm sad as hell about Forester."

"The firm is representing the estate, and we were wondering if we could ask you a couple questions about your treatment of him."

Dr. Loman didn't say anything for a few seconds. "Do I need to get separate counsel for this? Any chance I'm going to get sued here?"

Grady looked at me.

I shook my head and spoke up. "No, Doctor, it doesn't appear there will be any suit in this case whatsoever. In fact, everyone is very anxious to close the estate and move on. We just have a few questions."

"I've got a cabbage in forty minutes, but if you can make it quick, go ahead."

Cabbage? I gave Grady an inquisitive glance.

"Coronary artery bypass graft," he said.

I nodded. "We'll be brief, Dr. Loman. You signed the death certificate, is that right?"

"Yes, I got called to the E.R. Forester was already gone. I examined him, reviewed the EMT records and talked to one of the EMTs. Classic presentation of an MI, myocardial infarction."

"Did you order a tox screen as part of the autopsy?" Grady asked.

"No need," Dr. Loman said. "Common things happen in common ways. This was an MI."

"Why was there a risk of repeat heart attack in a patient like Forester who'd taken such good care of himself?"

"Well, there's always a risk. Even if you're on anticoagulants, like Forester was. Any number of things can increase that risk—depression, stress, other medications."

"Was Forester on any meds that could have increased the risk of a heart attack?"

"Not that I know of."

"Were you aware he saw a Chinese doctor who prescribed herbs?"

"Yes, he told me about that when he first saw her. In fact, there should be a notation in my chart about that. She provided a list of the herbs she mixed for him, and I didn't believe there was any contraindication for him taking them. To be honest, I didn't think there was any real upside either, but I'm not an integrated-medicine specialist."

"Could the anticoagulants that Forester was taking have in any way caused his heart attack?" Grady asked.

"No, they shouldn't. They can cause stroke, if not taken properly, but they should have only helped prevent an attack."

"So there's nothing really you can point to that caused his recent attack?" Grady asked.

"I wish there was. As I always say when I testify, medicine is not an exact science. You lawyers just try to make it one. So what's this new case you have for me?"

"You know what, Doctor?" Grady said. "I have to call you right back. I thought I had the file in front of me and I don't."

Grady and I thanked the doctor and hung up.

"Can you find the notation he made about Forester's herbs?" I asked.

Grady flipped through the medical records again, quicker this time, and found an entry in the office notes. "Here it is." He turned the records around to face me.

Patient seeing Dr. Song Li for Chinese holistic care. Dr. Li prescribed patient herbal tonic "Move Mountains."

I looked up at Grady. "Move Mountains? What's that?"

He shrugged.

The herbs in the tonic were also listed, things like, *astragalus root, schisandra fruit* and *dendrobium herb.*

"These mean anything to you?" I asked Grady.

"Nah."

Finally, the medical record listed an address and phone number for Dr. Li. I took a pen off Grady's desk and a scrap of paper and copied the herbs and the contact information. "Can we get on the Web for a second and see if there's anything there about this doctor?"

Grady turned toward his computer and ran the mouse over the pad. He went to Google and typed in "Dr. Song Li," then "Dr. Li" then "Dr. Li Chicago" and a host of other searches. None of the results that came up were for the right Dr. Li.

"Where in the heck did Forester find this lady?" Grady muttered.

"He said he was recommended by a friend after his heart surgery. He was scared of dying, and he was ready to try anything. He's been seeing her for a while."

I gathered up the records. I wanted to call Mayburn with all the info.

"Thanks for your help," I said to Grady.

He studied me for a second, and I wondered, again, if we should discuss Saturday night. "You let me know what else you need," Grady said.

I thought of the party at Prada that Mayburn wanted me to go to. The one I was supposed to bring a "husband" to. "Feel like going to a party tomorrow night?"

"Sure." No hesitation.

"It's a presale for some charity. I don't know much about it."

"Whatever." He shrugged. "I'll be your Sam stand-in."

I laughed uncomfortably. "Well, as a matter of fact, I kind of need you to pretend you're my husband."

Grady raised his eyebrows. "Now who's moving too fast?"

"It's kind of a long story. I'll explain at some point." I

stood. I felt better suddenly, just by doing something, moving, making plans. "I'll call you tomorrow."

Back at my office, Q was packing up case files with a forlorn look. My stomach dropped hard. He handed me a slip with Mayburn's name and cell phone on it. "Are we working with him on a case?" he asked.

"Um. Kind of."

Q waited expectantly.

"Just some things I'm closing up for Forester."

"You're having him look into Forester's death, aren't you?"

"I just talked to his heart doctor. He said it was a classic heart attack. But I just want to make sure. For Forester. I told you about those threats."

Q shook his head. Then, "Mayburn said he had information for you." He picked up a box of files. "I'll be back."

I called Mayburn and told him about the conversation with Dr. Loman and the fact that I'd gotten Grady to agree to the Prada party the next night. And to be my husband. I gave him the list of herbs Dr. Li had prescribed as well as her address and phone number.

"Good work," Mayburn said. Then he cleared his throat. "I've got some news, too. First, Alec Thornton's credit card hasn't been used in the last week."

I leaned forward onto my desk, feeling as if the air had been sucked from me. "I just thought…" I said. "I guess I thought this was the best lead on Sam."

"Yeah, I know. Not yet anyway. But I did get something for you."

I sat up straight. "Tell me."

"This sound familiar to you?" He read off a number with a 312 area code.

"That's Sam's cell-phone number."

"Yeah, well…I'll just get to the point. That number appears to be the last one called from Forester's study on the night he died."

My body froze. I literally couldn't move. My mind felt as if it was frozen, too. "What does that mean?" I managed to say.

"What time did you say Sam got to that wedding coordinator's office?"

I told him.

"Looks like Forester called Sam about ten minutes before that."

My mind struggled to regroup, to process what this could represent. "That makes sense. Sam was worried about something. And he said it had to do with Forester."

"And what time did Sam leave the office?" Mayburn asked.

I told him.

He grunted.

"But that phone call doesn't mean anything, right? I mean, Forester often called Sam after hours to talk about investments and stuff."

"What kind of car does Sam drive?"

"A Lexus."

"Kind of a white color?"

"Yes." My voice had gone quiet. That frozen feeling returned, and my body literally felt chilled along with it.

"Yeah, thought so. I went back to Lake Forest early this morning and spoke to the three neighbors in the vicinity of Forester's house. Told them I was with a detective. They thought I was the police. Anyway, two of the neighbors didn't remember anything from that night."

"And the third?"

"The third said she saw a white Lexus turning in to Forester's driveway. About fifty minutes after Sam left the wedding coordinator's office."

I stared straight ahead at the closed door of my office. "And?" I sensed there was more.

"You know how when Annette found Forester, he was already dead?"

"Yes." I could barely hear my own words now.

"The estimated time of death is sometime within the hour the white Lexus pulled in Forester's driveway."

47

The meeting with Jane Augustine would be my last, apparently, since I would no longer be representing Pickett Enterprises.

Since talking to Mayburn, a fear had taken up residence in my belly, leaving me with a hollow feeling. And yet as I gave my name at the office of Jane's lawyer/agent, Steve Severny, the moment had a strange, sweet, wistful quality now that I knew the Pickett work was going away.

Five minutes later, I gave a copy of the final contract to Jane, who looked stunning in a black suit and red scarf, her black hair falling over her shoulders. I handed copies to Severny, as well. I placed one before my chair and remained standing.

The meeting was being held in a conference room that overlooked the river. I glanced down for a moment at Fulton's, a restaurant where just two short weeks ago, Sam and I had gone after work for oysters and beer.

"Okay," I said, trying to focus myself as well as everyone else, "let's get down to business. Jane, we're so happy that you're staying with us for another three years." I went on to discuss how Jane was a star in the Pickett Enterprises family. I did not mention that very soon I would no longer be a member of said family.

As I started to wind down, I noticed Jane looking uncomfortable.

Severny, a tall man who'd had a lot of Botox and wore his

salt-and-pepper hair slicked back, held up his hand. "We've got an issue."

"With what? Jane told us she was ready to sign." I looked at Jane. She was studying the contract, her head down. "Jane told us to finalize everything, and I have."

"We'd like an out clause after one year," her agent said.

"What? You know as well as I do that fixed-term contracts are standard in this industry."

"True, but Pickett is an unknown entity now that Forester has passed away. We have no idea how the company will be run from here on out." He gave me a smug smile.

I hated to say it, but he had a point. I saw Shane in Forester's office. Could he handle the job? Or would he leave it to Walt and Chaz? Did either want the power so badly that they would threaten or harm Forester? In reality, it was too soon to tell how Pickett would be run.

But in the meantime, there was no way in hell I was granting a clause that would let Jane out of her contract in a year. "Sorry," I said. "Can't agree to that."

"I talked to Tanner Hornsby earlier, and he said Pickett Enterprises would consider it."

My blood started to simmer. "Tanner isn't handling this negotiation." *At least not yet.* "There will be no out clause."

"Well, then we're going to have to go back to square one," the attorney said.

I looked at Jane. She gave a helpless shrug.

I stood. "This meeting is over." I picked up my bag and left.

Jane ran into the hall after me. "Izzy, I'm so sorry about this mess."

I hit the button for the elevator and turned around. "Then tell your agent that you've already agreed to this contract. More than once."

"He just gets on those power trips. I don't know what's going on."

"Jane, get some balls and get your agent to say yes. You've

got until five tomorrow." I turned and got in the elevator before she could say anything else. I liked Jane. A lot. But my patience, with everything, had run its course.

I pulled my cell phone out of my purse. I'd had it on silent for the meeting, but now I saw that Mayburn had called three times. I also had a text message.

It was from Mayburn—The list of herbs you gave me doesn't match what was in Forester's house. The real herb mix was predominantly ma huang, which could have caused a heart attack. When are you seeing the doc?

I called him as soon as I got on the street. "What's ma huang?"

"It's ephedra."

"I thought ephedra was banned by the FDA?"

"Only for a few months. I got ahold of an herbalist. He said ma huang was linked to a couple deaths some years ago, but they lifted the ban. Apparently, the herb is great when taken in small doses and for a short period of time. It can be used for weight loss and even asthma. But it shouldn't be taken by a patient like Forester who has a history of a heart condition. Worse than that, there was a *lot* of ma huang in those herbs we tested from Forester's home. There was more ma huang than is usually seen in anything. Way more than should normally be prescribed. Like ninety percent."

"So why give it to him?"

"The herbalist told me there isn't any reason to give him this much ma huang at one time."

"If the ma huang caused the heart attack, why would Forester have had such normal test results a few weeks ago?"

"According to the date on that bottle of herbs, he'd started taking this batch of herbs around the same time. Even if he'd had it in his system for a day or two, the tests could have been normal if the herbs weren't causing arrhythmia at the time. In other words, the night he died, the amount of ma huang in his system could have caught up with him and caused an irregular heartbeat and then a heart attack."

"So, the big question is why did Dr. Li give him that herb and why so much of it?"

"Exactly." I heard him moving around. "How soon can you see her?"

I pulled the piece of paper out of my bag where I'd written Dr. Li's contact info. "I'm calling her now."

48

On Wentworth and Twenty-fourth Street, one of the main intersections in Chinatown, the streets were filled with hustling locals carrying plastic bags with vegetables and packets of noodles hanging from them. All signs were in Chinese; sometimes with an English translation listed below. The street lamps were white lanterns with gold dragons on top. Green-and-red pagodas decorated the end of the street, while the Sears Tower hulked in the distance behind them.

"We've got half an hour to kill," I said to Maggie. "Let's get something to eat."

When Dr. Li agreed to see me that afternoon, I had called Maggie immediately. She had represented a couple of drug runners—*alleged* drug runners—who operated out of Chinatown, and she'd gotten to know the area well. Plus, I wanted to update the attorney I hired for Sam and me on what I'd learned. More than anything, I needed my best friend with me.

In the cab on the way over, I told her about Sam's Lexus arriving at Forester's around the time he died, and the fact that Forester had been given an herb by the Chinese doctor that might have caused his death.

Maggie pointed at a restaurant where tiny English letters read Evergreen. "This is where they take me when they're looking to sign me up for a case." She was talking about the drug clients she represented.

"And when the case is over and you've won? Where do they take you then?"

She pointed up the street. "A place much less westernized, where they feed me food I can't recognize and get me drunk on Du Kang."

"What's that?"

"Don't ask."

Maggie's clients loved to take her out after she'd gotten someone a "not guilty." It always made me nervous, because she was a tiny golden-haired girl getting taken to places in Chinatown or in Mexican neighborhoods where she didn't speak the language and where we'd never find her if they decided they weren't so happy with her representation. But Maggie loved it. She insisted she had to spend quality time with her clients if she was going to tell a jury with a straight face that they should let them walk.

Inside Evergreen, the female hostess recognized Maggie and hurried us to a table with a white tablecloth topped with white butcher paper. The place had forest-green carpeting, and vases of fake flowers dotted the room. It was also decorated with religious-looking Chinese art and gold-leaf screens on which koi fish and storks were painted.

Soon, plate after plate after bowl after plate arrived in front of us—egg drop soup in white china cups trimmed in blue; pot stickers with gelatinous shiny skins shaped like cut onions; a yellow-and-pink mass of egg and shrimp, swimming amidst a warm brown broth in a glass pie tin.

Along with it, the hostess placed in front of us little glass plates of hot chili oil. "Use lots."

As we ate, I told Maggie about my talk with Shane and the phone call with Alyssa.

Maggie listened in that intent way she has—head down, bottom lip slightly open. She nodded, she stopped me, she asked me a thousand questions, especially about what I'd learned from Alyssa. She, too, was concerned that maybe we should tell the authorities, but when we reviewed our contact with them, it was clear that the cops had closed their case and therefore we had no duty to tell them anything. As for the feds, they hadn't subpoenaed me or asked me to report any information to them.

"And you don't think they're taping my phone conversations?" I asked. This had occurred to me after I got off the phone with Alyssa, and it bothered me.

Maggie shook her head. "Wiretapping is considered more serious than just tailing someone. You're not a suspect or a person of interest. Yet."

"Yet?" I stopped spooning the shrimp egg foo yong on my plate.

"Who knows what Sam is doing. He might have used your name or your information on certain documents." She drizzled a vast amount of chili oil on another pot sticker and popped it in her mouth whole. "Yum!"

I sat back, letting the spoon clank on my plate. "Are you serious?"

"I've seen it before," she said through her mouthful of food.

She stopped chewing and seemed to notice my stricken face. "Let's talk about something else for a second."

"What else is there?" That hollow feeling returned, despite the food in my stomach.

"Tell me about the Halloween party."

I filled her in on the costumes and Simone. And then I told her about Grady.

That lower lip of hers dropped farther away from her mouth. She pushed away her plate. "I guess I've always known that Grady was a little in love with you."

"What? No way."

"Yeah way. He's got those eyes when he looks at you. He just kept it under wraps, but now that Sam is gone…"

"I still don't know what to do about it."

She shrugged. "Let him love you. Let him help you. You could use it."

I couldn't argue with that.

When we were done, we'd barely touched all the food. The waitress packaged the leftovers in brown paper bags and delivered them with two fortune cookies. Mine read, *Get Ready for a Daring Adventure.*

49

Dr. Li's office was in a two-story white-brick building. On the first floor, a shop called Dong Cheng sold jade rings and gold bracelets. A red door to the right of the shop was surrounded by a pleasing archway of carved stone, but once we were buzzed inside, the stairwell looked seedy and contained a set of slanted stairs with dirt-covered rubberized treads. The smell that wafted as we stepped inside was hard to describe—part cooked meat, part pungent spice, part Pine-Sol. I had a hard time imagining Forester in this place. But then again, Forester had a taste for exploration. He was always on board for a daring adventure.

We climbed the flight of stairs and knocked on the plain wooden door at the landing.

A small woman in a white lab coat answered the door. "Hello, hello," she said. "I am Dr. Li." She gave us a slight bow and pointed to two chairs in front of a dinged-up wood-veneer desk.

We took our seats.

"Wow," I said, staring at the wall behind the desk. It was lined with white shelves on which stood hundreds of glass jars, filled with what looked like bark, moss and mushroomy-looking lumps.

"Forest in a jar," Maggie said under her breath.

The doctor took a seat. On top of her desk sat a few scales, some old-looking books and an old computer circa 1978.

She saw Maggie and me studying the jars. "I prescribe herbs based on your life and your problems in life."

"Physical problems?" I asked.

"Or mental or life problems. Human beings…we are essential parts of nature. Nowadays too many not remember that. Too many try to find way out of something difficult by inventing something new." She waved an arm at the jars. "No need for new. You tell me problems. Nature already has remedy."

Maggie and I began asking a number of questions—Were these herbs sanctioned by the FDA? (Not sanctioned, but no problem, Dr. Li said.) Did she have a medical license? (No, she was educated in Hong Kong on holistic healing and herbal medicine.) Was there any kind of patient who shouldn't take herbs? (Some patients needed different kinds or less, but everyone could benefit from herbs.)

I looked at Maggie. One of her eyebrows was raised, and I could see her thinking, *What a racket.* Her South Side Irish upbringing didn't permit much room for nontraditional medicine. Maggie's family was more the grin-and-bear-it type.

Dr. Li appeared to tire of our questions. "Okay, why you here?"

"I was recommended by a friend of mine."

The woman beamed. She had graying black hair, pulled back at the nape of her neck and wore no makeup. When she smiled, she showed a large gap in her front teeth, but it was a beautiful smile nonetheless, her brown eyes lit up and you couldn't help but feel a positive energy. "Who friend?"

I looked again at Maggie, who gave a slight shake of her head. We'd decided earlier not to say Forester's name right away, but rather to get the lay of the land first.

"This friend recommended me to you because I'm having a lot of problems in my life," I said.

"Okay, okay," she said with encouragement, bobbing her head.

I began talking. And talking. It was easy enough. My

fiancé had taken off, I said. I was having trouble sleeping. I was having trouble concentrating. I felt out of control. I didn't know what would become of me.

When I was done, Maggie squeezed my hand.

The doctor stood from her desk, walked around it and took my other hand at the wrist. "I listen to pulses." Her warm fingers probed the inside of my wrist. She moved them incrementally, her face scrunched in concentration. "Mmmph," she said a few times, as if stumped by the results. She asked me a number of questions about my health, my habits, my eating.

Finally, she dropped my hand and moved to the rows of jars. "Your heart is weak," she said. "Very weak. I will give you herbs to make strong. You feel better." She began opening them and pinching contents into a paper bag. "You make tea from this. Use only little. Drink every day."

I thought of the herbs Forester had in his house, the ones that apparently had ma huang in them. They were in a bottle already, which was perfect for Forester, who was always on the go and would rarely have time to stop and make tea, or even have it prepared for him.

"Is there any other way to take the herbs?" I said. "I travel a lot and it would be hard for me to make tea on the road."

She stopped. "Yes, I have liquid herbs, and I mix for you, but not as potent. More for long-term patient. You come back and see me?"

I could almost hear Maggie scoff.

"Sure," I said.

Dr. Li pushed the paper bag to the side and moved to a baker's rack of brown liquid in small tubes. Using an eyedropper, she began opening different tubes and squeezing droplets into a small bottle with a simple label, the kind in Forester's cabinet.

When she was done, she handed me the bottle. "You use twenty drops. Warm water. Two times day." She beamed as if she'd given me the key to the Forbidden City. "Thirty dollars."

I pulled cash out of my purse and handed it to her. "So, my friend who recommended you was Forester Pickett."

She blinked rapidly, but then her smile widened. "I love Forester! How Forester doing?"

I handed her the cash. "Forester is... Well, Forester passed away last week."

The blinking started again. The smile crashed. "Passed? You mean..."

"Yes, Forester died."

The blinking stopped and her face froze into a mask of shock. "He die? Why?"

"He had a heart attack."

Dr. Li turned abruptly and made her way to her desk. She sat down hard and put an elbow on the arm of her chair, her chin on her fist. "Forester was great man."

"Yes, he was."

"I am very sad."

"Yes, we are, too. Do you know any reason why he would have a heart attack?"

Her eyes, which had been staring vacantly toward the louvered blinds on her windows, bolted to me. "What? I am Chinese doctor, not heart doctor."

"But he was your patient," Maggie said.

"I give him herbs for energy and to make him strong. He is an old man."

"He was only sixty-eight. That's not so old these days. Did you give him ma huang?"

She swallowed hard. "I no discuss treatment of patients."

"But you just were discussing how you gave him herbs for energy."

"I no discuss treatment of patients." She shook her head. "No, no."

The room fell into an uncomfortable silence. Dr. Li stood. "Okay, you feel better soon."

I looked at Maggie, who shrugged.

I stood and held out my hand to Dr. Li.

She shook it, but barely looked me in the eye.

Maggie and I made our way down the slanted stairs. I heard the hard slam of Dr. Li's door.

"Maybe she gave Forester the ma huang because she thought it would make him feel good," Maggie said, "and now she's feeling guilty that she might have contributed to his death."

"Do we need to turn her in to the cops? Would they prosecute her?"

"Hard to say. She never admitted to giving him ma huang."

I stepped out onto the street and I saw him—the short guy with the wavy, black hair. Same guy I'd seen that night in my neighborhood. Same guy I'd seen at the playground. He was standing across the street now, under the shade of a blue awning. I recognized the jut of his elbows. I recognized the tan jacket.

And then he started to cross the street. He didn't look either way for oncoming traffic. He was staring straight at me, and I felt a jolt of terror run through my body.

I grabbed Maggie by the arm, waved frantically for a cab and practically pushed her into one when it stopped. "Let's get the hell out of here," I said.

50

Sam Hollings walked through the penthouse apartment, his bare feet padding softly over the yellow marble floors. The apartment was top-of-the-line, but it was empty, save for a few bland pieces of furniture placed by the real-estate agent in order to show it. There wasn't even a bed, and although he could have certainly purchased or rented one, he didn't want to make himself comfortable. And so he spent his nights on a blow-up raft under a towel. This was his residence until the new owners could close and move in. Or until the rest of the pieces slid into place. But when or whether that would happen was a mystery. In fact, his future, once so solid and happily predictable, was now a large gaping hole.

The only person who knew he was even here was the real-estate agent and the guard in front of the building. He'd been staying put so the other residents wouldn't see him, coming and going only when necessary and usually at odd hours.

Now, the mornings were the worst for Sam. It was first thing in the morning when his mind wasn't on guard, when the memories leaped into his mind like children unaware they had been banished from a room.

First, he would remember the phone call, that time when he had first known that something was wrong, something that would change his life.

And then he pictured Forester's house when he arrived that

night—the white of the front columns shimmering under floodlights amid a black sky. No one answered the doorbell. He crept around the side and then the back of the house, feeling terrified, ramped up with a foreboding that screamed relentlessly in his ears.

When he first glimpsed the patio bathed in soft light from Forester's study, he felt relief, and yet he knew it was false. He knew in his gut it was all going wrong, and he would have to do something he very much did not want to do.

He stepped lightly across the lawn toward the patio. Jazz music spun softly from Forester's study, out into the night. As he drew nearer and nearer to the patio, a tree still blocking part of it from his view, he saw a plate of food on the table along with a half-full glass of red wine.

His foot crunched on a fallen autumn leaf and he froze, gulping in crisp air, hoping it would somehow lessen his alarm. He stared at that solitary meal. And then he made his feet keep moving, until he was at the patio's edge.

Sam walked through the living room to the wall of glass that overlooked the blue-gray waters of the Gulf of Panama and in the distance, the Bella Vista and Caledonia areas of the city. Below him lay a majestic pool and fountain. The pool, and the surrounding cabanas and lounge chairs, were big and grand enough for a hotel pool that could accommodate at least a hundred guests, but there were only seven apartments in this complex—all of them considered penthouses—and the funny thing was that rarely did anyone use the pool. Most of the people who owned property here lived in the city during the week and then escaped to their second homes on the weekends. It was in those weekend homes where they lounged by the pool or gazed at the ocean. As a result, the pristine fountain, made from the same yellow marble in the apartments, splashed majestically without an audience.

Sam moved to his left and slid open a pocket door made

of cut glass and wood. Outside on the balcony, he stared down at the pool. He should hang out there, he decided. And he would start this afternoon. There was little else to do. He'd taken all the steps he'd been instructed to—the properties had been sold, the money transferred into a series of offshore accounts, mostly in the Cook Islands. Now all that was left was to wait and see if everything would be illuminated or if it would all fall apart. Maybe that had happened already.

51

After the visit to Dr. Li's I went home, although the place didn't feel like home so much anymore. With Sam gone, with the break-in, with that guy coming at me in that menacing way, I couldn't feel safe. Maggie wanted to cancel her court call that afternoon to stay with me, but I told her she had done enough already. I told her I'd probably just been imagining things. I told myself that, too, but I didn't believe a word I was saying.

I tried Mayburn's number but got his voice mail. I began to walk around my apartment, hoping the movement would inspire some thought, some *action.* I wore a path that went around the living room, into the office, down the hall to my bedroom and then back to the living room to start all over again.

In my head, I tried to hold together all the "pieces," as Mayburn would call them. All the bits of information we had learned. I made myself go over and over the visit with Dr. Li. She'd been shocked when she learned of Forester's death, but I couldn't tell if it was just the usual shock people experience when they hear bad news, or whether it was more of a shock because she knew she'd contributed to his death. It still made no sense that she would give an inordinate amount of ma huang to Forester.

I made a loop around my bedroom and was about to head down the hallway, when I stopped. I would have to talk to Dr. Li again, that was all.

I had noticed that the sign on her front door said she was open until six. I looked at my watch. Five-thirty.

I grabbed my coat, mittens and helmet and sprinted down the stairs. As I went around to the garage, I swung my head back and forth, trying to see if anyone was there. The sun was setting, but with all the buildings in my neighborhood, it was almost dark. Anyone could be behind a tree or in the shadows of the neighbor's porch. I ran to the garage and revved up the scooter. It was really too cold to drive it, but this was the fastest way to get around and I *had* to see Dr. Li…before she closed for the day.

On the street, I pulled hard on the gas. I sneaked around cars and blasted through yellow lights. When I got to the South Side, I wished I'd taken a cab. I sat at a light on Thirty-first Street, nervously looking over my shoulder. The El track loomed ahead of me, cold and rusted, the small apartments to my right were run-down, a few guys eyed me from a street-corner stance. Without many buildings to crowd the neighborhood, it was brighter here, the setting sun casting a blood-orange glow to the place, making it feel sinister and pulsing with danger. One of the guys on the street corner took a step toward me, a loose, laughing grin on his face that, if I wasn't mistaken, was fueled by booze. Or something stronger.

The light turned green and I floored the scooter, racing to Dr. Li's. When I got there, the front door was open and the light on the stairs still on. I took the steps slowly, trying to calm myself down and focus on what I wanted to ask her. When I got to the landing, I saw an old rusted scale in the hallway, her door open.

I stepped inside and saw that much of the office had been cleaned out. All the jars were empty. The books and scales were gone. The shelves were still there, as were the desk and chairs, but the diplomas were gone from the walls. I spun around a few times, wondering what was going on. I noticed a small window overlooking the side of the building. I looked out onto a parking lot, and there was Dr. Li, putting a box in the back of a small white car that looked at least a decade old.

I ran from the room and made my way as fast as possible down the front stairs. I bolted around the side to the parking lot. Dr. Li was just getting in the driver's seat and closing the door.

"Dr. Li!" I yelled and began running to the car.

She stopped and looked over her shoulder. Her expression registered fear. She shut the door and turned the ignition.

"Dr. Li!" I reached the car, pounded on the window.

Dr. Li shook her head. She looked terrified now. I took a step back and held my hands up. I didn't want to scare her. "Please!" I yelled loud enough so she could hear me through the window. "Please talk to me."

She rolled down the window about six inches. "We talk today. No more talk."

"Where are you going?"

"Going to be with family."

"Are you closing your medical practice?"

"Yes."

"Why?"

"I no want to do no longer."

"Can I please talk to you about Forester? I have a few questions."

Dr. Li bit her lip and looked straight ahead, as if someone there could give her the answer. "Forester one of favorite patients," she said. "I like Forester very much."

"I did, too. I loved him. And I'm not sure, but it looks like he might have died because of the amount of ma huang you put in his herbs."

Scared eyes zinged to mine. "I didn't want to hurt Forester."

"But you knew that a lot of ma huang could make his heart condition worse, didn't you?"

She bit her lip harder. "We just want to make him not feel so good for little while. That is all."

"We? Who is we?"

She shook her head. "I no say."

I thought of the threats Forester had been getting. Someone wanted him to step down from the company.

"Did someone pay you to put the ma huang in Forester's herbs?"

Panic flashed in her eyes. "Just to make him feel bad for little while. We no want to make him die."

"So someone did pay you?"

"Forester no supposed to die." Her hands gripped the steering wheel. She rocked back and forth a little in her seat, as if she couldn't sit still. "I no think he would die."

I stepped closer and tried to keep my voice low. "What did you think would happen?"

"He supposed to not feel so good. He get sick a little. But no die. Forester no supposed to die."

"Who wanted Forester to feel bad?"

"I no say." Her hands were shaking now. She gripped the steering wheel harder and began wringing her hands on it. Her whole body was trembling. "No, no, no."

"It's okay, Dr. Li. Please, just tell me who paid you to make Forester feel bad."

She pursed her lips. She looked on the verge of tears. "No, no," she said again. And then Dr. Li took her right hand off the wheel, put the car in Drive and squealed backward.

"Stop!" I said, standing in front of the car. "Please, just talk to me!"

She backed up farther and punched the gas. The car shot by me, narrowly missing me and disappeared down Wentworth.

52

Tuesday morning, exactly one week after my fiancé disappeared, it was Mayburn who I spoke to first thing in the morning, not Sam.

"Where were you last night?" I asked when he answered, unable to prevent the demanding tone in my voice. I'd called him after my showdown with Dr. Li and it had gone to voice mail again.

"Remind me not to date you."

"Seriously."

"Seriously, I was working the phones and three computers on your case, trying to see if your boyfriend used those credit cards."

"Oh. Thanks. Anything?"

Mayburn exhaled loudly. "A few red herrings. Nothing yet."

I rushed through the details of my two conversations with Dr. Li. "What do you think?"

"I think Dr. Li is closing up shop because she knows she's done something bad."

"Should I call the cops so they can put out an APB?"

"They won't."

"But someone paid her to put those herbs in there."

"She didn't say that. You just assumed that based on what she was saying and doing."

"And the fact that she'd cleaned out her office."

"Yeah, and that, too. And I think you're right. But what I'm saying is if you go to the cops, you've really got nothing— no admission, no real evidence. What they'll think is you're the slightly crazy girl whose boyfriend took off with her boss's cash, and now you're losing it and hoping to place the blame somewhere else. We're working this case better than the cops could. When we have enough evidence—about anything, even if it's something not so favorable about Sam— we'll turn it over."

"Well, what should I do now?" I said, agitated. I blinked against the glare of the bright streetlights. "I've got to do something. Tell me what to do."

"Go to work. Be careful."

Work, or what was left of it. When I got there, I found Q in my office sitting on one of the visitor's chairs. His elbows were on his knees, his bald head hung low between his arms. He straightened when he heard me. He wore a white shirt under a black blazer, his khakis pressed to a fine point. And yet, despite the sharp outfit, he looked lost.

"It's just about done," he said, gazing around the office. "All the files are gone except the Jane Augustine contract."

I closed the door and slid onto the love seat that was pushed against the far wall. That love seat used to be laden with files and stacks of depositions.

"I might have to start working for Tanner again," I said.

"You couldn't."

"I don't want to, but with Shane giving all the Pickett cases to his best friend, and with the fact that I really don't know how to practice any other kind of law, what am I going to do?"

Q pursed his lips. "Tanner isn't going to want you around,

Iz. You're too much of a threat to him, even with Forester gone. You know everyone at Pickett Enterprises. They all love you. I hate to say this, but..."

"What?"

"You're going to be lucky if you have a job."

His words trickled into my brain. Then they exploded, the enormity of them hitting me. "Oh my God. You're right." I felt the plates of my earth collide, screeching with a loud, painful noise.

I looked at Q's stricken face. "You okay?"

"Not really."

"Is it all this?" I waved a hand around the nearly empty office.

"Yeah. And it's Max." He looked down. "Max knows about my affair," he said. "It's over."

"Wow," I said. "So you were having an affair. How did it come out?"

"I told him. I had to."

"The guilts?"

"Of course. I feel horrible. But mostly I wanted to tell Max because I'm in love with him."

"Him, Max, or him, the other guy?" I couldn't keep the surprise from my voice. Q had always had a hard time with monogamy, but I thought he'd be with Max forever.

"Him, the other guy."

"But you love Max."

"Not like I love this guy."

"Who *is* this guy?"

"I'm not ready to talk about it."

"You're not ready to talk about it? But it's me here. We talk about everything."

"He doesn't want me to say anything yet."

"But it's me," I repeated. Q's holding back was so very unlike him.

He shook his head.

"Why won't you tell me?" I asked. "Is it because he's involved with someone, too?"

"It's hard to explain."

"Maybe to someone else it is, but we can talk about anything."

Q narrowed his eyes. "Give me a break, Iz. It's not like you've let me in all that much this week."

"Of course I have." But my voice died off fast. He was right. I hadn't told him about breaking in to Forester's house or seeing Dr. Li yesterday. I hadn't told him about working with Mayburn. Yeah, Mayburn had told me not to discuss that stuff, but there was something else…something seemed off between Q and me.

"I haven't been confiding in you as much because things have seemed weird with us," I said.

"How so?" he asked defensively.

"I don't know. You've been evading some of my questions." Dr. Li's frightened face filled my mind. Who had paid her? It couldn't be Q. It made no sense. Still…

"Relationships can't stay the same forever, Iz. Not romantic ones or friendship ones. Or professional."

A feeling of trepidation permeated my body. But then that was a familiar sensation. Lately, I was always waiting for the other shoe to drop. "Why does this sound like a break-up speech?"

He stared at me, then looked around the office. "It's time."

"You're breaking up with me?" I asked.

"Not from our friendship…"

The trepidation grew, forming a lead ball of anxiety in my sternum. "You're not quitting…"

He nodded. "Not right now, but…but soon. Yeah."

"But Forester just died. And Sam is…who knows where. And you're just…" I searched the cacophony in my mind for the right word. "You're leaving me?"

"Izzy, all this stuff that's going on doesn't just affect *you*.

At the firm, you and I have been operating like our own team. Now, with you losing the Pickett work... You know I never wanted to be a damn secretary. And now that's what I'll be."

"Is your new boyfriend part of this decision?"

"First off, he's not my boyfriend." He looked over me and out my window. "He's not really even out of the closet."

I leaned forward. "Excuse me?"

"Shut up."

"No way. Are you telling me you're in love with someone who isn't even out yet? Is he married or something?"

His eyes returned to mine. "Don't."

I made myself sit back. "And is this guy, who is not out of the closet, part of this decision to quit?"

"It's my decision, but yes, he's been encouraging me to do something more with my life. Professionally, anyway."

"And what is this person recommending? Would you go back to acting?"

"Oh, please. We both know I'm never going to make it as an actor. I've got to do something else."

"What else would you do?"

"I don't know, Iz, but it's not going to be at Baltimore & Brown."

Again, I felt a ripping away of the life I'd had such a short time before. I looked down at my engagement ring. The sparkle was definitely gone.

"So what are you going to do now?" Q asked.

I stood. "I might as well face it. I'm going to see Tanner."

When the elevator reached Tanner's floor, I hurried off. And ran smack into him.

"Oh!" I said. "I was just coming to see you."

He gestured at the floor's conference room. "I've got a meeting in twenty minutes, but we can talk in here for a second."

The conference room was sunny and bright, the light-blue

curtains open and showcasing the Sears Tower to the right, the sun glinting off it.

Tanner patted a high-back leather chair. "You want to sit?"

"Don't be nice to me." I crossed my arms.

"Hey, McNeil, I feel…well, I feel…bad."

"You feel *bad?*" I had to admit, he didn't look good. He was as tan as always, and the widow's-peak hair was perfectly coiffed, but he was thinner than usual, his eyes more weary.

He put down his briefcase on the conference table. "Here's the deal. I mean, let's get right to it."

I nodded.

"When you took the Pickett business away from me a few years ago, well…I'm not going to tell you it didn't smart— and hard—and I'm not going to tell you I didn't want the work back. But I'm really sorry about the way it's gone down. I feel bad that it's happened now, with Sam being gone and with him being possibly implicated in Forester's death."

"He is *not* being implicated." I was getting really sick of defending Sam. I leaned against the wall.

"Well, he stole the bearer shares." Tanner shrugged. "I mean, we're not in dispute about that, right?"

"Don't depose me." I wish I could have said it with some force, but all I had wanted was to confront Tanner and get some semblance of an apology, and that had now happened. Too fast, in fact. There was nothing worse than getting yourself lathered up over something, but achieving your objective too quickly. "You could have waited for all this to settle down before you let Shane pull everything from me."

"It's business. There's no waiting in business."

"There is if you're a good person."

He shrugged again, his shoulders lifting high up to his ears and falling back slowly. "I never pretended to be that."

That was true. Tanner never acted like anything but a jerk. An unapologetic one. And, if anything, he was less of a jerk now that he wasn't bitter about me having the Pickett work.

"I could talk to some of the other partners," he said, "and see who might need an associate." In other words, you won't be working for me. Q had been right.

I felt queasy at the thought of starting over, a young associate assigned to a new partner. I wasn't above working hard, and I wasn't above working for someone else, but I couldn't simply make a U-turn and go back to the place I'd been at Baltimore & Brown so many years ago. And without Q.

I stood. "Thank you, but please don't bother." I left the room, went to my office, and I didn't think twice about slamming my door.

53

I sat at my desk, doing nothing but muttering and swearing.

Mayburn called. "I've been checking out Dr. Li. She and her husband were in some deep financial trouble. Was there a store downstairs from her office?"

I recalled the store with jade rings in the window. "Yeah."

"Well, her husband's family opened that. They were from Beijing. Her husband took it over when his parents got older. After he did, the store fell behind on the mortgage payments. Looks like they were about to get foreclosed on."

"So Dr. Li needed cash."

"Bad. The husband was gambling, and they were in serious, serious debt."

Q opened the door. "Jane Augustine is here," he said.

"Really?" I had no appointment with her. Hell, I had no appointments with anyone.

"Call you later," I said to Mayburn.

Q led Jane into the room, her Amazonian frame clad in a winter-white suit and cornflower-blue silk blouse that showed a peep of her perfect cleavage and made her eyes an even more startling mauve-blue.

"Hi, Iz," she said sheepishly. She shook her long locks of black hair over her shoulders. "Got a minute for an old friend?"

"Not if you're here to pimp me for information about Sam."

"It's not that."

I nodded at my now-empty love seat. "Have a seat?"

"Nope." She dug in a large black alligator bag and pulled out a folder. She placed it on my desk.

I opened it. Inside was her contract. "You're back for more of my abuse?" I said with an attempt at a grin. I was feeling a little bad about my outburst yesterday.

"Look at the last pages."

I did. She'd signed them.

"It's the same contract you brought yesterday. I fired Steve Severny."

"Whoa, Jane. I told you to get some balls, but I was just angry. You shouldn't listen to me, especially not right now."

She threw her arms up. "No, don't you see, you were *exactly* right. I've been letting him run my professional life— forever—and I'm miserable. So I'm making some changes."

"Wow." I was impressed, but a little afraid for her. I'd learned to fear change in the last week.

My door opened, and Q stuck his head inside. "Joel Hersh called to say he's on his way to see you," he said in a low voice. "And Edward Chase."

"Oh, boy." Joel was the head of the firm's estate-planning section and a member of the firm's executive committee. Edward Chase was the head of that committee—the undisputed king of the B & B fiefdom.

I stood. "Jane, thanks for the contract. And congrats on the changes you're making." I went around the desk and hugged her.

"I'll get out of your hair," she said. "We'll catch up later."

She left my office. I heard Q introduce her to Joel, who said his wife watched her every night.

A second later, Joel Hersh stepped into my office. He was a short man, always well dressed. Today, he was in one of his "casual" outfits, which consisted of gray pants, a perfectly pressed navy jacket and loafers that looked so soft and supple you'd think they had just jumped off the cow. He was one of the nicest guys in the firm, but since the estate lawyers had offices two floors below us, I didn't see him often except at the occasional firm outing.

"Izzy," he said, an expression on his face I couldn't read, "may I speak with you privately?"

"Of course."

"Ed should be here in a moment."

At that moment, Edward Chase appeared. He was a large, round man, originally from Texas, who compensated for his weight with lots of bling. Today he wore a Super Bowl-size ring on his right hand and a tie clip that appeared to be made of an ancient coin.

Joel shut the door and they both took a seat.

Joel crossed his hands in his lap. "We're here about your mother."

Now I was surprised. "You know my mother?"

"We don't, but I understand she runs the Victoria Project."

I nodded. "My mom started the Victoria Project about five years after we moved to Chicago. It's a charity that helps widowed women who have children."

The charity had been my mother's sole passion for many years. Maybe Joel wanted to donate to the charity, or get the firm to sponsor an event. Joel was, I now remembered, on the firm's charitable board. But then I glanced at Ed Chase, who had no reason to babysit such a conversation, and my stomach clenched.

"I understand it's a wonderful organization," Joel said. "But I'm concerned about a bequest that's been left to the charity."

"I'm not sure I understand."

"I've been working on settling Forester's estate, and Forester left a large settlement in his will to the Victoria Project."

I felt myself relax. Wonderful, wonderful Forester. That he'd left the charity some money was such a sweet move. "Yes, Forester made donations to the charity before."

Joel shifted in his chair. He exchanged a look with Ed. "Had he donated fifteen million before?"

"Fifteen million?" My mother's charity was lucky if it raised two hundred thousand a year.

Joel nodded. "I'm concerned for a number of reasons, Izzy, which is why I've asked Ed to be here."

Ed remained impassive, looking down, apparently studying his massive ring.

"Normally, I wouldn't be discussing Forester's will with you," Joel said.

"I know." Joel was one of the few attorneys I knew who didn't gossip about his clients or his work.

"But there are a number of potential issues here that may draw litigation from the other beneficiaries of the estate. First of all, this is a very large bequest. Second, you were Forester's attorney, so there may very well be a conflict of interest. I've got some people working on that."

I knew what he meant. At this moment, two associates, probably one of them Erin, were scrambling to perform legal research about whether the mother of an attorney of a deceased client could be a beneficiary of the will. The law was full of sticky little questions like this, and I was sure Erin would be on Westlaw, searching high and low until the late hours of the evening.

"The last issue is the fact that your fiancé allegedly stole thirty million dollars of property from Forester," Joel said.

"Thanks for the 'allegedly.'"

Ed looked up now, a pissed-off expression on his face. "This is no time for sarcasm, Izzy. You've put us in a shithole of trouble here."

"I wasn't being sarcastic, but I do think it's humorous that you're asserting that *I* have gotten the firm in trouble. *I* didn't do anything except represent Forester to the best of my abilities, and make you guys a lot of money in the process. *I* don't know anything about what Sam has done."

"What about this donation to the Victoria Project?" Joel said. "Did you have prior knowledge of this?"

"None." I stood. "But if you guys will excuse me, I'm going to find my mother and get some current knowledge."

Joel began to sit forward in his chair, but Ed didn't move.

"Izzy, I think you need to take a leave of absence," Ed said. "Until all this business with Forester and Sam and your mom is sorted out." He twisted his ring around, but didn't take his eyes from me.

I looked down at my desk for a moment, remembering just last week when that desk was littered with files and notes and phone messages. I looked back up and met Ed's gaze. "I agree."

I grabbed my bag off the back of the door and left the law firm of Baltimore & Brown.

54

I called my mom as I hunted for a cab on LaSalle Street.

She answered on the first ring.

She wasn't always like that. With her melancholy—her depression, if we called a spade a spade—Victoria McNeil required a lot of time to herself. She wasn't the kind of mother who made herself indispensable. But since Sam had disappeared, she had taken all my calls quickly and let me know she was always available.

"Where are you?" I asked.

"At lunch with Cassandra." My wedding coordinator. Or should I now call her a disaster-relief coordinator?

"She's been calling," I said. "Tell her I know we have to make decisions… *I* have to make some decisions, but I need a little more time."

"Of course."

"I have to see you."

"We're at P. J. Clarke's." Which was only about a block or so from her house. "Why don't you take some time off and meet us for a salad. I'm afraid you're running yourself into the ground with all this."

"Will you meet me at your house in ten minutes?"

"We just ordered."

"I need you, Mom."

She didn't pause. "I'll see you there."

Soon, I was sitting in my mother's peaceful, ivory-colored living room. She looked beautiful, as always, in a crimson, wraparound designer dress that fit her as well as it had when she bought it thirty years ago. Her strawberry-blond hair was pulled back in a low ponytail. Large, square-cut diamond earrings, a gift from Spence for their last anniversary, were the only jewelry she wore aside from her diamond wedding band.

She sat next to me and pulled me into a hug. When I didn't return it as tight or as long as I normally would, she pulled back and regarded me, her chin turned to one side. "Has something happened?"

"Yes." I disentangled myself and moved back a few inches. I wanted to be able to see her expression. "Forester left the Victoria Project fifteen million in his will."

Her expression softened, a hand flew to her throat. "Are you…are you serious?"

"Yes. Did you know he was going to do that?"

"No." She gave almost a bemused laugh. "I didn't. But then you know Forester."

"But this seems overly generous, even for him."

"What an amazing man." She turned to stare out the front window at its view of State Street, the sun bathing her face as she did. I noticed for the first time a faint, crepelike texture around her mouth.

"Mom," I said, "why would Forester leave so much money to the Project?"

She turned back. "Because he was extremely generous. He had to leave his money somewhere."

"You barely knew each other."

"Forester knew how to help people. He loved doing it. And that's what he's doing, even now."

"And you knew nothing about this?"

"No," she said, a delighted but baffled expression on her face. "Not a thing."

I believed her. My mother was not an actress. She couldn't

fake a good mood or an inauthentic reaction if she'd tried. And I'd often wished she could have tried harder in those early days after my dad died when we first moved to Chicago and her depression was almost palpable.

I fell back onto the couch. "I'm happy for the charity and everything, but it's causing me some major problems at work."

"Why?" she said, distressed now. My mother was a very smart woman, but she had little business sense, and she'd never worked for a big company or in the law.

"Because I was Forester's attorney? And you're my mother? And my fiancé already has thirty million?"

"Good Lord." My mother's expression went stern. "I didn't think of that."

We sat in quiet for a moment.

"Do you want some tea?" she asked.

"No, thanks." A pause. "I quit today."

"You quit?"

"Well, they took all my cases away and then I sort of quit and then they suggested a leave of absence."

My mother shook her head. "I think we both need a glass of wine."

"What the hell."

My mother stood. "White burgundy?"

"Perfect."

My mind returned to Dr. Li. Who had paid her to put ma huang in Forester's herbs? I sat in my mother's warm, cozy living room, thinking over the possibilities that were cold and unwelcoming. Shane stood to gain much financially and professionally from his father's death. Chaz and Walt did, too, since they could control Shane, and therefore Pickett Enterprises, with Shane at the helm. Annette stood to come into a lot of money and could live the rest of her life without working for a living.

And then there was Sam, of course. Sam, with thirty million of bearer shares. But then Sam didn't need Forester dead to steal those. My fiancé might have been a thief, but I still had a hard time believing him a murderer.

"Do you want any food, honey?" my mother called from the kitchen.

I turned and yelled no. When I turned back, my eyes fell on a floor-to-ceiling bookshelf to the right of the front window. In particular, my gaze was drawn to a certain item on that shelf.

I focused in on it. I blinked repeatedly. I stood and I walked toward it.

I picked up the bowl. I ran my hand over the scalloped edges, and around its overly glossed sides. It was clearly handmade.

And clearly made by the same person who'd created the bowl I'd seen in Forester's study, the one that had looked so familiar to me somehow.

Now, the recognition came flooding in—my mother had taken a pottery class at Lillstreet Art Center when we'd first moved to Chicago and she was trying to find something to pull her out of her funk. She'd made one after another after another of these scalloped bowls, all in white or ivory. Her cupboards were still full of them. But I'd never known her to give them to anyone. Pieces started to fall into place. The bowl at Forester's. The money he left her in the will.

My mom walked back into the room then, carrying two long-stemmed wineglasses filled with golden wine.

"Were you involved with Forester?" I said when she'd reached me.

Her face fell. She seemed to sway on her feet. I wondered for a second if she would drop the glasses.

"Don't lie to me," I said.

She sat on the couch, and without letting go of those glasses, my mother started to cry.

55

Although my mom is a woman who carries her sadness with her, she rarely cries. When she does, she does so beautifully. Tears appear like tiny crystals at the corners of her blue eyes and slide gently down her face—a graceful, trickling waterfall. I have always been fascinated the handful of times I'd seen her cry, and this was no exception.

I watched her, making no move to comfort her, because that wasn't how she worked and also because I was profoundly surprised and confused.

Finally, I said, "You were cheating on Spence?"

She looked up, her mouth making an *O* shape. "No! It was years ago."

"You've been married to Spence for fifteen years."

She put the wineglasses on a side table. "It was before that."

Now I was bewildered. "You've known Forester all this time?"

"Yes. I met him when I worked in radio."

"When we first moved here? After Dad died?"

"Yes."

"So you were working for one of Forester's stations?" My mother's career as a traffic reporter was so far in the past that when I'd met Forester it never occurred to me they might have known each other. In fact, when I introduced them, they acted, vaguely, as if they might have met each other somewhere but didn't know each other well.

"We were friends first, the way Forester was friends with all his employees, but we were drawn to each other." She glanced down, smiling a small, secret-looking grin. I knew that smile. It was the one I made before all this, during times when Sam wasn't around, but when I thought of him, of his martini-olive eyes.

"He said there was something," my mother continued, "something about me that made him want to take care of me, made him want to hold me."

"He was married to Liv."

The smile disappeared, replaced by a short affirmative bob of her head. "We were truly just friends for a long time."

My *mother* was friends with Forester? She had an affair with him? A combo platter of emotions was served up in my head. The shock lingered. There was also a strange envy that my mother had experienced something even more personal, and apparently profound, with Forester than I. I realized now that I carried around a proprietary sense about Forester, and a certain image of him as a bastion of decency and values. Now I'd learned he'd had an affair? And with *my mother*.

And then there was something else, something that was beginning to grow—the realization that my mom lied to me. She had known Forester well. She'd had a relationship with him. If she'd been able to hide this for so many years, and so well, what else was she hiding?

"How did it start?"

It was as if my mother had been waiting to tell this story forever. She sat forward on the couch and began to talk in such an animated way I almost didn't recognize her.

Nothing happened between them, she said, until one night when he saw her looking in vain for a cab after a company party. He asked her if he could give her a ride home. She protested, but when no cabs appeared, she finally agreed.

When they got to her Northside brownstone, he bid her good-night and waited in the car while she trotted up the steps.

"Remember how we always had problems with the lock on the front door?" she asked, her eyes bright with tears.

I nodded. As a city kid, I'd had to learn to carry around keys, and I'd wrestled with that lock for years.

"Apparently, he could see me struggling," she said. "He got out of the car and helped me. When I turned around, we looked at each other, just looked, for a long, long…long time. And then he kissed me. I'd like to tell you that I resisted. But I didn't." She exhaled almost contentedly, remembering. "He turned and walked away, and neither of us mentioned it afterward."

She glanced at me, seeming to register my presence for the first time in minutes. I gave a nod for her to continue. It was as if I was watching someone on a movie screen, someone I didn't know, and I was compelled to see the ending.

Forester called her two weeks later, my mother said, and asked if she would have dinner, ostensibly to talk about her contract. They both knew Forester wouldn't have normally been talking to the traffic girl about her contract. They both knew what was going on, my mother said, but it was as if some unstoppable force was pushing them together. Their affair, the first he'd ever had, started that night. It was bliss for about a year and a half. Initially, he said he was a better husband to Olivia because of their affair. Eventually, he talked of divorce, and they began to plan a future together. It was when Olivia was diagnosed with cancer that everything came crashing down. The guilt rushed in, and Forester broke my mother's heart.

"Forester couldn't abandon Olivia," she said. "You know how he was."

"I thought I did."

Even though I hadn't known anything about her and Forester and had never met him as a kid, I remembered the time she was talking about. A few years after we'd moved to Chicago, my mother seemed to recover from my father's death, at least for a while. She played with Charlie and me with an ease that hadn't been there for a long time. She smiled; she even giggled. I could remember now how she brightened during those years, but then she dimmed again; she disappeared again.

"He nursed Olivia," my mother explained. "He took care of her day and night. We decided we would have to wait until after her treatment, and we cut off contact. But cancer was a battle Olivia fought for years. She would nearly recover, then another diagnosis would be made and another round of chemo would start and the tests would begin again."

My mother said that she finally realized she and Forester would never be together. Heartbroken, she moved on, eventually meeting Spence. By the time Olivia died years later, Victoria was remarried, and Forester refused to get her into another affair. The love they had was bigger than that, he told her. Despite how much he loved her, he was tortured by what he'd done to Olivia, even though she'd never known about the affair. My mother, again, was heartbroken.

"You would have left Spence for him?"

My mother smiled a sad smile. "Yes. I would have. Forester was my other half, literally someone who was so much like me and so perfect for me, even more so than your dad or Spence. I know it was wrong, doing what I did back then— being involved with a married man—but when you're truly in love like that, you will do absolutely anything to keep it."

For the first time in this conversation, my mother said something I understood. I loved Sam that way. At least I thought I had.

"I have to tell you something," my mom said. Her face was a mask of regret. She was looking at me scared, as if she was about to impart information that would not just anger me but shock me.

"What?"

She shook her head as if she couldn't bring herself to speak. The room swirled. Shades of ivory seemed to fuzz in front of my eyes, and for a moment I felt light-headed, as if I might faint. Sam was gone. Forester was gone. My job, probably gone. Could it be that I was about, in one way or another, to lose my mother because she'd done something to Forester?

"What is it?"

"That's the reason I've been pushing you for this big wedding."

"What's the reason?" I blinked, trying to clear my head.

"Forester." She clasped her hands on her lap and gave an embarrassed look. "We hadn't seen each other for such a long time, and I was using your wedding as an excuse to spend some time with him."

"Oh." I shook my head a little to clear it. "Is that it?"

"It's mortifying, I know. I'm old enough to be past these kinds of things."

"You're not old," I said in a distracted way, because just then something occurred to me. "Wait a minute. So the reason Forester gave me Pickett Enterprises work was because of you?"

My mother didn't respond immediately.

I laughed, a sparse, harsh laugh. It all made complete sense now. I hadn't gotten the job as lead attorney because I'd impressed Forester that first day with my hustle or the way I'd spoken to him on the phone. And it wasn't because I was a good lawyer. It was because my mother used to meet him in a hotel room.

"No, no, no," my mother said. Then she stopped and seemed to think about it a second. "Well, possibly the first few cases, but Forester adored you, Izzy, *adored you.* He looked at you as the daughter, the stepdaughter, he almost had. Forester gave you the rest of his cases because he was fed up with Tanner, but more importantly because he thought you were an exceptional attorney and you were going to be even better in the future. He respected you immensely."

"Don't flatter me." My cell phone rang from within my purse, but I ignored it.

"I'm not. That's absolutely true."

"True? What's *true?* I have no idea anymore!" I found myself almost yelling. I stopped. It was time to ask. "Did you hurt Forester? Did you know he was going to leave money to the Victoria Project?"

"What?" Her blue eyes flashed with hurt. "I *loved* that man. Right up until the day he died. I would never hurt him."

"But your charity is going to be fifteen million dollars richer."

"I don't need the money—you know that."

"I don't know anything anymore!" The words rang out in my mother's big house, and then we both fell into a silence that sang with such intensity it felt almost preternatural.

We sat staring, and for the first time I saw her as a woman, not my mother, but doing so meant I didn't know her the way I thought I had. She was someone different altogether.

My cell phone rang again. It stopped and then rang again.

Finally, I turned and grabbed it from my bag. It was a number I didn't recognize. I stared at the area code. Indianapolis, I realized.

I answered fast. "Izzy," Alyssa said. "I just wanted to tell you that I got the money and my brother's credit card back today. They were overnighted by Fed Ex."

"You're kidding. What about the passport?"

"He wrote a note that said I'd get that soon. I knew Sam would do what he promised."

I wished I had the same sense of surety about him. "Was there a return address?"

"No. But I looked on the packaging. It was sent from Panama City, Panama."

56

I told my mother I had to go. I needed to talk to Mayburn about Alyssa's call, and more than anything I wanted to tell him about this situation with my mom. I trusted his instincts, plus I couldn't sit there, looking at my mother, feeling shocked and flattened with all she'd told me.

I left her house, more confused than ever. She seemed to have told me the truth—about loving Forester, about how she would never hurt him. My gut instinct was to believe her, but it also seemed my gut instinct might be severely, severely out of whack.

I called Mayburn when I got to the street. It was chilly outside, the sky turning slate gray with dusk. I looked both ways for someone who might be following me. A hundred feet away an older woman stood with a white poodle that was sniffing around a tree. Two girls walked with coffee cups. Cars drove by slowly on State Street. No sign of the guy with the dark hair, but it could be someone else, someone who wasn't so obvious, was following me. The unknown aspect of that—of my whole life—made me jumpy.

"You on your way to the Prada party?" Mayburn asked when he answered.

I looked at my watch. Five-fifteen. "Damn."

"You didn't forget?"

"No. I mean, maybe I did, just in the last hour." I groaned.

"I'm on my way home now. I'll change and get there on time." I'd texted Grady earlier and he was meeting me there.

"What's up?"

I felt guilty, like I was gossiping about my mom, but Mayburn had told me more than once that he couldn't help me if he didn't know *everything*. And it seemed he was the only one who'd been able to help thus far.

I told him about the bequest to the Victoria Project. And about my mother's affair with Forester.

He whistled. "Damn. Didn't see that coming."

"Yeah. Me neither. What's your take?"

"It's another piece of the puzzle."

I groaned again. "You're maddening with that puzzle analogy."

"It's true. It's how—"

"Yeah, well, here's another one." I told him about Sam's package from Panama City, sent to Alyssa.

"Now *that's* a piece we can do something with. I've been watching the brother's credit card for activity, but we can do a more refined search if we know where the card was used before it was returned. You get to the Prada party, and I'll get started on this."

"Right. Okay."

I reached North Avenue and took a left, heading toward Old Town. Lincoln Park was on my right, and I let my eyes roam the walkways, the park benches, the trees, for signs of anyone standing too still, anyone with a camera or binoculars.

"You okay?" Mayburn said, making me realize I was still holding the phone to my head, almost like a protective shield.

"I guess."

"Hang in there. We're getting close."

I felt an unraveling in my mind. It was getting hard for me to keep all the pieces together and stay sane. "We'd better be."

* * *

At six o'clock I walked into the Prada store. The place was on Oak Street at the corner of Rush, a big money corner. Across the street was Barneys, where you could spend eighty-five dollars on a small votive scented like Himalayan wheat. The remainder of the block was lined with other high-end stores like Hermès and Frette.

I'd been in the Prada store only once before when I'd seen a white pleated skirt in the window, which I thought would be perfect for a firm outing to Arlington Park. When I found that the skirt cost as much as the gross national income of Romania, I promptly spun around, bolted out of the store and never dared look in their windows again.

Inside, the place was small, the walls lined with glass shelves holding shoes and bags. The few clothing racks normally in the center had been moved aside to make way for the party. The guest list, as far as I could tell, was made up of people who could easily afford to purchase Romania. And maybe Bulgaria for good measure. Everyone was coiffed to perfection, including the men, very few of whom had gray hair, even the guys in their sixties. Everyone wore beautiful clothes so crisp and well tailored they looked as if they'd been sewn into them only moments before.

And there, in the corner, was Lucy DeSanto, looking like a stylish little doll in a cobalt-blue dress with chiffon sleeves that puffed ever so slightly at the shoulder. She was gazing up at a man I assumed to be her husband, one of those dark-haired, dark-skinned guys I found handsome but only in a slick way.

I shrugged off my black wool coat and handed it to the coat-check person, then squared my shoulders and was about to make my way over to Lucy, when I felt a tap on my arm.

I turned to see Grady, handsome in a suit and pink tie. Most guys should stay far, far away from pink ties, but on Grady, with his tall body and his brown hair gleaming under the store's lights, he looked nothing but good.

"Wow," he said, sizing me up with his eyes.

After the talk with my mom, not to mention the talk with Alyssa, I'd broken out the big guns to make myself feel better—my Christian Louboutin black patent leather heels, so high they'd cause a lumbar laminectomy if you wore them too often, and my Dolce & Gabbana dress I'd bought for my bachelorette party. It was low cut and too tight and sexy as hell. The plan for the bachelorette outfit had been to get sauced up and then head over to Sam's and sauce him up, but I wasn't about to save the dress for something that might never happen.

"Thank you," I told Grady earnestly.

We hugged, and it was one of those hugs that lasts a nanosecond longer than normal. No one else would have noticed. But I felt it. We both did.

I pulled back first and smoothed the front of my dress, although, truthfully, it was too taut to need smoothing. Just then, out of the corner of my eye, I saw Lucy see me and point me out to her husband.

"Okay," I said to Grady in a businesslike voice. "You're going to have to go with me on this, but I need you to pretend that you're my husband, and my name is Isabel Bristol. Can you handle that?"

"Do I have to change my name?"

"You can be Grady Bristol." I saw Lucy moving toward me now, her husband in tow. "Got it?"

"What is going on with you, Iz?" he asked, but with a mischievous tone.

Lucy was three feet from me now. "Can you just go with it?" I asked Grady. "You know, just…go with the flow?"

He held up his hands in an exaggerated shrug. "I'm all flow, baby."

"Hello!" I heard Lucy trill.

I faced her and put on my best I'm-sorry-have-we-met? face.

"Lucy DeSanto," she said, putting a hand briefly on her

chest. "We met at the playground on Sunday? This is my husband, Michael."

"Oh, of course! How great to see you." I shook hands with Michael. Up close, he truly was handsome, one of those guys who makes the lines at the side of his eyes look sexy. But his attractive face didn't hide the sense of something shady behind those eyes. "I'm Isabel Bristol and this is my husband, Grady."

It suddenly dawned on me that I was wearing an engagement ring, but no wedding band. Would they notice? I kept my left arm firmly at my side.

Grady shook hands with them both and squeezed me affectionately around the shoulders like a good husband would.

"Thanks for coming," Lucy said. "I'm on the board for this charity. Have you been to our event before?"

Mayburn had filled me in on the cause—juvenile diabetes—and about the party they threw each year at a penthouse apartment considered one of the most striking in the city. The ticket prices were probably the highest of the year—nine hundred dollars each. I was determined to get out of this presale party without having to buy one.

"I haven't been lucky enough to attend before," I said, "but of course I've heard all about it."

"Well, thanks so much for coming, and for supporting the charity. It really means a lot to us. Our son has juvenile diabetes and it has been tough. Just so hard to see him suffer." Lucy blinked, and I could see her recalling her son hurting.

"I had no idea."

She shook her head sadly. "I don't mean to bore you at a party, but really it's nothing you'll ever recover from, seeing your child in pain. We're just doing everything we can to help ease the pain for other people."

Her obvious ache tugged at my heart. "How wonderful that you do that."

I glanced at her husband, who was staring at my breasts. I couldn't blame him, since, really, the dress was designed to get that response, but *C'mon, buddy, we're talking about your sick kid, here.* His eyes finally met mine and he gave me a sardonic grin with one side of his mouth. I could see why Mayburn hated the guy.

I felt so bad for Lucy—she was married to this dude and she had a child with a serious illness. "Of course, we'd like to buy a ticket." I put my hand on Grady's shoulder. In that moment, I remembered for a fleeting second what it was like to feel part of a couple, and I missed it.

"Thank you!" Lucy clasped her hands together. "You're amazing."

I gave her my credit card, and she handed it off to a woman circling the room. *Mayburn better reimburse me.*

"So, how often do you take your daughter to that playground?" Lucy asked, looking from me to Grady and back again.

I glanced at Grady, whose eyes had gone a little big. "Yeah," he said, giving me a wide smile. "How often do you take our daughter there?"

"Oh, usually once or twice a week." I slipped my arm around Grady's waist and squeezed it hard. *Go with the flow.* "I really want her to get to know more kids. You know, because she's an only child."

Michael DeSanto appeared inordinately bored with all the kid talk. "Excuse me," he said, kissing his wife absently on the top of her head, while he looked over at the door. He moved away toward two women entering the store.

Lucy seemed to flag a little, watching her retreating husband, but she turned back to me and smiled wistfully. "I love that playground. It makes me want to be a kid again."

"I know. Hey," I said, as if an idea had just come to me. "We should get the kids together for a playdate sometime. I know Kaitlyn was acting up a bit but, honestly, she's not like that usually." *Please, God, don't let her be like that usually.*

Lucy brightened. "I'd love to!"

"I wish I could ask you to our house…" I squeezed Grady tighter, willing him to stand there and look pretty. "But we're in the middle of a renovation. It's complete chaos."

"Oh, come to our place. We're right off of Fullerton." She named the address. "What days are good for you?"

"Wednesdays?"

"Would tomorrow be too soon?"

"No, that's great, actually."

Mayburn was going to love me. "One o'clock?" It wasn't like I had to go to work.

"Great!" Lucy said, her eyes bright. Honestly, the girl was the cutest person I'd ever met.

She pulled out her cell phone. "What's your number?"

"Uh…" I panicked. What would Mayburn tell me to do here? Give her a fake one? But then what if she called about our playdate? And wasn't that playdate the main reason I was here? I thought about my voice mail message, which only mentioned my first name.

I noticed Grady and Lucy looking at me strangely. "Uh…" I said again, and finally gave it to her.

She dialed it, and my phone started to ring. "There," she said with a pleased grin, clicking her phone off. "Now you've got mine, too."

"Thanks," Grady said to Lucy. "It'll be nice for Izzy and our daughter to have some new friends." His hand had moved up to my rib cage, and he held me with a startling familiarity.

The woman came back with my credit card and a slip for me to sign.

"I should make the rounds," Lucy said. "I'll see you tomorrow then. Nice to meet you guys, and thanks so much." She beamed a lovely smile at Grady.

"No problem!" He squeezed me tighter around the waist.

And then, as soon as Lucy was gone, "my husband," seemingly without a moment's hesitation, pulled me gently through the glass doors, and once outside, turned me to face him, slipped both hands around my back…and kissed me.

Later, I would think of my mother's words when she told me about that first night with Forester—*And then he kissed me. I'd like to tell you that I resisted. But I didn't.* My mother said that Forester had walked away then.

But that's not what happened with Grady.

It was as if something was released inside me with that kiss—something primal and passionate and angry. And it only made me want to kiss him more.

He drew away from me for a minute and looked at my face, trying to read it, but I just pulled his head back toward mine and kissed his lips that were so different from Sam's—wider, fuller. He kissed different from Sam, too. There was a hunger in Grady's mouth that could only be delivered with a first kiss.

A logical voice inside my head was now shouting, *Stop! You're just exhausted. You don't know what you're doing!*

But I knew exactly what I was doing—I was obliterating the week and whatever Sam might have done. Grady's kisses seemed to suck something out of me—the grief, the worry, the stress, the confusion—leaving behind an undeniable desire that managed to easily drown out the logic.

"Let's go somewhere." He took my hand. "Your place?"

A sliver of guilt sliced through my desire. "No, I couldn't."

"My place?"

I felt more desire getting cut away. "I shouldn't. I shouldn't be doing any of this."

"Fuck it. Come with me."

He got my coat, pulled me into Jilly's, a jazz bar only steps from Prada. Inside, it was dark, the walls deep-red. A sax player was blaring.

Grady found a corner table, ordered two gin martinis. Before I could think about it too much, we'd had two and were making out like high-school freshmen under the bleachers.

And for the next few hours, that's what we continued to do. There was little talking except for the few times Grady stopped, gazed at me and muttered something like, "I always wanted to do this," or "God, you're hot."

I let myself be consumed. I didn't think about the fact that Sam was apparently in Panama or the fact that my mother had slept with my client, thereby gaining me years of legal work that I thought I'd somehow earned. I didn't think about Dr. Li or who had paid her to hurt Forester.

Until the next morning.

57

Day Nine

I woke up at first with a feeling of calm that I knew, in those bleary initial minutes, was different than the way I had felt for a while.

And then it all rushed back. The kissing, the groping, the gin, the kissing.

What had I done? I'd been so quick to judge my mother the day before, and within hours of that judgment I'd cheated on my fiancé. Not cheating in a sex way, but cheating in a making-out-like-it's-the-last-day-on-earth way. But I couldn't even claim love, the way my mother had. I didn't love Grady. I did as a friend, of course, but it couldn't be more than that. Or could it? I guess I'd never considered it before. I looked at the clock. When I texted him last night about the playdate, Mayburn had asked me to come to his house that morning to prep me for it.

Cringing a little at a small headache, I made my way toward the shower.

My phone rang. Grady.

"So…" he said when I answered. "Are you freaked out?"

"No small talk, huh?" I gave a nervous laugh. Luckily, I'd managed to get home and get to bed after those two hours at Jilly's. He had said he would call first thing in the morning, and now he kept his promise.

"We're past the small talk, I think."

A memory burst in my brain—Grady's tongue in my mouth, his hands grazing my breasts through my dress. "Yeah, I guess…"

"You're freaked."

"No, I…"

He laughed. "Hey, it's still *me*."

"Thank God, because no one in my life seems to be who I thought they were."

He was quiet for a minute. "Look, I'm not going to push. I don't even want to talk about last night."

"Maybe we should. Maybe—"

"Nope. Don't even do it. You've got a lot going on."

He was right about that. I had to leave to get to Mayburn's place, and then I had to borrow Kaitlyn again and pretend I was a mother. And then I had to start facing the fact that Sam was in Panama, probably trying to sell a corporation, which owned thirty million dollars' worth of real estate.

"So, seriously," Grady said, "just do what you have to do. And you and I…well…we'll either talk about it or we won't."

I realized then that I *did* love him. At the very least, I loved him as a very, very good friend. He'd somehow known exactly what I'd needed in that moment.

"Thanks," I said. "Thanks a lot."

Mayburn's place was just off Lincoln Square, a predominantly German neighborhood years ago, which left behind great bars like the Chicago Brauhaus. Lately, however, the Starbucks, Gaps and American Apparels of the world had crept in.

The streets surrounding Lincoln Square were populated mostly with wood-frame, single family houses. When I pulled up in front of Mayburn's—three stories, white-painted wood with tan trim and a manicured lawn boasting a tall oak in the middle—I was surprised. It was so family looking.

"Nice house," I said when he opened the door.

He seemed to sense my question. "Yeah, I bought it when I was with Madeline. Kind of hoping she'd want to get married and have kids here, but hey, things don't always work out."

I thought of Sam. "No, they don't."

He led the way down a long hallway with old pine floors, past a sparsely decorated living room and into the kitchen.

The kitchen cabinets were old wood, painted white, but the appliances were all silver and new.

"I stayed because I like the neighborhood," Mayburn said, taking glasses from the cabinet. "It's getting more crowded, but it's pretty mellow, especially during the winter." He ran the faucet. "Water?"

I nodded.

He filled a glass, didn't ask about ice, and handed it to me. "So, how are you doing?"

"I'm going insane."

He half grunted, half laughed. "I hear that. I'd probably be the same."

"Did you find out anything about Sam, like where he might be in Panama?"

"Yeah."

I put the glass of water down with a plunk. "Tell me."

"Alec Thornton's credit card was used to check out of a hotel in Panama City a few days ago."

"What hotel?"

"The Decapolis. It's a nice one. I've been working the phones, trying to figure out what 'Alec' did while he was there. I did find out he was a blond guy, Sam's age, but the rest is a little tough because of the language barrier. Finally, I found some people who spoke English, though, and from what I could tell, he kept to himself, didn't charge much at the hotel and then left."

"Was he with anyone?"

Mayburn put a hand in his sandy-colored hair and rubbed it, like he was trying to shake something loose in his head. He said nothing, but looked at me, clearly thinking over his words.

"Tell me." I moved forward, leaning toward him. "Please tell me and do not hold back, because I am sick of not knowing, and I *don't* need to be coddled."

He made a face. "Step back, my friend, I'm not coddling you." He exhaled. "Fine, you want it straight, here it is. He had one charge at the bar. It was for four drinks, two were beers, two were wine."

Sam didn't usually drink wine. He was a beer guy. I bit my lip.

"I tracked down a bartender who was there that night," Mayburn said. "And since you don't want me to hold back, I'll just tell you…"

He paused, and I felt the pain in my heart, even before he spoke.

"He was with a woman."

58

"I gotta go." I turned and began walking from Mayburn's kitchen.

"Whoa, whoa." He caught my arm. "Where are you going?"

"To get a flight to Panama. If Sam thinks he's going to steal from my client and cheat on me, he doesn't get to do it without hearing a few select words. Like 'fuck you.'" My substitute phrase from my stop-swearing campaign had been "flub you," but that simply wasn't going to work.

And yet the news about Sam didn't all seem real. It couldn't be true. But clearly I had to stop tuning into that gut instinct that said, *Sam is a good guy. There has to be a reason for all this.*

"So you're just going to go to Panama?" Mayburn asked.

"Yep."

Mayburn gave me a skeptical look. "Been there before?"

"No."

"Speak Spanish?"

"No."

"Where you going to look for him?"

"The hotel."

"Anyplace else?"

"I'm not sure yet."

He pulled me gently by the arm, coaxing me back into the kitchen. "Let me do some more digging. We need to find out more before anybody starts booking a flight, okay?"

I groaned with frustration and confusion. I could feel despair clawing at the edges of my brain, wanting desperately to get in. I held it at bay, sensing that admitting it would let it overtake me.

He rubbed my arm in a kind but awkward way. "Hey, I'm sorry."

"Yeah. Thanks."

"He's a complete dumbass if he cheated on you, and who knows? Just because he was with a woman doesn't mean he was cheating. Trust me—never jump to conclusions on a case until you have all—"

"I know—*all the pieces.* It's all right. You don't have to baby me. You're the one who told me we'd probably find him with some girl."

He picked up the water and handed it to me. "Don't jump to conclusions."

I took a gulp and tried to imagine that the water was dousing the fire of my combustible emotions.

"Plus," Mayburn continued, "I need you, remember? You've got a playdate."

I looked at the clock above his kitchen sink. "I'm supposed to pick up Kaitlyn from preschool. Assuming I do that, and don't veer toward O'Hare, what do you need me to do when I get to DeSanto's house?"

"Well, here's the thing…" He leaned back on the counter, his elbows up. "I'm going to need you to hack into his computer."

I started choking up water. "Excuse me? You said you wanted *us* to get inside. You implied you'd be somehow getting into the house while I was there, and you'd be doing the dirty work."

"That's the thing. I can't figure out how to do it, even with you inside. The place is a fortress. It's not a normal house where you can just try to unlock the front door for me. They have huge walls and gates." He shook his head. "You're going to have to do it. You're not techtarded, are you?"

"I don't even know what that means, but I'm about as techie as a Buddhist monk. I don't even have a Facebook page."

"Well, it's not as much about being technical as it is about being smart and a good learner. And you're both of those." He clapped his hands together and rubbed them. "So let's teach you how to hack."

59

A few minutes after one o'clock, I was pushing the button on the DeSantos' buzzer. Mayburn wasn't kidding about it being a fortress. The place took up three city lots and was surrounded by spiked, stone walls. I knocked, thinking the door looked more suited for Buckingham Palace.

"Is this a jail?" Kaitlyn tugged at my hand.

"No, honey."

"Why are we here, Izzy?"

It would have been easier if she called me Mommy, but I told Mayburn that a) getting Kaitlyn to do anything she didn't want was impossible, and b) it would probably cause her to seek therapy later. Instead, we'd come up with a story that since I was her stepmother, she always called me Izzy.

"Hello?" I heard Lucy's high voice come through the intercom.

"It's Isabel and Kaitlyn."

She buzzed us in and the door swung open without me even touching it.

"Pretty!" Kaitlyn said.

The house was shaped like a huge *L*. Facing the door we'd just opened and, in front of us, was a courtyard full of bushes, windy stone paths and Japanese maple trees, blazing red. I'd never seen anything like it in the city. Lucy, or her expensive florist, had decorated the courtyard for autumn with cornucopias, garlands and grapevine wreaths, making the place look magical.

Lucy and her two kids came out onto their front porch, waving. "Noah and Eve, say hi to Kaitlyn."

Noah eyed Kaitlyn, then offered her a book he held in his hand. Kaitlyn trotted up the stairs, snatched it and dashed behind him into the house. Noah looked up at Lucy, who nodded and laughed, then he disappeared after Kaitlyn.

"I'm sorry," I said. "We're trying to get her not to be so grabby."

Lucy laughed again and shrugged. "They're kids. Kids do that. It's good to see you."

As I reached the top steps, she stepped forward and hugged me. I was sort of surprised at first, but then I returned it, and it was one of those hugs that makes everything in the world feel better.

"It's great to see you, too," I said, meaning it. "Your house is stunning."

"Oh, thank you! C'mon in. I'll show you around." With her daughter, Eve, holding her hand, Lucy led me around the house. Even though their furniture was predominantly dark wood, the home was filled with light coming in from the courtyard. The rooms were decorated in blue silks and gold accents. Lucy pointed out a blue rug they'd bought on their honeymoon in Portugal and yellow vases they'd brought back from a trip to China.

"And here's Michael's lair." Lucy waved her hand at an office as we passed by it. Unlike the rest of the house, the office was gloomy, the furniture heavy, the charcoal drapes only barely pulled back. On his desk was a brown leather blotter and on top of that, a black laptop, its cover closed. I felt a lick of apprehension up my back.

"Michael is at work?" I asked. *Please, please let him be at work, because I have to hack into that thing and make a duplicate copy of his hard drive.*

The bank told Mayburn that they had paid for a laptop, which Michael used at home. Mayburn then explained that the hard drive on such a computer carried information about every keystroke ever made. The only way to truly destroy that electronic information was to physically kill the computer. "You could burn it or smash it," Mayburn said, "or maybe throw it in a river, but beyond that, you can't get rid of the information that was once there."

"Don't people clean out stuff on their computers all the time?" I said.

"They try. If they're serious about it, they do something called scrubbing. But even with that, the files are no longer active, but the information can be found. So I just need you to get on DeSanto's computer and download everything off it."

I took one more look at the computer as Lucy led me toward the kitchen. God, I hoped I could I get in there and remember everything Mayburn had taught me. My palms felt slick with sweat at the thought.

The kitchen was huge, with taupe-colored granite and golden pine floors.

"I hope you didn't eat lunch," Lucy said. "I made some cucumber sandwiches."

"Sounds great."

Lucy told Eve to find Noah in the basement playroom, and after Eve scampered from the kitchen, it was just Lucy and me. For the next twenty minutes, we ate and talked, and I fell into my role as Isabel Bristol, average mom. I gave the story about how I'd become Kaitlyn's stepmother. Lucy told me about how she met her husband at an opening of a local restaurant. She was in town as part of her job at a New York PR firm, and they'd handled the opening.

"I'd never been to Chicago," Lucy said, "but I fell in love with it, just like I fell in love with Michael."

"Was it a hard adjustment?" I asked. "To move here?"

She bent her head to the side, a thin sheet of her gold-spun hair falling on a shoulder. "Yes, I suppose. I mean, it's so different here than New York, but in a good way. The hardest thing was realizing that we were here for good, while most of my family live in Connecticut now. I missed my sisters a lot. Still do. But this is my family now." She gestured around her vast kitchen. "You know how it is."

"Sure."

Lucy was so easy to be with. She had a tinkling laugh that made you smile, and she had such an uncomplicated and sweet air about her.

But as we finished our sandwiches any ease I'd experienced evaporated, and I started dodging glances at my watch. Assuming I could get into DeSanto's hard drive, which I had no real confidence about, the duplicate would take at least an hour, possibly two, to complete. I had to get in that office and on that computer now.

When Lucy stood to clear our plates, I grabbed my bag. It was heavy with the equipment Mayburn had loaded into it.

"Can I use your bathroom?" I pointed in the direction of a powder room that was just outside Michael's office door.

"Sure, and I'll go check on the kids."

"Thanks." I hoped desperately that Kaitlyn hadn't defaced a painting or taken apart a stereo.

I stepped into the bathroom and closed the door behind me. Nervous, I looked at myself in the mirror, struck by how little I'd changed over the last week. My hair was still red and curly and fell past my shoulders. My eyes were still large and green. I didn't look older, although I felt ancient. I didn't look jaded, although the loss of innocence was palpable.

My heart rate started to ratchet up as I looked at myself. How in the world had I gotten here? Last week, I would never, ever have agreed to hack into someone's computer, particularly someone who, as Mayburn had explained, might have some significant mob affiliations, but here I was about to do it.

Ignoring the hard *thump, thump* in the veins in my neck,

I pulled latex gloves from my bag and tugged them on. I turned off the powder-room light and opened the door as quietly as possible. I stuck my head out. I couldn't hear anything, which, hopefully, meant Lucy was still downstairs with the kids. My bag over my shoulder, I began stepping on my tiptoes in the direction of Michael's office. I gave myself five minutes until Lucy might come looking for me. Five minutes to dismantle a computer and start downloading the hard drive.

The computer was off, just as Mayburn had said it would be.

"How am I going to turn on the computer?" I had asked him. "Won't he have a password?"

"Oh, absolutely. And it's probably encrypted with a fingerprint swipe to get on. That's why you'll leave it off."

I unplugged the laptop and turned the thing over. It was a heavy one. The back had a number of panels screwed into place. I heard Mayburn's words, *Don't try to decipher the panels, just unscrew them all.*

I took out the set of screwdrivers he'd given me. My hands began to shake as I tried to match drivers to the different screws on the laptop. Finally, I found the right ones and unscrewed the four panels on the back. I got a shot of excitement, thinking I'd gotten to the hard drive, but all I found underneath was a sheet of metal, affixed with more screws.

Dammit. I shuffled through the screwdrivers again, finally unscrewing and lifting off the metal sheet. And that's when I recognized the hard drive—it was square and made of aluminum. Four more screws held it in place. I unscrewed those, but now I had to detach the flexible cables that held the hard drive to the computer, pulling them apart from the motherboard. But the space that held the hard drive was cramped and my fingers felt as big as sausages. The thing wasn't coming out.

"Okay," I said under my breath. "You can do this." I looked quickly over my shoulder. I heard nothing from the hallway or the kitchen. I looked at my watch. I'd been in there at least five minutes already. Should I return to the kitchen and try to get back to the office later? What if I didn't have a chance?

"Go, Iz," I said to myself, again under my breath.

I forced my fingers deeper into the bowels of the computer, gently twisting the hard drive from its place and, finally—*Yes!*—I extract the thing. It was surprisingly heavy—at least a pound in weight.

I rustled in my bag until I found the Logicube, a handheld hard-drive duplicator. It was blue with black sides and about the size of a large cordless telephone—roughly seven inches tall and four inches wide. An LCD screen covered the top of the device. At the bottom was a keypad.

I plugged the Logicube into the hard drive.

Don't turn it on yet! I remembered Mayburn saying. *If you turn that thing on before you attach the Write Blocker, we're screwed.*

You mean *I'm* screwed, I retorted in my head. I was the one sneaking around this house and breaking in to this computer. I was the one who'd littered the desk with a constellation of little screws. The pulse in my neck began tapping louder against my flesh. It felt like a drum in my throat.

Suddenly, I heard Lucy in the kitchen, singing a kids' song softly to herself. I drew in a sharp breath, swiveling my head and looking over my shoulder again. *Go, go, go!* In minutes, she'd be down the hall to ask if I was all right.

"You can do this," I whispered to myself.

I pawed through my bag until I found a box that looked like a black cigarette case.

The Write Blocker, I heard Mayburn say. *It prohibits any change in the appearance of DeSanto's data, so he'll never detect you were on the computer.*

I attached the Write Blocker to the Logicube and then, lastly, pulled from my bag a silver box, similar in size to the Write Blocker. An external hard drive.

Fix that to the Logicube, I heard Mayburn say. But then I

froze. Where was it supposed to attach? I couldn't remember. Frantically, I turned the Logicube this way and that, bumbling the hard drive and the Write Blocker in the process, cords twisting everywhere.

"C'mon," I muttered.

"Izzy?" I heard Lucy's sweet voice trill from down the hall.

My drumming pulse began beating wildly. I turned the Logicube over and over in my hand. Finally I spotted the open USB port at the bottom right side. It had been covered by a cord. I shoved in the attachment for the external hard drive.

Mayburn insisted that I run a series of checks before I turned on the Logicube, but he was crazy if he thought there was time.

I heard Lucy say again, "Izzy?"

I hit the Power button for the Logicube and watched as the LCD screen came to life. *Downloading,* it said.

"Yes," I whispered.

I jumped up from the desk, grabbed my bag and hurried down the hallway, pulling my gloves off and shoving them in my pockets. It would have been helpful if I could have hid the components and the mess I'd made of the laptop, but I had no time. I would have to keep Lucy occupied and away from that part of the house for at least an hour.

She was stepping from the kitchen into the hallway. "Hi," she said tentatively, her eyes concerned. "You okay?"

I patted my stomach. "Sorry I was gone for so long. Suddenly, I didn't feel so well."

"Oh, I hope it wasn't the sandwiches."

"No, no. I've been feeling off, almost nauseous, for a few days." This was absolutely true. Since Sam left, nothing in my body felt right.

"You're not pregnant?" she said jokingly.

"God, I hope not." The words shot from my mouth, from me and not my cover. There was no way I could fake wanting a pregnancy, even for Mayburn.

She laughed and led the way back into the kitchen. "You and Grady wouldn't want one of your own?"

"Kaitlyn is handful enough."

"Yeah," Lucy said. "She found the chest with Michael's Notre Dame memorabilia."

"Oh, gosh." I immediately started heading for the basement door.

"Don't worry about it. Seriously, leave it alone. It's just T-shirts and posters and stuff."

"Let me clean it up." Michael DeSanto didn't seem the type of guy who you wanted mad, and I knew that Domers (what we in the Midwest called Notre Dame grads and fans) could get pissed off quick if you messed with their school in any way.

"I put the breakable stuff up high." Lucy waved a kettle. "Are you in for some tea? Would that be good for your stomach?"

"Absolutely." *And hopefully our tea ceremony will last through the downloading of your husband's hard drive.*

Five minutes later, Lucy and I settled onto bar stools at the granite countertop. She had set out small china cups and tiny mint cookies on a china plate. "What else can I get you? How are you feeling?" she kept asking me.

We got talking about Chicago again, and Lucy admitted how lonely she was.

"Michael is great, of course," she said quickly, giving me the distinct impression that the opposite was true. "But he works a lot and he has a ton of friends here who always want him to golf or do guys' dinners."

"What about Bethany?" I remembered her friend from the playground.

"She's the best." Lucy sipped her tea, then stared into it with those cornflower-blue eyes, as if trying to glean answers in the tea leaves. "But she works, and so she's got a lot on her plate. Really, my best friends are my sisters, and we're on the phone all the time, but I'd just love to be closer. What about your family?"

I decided it would be easier to talk about my real mom and brother, rather than make up some crap. I said that my mother lived in Chicago. I tried not to think about my mom, and her confessions, and my wonderings about whether she'd had anything to do with Forester's death. I told her how we called my brother Sheets. She laughed, raising her face from her tea and throwing her blond hair back, exposing her white neck. That laugh seemed to ring through the kitchen and maybe the whole house, and in that moment I felt better than I had in weeks.

We talked for about an hour, and I kept thinking that Lucy was the kind of person I would love to be friends with. While our lunch looked like the perfect first meal shared between girlfriends, after her laugh died away, I felt horribly guilty that I was lying to her, that I was there for more than her friendship.

Then a rumbling came from the back of the house.

"What's that?" I said.

"The garage door," Lucy said. "Michael's home early."

60

"Michael is *home?*" I couldn't help it. My voice came out loud.

I looked at my watch. The download had been going on for fifty-five minutes. Was it enough? And how could I get to the office? I couldn't very well just sprint from the room without causing her to follow me. And it would take time to get the computer back together. Mayburn said that was the hardest part.

"Yeah, he is." Lucy bit her lip, then she stood. "It's great when he's home. Really." I don't know who she was trying to convince, but she wasn't particularly successful.

She started cleaning up the tea tray and the sweetener. Her gestures had a fast, nervous quality to them.

I stood, trying to figure out what in the hell to do. I was about to claim intestinal difficulties again, when the backdoor of the kitchen opened. And there was Michael DeSanto.

He was dressed in a black suit with a lime-green tie. I was struck by how technically handsome the man was, but how dangerous he felt.

"Hi!" My voice came out like a chirp. "I'm Izzy. We met at Prada last night." I advanced on him and stuck out my hand, physically blocking his path to his office.

What should I do? What should I do?

"Yeah, sure." He gave my hand a quick pump, his eyes cold and flat.

As I stood there, dumbfounded, I looked into those eyes and noticed how light they were—brown, certainly, but almost like a brown paper bag, a wet one, bordering on translucent. The effect was spooky, and the proximity of him put my nerves into overdrive.

I wanted to run down the hall, but that would be alarming and he'd follow me. I had to get him out of the house, or keep him away from the office while I got back in there. But there was nothing I could do now that wouldn't draw attention.

I went back to the stool in front of my tea. After I'd taken a seat, I saw that Lucy was hugging her husband, yet he was staring at me over her shoulder, those light brown eyes examining me in a curious and clinical way.

Michael DeSanto remained quiet as Lucy pulled away and began chattering about the kids and how well they were playing downstairs. He glanced at her and nodded at an occasional thing she was saying, but mostly he was looking at me.

Lucy seemed not to notice. She was anxious and distracted around her husband. She continued to chatter about the kids. She cleaned up the teakettle and the box of cookies.

Michael nodded blandly at her, but he kept staring at me. It was freaking me out.

Finally, he interrupted his wife. "I've got to get some work done." He took a step in the direction of his office.

The pulse in my neck banged so loudly, it was all I could hear in my head. I had to stop him.

I jumped up, blocking his path. "Kaitlyn destroyed some of your Notre Dame stuff," I blurted. "I'm so sorry."

I looked at Lucy, whose face had gone scared. "Oh, it's not that bad—"

"I'm really sorry," I said, talking over her. "She's still down there right now. I hope she hasn't torn up anything else."

Michael gave Lucy a murderous glance, which made her bite her lip. I felt terrible about throwing Lucy to the wolves, in this case one wolf—her husband—but I could think of no other way to get him out of the room. And like a good Domer, Michael bolted and headed for the basement.

Lucy bit her lip and looked at me. "You shouldn't have gotten him worked up…"

"I'm sorry."

"I suppose we should see how it's going?" she said with trepidation.

"I'll be right there." I put my hand on my stomach with one hand. "I'm not feeling so well again."

I picked up my bag and left. When I got to the bathroom door, I stopped and strained my ears toward the kitchen. It was hard to hear over the pounding pulse in my head, but it seemed everyone was in the basement now.

I ran from the bathroom to his office, pulling on my gloves. I looked at the LCD screen on the Logicube. *Download 99% complete,* it said.

"Go, go, go," I whispered to the thing. I tapped my foot, trying to ignore my ragged breathing. A minute went by, each second taking decades. Finally, the LCD screen changed and read, *Download complete!*

I ripped the hard drive from the Logicube, throwing the Logicube, Write Blocker and external hard drive—all still humming and attached to each other—into my bag. Now I had to get Michael's hard drive back in his computer. I wrestled with it. No matter how I turned it, it didn't seem to fit properly.

"Oh, God. Oh, God," I whimpered. My hands were shaking, which wasn't helping matters.

And then I felt something horrible.

It started somewhere in my belly and it crawled its way up through my chest and into my heart and then into my neck and my arms and legs until it finally reached my face.

"Shit," I whispered, the stop-swearing campaign completely abandoned. That little flop-sweating problem I had— the one that only showed its sad, pathetic self in the midst of public speaking—had decided to rear its ugly head. My face pulsed red with the flush, and my body started sweating hard.

I kept turning the thing and twisting the hard drive, trying to get it into place, but my hands were so clammy under my gloves I couldn't seem to hold it straight or fit it in.

The sweat trickled from my hairline and into my eyes.

I tried to blow my hair away from my face. *Fffff, ffff,* the upward shot of air did nothing to move it. I tried again and again, but my hair was sticking to my forehead now. The god-damned hard drive kept slipping around in my fingers.

Then *finally* it snapped into place. Now I just had to get the metal cover back on and the four panels. I looked at the debris on the desk. The panels were all lying there haphazardly, the screws strewn about. I couldn't remember which screws went with which panels.

"Fuck," I said.

Sweat dripping onto the components, I got the metal sheet on, and managed to figure out which screws held it in place. I lifted my arm and wiped my face with my sleeve. *Just ignore the sweat,* I told myself. *Think of all the detoxification and weight loss benefits.*

The panels were next. They were like puzzle pieces—all vaguely resembling each other, but none of them the exact same shape. I managed to get two on quickly, but the last two were impossible. Neither seemed to fit right. My hands, slimy under the gloves, kept trembling and slipping.

And then I heard voices in the kitchen. The thought of how close I was to getting caught shifted me into another mode. *Get it together,* I barked to myself harshly.

I didn't try to discern what the voices in the kitchen were saying. I ignored the sense that they were getting a little closer. I didn't think about the fact that I was probably starting to develop severe pit stains. I got the panels into place, tried one screw and then another and then another, working systematically until I'd secured both panels into place.

The voices were in the hall now, then one died away and all I heard was one set of footsteps.

Then suddenly the doorbell rang and the footsteps stopped, sounded as if they were going the other way. The break gave me just the time I needed.

Turning the laptop over, I plugged in the power cord. I pulled off my latex gloves, shoved them into my pockets again.

Heavy footsteps came from the hallway. They weren't Lucy's.

"Can I help you?" I heard Michael say.

I turned with a calm smile on my face. I heard Mayburn's words—*That's the number-one ticket to a successful cover—believing every word of it. No stumbling with your words, no embarrassment, just be confident about it and don't flinch.* But he'd never said anything about how to handle a spectacular bout of flop sweating.

"I've wanted this laptop for months," I said. "Is it the new model?"

Michael DeSanto took two steps into his office, his eyes sweeping the room. "Yeah. It is," he said in a cold, angry voice. Then he looked at my face. It was wet. I could feel that much. And I knew from the sheer heat that I was probably a lovely plum color. And yet I was determined to act as if there was nothing wrong.

"Sorry to be in your office," I said. "Lucy had given me the tour earlier, and I've been dying to see how heavy this is." I picked the laptop up and put it down again. "It's big, but you could definitely travel with it." I was relieved to find that my blush was somehow fading away as I went a hundred percent with the bold lying.

DeSanto took a few steps and touched the computer. I could tell he was touching it to see if it was warm, if I'd turned it on. He nodded slightly when the computer was cold. If he had touched me, he wouldn't have gotten the same result.

"You okay?" he said, a suspicious voice, a wary stare.

Although the sweat was receding, I was still positively glistening. "Great, great. I've got to get going."

But he didn't move. And he'd given me no room to stand from the chair, which had high leather arms on either side. He'd trapped me.

Michael stared down at me, his face impassive, those light brown eyes never wavering from mine, trying to see inside me, it seemed.

I tried to hear Mayburn's words in my head, but they were fading. I felt the sweat start running again under my arms.

"Anyway, I should go," I said.

Still he didn't move. Still he stared at me with those translucent eyes.

My pulse picked up again. Finally I stood up, fast, and he took a step back. "I should get going. I'll just grab Kaitlyn."

I left the office in what I hoped appeared to be a calm walk. In my head, I was yelling, *Run, run, run.* The sweat started again and ran in rivulets down my back.

I went down the stairs, where Lucy was laughing and officiating some kind of game between Kaitlyn, Noah and Eve. She looked so much happier here with the kids, away from her husband.

I grabbed Kaitlyn's coat from the floor and tugged it on her. "We have to leave. Thank you for everything, Lucy. I just remembered a doctor's appointment I have to get her to."

Lucy's face went concerned, whether from my quick exit or the fact that I looked as if I'd jumped into a swimming pool and quickly thrown my clothes back on, I couldn't tell. "Everything all right?" she said.

"Of course. Just a usual checkup with…" *What in the heck did you call a children's doctor?* Suddenly I couldn't recall.

As I hustled Kaitlyn up the stairs, she promptly began to bawl. "Thanks, Lucy, for everything," I called over my shoulder. I felt terrible leaving her like that.

I stopped short at the top. Michael blocked my way once more, standing still, looking down.

Don't stop, don't stop, I said to myself. I nudged myself and a sobbing Kaitlyn past him and didn't look back. I got outside the front door and through the courtyard, when I realized we were locked in.

I tugged at the huge brass knocker on the wood door to the street. My hands were wet, slipping on the knocker, and it didn't budge. Kaitlyn wailed. What had I just done? I'd possibly put a child in danger, while I'd illegally made a duplicate hard drive of a reputed mob figure.

I looked over my shoulder and there was Michael DeSanto, staring at me from the front door with his transparent eyes.

We gazed at each other for seconds that seemed years. Finally, he reached a hand out, the buzzer on the door sounded and the door swung open without a sound.

I hustled Kaitlyn down the street. "You're all right. You're all right," I crooned to her as much as to myself.

Strapping her into the car seat, my hands started violently trembling. In the front seat, I put the car in drive and pulled away from the curb. When I got to the next corner, I pulled over, put my head on the steering wheel, and then I cried just as hard as Kaitlyn.

61

When Mayburn got to my place, I buzzed him in and left the front door to my apartment open.

"Izzy?" I heard him call a minute later.

"In here," I yelled from my bedroom, my hands deep in a suitcase.

I heard him step into the bedroom. "What are you doing?"

"Packing for Panama."

"We went through this already."

"Yes, we did, but that was before all this." I went to my dresser top and picked up the mass of cords and boxes that was the Logicube, Write Blocker and external hard drive. I shoved it in his hands.

"Something go wrong?"

"Depends on how you look at it." I went to my closet, rifled to the back, where I stored my summer clothes, and grabbed a few dresses. I had no idea how I was supposed to pack for Panama City, Panama. What was the weather like? How did people dress? I had no time for research.

All of a sudden, something dawned on me. "Will the feds have my passport flagged?"

"I doubt it," Mayburn said. "They can't flag the passport of every potential witness in every investigation they have."

"Good." I kept packing.

I could hear Mayburn fiddling with the Logicube and the

external hard drive. "You know how nervous I was having you in that house by yourself?" he asked.

I was in the process of grabbing some T-shirts from a drawer, but I stopped. "*You* were nervous? You know what I went through in there?"

More fiddling with the Logicube. "No," he said distractedly, "but…" more fiddling… "I know that you did it. Yeah! Nice work!" Mayburn was practically bouncing on his feet now. "Damn, I didn't think you could do it."

"You didn't think I could do it?" I tossed the T-shirts on top of the pile of clothes already in the suitcase. "Then why in the hell did you send me in there?"

He laughed. "I'm kidding. I'm just trying to piss you off." He walked over and closed the suitcase. "Look at me."

I did. His eyes were compassionate. We stood still, a few feet from each other. "I'm proud of you," he said. "I want to hear all about it. Let's go get a beer or something to celebrate."

I turned and kept packing. "No way. Michael DeSanto caught me in his office."

"What happened?"

I told him quickly while I threw random tank tops and sandals into the suitcase.

"Holy shit," Mayburn said. "Maybe you should leave town."

"Exactly. They know my name is Isabel, but they don't know anything else about me, but it's not like I'm the hardest person to spot."

Mayburn eyed my red hair. "Good point." He stared down at the hard drive in his hands. "I can't wait to see what you got. You kicked ass here, McNeil. I have to thank you."

It was nice to hear. "You're welcome. Now, do me a favor and give me any information you can about what I should do when I get to Panama. Like the names of all the people you spoke to, and maybe those you have info for but haven't contacted yet."

"No problem." He pulled out a pen and small notebook.

Ripping out a blank page, he began copying a list of names he'd written in there. "And when you get to the airport, call your wireless company and ask them to turn on your international calling."

"Good idea."

Five minutes later, I took the list of names from Mayburn, threw my makeup on top of the pile in my suitcase and zipped it up. "I'll call you from Panama."

62

Day Ten

There were no available evening flights to Panama, so I stayed at an O'Hare Hilton. Strangely, I got the best sleep I'd had since Sam disappeared. No one seemed to have followed me there. I felt safe in the anonymity of an airport hotel.

During the flight the next morning, though, my anxiety returned like a train blasting into the station. The male flight attendant seemed way too accommodating for coach. And the guy behind me who glanced up over his paper when I went to the bathroom—was he someone to be careful of? I would probably never again think a man was simply ogling me for my looks, and I added this to the list of wrongs Sam had done me. I sat fuming in my seat.

The ride from the Panama City *aeropuerto* to the Decapolis hotel, where Sam had stayed, surprised me. Despite the billboards in Spanish, the highway looked as if it could have been in the States—a few industrial areas, a couple of impoverished-looking places. When we reached downtown and the avenue that ran along the bay, I was surprised to see its shore packed with high-rises.

"Does all of Panama City look like this?" I asked the cab-driver, who, blessedly, spoke English.

He laughed, looking at me in the rearview mirror. He was

old, probably in his seventies, and his entire tanned face creased when he smiled. "No, no. This is business area and Multicentro, for shopping. You make sure you see Casco Viejo, *sí?* And Panama La Vieja."

"Right. Great." I twisted in my seat and tried to see if any cars were lingering behind us. I saw nothing.

And then, for the first time in over a week, I got the feeling I was alone. That no one was watching me.

The hotel was a sleek tower made of stainless steel and glass. I thanked the driver and paid the fare using U.S. cash. The official currency was the balboa, I'd learned from the chatty flight attendant on the plane. But only coins were available, no balboa paper money, and the balboa was tied to the U.S. dollar 1–1, so they accepted American money.

As I stepped from the cab, the hotel loomed over me like a big mirror, reflecting the low-hanging gray clouds that peppered the sky. The temperature was pleasant enough— probably in the low eighties—but the humidity hung like a wet blanket. While the city had looked a hundred percent metropolitan from a distance, I could see now that sprinkled in between the high-rises were bodega-like shops, cafés with round plastic tables in front and video stores.

I handed my bag to the concierge and soon I was inside, checking in. So far, everyone had spoken nearly fluent English. My room, twenty stories up, didn't look so different from an upscale hotel in the United States—smooth maple furniture, crisp white linens on a low platform bed. The only thing that set it apart were the large photographs of what looked to be African natives in tribal dress.

The bellman saw me staring at the photos and explained, "Panamanian peoples." He pointed at a scary, colorful mask that hung between the closet doors. "Devil mask," he said.

An image flashed in my mind—Sam lifting the mask off the wall, wearing it.

I gave the bellman a large tip.

"If we can do anything for you during your stay—" he began to say.

"There is." I rifled through my carry-on for the two photos of Sam I'd brought with me. Both were close-ups of his face and torso. One, I'd taken in Mexico on the beach. His hair was almost white-blond from the week of sun and there was a streak of sand on his bare shoulder. The other photo showed him in a suit, before a benefit Forester had invited us to. His olive eyes matched the suit.

"Did you meet this man?" I held out the photos. I smiled at them as I did this, although really I felt like shredding them and tossing them at the devil mask as an offering. "He stayed here last week."

The bellman glanced at the photos, shook his head and shrugged.

I grabbed the list of contacts Mayburn made me. "Do you know any of these people?"

He studied it. "Alejandro? He does not work today. Fernando, no work. Pedro, I do not know. Dominga? She is downstairs."

A tickle of exhilaration crept up my back. "Downstairs where?"

"She is concierge." He looked at the rest of the list, shaking his head at many of the names. "Yes, and Mateo, he is bartender. He is working in—" he glanced over my shoulder at the bedside clock "—one hour."

"Thank you!" I gave him a few more dollars.

I changed into a black linen sundress, pulled my hair into a high ponytail to combat the humidity and took the elevator downstairs. I found the concierge behind a desk decorated with bold ethnic patterns.

Dominga was a nice woman who denied meeting Sam, and then immediately began trying to convince me to take a guided trip to someplace called Portobelo.

"No, thank you," I said over and over, continuing to slide

Sam's pictures in front of her. "If you could just look at these again."

She glanced at them. "I am sorry."

"But I thought…" I started to say that I thought she had given information to Mayburn about Sam, but then again, she might have simply given him information that *led* Mayburn to someone or something else. In my haste to leave, I hadn't asked Mayburn to decipher all the names.

I pulled out the list now and pointed at Mateo's name. "Bartender?" I asked.

She looked at me curiously but nodded. "Sushi bar." She pointed across the lobby to a chic bar that was lit from behind with a blue light. With its modern decor and the low thump of bass emanating from it, it could have been in Manhattan.

The sushi bar was nearly empty of patrons, save for one man wearing shorts and an untucked, cotton shirt that looked like something you might see in Havana.

I took a seat and smiled at the bartender, a small guy with a black ponytail. "Mateo?"

He shook his head and told me Mateo would be there in a half hour.

I ordered water, then changed my mind and asked for a Panamanian beer. He brought me a bottle of something called Soberana.

I poured it into a glass. It tasted like a light beer with a little extra flavor.

The man with the Havana shirt turned to me and smiled. He was older than me, with gray, thinning hair. Last week, I would have smiled right back at him. Now, I felt my heart rate jump.

He pointed at my beer. "Don't you think the name is funny? *Sober*-ana?"

I faked a chuckle. "Yeah, that is funny."

"Where are you from?"

I wanted to ask, *Don't you know already? Are you one of the people who are following me?*

But then again, I was here to talk to people, I was here to learn and I was here to find Sam. Even if this man was tailing me, I had nothing to hide. And again, I had that feeling of finally being alone.

"I'm from Chicago," I said.

"Hey, we're both Midwesterners. I live in Minnesota. You here on vacation?"

"Not exactly." I thought about showing him Sam's photo. "What about you?"

"I'm looking for property. My wife and I are planning on retiring in a few years, and we want to get a condo down here. It's a lot less expensive than Florida and all those places in the States. Hardly any taxes."

"How long have you been here?"

"Just got in last night. I'm waiting for my real-estate agent to go look at some places. You can't believe how much property is available."

We sat for a moment in silence and then he offered his hand. "Tom LaHaye."

"Izzy McNeil." I took Sam's pictures out of my purse and showed them to him. "You haven't seen this guy by any chance, have you?"

He said no and showed them to the bartender, who also shook his head. "Who is he?"

"My fiancé. I've sort of lost him."

Just then a short woman in a yellow suit rushed into the bar. "Mr. LaHaye!" she said. "I'm sorry I am late."

Tom LaHaye laughed. "Hello, Beatriz. You're always late. Isn't that what you told me? Panamanians believe in suggested time not being on time, right?"

"Yes." She patted his arm. "But you are not Panamanian—not yet, until we find you a home—and so I should be on time for you. Come, come."

Tom shook my hand again. "I hope you find him," he said kindly, before he was swept off by his agent.

My beer was gone by the time a new bartender stepped behind the bar and began tying his black apron. He was a young guy with a chiseled jaw, who looked as if he could have been in a boy band.

"Mateo?" I said.

He gave me a sexy grin and nodded.

"Hi." I tossed him my best *hey-there-hottie* look just for good measure, and ordered another beer. When he delivered it, I pushed Sam's picture toward him. "Did you meet this man?"

He looked at the picture. He scrunched up his gorgeous face and nodded. "Yes, and someone called the hotel about him recently."

"Yes! Exactly. That was my friend who called you. Can you tell me what you remember about this man?" I pointed to Sam in the picture.

The other bartender chuckled and moved away to serve a couple who'd just sat down.

"I told your friend that he was at the bar," Mateo said. "Over there." He pointed at a low black table surrounded by a cozy, blue velvet booth.

I felt my anger flare. I thought about giving Mateo the *hey-there-hottie* look again because who knew? Maybe, like Sam, I'd be finding my own Panamanian fling. But for now, I had to focus.

"Do you remember who he was with?" I asked.

"A woman."

I gritted my teeth. "What did she look like?"

"Black hair."

So far, nearly every woman I'd seen in Panama had black hair.

Was she pretty? I wanted to ask. Instead, I settled for, "Do you know her name?"

"No."

"Was she Panamanian?"

"Yes, I have seen her."

What did that mean? Was she a hooker? That seemed so very un-Sam, but what did I know anymore?

"Where had you seen her?"

"She is a real-estate agent."

I felt excitement. Maybe the woman wasn't a hooker or a new girlfriend, but possibly someone he contacted about the real estate owned by the Panamanian corporation. *Yeah,* I reminded myself. *That Panamanian corporation he stole from Forester.*

A woman in a tank top took a seat a few stools over from me, dumping a host of shopping bags on the floor.

Mateo began to move toward her.

"Wait!" I said. "Was the agent you saw him with the woman who just left here?"

He gave me a confused face.

"Just a minute ago," I explained, "there was an agent named Beatriz here."

He shrugged. "I do not know her name."

"Is she big? Small?"

He laughed. "She is a woman." As if that explained everything.

"How old was she?"

"She is maybe thirty? Thirty-five."

Beatriz had looked to be at least in her late thirties, but I couldn't be sure. "Can you tell me anything else about her?"

Now he looked impatient. "I don't know anything more."

"Okay, thank you." My energy flagged.

I sat there another minute, sipping my Soberana, wondering what to do next. And then I suddenly knew exactly what to do. I went to the house phone and asked for the room of Tom LaHaye.

63

Day Eleven

The next morning at ten minutes after eight, I stood on the front steps of the hotel, waiting for Beatriz.

Tom LaHaye had been happy to give me her contact information when he got back to the hotel and I told him on the phone I'd decided to look for a second home in Panama. "You're going to love her," he said. "You're going to love this place! It's the best."

I talked to Mayburn before I called Beatriz, and he thought my plan to pose as a wealthy American looking for vacation property was a good one, since it would get me in the ballpark of the properties owned by Forester, and we figured that if Sam was meeting with real-estate agents, it must have been about the properties owned by Forester through his bearer shares.

"I've been looking more into those types of shares," Mayburn told me. "Forester's estate could put liens on the shares if they'd been stolen. But since Sam had authority to possess them, at least while they were at the office, it's probably not entirely clear if the law would view them as stolen, and it would take a bit of time to work it out. In the meantime, Sam probably knows this and he's more than likely trying to liquidate the properties."

"And just take the money?" I'd asked.

"I guess."

I couldn't fathom it—not the money or the thought of Sam stealing it, but I was taking it one step at a time, I decided. First, meet with the agents and see if I could find him.

Meanwhile, Mayburn had worked the phones and the Web, and found five other real-estate agents who fit the vague profile Mateo had given me of the woman he'd seen with Sam. I'd meet with them, we decided, look at properties, and I'd try to figure out if any of them was the mystery woman.

Mayburn cautioned me not to bring up Sam right away when I was with the agents. "If they're involved in something shady with him," he said, "they're going to drop you off at a street corner—or worse—and disappear."

Beatriz pulled up wearing an orange suit this time. I'd worn my best heiress outfit—a white skirt, blue blouse, high black sandals and huge sunglasses.

Beatriz hustled me into her car, an SUV, and talked fast as we pulled away. "Okay, so you want a condo, you said on the phone. And you would like to spend one to two million. Is that right?"

"Yes." I knew from Sam's boss that the properties owned by Forester's Panamanian corporation were in that range and higher.

"Okay. I have showings at eleven o'clock, but I will take you to many places and if you don't like, I pick you up tomorrow, okay?"

"Perfect." Especially since I had three more agents booked that day.

She gave me a genuine smile through the orange lipstick that matched her suit, and I felt guilty for making her work when I had no intention of buying a thing.

"Don't worry about that," Mayburn had said when I mentioned the guilt last night. "All real-estate agents do is drive people around hoping that maybe, somewhere, someday one of them will buy property, and who knows? Maybe you will someday. Maybe you'll love it."

The truth was, I did find myself falling a bit for Panama City. The first place I saw was a development at Costa del Este, just outside the city. Driving up to the area, I marveled at the streets lined thick with palm trees and beachfront condominiums glittering white against the foamy light blue surf. The place Beatriz showed me boasted internal winding stucco staircases and huge curved balconies.

After touring the development, we got back in the car, and I finally mentioned my fiancé and pulled out his photo.

"He is handsome," she said vaguely, glancing back to the road. "Now, let's see. Where do I take you next?" She made a few turns. "Do you know that Panama has almost no hurricanes?"

"Really?"

"Yes. Is one of best things about our country. It is because where we are situated in the Caribbean."

We pulled up to another development, and once again I mentioned Sam's name, then Forester's. I got no reaction. I asked her if she'd met Alec Thornton, the name of Alyssa's brother. Not a flicker. I was pretty sure Beatriz wasn't my girl.

I repeated the process with two more agents that day—one named Gabriela, the other Pilar.

Gabriela suggested that if I wasn't going to spend a lot of time in Panama over the next few years, and if I would consider a more long-term investment, maybe I should think of a property in Casco Viejo.

"It is one of the oldest cities in the Americas," Gabriela explained when we got there.

She was a gorgeous woman—nearly six feet tall and exquisitely dressed in crisp linen pants and heels.

I followed her through the bricked streets of Casco Viejo, each of which seemed to lead to the Pacific. From many places, I saw boats entering the Panama Canal in the distance. I tried not to imagine Gabriela with Sam as we walked; I tried not to interrupt her history lesson or blurt out one of the many questions that batted about in my brain, like, *Are you sleeping with my fiancé?*

But my task soon became easier, because the charm of Casco Viejo was hard to avoid. Strolling through it was like walking back in time. Bougainvillea twisted itself around rusted wrought-iron fences and balconies. Old churches with flaking, carved red-tiled roofs sat in the center of the plazas. Bright paint crumbled from the side-by-side stone houses, some of which were empty hulls.

"The pirates," Gabriela said, gesturing at one house. "They stripped this city hundreds of years ago. And we have had many fires. We are just now building it up."

She pointed out a jazz bar and then a palace—imposing and scrubbed a gleaming white—which was now a museum. "You see, this is good area for investment," she said, stopping under a white square arch of another vacated building. "It is changing fast."

I pulled out a photo of Sam. "Do you think my fiancé would like it here?"

"Yes, of course. You need to build to specification—we have very strict rules about renovating in Casco Viejo—but you will enjoy it."

I held the photo a little closer to her. "But do you think *he* will enjoy it? His name is Sam Hollings."

No reaction, except another "Yes, of course."

"Have you ever met him?"

She looked at me quizzically. "I do not think so."

"Have you ever met Forester Pickett? Alec Thornton?"

Her expression morphed into full bewilderment that appeared genuine. "I am sorry. I do not believe so." She paused, her beautiful, nearly black eyes looked puzzled. "Maybe I take you to nicer place? A lovely condo?"

A few hours later, I was ambling through a host of other lovely condos in Punta Pacifica with Pilar, and I got no further with her. She had no response to Sam's, Alec's or Forester's names or Sam's picture.

At the end of the day, my white heiress skirt was smudged with soot from Casco Viejo, my skin coated with construction dust from the new developments. Exhausted and defeated, I thanked Pilar, went to my room and crawled into bed. I had another appointment the next day with an agent named Adelina, but what was the point? There were possibly hundreds of black-haired Realtors in their thirties in the city.

I stared at the white hotel ceiling. I picked up my cell phone and dialed Grady's number. Flashes of him had been popping in my mind all day—images of him kissing me, the sensation of him licking the side of my neck. I'd never thought of Grady in a sexual way before. Now I was having a hard time stopping such thoughts, probably because it took me away from the utter helplessness I was feeling.

Grady didn't answer, and suddenly I felt silly trying to come up with something to say. Be flirty or resort to our usual banter? And if you wanted to date a guy, which I wasn't even sure I did, weren't you supposed to wait for him to call you? I could barely remember all the rules, and the thought of dating again made me woozy. I hung up without leaving a message.

I called Mayburn, who answered right away.

"I don't think this was a good idea," I told him. "Finding this agent could take years."

"Yeah, well, it's not a good time for you to come home right now. Michael DeSanto should be arrested soon."

I sat up in bed, my eyes landing on the red-and-black devil mask hanging on the wall. "What?"

"Yeah. Money laundering, conspiracy and a bunch of other stuff that could put him away for a long time. He was working with a group that appears to be mob, and who were operating through a dummy company in the burbs. Whenever he worked at home, he got instructions on a secure phone and put the transactions through while he was there. He kept coded notes and things like that on another server at his house. The duplicate you made of the hard drive gave his bosses at the bank the direction they needed. When they started digging, they found enough to take their suspicions to the feds. DeSanto doesn't know it yet, but they're going to swarm his house any minute."

"But what about Lucy and the kids? This is going to be horrible."

Mayburn grunted. "I'm worried about her, too." A pause. "And I've never even met her."

I flopped back on the cool white sheets, picturing Lucy's innocent eyes. I thought of her telling me how she missed her sisters and how she was very lonely sometimes. What would happen when her husband was gone, too?

I felt a wave of bleakness.

Mayburn seemed to sense it. "Hang in there," he said.

"Hang in there? That's your advice?"

"Izzy, with your situation, that's the best I've got right now."

64

Day Twelve

The next day, my appointment with yet another Realtor wasn't until noon, so I spent the morning at the Miraflores Locks, part of the Panama Canal. I watched the massive gears of the locks operating as two monolithic ships passed through, then I strolled through the museum, reading about the enormous project that was the building of the canal. In order to link the Atlantic and the Pacific Oceans via the Canal, at least twenty-seven thousand people would die first. It was a massive undertaking that had produced one headache after another. And yet the builders and the engineers persisted and regrouped time and time again, changing their plans drastically, altering their thinking and their assumptions until they succeeded.

As I stood in front of a photo of the Culebra Cut—a man-made valley dug through the continental divide in Panama—I came to a conclusion. No matter what happened with Sam, no matter what happened with my job, no matter what I found out about Forester or who had paid Dr. Li, I was going to be okay. Like the builders of the canal, I would persist and I would regroup and I would change my plans and I would alter my assumptions and my thinking whenever I had to. Because I was not going to go down with this fight. I was not going to lose myself just because my world had been rearranged.

Feeling stronger and more determined, I went back to the hotel and got ready for my next appointment. I packed my bag and brought it downstairs with me. If I couldn't get a lead on Sam today, I was heading home to regroup.

The Realtor, Adelina, was a small woman with a soft, lyrical voice, who seemed to know everyone in Panama. At the hotel, she hugged two of the bellmen, and the manager rushed out onto the front steps to say hello. She took me to a café, where I choked down a dark cup of Panamanian coffee, and where every worker in the place came out to greet her. We spoke, and I told her how I'd already seen developments in Punta Pacifica, Costa del Este and the others. I liked Adelina. She leaned close and listened intently when I talked. She chuckled at the slightest thing that amused her. She reached across the table on a few occasions, squeezed my hand and said things like, "Don't worry, we will put you in the right place." Every time she said it, I felt as if she was promising to put me in the right place in my life.

"So," she said, paying the tab and picking up her purse from the floor. "Let's take you to some interesting places, yes? First, I think a tour of the Amador Causeway. There is American history with the causeway and a beautiful development there."

I liked her so much I decided not to wait to show her Sam's photo. I couldn't bear wasting her time anymore.

I grabbed my purse, took a picture out and placed it on the table.

Before I could even ask her a question, I saw the reaction—a deep blink of the eyes—then she leaned in again, this time toward the photo.

She sat up and looked at me quizzically. "Do you know him?"

"He's my fiancé."

"And so are you buying property now that he has sold the others? Why did he not tell me?"

My heart nearly jumped out from my ribs and through my mouth. "You sold property for this man?"

A careful look took over her face. "If you do not know, then maybe I should not say. We are very cautious here in Panama about our clients. We use…how do you say it?" She paused. "Discretion."

"Are you having an affair with him?"

"An affair? Do you mean sexual?" She tsked, clearly offended. "Of course not. I am a Realtor for Mr. Hollings, and for Pickett Enterprises."

"So, you've seen Sam? I mean, in the last week?"

She shook her head brusquely. "I cannot discuss this. I told you, we have discretion here."

Now it was my turn to squeeze her hand.

She gave me a nervous look like people do when they encounter a crazy person on the street.

"Please," I said, not letting go of her hand. I was *so* close. "Tell me what you know about him. Tell me if you know where he is."

She pulled her hand away. "Perhaps it is time for me to leave." She stood and walked out of the café.

Scrambling to put the photo back in my purse, I chased her onto the street. "Adelina, please help me."

She opened her car door. "If you do not truly want to buy property, then I cannot help you. I am sorry."

"You can't leave me here! We're miles from the hotel, and I don't know how to get back."

It wasn't entirely true—I was sure I could find a cab—but it stopped her.

She bobbed her head toward the passenger seat. "I will drive you to the hotel, and then I must go."

In the car, I began to pour out my tale as fast as I could form words. I told her how Sam had disappeared. I told her how it looked as if he had stolen the shares of Forester's corporation, which owned property in Panama.

She looked at me sharply. "That is not true," she blurted. "He did not steal. Mr. Pickett placed these properties in a Panama Private Interest Foundation. Upon his death, the documentation says that Sam became the temporary protector of this foundation. Mr. Pickett devised specific instructions through a very respected attorney here in Panama telling Sam how to dispose of the properties." She leaned forward a little, her face stern. "Sam has the right to hold those shares and to sell the assets of the corporation."

"He does?" I couldn't hide the surprise in my voice.

Adelina pulled over to the side of the road and turned the car off. "I want the truth. What is happening with this situation? Why are you here telling me this? Is your name really Isabel?" She looked scared now, and I felt terrible for her.

I took a breath and looked deep into her eyes. "Adelina, I am telling you the truth. I was supposed to marry this man—" I pulled Sam's photo from my bag again "—in a month and a half. He disappeared and did not tell me anything. I have wondered if he was hurt. I have been terrified that he was dead. I have been questioned by the FBI. I have been followed for weeks. I have lost this man, do you understand? And I *loved* him."

She opened her mouth a little as if she was going to say something, but she was silent.

I plunged forward with my words. "Is there someone you love with every piece of your body, with your whole heart? Because that is how I loved this man." I shook the photo a little. "I *do* still love him, and I need to know if he is okay, and I need to know if he has done something bad, because if he has I need to move on. I need to let him go. I need to stop loving him."

Tears began to roll down my cheeks. At the same time, I saw a tear spring from the corners of Adelina's eyes.

She exhaled long from between pursed lips. We gazed at each other. The car started to get steamy with the humidity seeping in from outside.

Adelina leaned toward me, and just as she had in the café, she squeezed my hand. "You asked if I loved someone like that. I did once, and he is gone, too. But I do not believe Sam must be gone for you."

She tapped a finger on her lip, like she was considering something. The car grew hotter, and I could barely breathe with the anticipation.

"Help me," I said softly. "I am begging you. Please tell me what you know if you know where he is."

She kept tapping, tapping. Finally, she nodded. "Yes," she said, as if answering an internal question. "Yes."

"Yes?" I asked quietly, afraid to push her in the wrong direction.

She started the car and pulled away from the curb. "I will take you to him."

65

As Adelina's car climbed the winding streets of Punta Paitilla, I grew more and more pissed off at Sam.

Over the course of the last half hour, I'd raced through an obstacle course of emotions. First came the excitement when Adelina said she knew Sam, then came the joy that he was alive and okay. Next in line was relief that maybe Sam hadn't done anything wrong—he had legal paperwork, which had been drawn up at the specific request of Forester— to possess the shares and to sell them and the property. Then there was the agony of living it all over again as I told Adelina what had happened. And then the fear had rolled in. Sam might have had the legal right, but Adelina said all the properties had been sold. Where was the money now? In his own bank account? Had Sam gotten rid of Forester by paying Dr. Li in order to make it easier for him to take and sell the shares? If not, why had he been at Forester's the night he died?

Anger was next and by far the most powerful emotion on the obstacle course, and it was the emotion I couldn't get around. It came when Adelina told me that, as far as she knew, Sam was living in a penthouse condominium in Punta Paitilla, one of the city's luxury areas.

"What's he doing there?" I'd asked.

We were still sitting in the car at the café's curb. It was hot, and Adelina had started the car, but the air-conditioning had yet to conquer the sticky air.

"I do not know exactly," she said. "I believe he is enjoying the city while we wait for these last properties to close."

And so, as the car now grew closer to Sam, and as I thought of him "enjoying the city" in a luxury apartment, my desire to kick his ass grew exponentially with each block.

"Flub him," I muttered, then, "Fuck him," then "Sorry," to Adelina.

I looked out the window and tried to calm down. Adelina had described Punta Paitilla as a luxury area, so I'd expected something like the Upper East Side of New York or the Gold Coast in Chicago. The reality was different. The streets were hilly and curved in a pleasing way, but the buildings and houses were rather nondescript, at least from the front. Some were five to ten stories high, and every so often there was a high-rise thrown in and then, randomly, a small vegetable market on a corner. Certainly, there were no designer boutiques or flashy restaurants.

"This is a somewhat older section of the city," Adelina said. "When it was built, it was during a time when Panamanians were afraid to flaunt their wealth. This was not because we don't like to do so." She smiled. "It was simply out of necessity."

"What do you mean?"

"There was more crime here at that time. If you flaunted what you had, you were asking for trouble."

As the car rose higher on the hills of Punta Paitilla my hands shook and my insides trembled with fury.

The car stopped in front of a white stucco condo building with a line of palm trees nearly obscuring it from the street. Brown-red metal gates protected the front of the building, a guard's station in the center.

Adelina pulled up to the station. She spoke in Spanish to the guard. He grunted and pushed a button, which parted the right side of the gate. We drove in and down a slope to a covered parking area. As we got out of the car, Adelina began to sift through a host of key rings in her purse.

"Okay," she said, finally deciding on one. "You are ready?"

"Oh, I'm ready."

She led me into the building—the foyer a cool oasis of yellow marble, decorated with palm trees and vases of fresh flowers—and into an elevator.

"You do not want me to call him?" she said. "There is a phone in the unit."

"Please, don't. In fact, I'd like it if you'd give us a little time to ourselves."

Adelina tapped her lip again. "I do not know."

I squeezed her hand again. I felt strangely comfortable doing it now, as if Adelina and I had grown close in a few short hours.

"I am very nervous about this situation," Adelina said. "I know Sam had the legal right to sell, but now you are telling me the authorities are looking for him, and Mr. Pickett is dead. I want to know the real story of all this."

"I do, too. And that's exactly what I'm going to find out. Believe me, I will tell you everything, and I will protect you if I can."

The elevator arrived at the seventh floor, the highest in the building.

Adelina stood still a moment as the doors opened to a small vestibule.

She nodded at a front door made of carved wood. Using her keys, she unlocked two locks and opened the door for me.

"Go," she said. "And I will be waiting in the car."

"Thank you," I said softly. "Thank you."

I walked through the apartment. "Sam?" My voice echoed off the vast amount of marble in the place. No answer.

The apartment was mostly empty except for a chair here and a couch there. In the master bedroom, a green beach raft lay in the corner. Folded next to it were a towel and a blue

T-shirt I knew very well. I walked over to the shirt and picked it up. It was powder-blue and silky soft from so many washings. On the front it said Coltrane and under that, the name of Sam's favorite John Coltrane album, *Dakar.*

But the place was empty. Except for an old piece of fruit and a bag of Panamanian chips in the kitchen, it barely looked as if anyone had spent time there.

"Sam!" My words echoed again.

And that's when something caught my eye. I was standing in an immense living room with dropped, molded ceilings. To my right were two cut-glass doors leading to a large balcony. I moved to the doors. I opened one and peered over the balcony, down to the pool and the sea below that.

And there he was, sitting at the side of the pool on a white chair, shirt off, reading a book. Just like a man of leisure should.

Rage coursed through me. I ran through the apartment and back to the elevators. I took one to the foyer. To the right was a sign that read Pool with a tiny gold arrow under it. I followed the arrow through a small hallway toward the back of the building. I pushed open the backdoor, the sunlight hitting me squarely in the face.

I blinked a moment to let my eyes adjust and when they did, I saw Sam's face turning up from his book, his mouth open. He looked shocked. There were other emotions in his face, but I couldn't read them. He stood and took a step toward me, the pool sparkling like diamonds behind him.

I realized I wasn't breathing. And I didn't care. My feet carried me toward him. It was almost as if they belonged to someone else. I could feel nothing in my body. I couldn't see anything now except Sam and that glittering pool. My purse slid from my shoulder and landed with a thud on the tile.

"Red Hot," he said, his nickname for me. And those two words—which used to make me feel wanted and loved and longed for—only enraged me.

I started running. Sam's face shifted from one of surprise to something more scared. But I didn't give him a second to react.

"You asshole!" I yelled.

My feet pounded on the marble as I sprinted toward him. And I tackled him right into the pool.

66

I have never hit anyone in my life. I don't know how. But as Sam and I sprang up from the water, both of us soaked now, I raised my fist, drew it back and punched him.

My hand connected with his cheek, but it didn't have the force I wanted.

"Izzy, stop!" he yelled as I raised my hand again. This time, he easily caught my fist as I swung. "Jesus, Izzy, stop it."

"You've got to be kidding me!"

I tried to raise my other arm, but he caught that, too. We were in the shallow side of the pool in about four feet of water.

Sam pinned my arms to my sides and spun me around so that I was facing the building. A beautiful building, I noticed, which just pissed me off more. He wrapped his arms around me while I squirmed and struggled.

"Iz, Iz," he kept saying, loud at first, then softer and softer as I realized how much stronger than me he was. And then I felt those arms—the ones that had held me every night for the last few years. And I felt his jawbone as it rested itself against the side of my forehead. And I felt his chest against my back. And I felt his breath in my ear. I heard him saying, "Iz, Iz, it's okay."

Finally, I was still. I closed my eyes and pretended for one moment that it was two weeks ago when I loved him unquestioningly, even though the wedding was making me nuts, when I would have sworn on my life that I'd never spend a day wondering if he loved me.

"Baby," he said. "God, baby." He spoke these words so quietly into my ear, it was like a dream.

Finally, he turned me around and bent down a little and stared into my eyes. His were so green—more green than I remembered. "I'm sorry," he said.

"What have you done? Just tell me. Now. Fast. I need to know."

"Let's get out of the pool."

Water dripped from my hair, running into my eyes. "No. Tell me. I'm going crazy. You have no idea what you've done to me."

"I didn't mean to, Iz. I swear." His blond hair, white-gold now, gleamed in the sun.

"Tell me!" I started to raise my fist again.

He pinned my arms to my sides once more. His face twisted as he seemed to struggle with what to say.

"Sam!" I yelled, my voice ragged with the agony of being so close and still not knowing.

"Okay, okay, I wasn't supposed to, but here it is. I'm just going to tell you quick." He took a massive inhale. "Forester told me about those letters he was getting, and that stuff the homeless guy was saying."

"Yeah, he thought someone might be trying to hurt him."

He nodded. "Before he got the letters, Forester had been buying Panamanian real estate—he thinks this place is going to be big—but in the last month, he bought even more property, sight unseen. He put it all in the corporation, knowing that it was easily transferable if anyone had possession of the shares. He sat me down and asked me if I would do something for him."

"What?"

Sam shuddered a little. His eyes looked over my head. And I could tell he was remembering.

67

Sam always loved the way Forester inhabited a room. It was impossible not to know when the man was around. He took up space, in part because he was tall and handsome, but even more so because he radiated an intense presence that no one could ignore.

That day, Forester sat in front of Sam's desk talking about his portfolio, the way they did every month. But at one point Forester paused, adjusting his silver tie and sitting forward ever so slightly. "Look, son, I have a favor to ask."

"Sure," Sam said. "Anything." He loved when Forester called him "son." And he meant it when he said he would do anything, because Forester was like a dad to him and, like a good parent, Forester would never ask anything of him that Sam couldn't, or shouldn't, do.

"Well, it's more than a favor." Forester glanced behind him, as if double-checking that Sam's office door was closed. "But I don't know who else to turn to."

"Anything," Sam said again.

Forester fixed him with an intense stare. "There are some people you simply can't trust in life—whether it's business or personal. We all know that's true, right?"

Sam nodded, yet he considered himself lucky. With the exception of his father, he trusted most people in his life.

"And that's fine," Forester said. "Those kinds of people

don't even pretend they're trustworthy. But I've learned from building Pickett Enterprises that there's also a different variety of people—people who appear to be trustworthy, people you believe in, but then later you find you were wrong. You shouldn't have trusted them at all."

Sam nodded again. He could see how true that would be if you ran a large company the way Forester did, and as usual, he was ready to soak up the words Forester said, to learn any knowledge he could from the man.

"The problem," Forester continued, "is that such people sometimes don't show their true colors. Not for a long, long time. And so, you don't know who those people are."

He told Sam about the letters, and the comments the homeless man had made about how Forester would join his dead wife if he wasn't careful.

"Who would do that?" Sam had asked, an indignant tone to his voice.

Forester opened his palms and stared at them, as if he could divine the future there. For the first time since Sam had known him, Forester looked helpless. "I don't know, son, but I've become…" He seemed to falter with his words. An expression, one that looked almost like embarrassment, crossed his features. "Well, let me tell you, these letters have me scared, because I've looked around at my life and I've realized something. Nearly everyone in my world has something to gain from me being gone."

"That's not true," Sam said.

Forester nodded. "It is. For so long, the opposite was the case. I was the head of the ship at Pickett Enterprises, and the ship couldn't run without me. There was no one who knew all its parts, no one else who could steer it. But now I've gotten this company running on autopilot. It doesn't need me anymore, not really. Chaz or Walter. They could run it fine. And Shane? Not yet, but someday soon. This was how I wanted it. But now…"

"Now?" Sam said, prompting him.

"Now, I'm frightened. And because you're not one of those people who has something to gain from my death, and because I am certain that you're not one of those people who has yet to show your true colors, and because you're one of the few people I can trust, I have this… Well, this favor to ask."

68

"He told me if anything happened to him, if it seemed that any of the threats had come true, I should take the shares to Panama, sell the real estate and hold the earnings until the whole mess could be figured out. He knew that would tie up the estate. He didn't want anyone to get the estate, especially not Shane, until it was obvious what had caused his death."

"He *asked* you to do this?"

"Yeah. But I don't think he believed anything would happen so soon."

"But…wait. You were at his house on the night he died."

"How do you know that?"

I shook my head. "Why were you there?"

"He called me that night—right before we went to Cassandra's office—and he sounded really strange. He asked if I was willing to do what we'd talked about. I said yes. Then he got off the phone pretty fast, and I couldn't stop thinking about it. I had a really bad feeling. That's why I left Cassandra's. I drove up there…" His mouth tightened the way it does when he was fighting tears. I'd only seen him do it a few times.

"Did you do something to him?" I asked softly. "Did you hurt him?"

He shook his head hard, and gave me an irritated look. "Of course not. I kept calling him on the way up there, and he wasn't answering. I had this terrible feeling. His place was locked up when I got there, so I went around back and..."

I brushed wet strands of hair from my face, then smoothed Sam's short hair. It was a gesture I used to make when I wanted to calm him. "What?"

"He must have been on the patio eating. The food was pushed away. And he was facedown. Like he'd fallen over. I touched him, but he was cold. He wasn't breathing. It was... It was terrible."

"Oh my God." I grabbed him in a hug. I wanted to take away the pain I saw in his face.

"I freaked," he said, his words muffled by my shoulder. "And then I heard someone inside the house."

"It must have been Annette. She's the one who found him."

"I thought someone had killed him, and they were still in the house. I got scared as hell and then I thought—*I have to do what I promised him,* and that's when I left. I heard later that the cause of death was a heart attack, but I still didn't know if there was foul play, or whatever you're supposed to call it. I just kept hearing Forester's words that night when he asked if I was willing to do what I promised."

I pulled back. "It was a hell of a lot to ask you."

"He felt terrible about it, but he wasn't sure who in his company, or his family, could be threatening him, and you know how much he loved Pickett Enterprises."

I nodded.

Sam looked intensely at me. "I am so sorry, Iz. When I saw him dead like that, I just went into action. I didn't really stop to think about anything except that I loved Forester. He'd been like a dad to me since I met him, and I'd made a promise."

"But you made a promise to *me,* too."

"I know." Sam squeezed my shoulders. Pain emanated from his eyes. "I don't know if I ever told you this, Iz, but when I met Forester, I was about to get fired by Mark Carrington."

"Are you kidding? I thought you'd always been the young star over there."

Sam gave a chagrined shrug. "I know you thought that, and I guess I *wanted* you to believe it. I wanted to forget that for a while I was a total screwup. I was drinking too much and playing too much rugby, and I just couldn't get serious about work. Forester took an interest in me like no one ever has, and he straightened me out. Everything I have—my job, you— was because of Forester."

"And now because of Forester," I said softly, "you might have lost both those things."

He shook his head fast, as if he was shaking away my words. Drops of water flew off him. "As each day went by I kept thinking how crazy it was that I was doing this. That I was wrecking everything. I wanted to call you so bad. I picked up the phone, like, a hundred times a day. Sometimes I would just stare at your number and imagine you and this face." He stroked my cheek. "Mostly, though, I was trying to work out how I could contact you without messing everything up, without making it somehow worse for you. But I'd promised Forester I wouldn't say anything to anyone, and once I started this whole thing I didn't want to violate that trust."

"But—"

He shook his head and kept talking. "I also knew that the government would probably question you, and if I started calling or e-mailing you, they might find out and it would just get you in trouble. I didn't want to put you in a situation where you had to lie to them."

"So you turned to Alyssa instead."

He swallowed hard. "You know about that?"

"I know about a lot of things."

"I didn't take time to think. I just acted. And I wanted to get out of the country without anyone knowing. Everyone has always said I look like her brother."

I decided to ignore the Alyssa issue for now. There was so much else. "Sam, Forester *was* killed. Someone paid his Chinese doctor to change the herbs he was taking to cause a heart attack."

"Are you serious? How do you know?"

I told him how Mayburn had been helping me with the case. I didn't mention that I helped him on other cases, too. I told Sam how I'd gone to see Dr. Li twice, how she'd essentially admitted getting paid to put the large amount of ma huang in Forester's herbs.

Sam took a step back and put a hand to his face. "Someone really did kill him. Dammit. Dammit."

His mouth tightened again, and this time tears slipped from his eyes.

"I know," I said simply.

He let his hand fall away, and we stared at each other. For the first time since this all started, we were on the same page—joined in our anguish. And I knew from that anguish that it hadn't been Sam who paid Dr. Li.

"Do you think it was Shane?" he asked.

"Could be. He's already moved into Forester's office."

"Yeah, I heard."

"From who?"

"This guy Forester hired before he died, a private investigator."

"What are you talking about? What guy?"

"Forester put the guy on a retainer and told him that if he died, and I took off, this detective should figure out what had happened with Forester's death. He told the detective to let me know when it was okay to go back to the States."

For a second, I thought of Mayburn. He'd worked for Forester, via me, before. "Is it John Mayburn?"

"No, some other guy."

And then I had a feeling I knew who the other guy was. Suddenly, I was cold, and it wasn't simply due to the fact that

I was standing in four feet of water. "Is this private investigator kind of a short guy?"

"I've only met him once, and he works with another guy, too, but yeah."

"Does he have dark, wavy hair?"

"Yeah."

"He's been following *me*."

He nodded. "He told me that. Between him and his partner, the guy was following *everyone*. He didn't have a lot to go on, so he was checking out every person who'd had significant contact with Forester. When he told me he was investigating you, I told him not to bother, but he said he had to. Eventually, he said he ruled you out."

"You mean after he was in my condo and on my computer?" My voice was rising, I couldn't help it.

Sam shrugged. "Yeah, but I told him to keep an eye out for you after he cleared you."

"You what?"

"I asked him to let me know if you were okay. But you weren't supposed to *know* he was following you."

"You had this guy following me?"

"Well, yeah. He was doing a lot of other stuff, too, but it's been a tough case for him. He said—"

"Wait just a freaking second," I said, interrupting him. "This guy broke in to my apartment and he scared the hell out of me!"

He shook his head a little. "I heard he was a renegade. He hadn't been working for Forester for long, so I guess he was doing anything he could to get a jump on the case. He didn't even have access to Forester's house..." Sam gave me a proud smile. "But I heard you did. He tailed you guys there that night. Nice work."

"Yeah, thanks," I said sarcastically. "But just so I get this straight, *you* had this person and his buddy following me?"

Another sheepish shrug. "Yeah."

I raised my fist again. Quickly before Sam could catch it. I punched him. And this time I got him good.

69

Upstairs, on his green raft, Sam moaned and cupped his cheekbone. "Jesus, Iz."

I handed him a washcloth full of ice. "Sorry," I said. But I wasn't. "You sent me a postcard."

He looked at me with the one eye not covered with cloth. "I told you. I promised Forester I wouldn't say anything to anyone. I did call the cops and tell them to check it out."

"You were the one who left the anonymous tip to 9-1-1 on the night he died?"

Sam nodded. "And then I couldn't just take off without telling you I was okay, so I sent you the postcard. I mean, do you know what it was like for me to watch you when I walked away that day at Cassandra's? I knew something was wrong with Forester, and I knew I had to check it out, and I also knew that my life was never going to be the same. It killed me. I thought about you, that look you gave me over your shoulder. Your smile." His voice broke a little. "I thought about that all the time. Every day. Fifty times a day."

I sat next to him on the raft, causing it to lurch. Across the room, the sun shifted, slanting a powerful beam through the glass doors and into the room. I hated seeing him sad. It was something I could never tolerate for long. I put my arms around his neck and we hugged. Feeling the heat of his skin, smelling that Sam smell.

We sat back and looked at each other.

"I still don't understand," I said. "Why would Forester tell me about the letters and all that, but not let you tell me what he wanted you to do?"

"He didn't want you to risk your law license."

"It's a little late for that." I told him how I'd made the duplicate hard drive from Michael DeSanto's computer and how I'd been in Forester's house that night with Mayburn. It felt good to tell somebody all of it.

Sam shifted the ice around. "Computer hacking, huh?" He grinned. "Impressive, although I'm not surprised. You could do anything you set your mind to."

I smiled a little, too. I realized then how much I'd missed Sam's ever-present cheerleading. "I was just so desperate to find you, and I made a deal with Mayburn—help him and he'd help me. And now I'm feeling bad about Lucy. I really like her. I hope I haven't screwed up her life."

"The way I did ours?"

My smile slid away.

"Do you still love me?" Sam asked.

"You know I do." It was an easy answer.

"Are we going to be okay?"

Not such an easy answer. I lifted my shoulders and let them fall. "I've been screwed up about the wedding. I mean, before you left."

"I know. I could tell." He gave me a half smile, the kind reserved for the times when he knew things would be all right. "But we were getting it done. We were on schedule."

I looked at the glass of the sliding doors, seeing the reflection of Sam and me in them. We looked like we'd always looked. And yet, so much had changed.

I looked back at him. "It didn't feel like *my* schedule. It felt like it was going too fast, like it was too much. I was going to talk to you about it that night you disappeared."

"You were going to talk about it like you wanted to *not*

have the wedding?" He laughed a little, as if he thought that couldn't be true, but his eyes peered at me.

I shrugged. "Maybe. I don't know. Look, let's not talk about the future. Let's talk about what we're going to do now." I found my phone in my purse. "I have to call Mayburn." I dialed his number.

"DeSanto was arrested," Mayburn said when he answered.

"I found Sam."

"Okay, you win. Where is he?"

"Sitting right next to me." I told Mayburn everything I'd learned in the last few hours.

Sam stayed with me on the raft, his bare shoulder touching mine. I could feel him thinking about what I'd said. He hung his head, his cheek in the cloth full of ice as I spoke to Mayburn. His posture seemed that of a boy caught doing something bad but who is relieved the jig is up. And yet wasn't sure about that. I'd lost the ability to read Sam's every emotion.

"Who's the P.I. Forester hired?" Mayburn said when I got to that part of the story.

I asked Sam and repeated the guy's name—Joe Medley.

Mayburn grunted. "I know Meds. Thorough guy, but a little radical. So's his partner. If you and Sam give us authorization to talk, I'll call him, and we can pool what we've learned. You guys stay put, and let us sort it out."

I told Sam that Mayburn suggested we stay in Panama.

"No way," Sam said, letting the cloth full of ice drop from his face. There was a deep-blue tint spreading under his right eye. "I'm ready to get the hell out of here. Let's go back to Chicago and figure out who did this to Forester. That's the whole reason we're in this mess. It's what we both promised him we would do."

Mayburn must have heard him. "I'd get legal counsel before you come home," he said.

"Actually, Sam doesn't know it yet, but he already has a lawyer."

I thanked Mayburn and dialed Maggie's number. "Your client Sam wants to talk to you."

"You're kidding me."

I handed Sam the phone. "It's Maggie," I said to him. "Tell her everything. I hired her for you. And in case there's anything you haven't told me yet, I'll leave."

"I've told you everything."

I left anyway.

I walked through the rest of the apartment. I could imagine the place filled with sumptuous couches, plush rugs and gauzy curtains. In the kitchen, I got myself a plastic bottle of water from the fridge. I opened some cupboards and drawers, noticing there were no utensils, plates or glasses. Aside from the fact that the apartment itself was spacious, Sam had been living with almost nothing. In a way, I knew how that felt, stripped of all the basics in life.

But how I felt now, I couldn't seem to figure out. I was relieved that I'd found him; that he was all right; that he had done something he believed was honorable; that he hadn't hurt Forester or stolen from him at all. I was relieved I had told him what I'd been thinking before his disappearance. In a way, that made me feel closer to him. But there was still the fact that he hadn't turned to me. He hadn't trusted me.

I walked back into the bedroom and poked my head inside. Sam gestured me in.

"What does she think?" I asked.

"Hold on, Mags." He hit the Speaker button. "Izzy's here. She knows everything." He looked at me pointedly.

"Okay, let's all get up to speed." Maggie's voice was clipped and assured. I could tell she was in full criminal defense–lawyer mode. "Here's the deal. If Sam's got the right paperwork, then he hasn't done anything illegal by taking the shares or selling the corporation and the properties. From what I can tell, he's got two potential problems. One is that if Forester was killed at his house that night, Sam could be on the hook for leaving the scene of the crime."

"No," I said, "it was definitely a heart attack. The crime was what Dr. Li did, and hiring her to do it."

"Fine. The other problem is traveling with a passport that's not his. That's a big one, if he's going to have to do it again to get back in the country undetected, because the feds will have tagged his passport for sure."

"I can use Alec's passport again," Sam said. "No one knows about it other than Alyssa."

"Think she'll talk?"

Sam and I looked at each other. "No," we said in unison.

"So, can we come back?" I asked Maggie.

"If no one knows you've gone in and out of the country with that passport, Sam, you're in the clear," Maggie said. "But if the feds keep following Izzy when she's back, they'll notice you're back, too."

"I won't go home or to Izzy's," Sam said. "I'll stay out of the way until we get this figured out."

"Up to you," Maggie said again. "I can't give you advice that would make it illegal for you to do anything. All I can do is advise you that the federal government is looking for you, and they will take you into custody if they know you've returned. It's possible they may have already followed Izzy there and are ready to follow you back to the States. Izzy, have you seen anyone?"

"No one. I haven't felt followed here at all."

"Well, I'd still act fast when you get home. Do whatever you need to do before they find Sam and pull him in."

"Mags," I said. "Can I ask you for a favor as a friend and not a lawyer?"

"What is it?"

"Can you get on the Internet and see if there are any flights from Panama to O'Hare this afternoon?"

Silence. "As a friend? Yeah, I can do that." We heard the *clack, clack, clack* of her fingers on a keyboard.

"Three hours," she said, naming an airline.

One more look between Sam and me, and this time I could read him perfectly.

"Let's go for it," I said.

Sam thanked Maggie and hung up the phone.

I started to turn, but I heard Sam say, "Wait."

I stopped, standing in the doorway of a foreign apartment in a foreign country, and with my fiancé coming toward me. He was foreign, too, and yet oh so familiar.

Sam touched my hair, then my cheek. "The airport isn't far. We've got a few minutes."

"Meaning?"

He said nothing. He drew his fingers down and brushed them over my mouth. I could barely breathe with his proximity. I'd always found him gorgeous. He'd always turned me on. And now we stared at each other with an electric intensity we hadn't known before. The highs and the low-low-lows of the last couple of weeks crashed together in my mind. They combusted with the fact that I'd now found Sam and with the other fact that I might lose him again if I couldn't live with the way he'd handled the situation, if we couldn't get over the fact that I'd been thinking of pulling the plug on the wedding. The uncertainty of it all, with the sun now blazing through the glass doors, made for a moment so powerful that everything in the world stopped. The truth, if we admitted it, was that neither of us knew whether we would get such a moment again.

Sam cupped my cheeks with his hands. I felt the calluses on his fingers from playing guitar. I smelled the chlorine and the sun from the bare skin of his chest. I felt his breath as he slowly—so slowly—moved his face to mine.

He kissed me. And it was as if he'd never kissed me before. His lips were softer than I remembered. His tongue was like a pillow. Our mouths touched, as light as ocean spray, but then he bit my bottom lip, and I felt the danger that was now Sam, that was part of him no matter what might happen. That danger made me kiss him harder, made me suck his tongue into my mouth. We grabbed at each other, clutching at arms, ass, shoulders.

I stopped for a second and stared at those martini-olive eyes fringed by brown lashes—different than I remembered and yet the same. There was so much to say, and yet I wanted nothing but silence, to feel nothing but the weight of Sam's body.

I pushed him toward the raft, and I fell onto him.

70

The Chicago night was gray and cold when I came outside the international terminal at O'Hare. I looked up at the orange streetlights, at the spitting of rain that misted against them. I got in the cab line. Out of the corner of my eye, I saw Sam, wearing a baseball cap pulled low, getting in the same line. Alec Thornton's passport hadn't been flagged. The feds must not have known about it. We spent the flight in different seats, never looking at each other, just as we'd decided. Feeling him near, and yet not having him, was something I'd gotten used to over the last few weeks.

In the cab, I asked the driver to sit at the curb for a moment. He grumbled that the cops would make him move soon, but he did as I asked. A minute later, I turned around and saw Sam getting in another cab.

"I'm ready," I said to the driver. I gave him my address and hoped I wouldn't be going there just yet.

As we pulled away and onto the Kennedy, I glanced behind me and saw that Sam's cab was following as planned. It was ten o'clock at night, but because it was Friday, there was a healthy stream of downtown-bound traffic. The cab carved slowly but steadily through the light rain, the tires making a swishing noise.

I pulled out my cell phone and called Shane. It rang, but no answer. I sent him a text. It's Izzy. Need to see you ASAP.

Time went by. I spent it gathering details of everything we'd learned in my head. As if preparing for a trial, I collected each tiny bit of evidence, wrapping my mind around the places where there were assumptions instead of facts. The biggest assumption, but one I felt nearly certain of now, was that Shane was responsible for his dad's death. It was the logical guess all along, but the fact that Forester had believed it, too, and had gone so far as to ask Sam to take such strong actions, solidified it. Forester had rarely been wrong. He'd suspected Chaz and Walter, too. Maybe they were all in on it together. If so, it would be Shane who would crumble first from the pressure.

I kept looking at my phone. No response from Shane. I decided to make another phone call that had been on my mind. I dialed Lucy DeSanto.

"Hello?" she answered, her voice wary.

"Hi, it's Izzy."

Silence.

"I heard about Michael."

"When he was getting taken away he said that it was you who brought him down. He said he thought you had gotten into his computer."

I cleared my throat. I didn't know what to say. Mayburn and I had never discussed whether you could talk to a subject after an investigation had closed. I hadn't wanted to have that conversation with him, I realized now, because I very much wanted to call Lucy and see if she was all right.

"How have you been?" I said.

She was silent a moment, acknowledging my unspoken admission. "I'm scared."

I felt a wave of guilt.

"But you know what?" she continued. "I feel hopeful for the first time in a long time."

"Why?" I asked, surprised.

"Because Michael was a nightmare to live with. He was abusive. Not physically. Well, just a few times, but mostly it was just this constant verbal abuse, always telling me how stupid I was and how I was messing up. I could never do anything right in his eyes."

"I didn't know that."

"When he got taken away, it was the most scared I've ever been. But as each minute passes, I realize how nice it is to not have him around. I feel like I can breathe again. I hate to say this, but I'm almost hoping he gets denied bail."

"Wow."

"I know. It's weird."

"Well, I called to say I'm sorry."

"No, don't apologize."

"I really do like you, Lucy. A lot."

"Thanks. So, is Grady really your husband?"

I could hear Mayburn screaming not to admit anything. "No."

She laughed. "I could tell."

"How?"

"I saw the way he was looking at you. Like a kid in a candy store. No one looks at their wife like that, even if you've only been married a few years."

I wanted to say, *You should have seen him later when I let him in the store.* I felt a wave of confusion then. What would I do about Grady, now that Sam was home? An even better question, what would I do about Sam?

"I'd like it if we could be friends, Lucy. You know, apart from all this stuff."

She was quiet a second. "I have a lot to sort out right now."

"Of course."

The skyline of the city came into view—the Sears Tower and the Hancock glowing gold behind a swirling fog. My phone trilled to let me know I'd received a text.

"I've got to run," I said, "but I'll touch base in a week or two, if that's okay. Good luck, Lucy."

I hung up and scrolled to my text. It was from Shane— What's up?

Need to see you, I replied.

It's late. Tomorrow?

It's about Sam. I know where he is.

And then nothing. A few minutes later the cab got off the highway at North Avenue and sped east toward the city. I looked over my shoulder and saw Sam's cab still trailing.

I'm at my condo downtown, came Shane's next text. Should we meet somewhere?

Shane's place, I knew from attending a party over the summer, was on Dearborn. Why don't I just stop by, I texted. This won't take long.

More minutes ticked away. The cabbie was approaching my street. "Wait," I said. "Just pull over to the curb, please. I might be heading somewhere else."

The driver began grumbling about it being Friday night and how he needed to make money. "I will tip you big," I said, cutting him off. "Just pull over, please."

He did as I asked. Sam's cab did the same.

More time ebbed away. "C'mon, Shane," I muttered. Still nothing.

I picked up my cell phone again. I'm a block away, I wrote. I know what Sam did with your dad's property.

This time, he texted back right away. You've got 5 minutes.

"Yes!" I directed the cabbie where to go.

The doorman gave me a raised eyebrow when I entered, pulling my suitcase. I was wearing a navy sundress that I'd put on in Panama that morning, along with the high-heeled sandals I thought would go with my heiress-shopping-for-a-crash-pad look. I'd thrown a sweater over the outfit on my way home, and now my teeth chattered from a combination of the cool November night and the fact that we were about to confront Shane Pickett with the murder of his father.

Sam followed me into the white-marbled lobby. He wore shorts and a jacket, along with a duffel bag thrown over his shoulder. The cap was still pulled low, but there was no hiding his black eye.

The doorman's other eyebrow lifted at the sight of Sam's face.

I acted as if there was nothing amiss and gave him Shane's name, then mine. "He's expecting me."

But then I got nervous. Could we get Shane to confess? And if we did, could things get ugly?

I turned to Sam to say I was having second thoughts, when I heard the doorman say, "I'll send her up."

He pressed a buzzer. "Fourteenth floor," he said.

I looked at Sam. His eyes were somewhat wide, the way they got when he found himself processing something new. The blond stubble stood out on his tanned face.

He met my eyes, and I knew he could see the question there. He nodded. "We're going to do this. For Forester."

In the elevator, he held out his hand to me. "I'm here now."

I didn't take it. "Yeah…*now*."

"That's all we're talking about, right?"

He stretched his hand out farther.

He was right. We were talking about now. Only now. I took his hand.

The elevator dinged, and the doors opened. Our footsteps were silent as we moved down the hallway that was carpeted. I knocked at Shane's door.

He opened it, his face stern with thought. But it went slack at the sight of Sam. He looked back and forth between Sam and me. "I'm calling the cops."

"Don't do that, Shane," Sam said. "I'm here to tell you everything."

Shane hesitated, but not as long as he would have in days past. He gave an abrupt nod. "Five minutes," he said with authority.

He stepped back to let us in. The condo was a large one. I remembered views of both the lake and the Loop from last summer, but now the sky was blocked with fog. It felt as if there was no one around, only us, and I became very scared. If Shane had plotted the murder of his father, what else was he capable of? I tried to signal Sam, but he was like a man released from chains. He charged into Shane's living room and stood in front of the windows, his arms crossed.

Shane didn't offer us a seat. Wearing crisp, dark jeans and a blue shirt, he took the same posture as Sam and stood in front of an antique sofa table. He was a short man whose lack of self-assurance usually made him seem even shorter. But today Shane appeared confident and poised. He leaned on a two-hundred-year-old table from France. A few weeks ago I thought that the entire apartment, which had been meticulously decorated down to the antique silver wine coasters, was too adult for Shane. Now, something about the confidence he exuded made it seem as if he'd outgrown the apartment.

I stood near a contemporary oil painting and watched the two men.

"I'm listening," Shane said. "And now you've got four minutes."

"Don't tell me what to do, Pickett. Not after what you've put me through."

"What *I've* put you through?" Shane picked up a phone from the table. "I'm calling 9-1-1 if you don't get talking."

Sam's jaw flexed and tensed. An enormous moment of silence passed.

"Maybe I should explain," I said. "Sam—"

"No, Izzy, please," Sam said, interrupting me. "Let me." He looked back at Shane. "Your father asked me to take the Panamanian shares in the event he died suddenly. He asked me to sell them so that the estate would be tied up."

Shane scoffed. "Are you crazy? You must be seriously unhinged. Why in the hell would he want to do that?"

"Because he was concerned that someone wanted to kill him. And he wanted to make sure whoever that person was didn't get the estate or his company."

Shane exploded. "How dare you come here and make up crap about my father. He was nothing but good to you!"

Sam began yelling now, too. "You *wanted* him to retire so you could take over the company, and when he didn't, you killed him!"

Shane lunged at Sam.

I threw myself between them and managed to shove Shane backward. "Wait, wait!" I yelled. "Shane, listen. Your father spoke to both Sam and me before he died about letters he was receiving at Pickett, letters telling him he should step down from the company."

Shane's gaze swung from Sam to me and back again. "I want you out of my house right now."

"Just listen, Shane," I said calmly. I explained what the letters said. I explained what the homeless guy on the street had said, how his father had been very concerned. Shane did not look surprised.

Sam and I glanced at each other. Sam spoke up. "He thought it might have been you behind it. After all, you were the one who stood to take over Pickett Enterprises."

Something in Shane's face crumbled. "But I *never* wanted that. I mean, I told my father I did, that I was ready, but I only said that because I knew that's what he wanted to hear. I've been trying my whole life to be the man my father wanted. I knew he had designed Pickett as a family business, and he wanted to keep it that way, but I have no head for business." He looked at me. "Izzy, you know that. I'm struggling now to learn the business and to take control of the company, but only because that's what my dad wanted." He looked at Sam again. "But I can't believe he also wanted you to steal thirty million from him."

Sam explained Forester's plan. He told Shane how his dad had called that night he died, how he'd found Forester face-down on his patio table, how he'd sprung into action and taken off to Panama. "I have documentation that your father drew up," Sam said. He reached into his jacket and withdrew a sheaf of papers. He handed them to Shane. "These are copies, and they were translated into English, but you can see your father's signature there at the bottom."

Shane flipped through the pages. "I have no idea what these mean."

"They mean that your father gave me the authority to possess and sell the Panamanian corporation that owned the real estate. And I did what he asked." Sam's voice was getting louder again. "What we're here to talk about tonight is what *you* did to your father, Shane. And I want you to quit playing dumb about it!"

"Enough!" came a familiar voice somewhere behind Shane.

We heard footsteps in the hallway. I looked at Shane, whose expression turned to one of fear.

Sam moved closer to me, as if to protect me. "What's going on?" he said softly.

Shane turned in the direction of the voice, then back to us. He didn't seem to know what to do. "Don't!" he called out.

But it was too late. "Leave him alone," said the voice, that voice I knew somehow.

The owner of that voice stepped into the room.

It was Q.

71

The living room pulsed with tension. None of us said a word. I watched as Q stood beside Shane and placed a hand on his shoulder. Shane's face twisted into a mix of panic and helplessness, the face of someone watching the beginnings of a car crash and unable to do anything to stop it.

Sam pointed at Q and then Shane. "Are the two of you…are you involved somehow?"

"Yes," Q said at the same time Shane said, "No."

Q turned to Shane and bent his head toward him. His skin looked deep-black against Shane's pallid white face. "Listen to me," Q said, low and insistent. "It is going to be okay."

Shane breathed in deep, seeming to draw strength from the sight of Q and the sound of his words. He nodded, a small fast movement.

"Yes," Q said, turning to us, "Shane and I are having a relationship."

I felt my mouth form a surprised *O*. "This is who you were cheating with?"

Q bowed a little. "Yes. And I love this man."

Shane's eyes fluttered closed. But then he opened them, looked at Q and nodded again.

"You were together the night Forester died," I said to Shane. "That's why you weren't that surprised at the news of his death, and why you were being so evasive after that."

Q nodded again.

"But wait a minute." I pointed at Q. "When I told you Shane was giving Tanner the Pickett Enterprises work, you were pissed off. So you were just pretending?"

"No. He hadn't told me because he knew I would try to stop him." Q glared at Shane. "We're in love, but we're not perfect yet."

"Did the two of you plan Forester's death?" Sam blurted.

"No!" Q shouted. "And I'm sick of all these accusations against Shane. No one killed Forester. I've seen the autopsy, Izzy, so have you. Why have you been so caught up in the idea that someone deliberately hurt him?"

"You know about the letters."

"Yes, and I told Shane about them after I learned about them from you. He had never seen the letters or heard about them. He certainly didn't write them. The autopsy showed a heart attack, Iz."

"Yeah, but we believe someone caused that heart attack."

"How do you cause a heart attack?" Shane looked thoroughly confused and distraught now.

"You know those herbs your father got from Dr. Li?"

Shane nodded. "He was always putting them in water and drinking them. But those couldn't have caused it. He's been on those for years."

"He was on certain herbs for years. The last batch he got from Dr. Li, though, contained what was essentially an overdose of an herb that can cause heart attack, especially in patients with a history of heart problems. I think Dr. Li did that deliberately."

"Why?"

"Because someone paid her. It turns out she and her husband had serious financial problems. They were in debt. Their building was about to be foreclosed and now they've taken off. When I spoke to her, Dr. Li basically admitted that she had given your dad too much of this herb, and she said that 'they' only meant to make your dad sick. She seemed very upset to learn that he died."

"Who would have paid her?" Shane asked.

"It's better to be violent than impotent, isn't that right?" I said.

"What are you talking about?"

"It's part of a Gandhi quote that was in one of the threatening letters your dad received."

"*I* didn't write them!" Shane yelled. "I loved my father more than anything! I was never the man he wanted, I know that, and I know he wouldn't have been happy to find out about this." He pointed between him and Q. He looked at me, deep into my eyes. "Izzy, I *loved* my dad."

I glanced at Q, whose expression was one of pain. I knew that expression. It was how I'd felt when Sam told me about finding Forester dead. It was the expression made by a person who sees someone they love in agony.

Slowly, without breaking my gaze with Shane, I nodded. I believed him. Not just about his adoration of his father but about not hurting him. I shot a glance at Sam, and I could tell he believed Shane as well.

Q put a hand on Shane's shoulder, a silent support.

"If it wasn't you, who would have paid Dr. Li?" I said. "Who stood to benefit from your father being ill enough to step down from the company, assuming Dr. Li was telling the truth about just wanting to make him sick?"

Shane shrugged. "Chaz and Walt run the place now that my dad is gone."

"And your dad and Walt had been warring for years," I pointed out.

"Yeah, but in a healthy business way, I'd always thought."

We stood quietly, working over the other possibilities. "Chaz is a goddamned bulldog," Q said.

Shane nodded. "He did orchestrate the recent sales of all those TV and radio stations. It was like he'd been planning it for years."

I spoke up. "I should tell you that my mother's charity was given fifteen million by Forester's will."

Shane's eyes went big. "Jeez. That's a lot. But then again, my dad always said that was his favorite charity."

Sam and I exchanged glances. I'd told him about my mother's affair with Forester, but I wanted to keep her secret from everyone else unless it was absolutely necessary.

"My mom had no idea that money was coming to her charity," I said, "and she adored Forester."

Shane nodded.

"What about Annette, your dad's housekeeper?" Sam asked. "Izzy said she'll get two million from the estate."

"I just can't believe Annette would hurt my dad. I can't believe Dr. Li would either. I've never met her, but my dad had been seeing her for a while, and he really liked her."

"How did he start seeing her?" I asked.

"She was highly recommended by Tanner, who saw her for anxiety or something. Tanner said—"

We all froze. I looked from Sam to Shane to Q.

"Tanner has been seeing Dr. Li for years," Shane said, his voice slowing down, as if he was reading the words off a sluggish teleprompter. "And then, right around after my dad died, Tanner started going to see a psychiatrist. Now he's seeing this shrink twice a week. He says he was having depression and feeling guilt. When I asked him why the guilt, he mentioned his ex-wife."

Q scoffed.

"I know," Shane said, his eyes fixed on a point on the floor. It was as if he was seeing Tanner, listening to him in his mind. "I couldn't believe it when he said it. He's never felt guilty about either of his ex-wives or what he did to them, although he's had a lot of anxiety since the last divorce."

"When was that?" Sam asked.

"About the same time I began getting the Pickett work," I said.

Shane nodded. "He started doing all sort of things to cope

then. He went to see Dr. Li. He read all this spiritual stuff, although he thought most of it was crap." Shane laughed, but it was raw and full of agony. He looked up at me. "He was reading Gandhi."

He looked at Sam, then Q, then back at me. None of us seemed to have the power of speech.

"If Tanner had been seeing Dr. Li for a while, she might have told him about her financial problems," Sam said.

"And he also knew that if Forester was too ill to run the company, Shane would have to take over," Q said, his voice raw. "And who better to help out his friend during his dad's illness? Who better to take over all the Pickett legal work again and get his life back on track?"

"Oh, God." Shane put his hands over his eyes, as if he couldn't look at what we were all seeing. "It was Tanner."

72

The four of us marched down Dearborn Street—Shane and I in the middle, Q and Sam on the outside. It was still misting rain, but the low rumble of thunder in the distance promised a storm.

"Tanner is at Hugo's Frog Bar," Shane had said in his apartment. "Right now. He called me half an hour ago and asked me to come out."

Hugo's Frog Bar was in the Viagra Triangle, about six or seven blocks from Shane's apartment.

"I'm going to kill him," Shane said now as we pounded down the street. "I know I'm not a violent person, and I know I'm not very strong, but I am going to *kill* him." He glanced at Sam and Q. "You guys have my back, right?"

Sam and Q mumbled "of course," and our feet continued their fast march, but I don't think any of us knew what to do now. The air hissed with electricity.

"Should we call the cops?" Q asked.

"They'll call the feds and arrest Sam before we could explain anything about Tanner," I said. "And the fact is, without Dr. Li, we don't have any evidence."

"We're confronting that son of a bitch, and that's it," Shane said. "And we're not waiting for the cops or anyone else."

Rush Street was packed with partygoers. As we crossed at State Street, the sky lit up with a bolt of lightning, followed by a loud boom. There were groups of people everywhere—

some standing on corners, others making their way from bar to bar. The rain continually sprayed the masses. No one seemed to care.

We pushed past girls dressed in sky-high heels and fall coats. They giggled lightheartedly. I remembered, in a distant way, when I had been like that.

Hugo's was packed as usual with a blend of tourists and locals. The bar at the front was ten people deep. We rammed our way inside, searching for Tanner.

"He must be sitting down," Shane said. "He likes the booths." He pointed to the left and led us that way.

The dining room was less crowded but still buzzing with activity.

"Can I help you?" the maître d' asked.

None of us answered as we stood at the entrance of the room. Our eyes scanned the white-clothed tables, the blue leather booths.

"There he is." Sam pointed to the back of the room.

And sure enough, there was Tanner, sitting in a rear booth, with two other men. He was clearly intoxicated—you could always tell when Tanner got drunk because he actually smiled. Now he was laughing and telling a story, gesturing with a fork that held a chunk of red meat.

Shane bolted for the table before we could devise a plan. The rest of us charged after him, the maître d' behind us, calling, "Wait! Excuse me!"

"You!" Shane said when we reached the table.

"Hey!" Tanner said in a boozy salute. But then his eyes landed on Sam and his smile slipped away. He looked at the four of us, his expression growing cautious.

"You killed my dad, you son of a bitch!" Shane said.

Patrons at the nearby tables stopped their conversations and stared.

Tanner looked at his two buddies. "I'm going to need a minute."

"Sure, sure," they mumbled, getting up from the booth and making a quick exit toward the bar.

Tanner started to stand, but Shane shoved him. "No!"

The four of us closed ranks so that we were looking down at Tanner. His eyes were bloodshot from booze, but they still processed everything going on. I'd seen him do that during trials. No one was more accomplished at dealing with last-minute surprises than Tanner. He could always figure out precisely what was being planned by the opposition and exactly what he would do in response.

"Why don't we all sit," Tanner said.

"No." Shane's voice was hard. "I want you to be honest. Did you pay Dr. Li to give my dad an herb that would make him have a heart attack?"

"No," Tanner replied cautiously, but I knew what he was doing. He was denying that he had paid Dr. Li to actually kill Forester. Shane hadn't accused him of paying her to make Forester ill. His denial was a trick lawyers used when they coached witnesses—if you can say no to part of the question, then just say no and let the other side work out exactly what you're denying.

"You paid Dr. Li to make Forester sick, didn't you?" I said.

Tanner looked at me with hatred. "You're just a little girl who's bitter because her sugar daddy isn't around anymore."

Sam started to say something, but I put a hand on his arm and pulled him back.

Tanner's response had been another tactic—divert the questioner, make it personal.

"Tanner," I said, "you were the bitter one." I thought of everything we had figured out in Shane's apartment, and I let it fly. "You were losing everything in your life—your work, your wife, your house, your status at the firm. Between the lack of bonuses and your divorce, you were broke. You'd hit the bottom of the barrel. Believe me, I know how bad it can be to lose your world, but you couldn't handle it. You thought if you could just get the Pickett Enterprises cases, you'd be on top again. You'd start making money, you'd regain respect at the firm, you'd have money to pay off your ex-wives, buy a great place and start dating again. The way to accomplish that was to put your friend Shane in power at Pickett Enterprises. And the best way to do that was to make Forester sick so he'd retire."

"You're out of your *mind,* McNeil." He spat the words with venom, his eyes narrowed and crazy with anger…and something else that I couldn't read. Tanner gave me a disgusted look, then his eyes flicked over to Sam. "Your boyfriend here stole from Forester, probably killed him, too, and now you're trying to put the blame somewhere else."

"Yeah, my disappearing worked out perfectly for you, didn't it?" Sam said. "When I was gone, it looked like I was the guilty one."

Something dawned on me then. I looked at Tanner. "And you leaked the news of Sam taking the shares to the press, didn't you?" I said. "Because the more heat there was about Sam, the less anyone would ever look in your direction."

Tanner's face was unreadable.

"What you didn't realize," Sam said, "was that I have paperwork from Forester authorizing me to act as I did. Do you have paperwork giving you the power to mess with his medications?"

"I don't even know what the fuck you're talking about." But Tanner's eyes twitched from one of us to the next. I could see his mind scrambling over everything that was happening. He was looking for an out, either intellectually or physically. The four of us pushed closer around him. His jaw clenched, his eyes continued to seek refuge, making him look like a trapped rodent. I knew we'd hit the mark. He wasn't protesting enough. He didn't appear at all shocked by our allegations.

"You know what I'm talking about," I said. "You've been going to Dr. Li for years. She must have mentioned to you that she was in financial trouble, and you decided to use that information to your advantage. You gave her money and in exchange she gave Forester herbs that exacerbated his heart problems. You didn't count on him having a heart attack and dying."

There was panic in Tanner's eyes, but he was trying to cover it. Tanner looked at Shane, the one person he could always manipulate. "I hope you're not listening to her, Mouse."

"Don't you ever call me that again!" Shane swung at Tanner with his fist.

"Shit!" Tanner said, ducking.

Sam yanked Shane away.

"You're going to have to leave," the maître d' said, appearing at our table, her face creased with a deep frown.

I turned to say something to her, but all the movement had caused a break in our formation around Tanner. He bolted to his feet and began running for the door.

"Stop him!" Q yelled. He ran after Tanner, the rest of us right behind him. Shane knocked into a waiter, sending a tray of food into the air, the plates shattering on the floor. The entire restaurant watched in fascination. The maître d' screamed.

Out on Rush Street, it was even more crowded. The scent of burned leaves hung in the air. Another bolt of lightning pierced the sky.

"There he is!" Sam yelled.

Tanner was near Gibsons restaurant. He rounded the corner and began running west. We ran after him, pushing by the drunks and revelers. The sky boomed with lightning and started pouring rain. I nearly slipped in my high-heeled sandals as I ran after the guys. I could see Tanner sprinting down Maple Street, Q close behind him and Sam right behind Q. Shane was just in front of me.

The sky began dumping rain, making the streets a watery blur of light. Luckily, Maple Street was less crowded. Tanner turned right when he hit Clark and kept going.

Shane stopped ahead of me and doubled over, sucking in breath. "C'mon, Shane!" I yelled at him, dragging him along.

"You always wanted to make your dad proud? Well, now's the time. We can't let him get away like Dr. Li. Let's go!"

My words spurred Shane into action and he ran past me. I took off after him, panting and pushing my wet hair out of my face. I saw Tanner run down the steps of the El platform at Clark and Division. Q and Sam hit the stairs right after him and disappeared below.

When I caught up with Shane at the gate, he looked befuddled. "I've never taken the El before," he said, panting. "Should I just jump the gate?"

I pulled out my wallet and found my CTA card. I dipped it into the slot and pushed Shane through, then repeated the action for myself. "Which way did they go?"

Shane pointed at the southbound Red Line.

We ran down the steps to the island platform, where the tracks ran on either side. There were a few people waiting for trains. Shane and I spun around, looking for the group.

"There!" Shane said.

On the island, near the place where the southbound train would enter, was Tanner. He was standing with his hands out, Sam and Q maybe ten feet away.

We sprinted to them, but I stopped short when I saw Tanner. His black hair, always combed perfectly back from his widow's peak, was messed, wet strands clinging to his face. His eyes had a wild tinge to them.

"Just get the fuck away from me!" he screamed. "All of you. Get the *fuck* away from me."

Shane took a step forward.

"Shane, stay *right* there!" Tanner shouted.

Shane stood, panting for a moment, he and Tanner locking eyes.

Shane caught his breath. "Do not tell me what to do," he said in a voice that was authoritative and contained but clearly livid. "Don't tell me what to do *ever* again. I have been following you around since we were kids, Tanner. I worshipped you. I shared everything with you. Anything that was mine was yours. I got my dad to give you all that legal work. I stuck by you when you got divorced and then divorced again. I moved into my dad's office this week because *you* told me to. And what did you do? You killed my father."

Tanner's eyes glittered with what looked like fear. "You have no proof," he shouted. "I didn't give him those herbs. That crazy doctor did."

"She'll testify you paid her," I said. "She's already given a statement." It was totally untrue, of course, and lying was not something I did often, but Tanner looked on the verge, and if we could force him into a confession, it would be a start to prosecuting him for Forester's death.

Tanner's eyes skittered to me then back to Shane. "You're bullshitting."

"It's over," I said, my tone calm. "Dr. Li is telling everything to the cops."

"So then why haven't they arrested me?" Tanner yelled. "This is bullshit!"

"I can't believe you did this to me." Shane's voice trembled now.

In the distance, we heard a rumble of a train.

"I cannot believe that you, my best friend, would hurt my dad." Shane started to cry. "How could you do that to him? He was a great man. How could you do this to me? How can you live with yourself? How can you stand there, knowing what you did? I mean, even *you*. You're such a jerk, Tanner, but I never thought you could kill someone."

Tanner's expression became one of agony as he watched Shane drop to one knee and begin to sob openly. The rumble of the train got closer, louder.

"I can't believe you did this," Shane said, yelling now over the sound of the approaching train. "You killed my dad. You killed him. You *killed* him."

The roar of the train was deafening. The sound filled the

platform, and there was nothing but that roar and the sight of Shane on his knee, Tanner watching him in horror.

And then Tanner's expression cleared, like a man who's made a decision he'd been struggling with for decades. He gave a slight nod of his head. His mouth moved, forming the words *I'm sorry.*

He turned away from Shane and took a few steps. A short pause. And just then, as the train barreled into the station, Tanner leaped in an almost lighthearted way, a way that made him look like a child skipping into a field of flowers.

73

I am standing in front of the police station at Larrabee and Chicago Avenue, ten hours after that awful moment on the El tracks. I'll never forget the details—the way Tanner jumped with ease; the vicious crack of bones; the long, uninterrupted blare of the train's horn; the way his body soared ahead of the train like a bird in flight; the shriek of the brakes and the screams of those nearby; the powerful thud as Tanner landed on the tracks.

My sundress is now as limp as I feel. When all this started on that Tuesday, twelve days ago, I saw how fast a life can change. But now I'm amazed by that reality once again. Twelve days ago, I rode my scooter to work, the wind whipping my hair, secure in the fortress that was Sam and me, ready for another day on top of the heap at Baltimore & Brown. Yesterday morning, when I pulled this dress over my head, I was in another country with no knowledge of who had hurt Forester, with no knowledge of whether I would ever see Sam again.

I am exhausted to an extent I have never known; a tiredness that has settled into the very back of my eyes, the deep well of my ribs. It's an exhaustion born of grief—for Forester, for the simplicity of the life I'd led only a short time ago and even for Tanner. He had been a flawed man, and although it seemed as if he'd been driven by pure greed, I'm not sure pure greed exists. I think instead that, like most people, Tanner

wanted to be happy, and in the past he had found a certain
type of happiness in money and status. To have those stripped
away was like watching *himself* be stripped away piece by
piece. When he couldn't regain those things, he grew reckless,
grasping at anything that might help him recover some semblance of joy, maybe a few stray moments of peace. I suppose
he's found that peace now at last.

Outside the police station, I stop and turn around. The
station is one of the newer ones with an architecturally pleasing
glass front and a smattering of sculptures. The group files out
onto the sidewalk with me, everyone blinking in the sun.

There is Q and Shane. They seem very much like a couple
suddenly with their shared gazes and subtle-but-certain
touches. Shane is shell-shocked with the news that his best
friend killed his father, but I sense that later, somehow, Shane
will be okay. With the new confidence he's had to acquire and
with the support of Q, I think he's going to make his father
very proud, even if it's not exactly in the way Forester had
envisioned.

Maggie squints at the bright Saturday morning. Of all of
us, she should be the most tired, since she spent the night
managing the cops as only a magician could, running between
interrogation rooms where each of us was until the cops could
untwist the entire story. Instead, Maggie is jazzed up and
buoyant, looking more like a college student in her jeans and
big sweater than a top-notch criminal lawyer. She gives
everyone her card with instructions to call with any questions.
She grabs Sam and whispers something to him, their heads
bowed. I'm sure it's something to do with the fact that now
she'll be taking him to the FBI.

After a few hours of questioning last night, the police went
to Dr. Li's house where they found her and her husband packing their belongings. They had two one-way tickets to Beijing.
After being taken into custody, Dr. Li confessed everything,
including the fact that Tanner had paid her.

Andi Lippman arrived at the police station shortly after we learned about Dr. Li, and she is now waiting at the curb for Sam with an unmarked car and two federal marshals. Sam will be questioned, but given Tanner's actions, Dr. Li's confession and the documentation drawn up by Forester, Maggie doesn't expect him to be held for long.

My mother touches my arm as she steps outside the station and hugs me. I'd called her last night and asked her to come. Maggie told me my mom was worried about me while I was in Panama, calling every few hours. I felt terrible that I'd made her worry, that I'd even for a moment accused her of hurting Forester.

"I'm sorry you lost him," I say as I squeeze her, smelling that fresh citrus smell from the light perfume she always wears.

She squeezes me harder, and I cannot see, but I can imagine, those crystalline tears trickling from her eyes.

When I pull away, my eyes land on the head of the executive committee at Baltimore & Brown.

Edward Chase steps forward, dressed in slacks and a blue sweater too tight for his ample belly, and shakes my hand. "I want to thank you for notifying me, Izzy. You did the right thing for the good of the firm."

I nod. I'd tracked down Chase's home number last night. The suicide of one of the firm's partners, soon to be followed with the news that the same partner had killed one of their biggest clients, was a major blow. I knew they'd want to manage the situation as quickly as possible.

"So, listen," Chase said. "Why don't you keep that leave of absence going. You know, take it easy for a while."

"Sure, Ed." His words seemed kind, but I know that Chase, no matter what the circumstances, never lets his attorneys take a few months off. The truth is, there is no great reason to fire me, and it would reflect poorly if he did so right now. But if I'm around, I'm a reminder of all the messiness.

Strangely, his implied dismissal doesn't hit me as hard or as much as I would have thought. I couldn't imagine life at Baltimore & Brown if I returned—no Q, no Forester. I would always be the girl who was involved somehow in that business with Forester and Tanner.

And now that I'd been walking around, stripped of everything that had defined me, I realize I didn't have to hold so tight to it all. I'll find another job, maybe do something entirely different, follow a different path I can't even see right now. Maybe I'll start my own firm and Shane will let me keep representing Pickett Enterprises.

"I don't think I'll be returning to Baltimore & Brown," I say to Chase. "I think it's time for something new."

He doesn't look surprised. Or disappointed. "Can I ask what you'll do?"

"Can I let you know when I figure it out?" Despite the grief that lies deep inside me, I find myself inhabited by the power of potential, a strange exhilaration for the unknown.

Chase smiles. "You bet." He shakes my hand, wishes me good luck and leaves.

As I turn back to the group, I see Sam. He is standing slightly apart from everyone now, just watching me with those olive eyes, but getting ready to leave me again, at least temporarily. He glances toward the federal marshals, then back at me.

He looks drained and yet somehow very sexy. The sexiness is due in part, I suppose, to the danger he's brought back with him to Chicago, a sense of mystery. I'd been sure that I knew everything about Sam Hollings. And I had been wrong. I hadn't known his capacity for generosity, for loyalty, for adventure, for stupidity. I find the new mystery of him intoxicating.

But...but...but...there is no going back to the way we were before this all happened, before the craziness of the wedding. That much is evident. I squeeze my left hand, feeling my engagement ring digging into my skin. There are so many questions—questions about why he didn't trust me, even if he was following the directives of Forester, questions about how he could put me through what he did, questions about what my reluctance toward the wedding says about us. So if we stay together, if we look deep for the answers to those questions, *we* will be different, and I don't know what that "different" will look like or if we'll even want it.

As I look at Sam on this quiet, crisp morning, I realize that life in general is not only volatile (sometimes wonderfully so, sometimes tragically), it is also irrevocable. There is no returning to yesterday when my dress was fresh. There will be no rebound to two weeks ago when Q and I ruled the roost at Baltimore & Brown. I can't rewind to a year ago when Sam and I got engaged and when my feelings for him were rock solid. Now, it's all slithering through my fingers as I try to get a hold on something, anything, that is here to stay. The only thing I can come up with is that I love these people I'm surrounded by, and they love me, and maybe love is the only real comfort, no matter what form you receive it in, no matter that you might not find it again tomorrow.

Now, I say to myself. *Now is enough.*

I cross the ten feet that separate Sam and me.

"I *will* be home soon," he says.

"I know." And then I kiss him.

I pull back, and we share a smile. I'm pretty sure he's thinking the same thing as I, wondering where we will go from here, wondering what the world now holds for Sam Hollings and Isabel McNeil as soon as this all clears.

The sun moves around the corner of the building. I lift my face to it, and I close my eyes. I know now that what I told myself at the Panama Canal is true—no matter what's in store, I'll be fine, though perhaps "fine" in a way I'd never thought about before.

In my mind, I look at the great open space that is my future. And I find myself thrilled at the prospect of dipping my toe into that deep chasm, just to see what it feels like.

* * * * *

We hope you enjoyed this novel by Laura Caldwell.
See the discussion questions on the following pages
to further enhance your reading enjoyment.

QUESTIONS FOR DISCUSSION

1. Is this a novel you would like to see made into a movie or television show? If so, who do you think the actors and actresses would be to play the main characters?

2. If you had everything in your life pulled away from you in one day, as Izzy did, how would you respond?

3. What was your favorite scene in *Red Hot Lies?*

4. What was your favorite twist? Did you anticipate the twists in the end?

5. What did you think of Izzy's mother's character? Could you feel the sadness in her?

6. Did you like the subplot of Izzy's venture into detective work?

7. If you are not from Chicago, did you get a good feel for it? If you live in Chicago, did you like the descriptions of the city?

8. Did you feel as if Izzy was someone you could be friends with?

9. How did you like John Mayburn as a character?

10. Do you think Sam and Izzy should make it as a couple? Could you forgive him?

11. While reading the book did you have a different ending in mind? If so, what was it?

RED BLOODED MURDER
is the next book in the
Izzy McNeil series by
Laura Caldwell
Turn the page for a sneak preview
RED BLOODED MURDER
will be available in bookstores
July 1, 2009

The hands that grabbed her were greedy. They shoved her, pushed her, not caring when she cried out. And although she wanted more—more now, more later—she felt the need, even in this faraway moment, to say the truth. "We shouldn't be doing this again. At least I shouldn't. This is the last time, just so you know."

"Shut up," came the reply.

"I'm not kidding. I want you to know that this is it. It's over after today."

"Shut up."

Those hands moved lower, clawing and probing as if they'd been waiting for this, lying in wait until she was vulnerable, when they could strip her bare and plunge her into oblivion.

She threw her head back and clutched at the bedsheets, holding herself down until the moment when she would step into the void that she so craved.

A breeze trickled in the window, enticing after the biting winds that had battered Chicago for months. Yet nothing could touch the heat that boiled inside, carried her in small but growing crests, reaching her in places she always forgot until moments like this.

The hands stopped suddenly, startling her.

"Why?" she said, desperate.

A mouth crushed against hers, bit her. "I said shut up."

And she did.

* * *

*Later, when she was alone, she slipped into her clothes for
the evening—white, ironically. Tonight she would smile, and she
would be engaging. After all these years, she knew how to do
that—how to shine her eyes at someone, how to direct her energy
so they felt seen and heard and touched. No one at that event
would know what she'd just done. She would carry the last two
hours in her head, like little packages whose pretty wrappings
hid the shame, and the pleasure. Those thoughts would please
her when she mentally unwrapped them; they would send pangs
of delight throughout her body. But they would remove her from
everyone, too. Secrets were always like that. They put a film
between you and the rest of the world, so that you could see
everyone else, but no one could see the whole of you.*

*Searching for her bag, she walked through her place and
found it by the door. She remembered now that she'd dropped
it there in the heat of that first moment, when she had let
herself be devoured by her wants.*

*She sighed and picked up the bag. She took it into her
bedroom, where she transferred a few essential items into
a smaller bag more appropriate for the evening. She
brushed her hair.*

*For a second she studied herself in the mirror. She didn't
look any different than she had that afternoon. There wasn't
a blush to her cheeks or a shine to her eyes. She'd gotten so
good at hiding the evidence.*

*Her gaze dropped. It was hard to look at herself these days.
She walked to the front door, trying to let her mind clear of
the last couple of hours, of everything.*

*She stretched out her arm for the doorknob, but suddenly
it turned on its own, surprising her, making her gasp.*

The door opened.

*"You scared the hell out of me," she said when she saw
who was there.*

She stopped short, looking into those eyes—eyes that saw

her, knew what she was really like. She opened her mouth to say something sexy, but when she looked again, she saw those eyes shift into an expression of cold anger. She paused and turned away for a moment while she collected words in her head and shaped them so that they would be earnest, pacifying.

But before she could form the sentences, she felt something strike her on the back of the head. She heard herself cry out— a cry so different from those she'd made earlier, a cry of shock and of pain. Instinctively she began to raise her hands to her head, but then she felt another blow. Her mind splintered into shards of light, the pain searing into pink streaks. She felt her knees buckle, her body hit the ground.

She felt a tightening around her neck, something squeezing her larynx with more and more force, stealing the breath from her. The light in her brain exploded then, filling it with tiny spots. Strangely, it seemed as if each of those spots encased the different moments of her life. She could see all of them at once, feel all of them. It was a beautiful trick of the mind, a state of enlightenment the likes of which she hadn't known possible. She felt more alive than she ever had before.

1

Three days earlier

The patio of NoMi, on the seventh floor of the Park Hyatt hotel, had its doors propped wide, as if boasting about the suddenly dazzling April weather.

We stepped onto the patio—an urban garden illuminated by the surrounding city lights.

"Spring is officially here," I said. "And man, am I ready for it."

The thing about spring in Chicago is that it's fast and fickle. A balmy, sixty-eight-degree Friday like tonight could easily turn into a brittle, thirty-five degrees on Saturday morning. Which is why Chicagoans always clutch at those spring nights. Which is why a night like that can make you do crazy things.

The maître d', a European dressed in a slim black suit, spotted the woman I was with, Jane Augustine, and came hustling over. "Ms. Augustine," he said, "welcome." He looked at me. "And Miss…"

"Miss Izzy McNeil," Jane said, beaming her perfect newscaster smile. "The best entertainment lawyer in the city."

The maître d' laughed, gave me a quick once-over. A little

smile played at the corner of his mouth. "A lawyer. So you're smart, too?"

"If so, I'm a smart person who's out of a job." I'd been looking for six months.

"Maybe not for long," Jane said.

"Meaning?"

Jane shrugged coquettishly as the maître d' led us to a table and said, "For the best." He put down two leather-bound menus and left.

We sat. "Do you always get this kind of treatment?" I asked.

Jane swung her shiny black hair over her shoulder and looked at me with her famous mauve-blue eyes. "The treatment was all about Izzy McNeil. He's hot for you."

I turned and glanced. The maître d' was watching us. Okay, I admit, he did seem to be watching *me*. "I think I'm giving off some sort of scent now that I'm single again."

Jane scoffed. "I can't stop giving off that scent, and I'm married."

I studied Jane as the waiter took our drink orders. With her long, perfect body tucked into her perfect red suit, she looked every inch the tough journalist she was, but the more I got to know her, the more I listened to her, the more she intrigued me by the many facets of Jane. When I was lead counsel for Pickett Enterprises, the Midwest media conglomerate that owned the station where Jane worked, I'd negotiated her contract. And while she was definitely the wise-cracking, tough-talking, shoot-straight journalist I'd heard about, I had also seen some surprising cracks in the veneer of her confidence. And on top of that was the sexiness. The more I knew her, the more I noticed she was simply steeped in it.

"Seriously," Jane said. "I know you're bummed that you and Sam had that little problem—"

"Yeah, that *little* problem," I interrupted her. "We're seeing each other occasionally, but it's just not the same."

Six months ago, my fiancé, Sam, disappeared with thirty million dollars' worth of property owned by my client Forester Pickett, CEO of Pickett Enterprises, and it happened on precisely the same night Forester suddenly died. After nearly two agonizing weeks that seemed like two years— weeks in which my world had not only been turned upside down, but also shaken and twisted and battered and bruised, weeks during which I learned so many secrets about the people in my life I thought I'd been dropped into someone else's life, the matter had been resolved and Sam was back in town. But I'd lost all my legal work in the process and essentially had been ushered out the backdoor of my law firm. As for Sam and me, the wedding was off, and we weren't exactly back together.

"Whatever," Jane said. "You should enjoy being single. You're dating other people, right?"

"A little." I rubbed the spot on my left hand where my engagement ring used to rest. It felt as if the skin was slightly dented, holding a spot in case I decided to put it on again. "There's a guy named Grady, who I'm friends with from my old firm, and we go out occasionally, but he wants to get serious, and I really don't. So mostly I've been licking my wounds."

"Enough of that! Let someone do the licking for you. With that red hair and that ass, you could get anyone you want."

I laughed. "A guy at the coffee shop asked me out the other day."

"How old was he?"

"About forty."

"That'll work. As long as he's eighteen, he's doable."

The waiter stepped up to our table with two glasses of wine.

"Would you go out with her?" Jane asked him.

"Uh…" he said, clearly embarrassed.

"Jane, stop." But the truth was, I was thrilled with the randomly warm night, with the hint that the world was somehow turning faster than usual.

"No, honestly." Jane looked him up and down like a breeder sizing up a horse for stud. "Are you single?"

The waiter was a Hispanic guy with big black eyes. "Yeah."

"And would you go out with her?" Jane pointed at me.

He grinned. "Hell, yeah."

"Perfect!" Jane patted him on the hip. "She'll get your number before we leave."

I dropped my head in my hands as the waiter walked away, chuckling.

"What?" she said. "Now you've got three dates when you want them—the waiter, the coffee-shop guy and that Grady person. We're working on the maître d' next. I want you to have a whole stable of men."

A few women walked by. One of them gasped. "Jane Augustine!" She rushed over. "I'm so sorry to bother you, but I have to tell you that I love you. We watch you every night. You were great on the six o'clock tonight."

"Thank you!" Jane extended her hand. "What's your name?"

The woman introduced her friends, and then the compliments poured from her mouth in an unending stream. "Wow, Jane, you're attractive on TV but you're even more gorgeous in person… You're beautiful… You're so smart… You're amazing."

"Oh, gosh, thank you," Jane said to each compliment, giving an earnest bob of the head. "You've made my day." She asked what the woman did for a living. She graciously accepted more compliments when the woman turned the conversation back to Jane.

"How do you do that?" I asked when they left.

"Do what?"

"Act like you're so flattered? I know you've heard that stuff before."

Jane studied me. "How old are you, Izzy?"

"Thirty this summer." I shook my head. "I can't believe I'm going to be thirty."

"Well, I'm two years away from forty, and let me tell you something—when someone tells you you're beautiful, you act like it's the first time you've heard it." She looked at me pointedly. "Because you never know when it'll be the last."

I sipped my wine. It was French, kind of floral and lemony. "How's your new agent?"

"Fantastic. He got me a great contract with Trial TV."

"I've seen the billboards."

Trial TV was a new legal network based in Chicago that was tapping into the old Court TV audience. The billboards, with Jane's smiling face, had been plastered up and down the Kennedy for months.

"It's amazing to be on the ground floor of this," Jane said. "They've got a reality show on prosecutors that's wild. It's gotten great advance reviews. And we're juicing up trial coverage and making it more exciting. You know, more background on the lawyers and judges, more aggressive opinion commentary on their moves."

"And you'll be anchoring the flagship broadcast each morning." I raised my glass. "It's perfect for you."

Jane had always had a penchant for the legal stories. When she was a reporter, she was known for courting judges and attorneys, so that she was the one they came to whenever there was news. She got her spot as an anchor after she broke a big story about a U.S. senator from Illinois who was funneling millions of dollars of work to one particular law firm in Chicago. It was Jane who figured out that the head partner at the firm was the senator's mistress.

Jane clinked my glass. "Thanks, Iz." She looked heavenward for a second, her eyes big and excited. "It's like a dream come true, because if I was going to keep climbing the nightly news ladder, I'd have to try and go to New York and land the national news. But Zac and I want to stay here. I love this city so much."

Jane looked around, as if taking in the whole town with her gaze. This particular part of Chicago—the Gold Coast and the Mag Mile—had grown like a weed lately as a plethora of luxury hotel/condo buildings sprang into the skyline.

"Plus, aside from getting up early, it's great hours," Jane continued. "I don't have to work nights anymore, and trials stop for the weekends. They even stop for holidays."

"Is C.J. going with you?" Jane's current producer was a talented, no-nonsense woman who had worked closely with Jane for years.

She shook her head. "She's staying at WNDY. That station has been so good to me I didn't want to steal all their top people. Plus, I wanted to step out on my own, start writing more of my own stuff." She gave a chagrined shake of her head. "You know how I got all this?"

"Your new agent?"

"Nope. He only negotiated the contract. It was Forester."

Just like that, my heart sagged. I missed him. Forester Pickett had not only been a client, he'd been a mentor, the person who'd given me my start in entertainment law, the person who'd trusted me to represent his beloved company. Eventually, Forester became like a father to me, and his death was still on my mind.

"I miss him, too," Jane said, seeing the look on my face. "Remember how generous he was? He actually took me to dinner with Ari Silver."

"Wow, and so Ari brought you in." Ari Silver was a media mogul, like Forester, but instead of owning TV and radio stations, newspapers and publishing companies all over the Midwest, as Forester did, Ari Silver was global. His company was the one behind Trial TV.

"Forester knew I loved the law," she said, "so he brought me to dinner with the two of them when Ari was in town."

"Even though he knew it meant he might lose you."

"Exactly." Jane put her glass down and leaned forward on her elbows. "And now I'm bringing you to dinner because I want you."

I blinked. "Excuse me?"

"The launch is Monday. We've been in rehearsals for the last few weeks." She paused, leaned forward some more. "And I want you to start on Monday, too."

"What do you mean?"

"I want you to be a legal analyst."

"Like a reporter?"

"Yeah."

"Are you kidding? I've never worked in the news business. Just on the periphery." And yet as logical as my words sounded, I felt a spark of excitement for something new, something totally different.

Months ago, after Sam disappeared with Forester's property, I'd been guilty by association and lost all my legal business. After everything was settled, Baltimore & Brown, the huge, glitzy law firm where I had worked, made it clear that it would be better for everyone if we parted ways. The fact was, if I had stayed, I would have started at the bottom again, and I couldn't face the thought of sliding backward down the corporate ladder I'd scaled up so fast.

"We had someone quit today," Jane said. "A female reporter who used to be a lawyer."

"And?"

"Well, let me backtrack. Trial TV has tried to put together a staff that has legal background in some way, including many of the reporters and producers. We have reporters in each major city to keep their eye on the local trial scenes. You know, interview the lawyers and witnesses, prepare short stories to run on the broadcasts. But one of our Chicago reporters hit the road today."

"Why?"

Jane waved her perfectly manicured hand. "Oh, she's a prima donna who wants everything PC. She couldn't handle our dinosaur deputy news director." Her eyes zeroed in on mine. "But you could. After working with Forester and his crew, you know how to hang with the old boys' network."

"Are you talking an on-air position?"

"Not right away. We'll give you a contributor's contract, and you'll do a little of everything. You'll assist in writing the stories and help with the questions when we have guests. But eventually, yeah, I see you on-air."

"Jane, I don't have any media experience."

"You used to give statements on behalf of Pickett Enterprises, and you were good. Either way, the trend in the news is real people with real experience in the areas they're reporting on. Think Nancy Grace—she was a prosecutor before she started at CNN. Or Greta Van Susteren. She practiced law, too."

The spark of excitement I'd felt earlier now flamed into something bigger, brighter. If you'd asked me six months ago what the spring held for me, I would have told you I'd be finishing my thank-you notes after my holiday wedding, and I'd be settling into contented downtime with my husband, Sam. But now Sam wasn't my husband, and things with him—hell, things with *my future*—were decidedly unclear.

"What would it pay?"

She told me.

"A month?" I blurted.

She laughed. "No, sweetheart, that's a year. TV pays crap. You should know that. You've negotiated the contracts."

"But I'm a lawyer," I said.

"You'd be an analyst and a reporter now."

Just out of principle, I considered saying no. I *was* a lawyer; I was worth more than that. But the fact was, unless I could find entertainment-law work, I was worth almost nothing. I knew nothing else, understood no other legal specialties. I'd been job hunting for months, and trying to make the best of the downtime—visiting the Art Institute, the Museum of Contemporary Art, the Museum of Science and Industry and just about every other museum or landmark Chicago had to offer. But, depressingly, there was no entertainment work up for grabs in the city. Though most Chicago actors and artists started with local lawyers, when they hit it big, they often took their legal work to the coasts. The business that remained was wisely hoarded by the lawyers who'd had it for years. And Forester's company had decided to use attorneys from another firm, saying they needed a fresh start and a chance to work with someone new. I couldn't blame them, but it had left me in the cold. My bank statement had an ever-decreasing balance, teetering toward nothing. I hadn't minded the lack of funds so badly when I couldn't buy spring clothes, but soon I wouldn't be able to pay my mortgage, and that would be something else altogether.

For the first time in my adult life I was flying without a net. Fear nibbled at my insides, crept its way into my brain. I was buzzing with apprehension. But the job offer from Jane was a bolt of calm, clean sunshine breaking through the murky depths of my nerves.

I knew, as the negotiator I used to be, that I should ask Jane a lot of other questions—What would the hours be? What was the insurance like? But in addition to needing the money, I needed—*desperately* needed—something new in my life.

So I leaned forward, meeting Jane's gaze and those mauve-blue eyes, and said, "I'll do it."

It's going to be a

RED HOT
SUMMER

LAURA CALDWELL

REQUEST YOUR FREE BOOKS!

2 FREE NOVELS
FROM THE ROMANCE/SUSPENSE
COLLECTION PLUS 2 FREE GIFTS!

YES! Please send me 2 FREE novels from the Romance/Suspense Collection and my 2 FREE gifts (gifts are worth about $10). After receiving them, if I don't wish to receive any more books, I can return the shipping statement marked "cancel." If I don't cancel, I will receive 4 brand-new novels every month and be billed just $5.74 per book in the U.S. or $6.24 per book in Canada. That's a savings of at least 28% off the cover price. It's quite a bargain! Shipping and handling is just 50¢ per book.* I understand that accepting the 2 free books and gifts places me under no obligation to buy anything. I can always return a shipment and cancel at any time. Even if I never buy another book from the Reader Service, the two free books and gifts are mine to keep forever.

185 MDN EYNQ   385 MDN EYN2

Name	(PLEASE PRINT)	
Address		Apt. #
City	State/Prov.	Zip/Postal Code

Signature (if under 18, a parent or guardian must sign)

Mail to The Reader Service:
IN U.S.A.: P.O. Box 1867, Buffalo, NY 14240-1867
IN CANADA: P.O. Box 609, Fort Erie, Ontario L2A 5X3

Not valid to current subscribers of the Romance Collection,
the Suspense Collection or the Romance/Suspense Collection.

Want to try two free books from another line?
Call 1-800-873-8635 or visit www.morefreebooks.com.

* Terms and prices subject to change without notice. Prices do not include applicable taxes. Sales tax applicable in N.Y. Canadian residents will be charged applicable provincial taxes and GST. Offer not valid in Quebec. This offer is limited to one order per household. All orders subject to approval. Credit or debit balances in a customer's account(s) may be offset by any other outstanding balance owed by or to the customer. Please allow 4 to 6 weeks for delivery. Offer available while quantities last.

Your Privacy: Harlequin is committed to protecting your privacy. Our Privacy Policy is available online at www.eHarlequin.com or upon request from the Reader Service. From time to time we make our lists of customers available to reputable third parties who may have a product or service of interest to you. If you would prefer we not share your name and address, please check here.

BOB09

Read *New York Times* bestselling author Lori Foster's very first Harlequin® book, *Impetuous,* originally from the Harlequin® Temptation line.

For a costume party, Carlie McDaniels trades in her frumpiness for the look of an exotic dancer—and says so long spinsterhood, hello handsome Tyler Ramsey. Even after the best night of their lives, Tyler doesn't guess the identity of his harem hottie, and Carlie plans on keeping it that way—because a gorgeous guy like Tyler would never fall for his smart-talking *best friend!*

Available June 2009 wherever books are sold.

LAURA CALDWELL

32183	LOOK CLOSELY	___ $6.99 U.S. ___ $8.50 CAN.
32309	THE ROME AFFAIR	___ $6.99 U.S. ___ $8.50 CAN.

(limited quantities available)

TOTAL AMOUNT	$ _____
POSTAGE & HANDLING	$ _____
($1.00 for 1 book, 50¢ for each additional)	
APPLICABLE TAXES*	$ _____
TOTAL PAYABLE	$ _____

(check or money order—please do not send cash)

To order, complete this form and send it, along with a check or money order for the total above, payable to MIRA Books, to: **In the U.S.:** 3010 Walden Avenue, P.O. Box 9077, Buffalo, NY 14269-9077; **In Canada:** P.O. Box 636, Fort Erie, Ontario, L2A 5X3.

Name: _____
Address: _____ City: _____
State/Prov.: _____ Zip/Postal Code: _____
Account Number (if applicable): _____

075 CSAS

*New York residents remit applicable sales taxes.
*Canadian residents remit applicable GST and provincial taxes.

MIRA®

www.MIRABooks.com

MLC0609BL